The Secrets We Keep

The Hidden Jules Series #2

I

CONTENTS

To Robyn Alisa.

Once a Princess, always a Princess.

AUTHORS NOTE:

Please note that this story has mentions of abuse, child death, substance abuse, child murder and mentions of adoption.

If that is something can't read right now, I completely understand. Please take care of your mental health, that is more important.

While I have tried to get it as close as I can to the American justice system, there maybe a few things wrong. Everything mentioned in this book is all fictional and not placed on any actual event.

TJ X

PROLOGUE

Arielle Laudierre, Princess of Donevia
June 2000

Guilt consumes me.

I wanted to stay, take her home with me.

Raise her.

But what would my father think? He would call off the engagement that he has planned, not to mention cancel the wedding.

I feel so guilty for lying to the Quinten's for so long. Giving them a fake name, not to mention a fake age. I do believe that towards the end they started to see it was all lies. Or they could have seen it from the start and never said anything.

I disappointed them. Especially Robert. He must hate *me*.

I lied to him. I lied to his family. I betrayed his trust.

I left. I will forever feel guilty of that.

I never told them who I really was, where I came from, who my family is.

My daughter will never know who I am, or where she comes from. I'm hoping she never finds out, although that was always the plan. To give her to a family that loves her, to a family that would be able to keep her safe.

Never did I think I would end up pregnant a month after landing into London. This year off from my overbearing parents was meant to prove that I am a worthy daughter, and wife to my soon to be husband, Edward.

The marriage is meant to bring union to both of our countries. There had been a rift in the families for generations. From greed to infidelity not to forget about the stealing.

Our marriage is meant to bring peace. And I honestly hope it does. Since we found out about the marriage, Edward has been all for it as have I. We want what's best for our countries. I marry the Haroux's, and my brother takes over as King of Donevia once my father passes on. That has always been the plan.

Now, I only agreed to the plan because I said I wanted a year to myself, in a new country where I get to explore for a full year before committing to the marriage.

Of course, my father was very against it. I a Princess, out galivanting without a security detail, getting up to all sorts of mischief? He *hated* the idea.

But thank God for my mother, who agreed, I needed to get out of here. I was a wild teenager; I was rebellious as a Princess. I never wanted the royal life growing up. I wanted to be free, away from all the titles and the greed and the lying.

But I have always known deep down that I will need to *'suck it up'*, as Robert would say.

I have to do this for my family, whether I want a different life or not. My daughter will have the life that I have always wanted. She will be normal.

I run towards the nearest black cab I can find and jump in, not caring whether or not it was for someone else.

"Where too, love?" The taxi driver asks sweetly while looking through the rear-view mirror. I look to him, clearly quite panicked as I settle into the taxi and take a deep breath.

"The airport, please."

CHAPTER ONE

Juliette Sanders

Michigan, USA

I feel as though my life is currently a movie.

Not even 6 weeks ago, I found out I was adopted, that I'm not related to my sister and my father is the leader of the American mafia.

Three days ago, I found out my birth mother, married a Prince, called Edward of Haroux and she was a Princess when she met my birth father, Robert.

I am trying to tell myself this is nothing like *The Princess Diaries*. However, instead of Mia's father, it's my mother. I don't even know if I have some rich grandmother. If I'm brutally honest, I don't want to know.

Robert has been a nightmare to live with

these past few days. He has been shouting at everyone, taking the littlest things out on any of the boys. He even had that conversation that needed to happen about how I found out about my adoption... And no one has seen Rodger since. Either he left on his own free will or, he is buried six foot under. Don't get me wrong, I hate Rodger. Hate is a strong word, but it's true. I hate him. But not enough to see him 6 feet under.

My siblings have been insufferable these past few days after they were forced to leave the room. I've been told I can't say anything. I think that is because Robert needs to find out if it is true or not and it is proving difficult.

Felicity had mentioned that every time Robert thinks he has managed to get in contact with somebody from Haroux, it is a dead end. I think the last thing he wants to do is have to fly out there, see what kind of life she has after she left him.

He will never admit it. But this is extremely hard for him. We all believed he loved her, or even better *still* loves her. I can't begin to image how he felt when she left and how he had to hand me over to my parents on his own. I can't even begin to pretend how I would know how that feels.

He was young. So was Arielle. Young dumb kids who tied themselves up in something they didn't know how to handle.

What did they do? They handed the responsibility to someone else.

I slightly resent them for it, I can't explain it. How could you say you love something, a baby, then not take responsibility for bringing it into this world?

I love my parents, Amy and Paul, I really do. But I am still angry as to why I was left in the dark about my family. Why was I sent away while he adopted my siblings?

Granted, I did get some sort of explanation, but not one that I would say is a good enough or one that would make me feel better.

I am not an angry child; I never have been. But the more I'm being silenced in this house and kept in the dark, the more I realise that this might have been a mistake to come here. It was all sunshine and rainbows until Peter had uncovered Arielle's mysterious identity.

Was I excited to understand 'Operation Redhead'? Of course. But never did I think it would have messed up my life more than it already is. My father a leader of the American mafia and my mother a Queen?

I can say for sure that if I do end up having a relationship with both Arielle and Robert and it was to be made public, I would be kissing any thought of being a Detective or working in the police force goodbye. Because no one would hire someone whose father is a murderer, not even Officer Bradley.

CHAPTER TWO

Juliette Sanders

Michigan, USA

I take another look around the library, for something that could take my mind off the mess that is my life right now.

There is a slight chill in the room and as I pass the basket in the corner, I grab a blanket to take with me to the chair.

I've spent a lot of time in here. It is a sanctuary as such from the chaos outside. I've kept to myself these past few days, not wanting to upset or anger anyone but also because I feel like I'm about to explode. I feel the anger simmer within me, that I am so uncertain of where I stand in this family or at all.

I decide to grab Jane Austin's *Pride and*

Prejudice. Something I've never read, and I feel like the silence I've been put under these past few days may help me focus on finally reading one of the classics.

I carefully remove it from the shelf and make my way over to the chair and wrap myself in the blanket. I feel comfortable today, my choice in jogging bottoms and a hoodie, was a great choice to pack. I decided to throw my short blonde hair into a bun. It may be hot outside but inside the Quinten *palace*, it's cold in some areas of the house.

I take a seat on the chair and begin my new book. I've always heard great things, but never decided to pick it up in Waterstones or the library at school.

"Educating yourself on the classics, huh?" A voice breaks through the silence of the room, and I look up to see Serena standing in the doorway. Her long brown hair is in a ponytail, and she is in some fluffy pjs, even though it is 2pm.

"Thought I'd do some reading since I'm banished from talking to anyone." I say as I shut the book and look down at the cover. Tracing the outline of the words trying to avoid the talk that is about to happen.

"Juliette. I understand you're angry. You have every right to be. Your whole life has been shattered in the space of a few weeks and you are feeling unwanted and misunderstood." She softly

9

explains while making her way over to the chair opposite.

I take a moment to give myself the courage to ask. "Is that how you feel? Misunderstood?" I ask as I place the book on the table and pull the blanket up closer to my chest. She laughs slightly at my question but follows it is a deep breath. Like she's been waiting for someone to ask her that.

"Yes. I feel everything you're feeling right now." She admits. Suddenly I feel speechless. Like all my anger calms down and I finally feel understood. I was given the indication that Serena was battling her own demons, and what I'm assuming is going to be a tough conversation about to emerge; I get the sense I'm about to get a deeper understanding as to who Serena is as a person. "You know I'm not always drunk." She admits in the silence, slightly catching me off guard, but also frightening me as it was exactly what I was thinking.

"I- I never." I begin to stutter, she holds her hand up, in a way to silence me, undoubtably stopping me from digging myself into a hole.

"I know. But I know what you were thinking." She says softly. "I deal with my own problems and the way I deal with that is a drink to forget." She admits sheepishly.

"I'd never judge you, Serena." I admit while she pauses, unsure on how to continue. My sudden admission catches her off guard and she looks up to me; like she has been waiting her entire life for someone to say that.

"You mean that?" She says as a whisper. I nod, knowing that by the way she's looking at me she's on the verge of tears.

Taking a long exhale, she stands and wipes a few tears that have fallen to her perfectly contoured cheeks. "Well then." She says almost as a breath.

"I never meant to upset you, Serena." I say, holding my hand to my heart. I watch her shake her head, still trying to compose herself.

"Oh sweetheart, you've not upset me. I've just waited a lot of years for someone to say that they won't judge me for my ways. Granted I've tried to be better, but I can't stop myself from feeling the way I feel." She admits, while wiping the tears away. I can't help my actions.

I get up from my chair and hug her. I can sense from her body language she's taken back by my action, so I don't move for the moment in the hopes she hugs me back.

I feel a wave of relief when I feel her hands wrap round me and she hugs me tight, something that I think both of us needed.

"Thank you for that." She says sweetly before releasing me from the hug, taking a long look at me, cupping my face giving me a reassuring smile.

She doesn't say anything for a moment while she looks around my face intensely, like she's trying to uncover the side of the mask that is currently on my face with a smile.

"You look so much like her." She quietly admits, and it comes out as a whisper. I'm taken back by her admission and am not sure how to respond back to her. She quickly notices my change in expression and shakes her head to me. "But you aren't her." She reassures me.

After a moment of silence between us, she releases me from her grasp and pulls herself together before giving me a smile.

"I will let you read, if you need anything, I'm only down the hall in my office." She says sweetly before turning to walk towards the door.

"Serena?" I call after her, stopping her in her tracks. She looks at me, eyes begging me to continue.

"What do you do for the organization?" I curiously ask.

She hesitates, looking at me, trying to come up with some sort of lie because I'm a kid and I shouldn't know any of this.

"I'm the troublemaker." She says with a grin. "I make sure that nothing goes right at the start so everything can eventually." She says before exiting the room, leaving me in silence once again.

CHAPTER THREE

Juliette Sanders

Michigan, USA

Walking through the corridors of the Quinten mansion, I find myself struggling to find or hear anyone. This place is gigantic, but I can always hear someone down some corridor.

Silence fills the house and I begin to become nervous as to the sudden eeriness that lingers.

I make my way down the staircase and into the study; the same study I saw Peter come out days earlier when he introduced himself. I am stunned when I realise that all of them are sat looking at me as I enter the room. I feel fourteen pairs of eyes on me, and my stomach is in knots.

"What have I missed?" I ask eventually. My

mouth is incredibly dry and the atmosphere in the room is cold, and dark. Like some bomb had just landed in here, exploded and this is the aftermath.

"Glad you could eventually join us." Robert says with a smirk on his face as he sits back in his seat. I look to him, confused which only makes his brows frown.

"I told Clarissa to tell you about the family meeting over 30 minutes ago." He says while making direct eye contact with her. The smile on her face tells me everything I need to know. She had no intention on telling me there was a family meeting.

"Well, I never knew. Sorry for being late." I express as I stand against the door.

"It's alright, Juliette." He reassures me. "The meeting was called to discuss you actually." He admits. I feel my heart sink as all eyes are now on me. I thought he had told them which is why there was tension in the air.

I know what this meeting is about, and it isn't about inviting on the next Quinten family holiday.

"What now?" Clarissa whines as she sits back in her chair annoyed. "She's all we have talked about for months. She's nothing special." She snaps. "Just because she's your birth child doesn't mean she is worth any of this." She complains.

I don't look at Clarissa, I look to the rest

of the siblings who either shake their heads or a loud exhale leave their mouths. I decide to look to Robert. His face is now filled with anger, staring down at Clarissa, warning her.

"Clarissa Brady Quinten." He says through his teeth. The tone of his voice low and harsh which sends a chill through my spine. "How would you feel if Alexis wasn't accepting of you when I brought you home?" He says leaning forward staring into deeply.

"She wasn't." Clarissa snaps which earns her a sarcastic grin from Alexis.

"You have isolated yourself from the entire family with your lies, you're deceiving and your reckless behaviour. Now where this has all come from, I don't know. But this needs to stop." He warns her. Her face doesn't move from a state of anger. "Until you are going to give, us, your family, some answers to your endless amounts of secrets-you don't get a say in anything. Especially about your sister." He warns. But I get the sense it isn't the first time he has had to warn her about this.

An uncomfortable silence fills the room for a few moments. I look around and catch my eye with Marcus who gives me a reassuring smile and a wink. I can't help but grin at the gesture. I get the sense he is trying to assure me that Clarissa's behaviour is her own fault and not mine, especially not because I came into the family.

"Now, with Clarissa's tantrum out the way." Robert says sarcastically in the silence causing a few chuckles. "We need to discuss Juliette's birth mother." He says as he turns to the tv behind him and shows a photo of Arielle.

She looks happy on this photo. Free. It looks old, like the photo was taken on a film camera, possibly something from Robert's photo collection.

"This is Arielle Henderson." He says towards the family. "Well, that's not her real name." He admits before moving the photo over to the next slide. I feel my mouth fall open as the photo on the screen captures me in a trance.

A portrait of a very young, beautiful Arielle. She's in a sapphire blue gown with diamonds. I suddenly feel sick when I notice the date at the bottom of the photo. 1999. The year before my birth.

"Arielle Henderson's real name was Arielle Laudierre, Princess of Donevia." He says pulling up a family photo of what I'm assuming is her family. I feel physically sick. *A Princess?*

"To all of us, Arielle was a 16-year-old who was travelling before going back to her family, that she said were overbearing. Granted we never pried into her life, and we take responsibility for that. But we never thought that she would have a title or belong to one of the biggest Royal families." Peter explains while putting up another photo of Arielle. My legs are starting to feel like jelly.

"Wait a minute, you're telling us that you had a child with a Princess?" Nathaniel pipes up. Robert shoots him a warning look. A one that says, don't interrupt Peter.

"Not much is known on the family, it is quite old fashioned in the sense they don't have a lot of technology. They grow what they eat. They are barely in touch with the digital world." Peter begins to explain while pulling up old photos of the country Donevia. It is beautiful.

"Now, fast forward to September 1999, where we meet Arielle in London. We know nothing about her trip, all we know is that she had a fake identity, and she was living her best life until she met us." Peter explains with sarcasm while looking at Robert. He rolls his eyes before taking the device off Peter and clicking the button to the next slide.

"Juliette was born in June of 2000. And within twenty-four hours, Arielle was nowhere to be seen." Robert admits, taking a second to compose himself. To everyone else in the world, even his children, Robert comes across as a cold, calculated leader. But to me, I see right through the frightening persona.

I look around the room and notice everyone staring at me, like I'm a freak. The looks catch me off guard and I stand up straight, unsure of how to handle the sudden judgement.

"Then what?" Marcus asks in the silence. I'm grateful for a moment because I watch as all eyes move to Robert for him to continue.

"Then she married a Prince from another country. It's not far from Donevia, but she became Queen of Haroux. That's as much as we know right now." Robert explains.

"So, what's going to happen now? Marcus asks again. Robert stands up from his chair and elegantly buttons his blazer while making direct eye contact with Marcus.

"I'm going to find that out. Arielle has agreed to meet me tomorrow." He explains and I feel my heart drop to the floor.

The sudden admission shocks even his siblings, especially Felicity and Peter who stare wildly at each other.

"Robert, you haven't seen Arielle since Juliette's birth. Are you sure meeting her so soon is a good idea? Have you thought about this fully?" Peter questions. Robert stops in front of his brother, he's quiet for a moment, and I'm now standing away from the door in shock.

Suddenly Robert grins, a wild and unhinged one that makes the hairs stand up on the back of my neck. "Of course, brother," He admits. "I think that this meeting will be good for both of us." He smiles before moving past his brother and walking towards me. I stare blankly at Robert; unsure of whether I'm witnessing a man who is about to go on a rampage.

He stands inches away from me, the silence in the room becoming so deafening you could hear a pin drop. "You're staying here." He admits before moving past me and opening the door, exiting out the room.

The look of surprise on the rest of the family's face is something I am sure doesn't happen often. "What?" I ask while following him through the door. "Why can't I come with you?"

"Because this is the first time, I'm seeing your mother in fourteen years, I'm doing this, so we have a understanding. I don't know anything about her, I want to make sure that if I was to introduce you properly, I understand her and her intentions with you. I know nothing about her Juliette, I *need* to keep you safe." He admits, which catches me off guard. I find myself trying to scramble for something to stay, but I can't seem to find the words.

"Yet, you still jumped into bed with her." Clarissa mutters behind me causing Robert's eyes to switch. The look of concern quickly turns to anger.

"Clarissa, leave please," Felicity warns. "Now." Clarissa smirks before walking up the stairs with a smug look on her face. She stops at the top of the staircase, Rodger not far from her trail.

"I can't wait for the day you see she's not good enough for this family." She says coldly while looking directly at me. "She won't be the perfect daughter you're trying to sculpt her into. She will always be," She pauses while the grin on her face gets unnervingly bigger. "An abomination."

"Clarissa, now!" Felicity shouts. Causing me to jump slightly and to advert my eyes to anywhere but the staircase, my eyes teary and my heart pounding. Clarissa's demonic laughter is the only thing I can hear as she makes her way up the stairs and down the corridor upstairs.

I look down at my fingers, my heart beating out of my chest. I've tried to avoid Clarissa as much as I can since arriving here just over a week ago, I still don't know what I've done to deserve this much hate from someone who has never bothered to get to know me the whole time I've been here.

Suddenly I feel a set of hands on my shoulders and notice Spencer standing behind me. He looks down before giving me a wink and turning his attention to Robert. The gesture makes me feel a little bit better. He had my back with Oliver and now with Clarissa. Although he has never said anything, the gesture itself gives me some piece of mind that it is only a few people in this house that don't like my presence or my existence. But I can't help that.

"When do you leave?" Spencer asks, his hands still firmly on my shoulders. Robert moves from where he's standing and grabs his coat off the bottom of the staircase and a suitcase that has been placed underneath the table in the hallway,

"Now, but before I go; Juliette I'm going to make sure you keep yourself busy." He admits while grabbing something of the table. "I will be gone no longer than 24 hours, but in that time, I have already given a lot of the family tasks to do." He says before handing me an ID badge. "For the next week and a half, you'll be volunteering at the local police station. I want you to get a better understanding of the criminal justice system in America." He explains.

I raise my eyebrow at him. "So, I can help you avoid any criminal charges when psycho in the corner decides to go on a murderous rampage again?" I ask. Everyone chuckles and I can't help my smile as I look to Oliver, who isn't impressed. Spencer lets go of my shoulders and I feel myself relax.

"Not at all. If you want to be in the criminal justice field, understanding other counties laws will keep you interesting to potential departments in the future." He explains. "I just have two rules that I expect you to follow." He warns and I frown my brows at him.

"Go on." I encourage. He smiles as he puts his coat on.

"Even if we upset you within the next week and half, you can't help them try and nail us to any crimes." He warns seriously. I look around smiling, hoping that is a joke. No one smiles with me; he is deadly serious.

"Okay, deal. What's the second one?" I ask while turning back at him.

"Under no circumstances do you tell any of them you're a Quinten."

CHAPTER FOUR

Robert Quinten

Spain, Europe

I take a sip of my coffee while listening to the Spanish music in the local café. She's late, but am I surprised? Of course not. I don't think she was ever on time for anything in the almost 9 months I knew her. I decided to wear something less boss like of me. Shorts, a white shirt and sandals, something she'd never expect.

I'm nervous. It's been fourteen years since I last saw her face. Granted she will be 30 now, she's married, and she has a daughter, an heir, Princess Robyn of Haroux.

I know she never fell for me the way I fell for her. How could she? A few months after Juliette was born, she became a Queen, something she had signed up for long before she met me or my family.

"Sir, she's over an hour late, would you like me to get the plane ready?" My security, Thompson speaks behind me. I shake my head while trying to get comfy in my seat.

"Not needed, she'll turn up. She just can't read a watch." I smirk while rubbing my thumb on my rough hands.

"You know your sarcasm never got you very far Rob." A gentle voice speaks. I feel my heart drop as I look up to the doorway of the café.

There she stands, the beauty that is Arielle. She stands tall in her tightly fitted patterned dress, curled long red hair and button up shoes. She's almost unrecognizable. Not the Arielle I knew all those years ago. But still as sharp as a pencil.

I stand to meet her, not sure as to whether to bow with her title. She shakes her head at me while removing her sunglasses, walking elegantly towards me. I can't help but feel my breath get stuck in my throat. She is, as she always has been, breath-taking.

"Robert, I swear if you bow to me, I will smack you with my purse." She smiles as she meets me. I can't help but grin, words failing me as I take in her beauty. Fourteen years, and she's never changed a bit. "Well, are you going to give me a hug?" She asks, which only makes my smile grow wider.

I open my embrace which she gladly accepts.

Her perfume is sweet, but also rich. My guess is it would be a Chanel of some kind. I hear a shift in the room and look up to see her security, getting closer to us. I decide to exit out of the embrace quickly, not wanting to upset the Royal security and she notices. She quickly turns to them and waves them away. They hesitate for a moment, but the look she gives them makes them realize they may not want to question her, and they move to stand outside.

"Ignore them, they are just extra protective." She smiles as she takes a seat. "You've not changed one bit Robert Quinten." She smiles as she nods to the owner. We're alone in the café. With her title, I thought it would be best seen as she might have all these newfound fans. I take a seat, trying to get comfortable and for the first time in my life, I find myself struggling to make conversation with someone.

The owner brings her a coffee and her tiny hands gently pick up the cup, taking a sip of the liquid gold so carefully. I'm in awe, and I shouldn't be. But the woman I met fourteen years ago was throwing back shots of alcohol like they were shots of juice.

"You've changed." I manage to say eventually. My tone comes across as harsh, and I quickly clear my throat. "I mean, you've changed in a good way." I say with a smile.

She sees right through me and narrows her eyes. I could never lie to her, or even attempt to lie because she could tell. I think that was her superpower, even when we thought the hit on us was getting close, I couldn't be the one to lie to her, I had to get Peter to do it.

"How long has it been?" She asks sweetly.

"Fourteen years, three months and 2 days." I say unfazed looking down at my coffee cup. I feel my heart sink with how quickly I answered and look up to find her smiling at me. I feel my cheeks go hot immediately and I clear my throat. "Not that I've been counting." I stutter.

She laughs, and what a beautiful laugh it is. It's her natural laugh, not one that has been forced and sculpted for when she's in the public eye. It's a hearty laugh and I feel my heart swell with how much it makes me happy to hear it after all this time.

After a moment, I watch her smile fade. She hesitates for a moment, the silence between is becoming unnerving. "Well, I never really told you the truth as to who I really am." She admits. I take a sip of my coffee, knowing that this subject was quite possibly going to be a very painful one.

"I managed to find out eventually." I say, my tone slightly bitter and she notices.

"Robert, I had to lie to you. As much as I didn't

want to, I couldn't reveal my identity or my title. That could have put me in danger, or worse I could have ended up dead." She says she leans forward so I can smell that sweet perfume again and my head goes all dizzy. The tone of her voice is more annoyed than anything. "You of all people should know about that." She says coldly and I look deep into her eyes.

"Arielle, you should have told me. Just me. Afterall, we did produce a child together." I snap at her which causes her to move back. My tone wasn't meant to frighten her, but to show my frustration for the last fourteen years. All I had was questions and not a lot of answers.

"I'm sorry I lied to you." She admits after a moment. The air between is now thick with tension. This is not what I wanted. I wanted to sit here and listen to all the amazing things she's gotten up to since becoming Queen. Her marriage, the birth of her daughter, Robyn. But I can't help but feel some jealousy.

Arielle was my first and only love. Admitting that even to myself took years. Because for a while I hated her. I don't feel love, not usually but every time she smiled my heart skipped a beat.

"Would you like to know what happened after you left?" I ask her eventually. She meets my eyes, and hers are filled with curiosity.

"Please. I have to know." She admits with

a nod before sitting straight in her chair. I lean forward, after all, Juliette is still a secret.

"After you left, I had to greet her adoptive parents, Amy and Paul Sanders. Amazing and loving couple, they were great with me too, handing her over was—" I pause for a moment, unsure on if to be this raw with her. But she notices and places her tiny hand gently on mine. "difficult." I admit. I look up at her eyes and I notice tiny tears forming in her eyes.

"From there, she has had a loving life. She's doing well in school; she has good friends. She has a younger sister called Ava. She's happy." I tell her. That seems to make her smile.

"Happy?" She cries and I nod. I watch as she begins to become more and more emotional. "Wow." She smiles. "You kept a close eye on her, didn't you?" She laughs for a moment. I laugh too, I can't help it. I always said I would keep an eye.

"Yes, admittedly. She is my daughter." I say without thought. Suddenly her smile begins to fade as she looks to our hands, hers still holding mine slightly.

"Our daughter." She says after a moment. She looks up at me, those big blue eyes and long black eyelashes give me a sense of happiness.

"Yes, ours." I agree. She smiles once again, and I feel my heart swell just that little bit more.

"So, what do you know about her? Tell me everything." She asks enthusiastically. I can't help but laugh at her excitement.

"Well, she looks more like you than me. Yet, she has neither of our hair colour." I laugh and Arielle joins in.

"How do you mean?" She laughs. I can't control my laughter because it is the most ridiculous thing. I pull out my phone and find a photo that I took of Juliette the night she arrived in Michigan. Her beautiful blonde hair is in a bun and the smile on her face is exactly like Arielle's.

I watch as her smile only grows wider as she takes my mobile from my hands gently cradling it as if it was a child.

"Oh, my goodness." She says smiling, the tears falling down her perfectly sculpted cheeks. "She really does look like me." She laughs while zooming in on the photo a little more. "A blonde?" She asks curiously. I shrug my shoulders and smile; never did I expect for her to have blonde hair, none of us did. "She is beautiful, how did you get that photo?" She asks curiously.

I hesitate for a moment – I had spoken to Arielle's personal secretary and kept the details brief, mentioned it was a private matter, but I needed her to meet me.

So, telling my siblings and children that she

had agreed to meet me was all a lie, she never agreed. I just hoped she'd turn up. But had mentioned our code word we had created while in hiding.

Our code word was more of a nickname. Arielle, a red head who was 16? I called her the *Little Mermaid.* It only seemed logical.

"That was taken when we had a party for her at the house in Michigan last week." I say sheepishly.

I watch as her face changes. The look of curiosity is now filled with what looks like anger. I understand why she's angry, the agreement was for her to not know who either of us were, but that clearly didn't happen and that is, after all, my fault.

"You have a relationship with her?" She grits through her teeth.

I nod. "She found out she was adopted not long after her recent birthday."

Arielle's face is furious, and rightly so. I went back on our agreement, and her reaction was entirely what I was expecting.

"Robert," She begins but takes a second to compose herself. "Does she know about me?" She asks.

I'm taken back by her question for a moment. Why wouldn't I tell our daughter about her birth mother?

"Arielle of course she does, she was there when I found out about your little secret." I say while pointing down at her outfit.

"Does she hate me?" She asks quickly and I pause, startled by her answer.

"Hate you? Why would she hate you?"

"For leaving her?" She questions. I fall back into my chair, stunned by her questioning.

"Arielle, how could she hate you?" I question, frustration clearly in my voice. "She doesn't know you, neither do I!"

She sits back in her back in her chair, staring blankly at me, like my words are a shock. "I never meant to disappoint you, or her." She says softly.

The frustration hits me, and I stand up out of my chair and begin to pace, how could she make it about her? "Arielle, I only know so much. I know that you married into the Haroux family so your brother could take over as king of Donevia. But what I need to understand is where does our daughter stand? Is she some sort of royal?" I question.

She sits for a long moment, before nodding very slowly.

"Since I was a Princess prior to becoming Queen, yes that makes her royal, by blood. Although she has not officially been given a title." She explains.

I move myself to stand against the wall, taking all this in. I, unknowingly, created an heir to a throne. She's silent for a moment, I feel her eyes watch me carefully, but I never look up; I don't need to. I just know.

"Don't give her a title."

I look up at her through my lashes to see the surprised look on her face.

"Robert, by my law I must give her one. It's her birth right." She explains. I shake my head.

"No, Arielle. You don't understand." I say while moving forward to grip the chair. "You give her that title, her life is over."

She laughs in my face. "Robert don't be so dramatic; this could be good for her! She could get to know her sister, my husband Edward. We have a great school in the palace," She begins to explain before I cut her off.

"You can get that ridiculous idea out of your head." I warn her. She's taken back by my tone, like what she said is some sort of surprise. "She's not moving to Haroux, you're not taking her away from her mom."

She laughs in my face. "Robert, I'm her mother." She says with a psychotic smile. *Jesus Christ who is this woman?*

"What's her name?" I ask her, my eyebrow raised. I watch as the smile falls from her face so slowly as the realisation sets in. "You couldn't care less Arielle. You see this as a something that could work in your favour."

She scoffs in my face and laughs once again. "Robert, please. Do you know what will happen to me when the country finds out I had a daughter out of wedlock?" She questions and I laugh back at her.

"You're making this about you, again!" I shout at her. She stands to meet me clearly annoyed now. "Go on, tell me what will happen."

"I will be publicly shamed. Publicly. But it is a price I'm willing to pay to get to know my daughter."

"Does your husband even know you're here?!" I shout.

"Course he does, Robert! He had to force me on the god damn plane!" She screams back. Her response takes me by surprise, and she can see that. "I never lied to him. I told him before the wedding that I had had a daughter when I was in London."

Her admission is a shock to me, admittedly. *She told her husband.*

"Must be nice not to be lied to." I say without thinking. My tone is harsh, and she begins to get upset.

"I've apologised for that, but clearly you

won't ever let me live that down." She says while grabbing her tissue and dabbing it on her cheeks to get rid of the tears that have fallen.

"I'm sorry." I say quietly. I hated seeing her upset, and a lot of the time during her pregnancy. A lot of her sadness was caused by me, my family and the stress of the hit that was on our family.

"I know." She says softly, still wipes the tears that fall. "I always wanted to know that she was doing well, but I couldn't ever bring myself to look for her," she says while placing the teary tissue in her bag before looking up at me directly. "Or you." She admits.

I take a deep breath, why didn't she just say that? Arielle can be so ridiculously selfish. But it is never intentional. It is because she doesn't know how to deal with her emotions so she turns the attention onto her so the topic she can avoid gets changed.

"So, he knows about her?" I ask while taking a seat. Her eyes follow me, and I see the confusion slightly on her face. "Your husband, does he know about Juliette?"

I watch as her eyes widen, and for a moment I get slightly confused until the realization hits me. I just said her name.

"Juliette? That's what they called her?" She asks, teary once again. I nod slowly. I want to kick myself, that was the only thing I had over Arielle.

"Yes." I admit. My tone is so bitter like I can taste the lemon in my mouth. "Her full name is Juliette Amanda Sanders."

"Wow." She says after a moment. "Is that the name you gave her too, or did you not give her one?" She asks.

The question itself catches me off guard for a moment. "Well, I gave her one before handing her over to her parents."

She smiles to me. "What was it?"

"Julianna Eleanor Quinten." I admit with a smile. Saying it out to the woman I loved makes this so much more real. I watch as she takes a long deep breath. "I didn't know she'd have a title so never bothered adding that in there." I joke.

She laughs lightly, revealing the smile that makes my whole world stop. Even after all these years, she is still to me the most beautiful woman to walk this earth.

"She doesn't officially. But that's not important." She says quickly. She moves her hair back and sits in her chair properly. She was slightly hunched over before, a more relaxed version to what her people see, I'm sure. "I'm not wanting to take her away from her family. But I'd like to have a relationship with her. So would Edward and Robyn."

Her response is so mature, yet startling. Not

even 10 minutes ago she was talking about Juliette attending a school on the castle grounds. Although I'm unsure. I nod, I can't deny her a relationship with her birth mother.

"I'll speak to her, I can't guarantee anything, but I'll talk to her when I get back to the US." I say gently. She nods to me, and admittedly I'm pleased she doesn't fight me on it. "Are you happy?" I ask, not looking up at her because I know the answer is going to hurt my soul.

"Yes." She admits honestly. I decide to look up to her and my heart aches even more. I knew I could never be the man she married, but I would have liked for her to be the woman to change me and my ways. But she left. Something she had to do.

"Good." I say quietly, ending it with a fake and painful smile. She sees right through me once again and laughs.

"Robert, I can tell when something hurts you. Is there something you want to get off your chest before we leave?" She asks honestly.

I hesitate for a moment, even admitting my feelings to myself took years and admitting them to her now would cause nothing but an uncomfortable atmosphere. She's married, has a child, a life and a country to look after.

"Nothing that needs to be said. Not anymore." I say with a smile, enough to convince her to drop the subject. I don't want her to leave, I want her to stay, and we talk for hours and eventually that might be case. But I know that right now, if I was to hear how perfect her life is, I might crash and burn with jealousy which isn't intended and the emotion I never knew I would be feeling.

"Before I go," She begins to say before opening her purse and pulling an envelope from her bag. I watch her every move and no doubt so are my security. "Will you give this to her?" She asks while handing me the envelope. I take it with caution and my eyes wide like a deer in headlights. "I just want her to understand why I left."

I can only nod my head; her response makes me angry. I can't help it. Although I now understand why, I still had all those questions for so many years as to who she was and where she ended up. But at least Juliette will know.

She kisses me on the cheek gently, causing me to look up at her startled. "I always loved you. Even when I hated you." She admits; causing whatever I was going to disappear along with my dignity.

She quickly picks up her purse and walks out of the door she walked through only 30 minutes prior. I feel deflated, shocked, and more broken than I was all those years ago. She always knew how to leave me speechless.

CHAPTER FIVE

Juliette Sanders

Michigan, USA

I walk through the doors of the police station to a strong scent of coffee. The smell makes my nose tingle and I sneeze. Americans really do love their coffee. I am quickly torn from my thoughts as I watch a man be dragged through the police station threatening to sue.

"You'll be hearing from my lawyer! Do you understand?!" He shouts through the station causing everyone, including myself to turn in his direction.

"Shut up!" A man shouts from beside me. He's tall, with dark hair and a moustache.

He looks down to me and smiles, a friendly one, that eases my nerves. He's dressed like a classic Detective you'd see on a TV show. Suit pants, shirt, and suspenders. A classic.

"You look lost?" He questions me while looking me up and down. I decided to wear something that was going to be smart yet casual, as no one had given me any pointers on what to wear.

"I'm looking for a Detective Gomez?" I ask looking up at him. He smiles and shakes his head before looking over in front of him at a man hunched over a desk talking to a woman. He's in the same attire, except his shirt is a pale shade of blue.

"There you go, sweetheart." He says in a strong southern accent. I give him a warm smile and begin to make   my way over to the desk. It's not as busy as I was expecting.

As I approach the desk, the woman he's talking to looks up at me and flashes a warning look with her eyes, causing me to stop in my tracks.

"Tracey, do you honestly think the Quinten family had nothing to do with that mass shooting last week?" The Detective asks her. She moves her gaze from me and stares back at him intensely. He clearly doesn't catch on and continues to shake his head. "I just know that they have to be involved. There is no way it can't be them." He says dumbfounded. He still doesn't make eye contact with her, until she clears her throat, to which he eventually catches on. I watch as she makes a clear sign to look in my direction and after a while, he does.

The man is tall, dark brown hair and has a moustache. He meets my face with horror and places his hand on his chest. "You okay there?" He asks nicely.

I pull out my badge and show him it, almost fumbling to try and get out of my pocket. "My name is Juliette Sanders, I'm here to volunteer?" I question him. He looks to me and the only thing I can see is utter confusion on his face. He has no idea who I am or that I was coming, and his face shows it.

Just as he is about to explain, his name is called from somewhere and we both look to the right and in that direction. From what I can see on the front of the door, it says Lieutenant Daniel Huntsman. I'm going to assume that's Detective Gomez' boss.

"Gomez, er," The man stutters as he pulls a piece of paper from his shirt pocket and puts his glasses on that hang from a chain around his neck. "Miss Sanders. My office please." He instructs.

Detective Gomez hands me my badge back and I take it gratefully.

We enter the room and this time, the room reeks of coffee, like this is the source of the stench that lives outside in the ballpen. I sneeze once again, and Detective Gomez is quick to hand me a tissue that is on the Lieutenant's desk.

"Thank you." I politely say as I blow my nose, turning away from the Lieutenant and the Detective.

"Okay, so Miss Sanders, it is to our understanding that your uncle would like for you to learn more about American crimes and the criminal justice system in general is that correct?" He asks while pointing to a seat indicating for me to sit down, and I do just that.

"Yes, that's correct." I lie. I've just lied to a Lieutenant. Robert is really going out of his way to make sure I end up in jail.

"Okay, great. Detective Mike Gomez, I'd like for you to meet your new intern slash volunteer. Juliette Sanders." He introduces us. I see a flash of fear go off in Detective Gomez' eyes.

"Lieutenant with all due respect, I'm handling a murder case that I am sure can be linked to the Quinten family. There was fingerprint evidence of the younger one," He begins to say before pulling out his notepad from his back pocket and flicking through frantically to land on a page. "Oliver. Oliver Jude Quinten."

I turn my attention to the Lieutenant who's shaking his head. "You and I both know Gomez, that we will never be able to link anything to the Quinten family, especially that unhinged one." He explains.

I press my lips together to hold back a laugh. I don't get on with Oliver, but, knowing that the police call him the unhinged one, has to be one of the funniest things I have heard on this whole trip.

"I don't want Juliette here to see the carnage that erupted from that crime scene. We will deal with it eventually, but even you know that trying to solve a case in the middle of a war between two high ranking families. You just don't get involved." He instructs Detective Gomez.

His face is furious, I'm going to assume he had some solid leads too. I suddenly feel guilty and turn my attention back to the Lieutenant.

"Sir, I don't want to be a pain, or get in the way of an investigation." I say while looking at Detective Gomez. He meets my eyes quickly and turns to his boss, with a hopeful look in his eyes.

"Not at all Miss Sanders, you're welcome to learn as much as you can from the old toad here." He says with a smile to his colleague.

I watch Detective Gomez take a long deep breath. "Fine, you can learn a thing or too." He says with a fake smile before getting up out of his chair and storming out of the office.

I stand to meet the Lieutenant, and he extends his hand which I gladly take.

"Miss Sanders, don't worry about him; or his

attitude." He tells me. "There are some cases that need to be solved, and some that need to go cold. That's just how this world works."

The admission makes me feel sick to my stomach. I may only be fourteen, and I understand that a lot of the time, the reason a case goes cold is because of lack of funding, lack of evidence and lack of witnesses to the crime itself. But now knowing that sometimes they don't even bother to try, makes my heart hurt even more for the families that are still waiting for answers about their loved ones.

CHAPTER SIX

Juliette Sanders

Michigan, USA

As I leave the Lieutenants office, I make my way over to the Detectives desk, and take a seat. He begins to put files and evidence into a box quickly, a clear look of frustration settles on his face, and I feel incredibly guilty. Not only for lying to him, but for the fact he won't ever be able to convict my psychotic family member.

"I'm sorry if I interrupted your case, which wasn't my intention." I admit to him. He doesn't acknowledge it and still packs up evidence and crime scene photos.

One of them catches my eye and I move the photo quickly to reveal the absolute carnage that was left from my uncle on the night I arrived in Michigan. The bodies are displayed everywhere and there is blood up and down the walls. 6 bodies in this photo, to reveal the massacre that was started only because I came into this family.

"It's not all sunshine and rainbows in Homicide, Miss Sanders." Detective Gomez says causing me to look up at him. The clear distress on my face causes him to quickly move the crime scene photo away and into the box that he then places onto the floor.

He takes a seat, before picking up a pen and paper and placing it in front of me. I'm clearly a ghost and he can see this. *How could someone do that to another human being?*

"I want you to take notes for our next case." He says quickly causing my eyes to widen. "You want to be a Detective? Catch the killers? Understand their motives?" He asks. My mouth is dry, and instead of speaking I can only nod my head as I know my words would fail me. "Then you're going to be my right-hand woman."

I pick up the pen and paper and place it on my lap before looking up at him. "Is there a case that needs to be worked?" I ask him.

He laughs. In my face, and it's a hearty one too.

"No, Miss Sanders. That case was the only active case we have here in Michigan." He admits before getting up from his seat and going over to the table with the pot of coffee. He turns his head and raises his eyebrows to me. I'm assuming in his way of asking if I'd like one.

"Oh no thank you." I politely say. Once he pours himself a cup and turns back to look at me. "Why do I get the feeling that that's not true Detective? It may not be an active case, but surely there are cases down in evidence that could be solved?" I question.

He stares at me intensely giving me the hint that I may have crossed the line with my questioning. "Miss Sanders, you have to understand that not everything is like the movies, TV shows or books that you see or read." He states.

His answer to my question is a clear dodge and I can see it. He's assuming that because I'm young, that I don't understand anything about the criminal justice system or how cases are solved. In some aspects of it he is right, I don't understand the American justice system.

"Detective Gomez, I didn't realise that justice had an expiry date?" I question him. He looks to me, started by my question. "Granted I'm young, so I couldn't possibly know anything about solving a crime." I say sarcastically.

He doesn't answer me, but only stares at me in a state of shock. "I just know Detective Gomez, that the case that I worked on in London, and the officers that I had the pleasure to work with; all made sure that everyone was kept in the loop, and nothing was left out of the investigation."

I can hear it go quiet around me for a moment, but I don't bother to look around. "Granted, not every officer is the same. You do have your lazy ones who only come in to get their pay and then go home. But I wouldn't see you as lazy Detective, would you?"

The silence in the bullpen now is deafening and by the look on Detective Gomez' face; I have clearly said something to upset him.

He looks down on me, before grabbing his jacket from the back of his chair and walking away and out of the building. I now stand, in the middle of the room surrounded by Detectives and police officers. I feel myself become anxious, and I can't help but think I have screwed up my chance.

"You know darlin'," I man in front of me speaks while leaning against a desk, "He needed that kick up the arse. So well done you." He applauds before the rest of the precinct join in.

I instantly become embarrassed, and I feel my cheeks become hot as I look down to the floor trying to ignore the stares.

"Don't worry darlin,' he'll be back." The man speaks once more in front of me. "You've just given hm the biggest reality check that even he knew he needed eventually."

I watch as the room scatters slowly, and new conversations start throughout the room. I look to my right and catch the eye of the lady, Tracy I believe, who begins to walk in my direction, a slight smile on her face.

"So, Miss Sanders, is it?" She questions me.

"You can call me Jules."

She smiles to me as she gestures for me to take a seat at the Detectives desk. "Well Jules, how about I give you some tasks to do till Detective Gomez comes back?" She asks.

I nod at her and in front of the desk she picks up a load of files. "You can start by sorting these statements into piles of sorted, need followed up and not needed." She says while placing the stack of files in front of me. There could be quite a few. "The ones that have been sorted will have a date on the right-hand corner. That's all you need to do. It will keep you busy." She says with a smile.

I nod to her, not wanting to upset anyone else. I watch as she walks away from the desk and down the corridor. I begin to look around and find a few of the Officers laughing at me. I'm going to guess that this is the job no one wants and with me being the volunteer, I've been left with it.

I decide instead of complaining I might as well do what I've been instructed. I look around the room and find a conference room that is empty and decide since there are a lot, I might as well do it properly.

I get up from the desk and knock onto the Lieutenants door. "Sorry to bother you sir, I'm just wondering if I could use the conference room to do my task I've been given?" I ask politely. A confused look appears on his face as he begins to look out of the window of his office. "One of the other Detectives gave me a task to do till Detective Gomez comes back. I just wanted to make sure I was okay to use the meeting room and that no one else needed it?" I explain and I watch the confusion turn to realisation. He smiles to me.

"Of course, Miss Sanders, thank you for checking." He says before hinting at me to get out.

I do just that and pick up a stack of files I know I'll be able to carry and make my way over to the conference room. I place the stack of files on the desk before going back for the last 2 and pulling out a seat. I grab a bottle of water that is on the table behind me and decide to get to work. After all, I'm only a volunteer.

CHAPTER SEVEN

Detective Gomez

Michigan, USA

I take one more deep breath before I decide I need to get a grip and get back to my job. Never did I think a kid would give me a reality check. And instead of getting angry at her, I decided to do what I do best and go and sit in my car and drive around.

I don't understand why they have decided to give me the task of babysitting and teaching a teenager. Not only is she stubborn and determined to try and help people but she also has the drive that I had at her age and that makes me angrier at myself.

I let this job and the cases take over my life for so long. I lost myself and I've lost my family over it.

I pull the sun visor down and pull the photograph that sits next to the mirror of my family.

My beautiful daughter, Riley looks like that British girl I'm now teaching. She looks like her mother more than anything and that causes me more pain the longer I stare at the photo. My son, Steven, he looks like me, and to everyone else my kids are the opposites of each other. *Or they were.*

I decide that all I'm going to do is upset myself the more I look at the photo and put it away.

Taking a deep breath, I decide to make my way into the police station in the hopes that someone else has taken on the responsibility of that girl.

To my surprise, I notice my desk is empty and there is no 5-foot odd British girl sat waiting for me to return. My heart slightly does a jump and I realize that I might be able to do my job in peace. I take a seat at my desk and take a deep breath.

"You're not off the hook." Tracy speaks behind me, causing me to turn around. "She's doing the job that no one wants." She explains and I look in the direction of where her eyes are looking and turn to see Juliette through the window of the conference room.

I let out a loud groan and slam my head on the desk. *Why me?* "Is it because I haven't been on my game for a while?" I turn to ask her, causing her pale green eyes to meet mine. "Is this punishment?" I ask.

She laughs lightly, shaking her head while standing up from her desk collecting her files. "No, Mike. It's not. I think all the Lieutenant wants you to do is realize that in this world there are people that want to do right. And that girl is one of them." She explains while her eyes dart between the conference room and my face. "She may not understand the American way of being a Detective, but I've heard a rumour that she brought down a drug ring within her school. So, you may wanna ask her about that."

She walks away from me and down towards the evidence room and I turn my chair around and watch as the girl, without an argument, begins to put all of the witness statements into piles.

I run my hands through my hair and take a deep breath, whether I like this or not, I have to be her mentor for the next however long.

I decide to pick up a donut from the side and grab a bottle of water in case she's thirsty. I pour myself a coffee and begin to make my way over to the conference room.

I knock, not wanting to barge in and startle her. After a moment, I hear a polite 'come in!' and I open the door gently while meeting her startled eyes. I'm going to assume she thought I wasn't coming back.

"Hello." I greet her properly while placing my coffee on the desk and her bottle of water that was under my arm. "I didn't know if you were hungry, but I brought you a donut." I say while handing her it which she takes.

A smile appears on her face as she looks down at the donut. "Thank you." She politely says before taking a bite and turning back to her task unfazed. I begin to panic, like my actions might have upset her with the way I stormed out and I find myself pacing the room with the uncertainty of my feelings.

"I'm sorry, I can't remember your name." I admit to which she smiles, not taking her eyes off the paper in front of her.

"My name is Juliette, Detective. But you can call me Jules." She says before looking up slightly at me.

"Jules, right." I begin to stutter while pacing. "I'm sorry if I upset you or startled you earlier." I admit unexpectedly. She looks up to me, this time caught off guard by my admission. "I don't want you to have those first impressions of me, and I would like to introduce myself properly if I'm going to be your teacher, as such." I say quickly.

After a few moments I watch as she smiles to me. "Detective don't be silly. I know you were given this task without being consulted. It's a shock. But

I hope you can teach me a few things." She says politely.

Admittedly, my face doesn't match how I'm feeling. I feel elated that she's not upset with me, but I feel my face is showing a state of shock, and the smile drops from her face. "Have I upset you, Detective?"

I stutter, not being able to find my words correctly. "N-no, sorry." I say while sitting down next to her and peeking over the piles.

She's placed them into 3 piles and placed sticky notes on each of them on whether they have been dealt with, a follow up needs to go on and not enough information.

"You've been busy." I say to her. She looks up from eating her donut and nods at me.

"Just doing what Tracy told me to do." She says, her mouth full. I can't help but laugh as it reminds me of my daughter.

"Sorry, that was terrible manners." She says while placing down her donut. "Some of these are horrible." She explains looking amongst the piles before meeting my eyes again. I follow her gaze and realize that I don't know what kind of statements she's been reading, and they should have been checked.

"There are some awful people in the world." I explain. She begins to pick one up off the pile and read it to me. "This woman's husband hit her because she asked if she could go out with her friends." She says before putting it down and picking up another from another pile. "This man shot his friend over money." She says before placing it back on the other pile. "The world is full of uncertainty." She admits before looking over in my direction. "How long have you been a Detective?" She asks.

"15 years." I say with a small smile. She sits back in her chair before picking up her donut again.

"Do you enjoy it?" She asks.

I struggle to find my words for a moment. I don't know if to lie to her or be truthful with her. Afterall, she is wanting to do this as a career, or she is doing this as experience. "Not as much as I used to." I answer honestly.

She doesn't say anything else, just takes a bite of her donut and nods. But that is all I need. I get the sense that she understands more than what she's letting on. "Jules, why is it you want to learn about the American system? Is it cause your curious?" I ask her.

She finishes her donut and wipes her face with the napkin. "I guess you could say that. I think that my family is wanting me to have a better understanding of this country as well as my own."

I can't help myself but become intrigued. A British girl wanting to get a better understand of the American system? Curiosity begins to fill my veins. "So, your family? What are they like?" I ask her and I watch fear suddenly flash in her eyes for a moment before she looks away from me.

"They can be a bit much, but they have good hearts." She says giving me a fake smile before picking up another statement and reading it intensely.

"You don't get on with them?" I ask her, to which she shakes her head.

"It's not that, I'm only visiting this side of my family for a few weeks, I go back home to London soon." She explains.

I can only nod, although she's being quite closed off, I do believe her. If she had more to say on her family, I'm sure she would probably be more forthcoming.

"Would you like me to give you a hand with the rest of these statements?" I ask her politely, not wanting to sit in silence and it makes me uncomfortable.

"No, it's okay. I'll get on with these, I only have a few more to do. Thank you for offering." She says with a smile, which I return. She seems like a good kid. Polite, kind natured, hard working. She reminds me so much of Riley that I can feel my heart hurt the more I look at her.

"Dad! Dad! Watch me!" Riley *shouts from the tree house towards kitchen where I'm standing. "I'm gonna catch the bad guys."* She screams before taking her brother out by diving on him and he falls to the floor. *"Gotcha!"*

"Get off me Officer! I didn't do nothing!" Steven *shouts while still being on the floor, struggling to move from Riley's grip.*

"Never! You're going to jail! Dad! I need your handcuffs." She shouts confidently while pulling her brother up.

"Riley, you know I can't give you, my handcuffs." I say while walking out into the back yard. *"But I can make sure the criminal goes to jail!"* I say while throwing Steven over my shoulder, hearing his little giggle ring in my ear. *"Officer Riley, well done for catching the criminal. You get to stay up an extra 10 minutes tonight."* I applaud her.

Steven then decides to struggle till I put him down. *"What about me, dad?"* He asks while I walk through the house, the sound of their feet following me like penguins following their huddle.

"Well since you played a good criminal, I'd say you get the same." I say with a smile while walking up the stairs and they follow. They both cheer as we walk up the stairs together and onto the landing.

"Okay my little people, I need you both to get

your pj's on and brush your teeth. Otherwise, I'm not reading you both a story." I say sternly. I watch as they both scatter into their rooms and quickly change.

Just as I am about to walk into my bedroom, Riley comes out of her bedroom and smiles at me. "I can't wait to be like you dad." She exclaims before running back into her room and out of sight.

"Is everything okay, Detective Gomez?" I hear a voice ask, breaking me from my flashback. I look up to meet those ocean blue eyes and I suddenly feel myself become embarrassed as I can feel my cheeks heat up.

"Yes, fine." I stumble knocking the bottle of water onto the table that I had apparently unopened, and it spill all over the table, ruining multiple statements in its path. "Crap!" I exclaim, while quickly picking up some paper towels from behind me and lightly dabbing the statements, attempting not to ruin them anymore. "Sorry." I apologise and I watch her shake her head.

"It's okay, I just hope I don't get in trouble for it." She laughs slightly while helping me dry the table. I don't pay attention for a second, before I watch a confused look take over her face. "Jules?"

"Detective, does this paper look slightly discoloured to you at the side?" She asks, turning a statement towards me. I can see a slight difference, but nothing too much.

"Nothing gigantic, why?" I ask her. I watch

her face carefully as she moves the paper away and looks up.

"This is a stretch, but when I was little, we had invisible ink and would have an ultraviolet light, and I think that that is what it is. The colour used to change slightly to a more cream, and yellow toned. It's hard to see but something is definitely there." She explains. I look at her, my face full of confusion as I honestly do think this is a stretch. "Detective, do you have an ultraviolet light?" She asks quickly and I frown.

"Yes, in my desk draw." I say placing the wet paper towels that were on the desk now in the bin beside me. "Jules, it's probably the water." I explain to her.

She nods to me, her face less determined but also, she has a look in her eye hinting that she would like me to get it. "Hang on." I say before turning around, opening the door, and going into the office and straight to my desk, internally rolling my eyes on how stupid this is going to look.

I get the ultraviolet light from my desk and walk back into the conference room, closing the door and I begin to pull down the curtains.

"I am probably wrong, but I would like to rule it out." She says to me in the dark before I put the light on. I decide to ignore her as I walk round towards the desk and place it over the statement.

I feel my heart plummet when I realize this

kid is right. Clear as day, in invisible ink, the words *'save me'* lie on the side of the statement.

"Good god." I say as I turn off the light, unsure on what to make of it. "Well, aren't you smart." I say without thinking.

She doesn't respond to me, only goes up to the window and pull up the blinds revealing the sun. "Who would have an invisible pen or something with invisible ink on their desk?"

I suddenly feel a wave of realization flow through me. "Stevens has one, keeps his kids entertained."

I stare blankly at her, because in the truth, I don't know who could. "This woman, Melissa Wilson, she came in a week ago making a statement against her husband." Jules explains while reading off the statement. "He hit her, threw her down some stairs. It says here there is noticeable bruising on her wrists but inevitably not enough evidence to arrest Francis Wilson." She continues.

I quickly take the piece of paper out of her hand and look for the badge number, or a name linked with whoever took the statement. Banks. Officer Banks. He's relatively new. And his desk is right next to Officer Stevens. I quickly turn on my heel and open the door, leaving Jules in the conference room and making my way straight towards Banks who sits flirting with one of the female officers on his desk.

"Banks!" I say loudly to which he turns around and I hand him the statement. "Why did you let this woman go back to her husband?" I ask him frustratingly.

He quickly looks down at the statement and shakes his head. "There wasn't evidence to say he was assaulting her." He explains handing it back to me almost laughing as he does it.

I turn to Jules who doesn't even need to be given an instruction and turns off some of the lights before making her way over with the UV light. "So, tell me why she's wrote 'save me' on the side of her statement?" I ask him honestly. I see the look of panic fall onto his face and a nervous laughter escapes his lips.

"Clearly, I wouldn't have sent her home to him if I saw that, but she was fine." He explains while looking around the room noticing the eyes on him.

"No, she wasn't, she had bruises on her wrists where he clearly had grabbed her, but you took her statement and said at the bottom, that 'nothing more needed to be done, apart from a few minor bruises, the woman was fine to return to her husband.'" I read, quoting his notes at the bottom. I feel myself become angry at him, the lack of care for this woman who clearly showed signs of being assaulted that he ignored. "The side of the statement aside, you let a woman go back to her husband who was clearly abusive." I state to him, and he avoids my eyes, which are clearly filled with rage. "I'm about to go and do a welfare check on this woman, I just hope she's alive."

I grab my coat and begin to walk out of the precinct, leaving Jules there on her own, gripping the statement in my hand that I just took out of his. I turn back and notice Jules still standing in the same spot as before. "Come on, I don't have all day." I say, hinting for her to follow me.

She does just that, like a puppy following its owner, she meets me at the car. "Are you normally this angry?" She asks as I open the car door and I can't help but laugh.

"Only every day, Juliette."

CHAPTER EIGHT

Juliette Sanders

Michigan, USA

I watch as we drive through the streets of Michigan. I've never been on this side of the city, and I watch closely as we pass bookshops, local cafés and businesses.

The silence in the car is unnerving as Detective Gomez drives carefully through the streets. I can't help but glance over every once in a while. I wonder what is going on in his brain, how to handle this and how to go about speaking with the victim.

We turn into a street, and I watch as he looks out of his window and slows down the car, I'm assuming looking for the house numbers.

"What number was it again?" I ask him.

"405."

I turn my attention the left-hand side of the car and count down the numbers in my head. I notice that on the end these are even numbers, and just like London, normally the odd numbers are on the other side.

"Got it." He exclaims before pulling in the car a little further down the street and putting the car in park. "I have a plan, but I need to use you as bait." He says before undoing my seatbelt and turning me towards him.

"Why?" I ask him as he gives me a look.

"Ask to use their phone, and then see if there are any bruises on the woman." He explains to me. My eyes widen, he really is using me as bait.

"What if she isn't in?" I ask him and he shakes his head.

"The car is there. Look, it might just be a dead end, but we won't know till we try." He explains to me, putting his hands firmly on my shoulders. "I trust that you can put on an American accent."

"Detective, you have to be joking?" I ask him seriously and he only shakes his head. "Detective, this is insane." I say to him, clearly panicked.

"Juliette, you are gonna have to be the girl who saves this woman. Just go to the door, say your lost, you've moved in around this area, and that you need to use a phone to contact your parents."

I feel my mouth go try but the adrenaline pushes me to nod my head, even though I am panicking inside.

"That's it, okay. You'll be fine." He says before pulling out his notepad and writing down his number on the piece of paper. "Remember, use your American accent, I'll answer, and I'll ask you yes or no questions. Just make it as believable as you can. If you see anything that shows she needs removing from the home, say nail polish." He explains.

I can feel myself nod, but not answer him trying to retain all of the information so I don't make a mistake.

"You've got this." He encourages me, before hinting for me to get out of the car. I do as he instructs, and I begin to walk towards number 405. I feel my hands become sweaty and my heart pounding out of my chest.

I'm going to assume that the reason that he has sent me in is because if there was a male presence, she may not ask for help if she feels like she's been denied it.

I walk up the steps to the house, an unsettling feeling coming over me making me shiver. I knock on the door and wait patiently, in the hopes that she might answer the door.

I wait for what feels like a lifetime before slowly the door opens and a woman peaks from behind the door. "Can I help you?" The shaken woman asks. I can see clear as day that she has a bruise on her eye, even though she's tried to cover it with makeup.

"I'm sorry to bother you ma'am." I say in my best American accent. It probably sounds fake, but I decide to keep going. "I've just recently moved to Michigan, and I'm lost getting back home. I think I took a wrong turn." I say light-heartedly.

She doesn't laugh, only hides behind the door more. "I can't help you, I'm sorry." She says quickly before almost slamming the door.

"I was just wondering if I can use your phone to call my Dad." I say quickly before she closes it. "That's it."

After a few moments she opens the door a little further, hinting for me to enter and I thank her kindly. I stand in the entrance as she shuts the door and scurries towards the kitchen and I follow her, taking in anything that I think I can mention to Detective Gomez.

"There." She says quickly before removing herself from the room. I thank her once again as I move towards the phone.

I pull out Detective Gomez's number and begin to put it into the phone. It begins to ring and within a second it answers.

"Act normal." He asks quickly.

"Hey Dad, I went out for a walk, and I got a bit lost. This lady has let me use her phone, but I'm not sure where I am. Can you come pick me up?" I ask quickly, in my fake American accent.

"Jesus, that American accent is terrible." He almost laughs and I roll my eyes. "Okay, ask for the address."

"Sorry ma'am, what's the address?" I ask her and she stutters while telling me the address and I say thank you.

"Jesus, she sounds shaken up. Is she covered in bruises?" He asks me.

"Yeah." I say while giving the woman a smile, which she doesn't return she is just hugging herself.

"Do you see anything that would warrant me being able to enter?" He asks and I subtly try and look around for something, trying to avoid the eye contact of the woman. I quickly scour the room for something and notice a white substance on the coffee table.

"Sorry Dad, did you manage to get that nail polish from the store?" I ask quickly. Suddenly, I hear a door from upstairs open and I look to the woman who's face fills with panic.

"Jules, what's going on?" The Detective asks. I

watch as the woman moves quickly towards me.

"You need to leave." She says quickly dragging me from the phone. I stutter trying to protest while she moves me quickly towards the door. "He will kill you." She whispers to me while grabbing my face.

"He'll kill you if you stay. Please." I plead her and she shakes her head. "You went into the police station last week to make a statement; you want to leave. So, come with me." I plead with her.

"I can't." She almost cries and I take a hold of her hand.

"If you leave with me, I promise he can never hurt you again. I'm making you that promise. Please believe me." I plead once more. She looks deep into my eyes, like she's looking for some indication that I'm lying.

"He will kill us both." She cries. I take her hand tightly and look into her eyes once more.

"Let's not give him that option."

I watch as she turns around and at the top of the stairs stands a tall broad man who comes booming down the stairs. Compared to me and Melissa, this man is double our size.

"Who the fuck is this!" He exclaims as he walks towards us, anger fuelling his face while he glares down at me.

"S-she needed to use the phone. She's lost."

The woman cowers in front of me. I watch as his face fills with more anger before he grabs hold of her tightly around her arm and drags her away.

"Why would she need to use the phone huh?" He mocks her. "Stupid woman!" He screams in her face. I try to pull him off her only to be shoved into the door.

"You little bitch! Coming into my home!" He says before grabbing my arm tightly and opening the door. Just as I feel as though he might let go, I watch his face drop so slowly and he goes extremely pale. I turn around and see Detective Gomez standing at the door, gun raised straight at Francis.

"Francis Wilson, you're under arrest for assault and battery. Now, I suggest you get your hand off my volunteer."

CHAPTER NINE

Juliette Sanders

Michigan, USA

I watch carefully as the paramedics take a look at Melissa Wilson and her injuries. Thankfully, apart from a few bruises she is going to be just fine they said, apart from the trauma.

I know I'll have a lovely bruise that I will have to hide from Robert and my family, but it was worth it seeing that woman smile with the paramedics. She has a long way to go, but I'm assuming she's tough.

I feel someone stand beside me, looking in the same direction of me. For a few moments we sit in silence and it's nice. The quiet. For Melissa it's probably peace.

"I was stupid for sending you in." Detective Gomez finally speaks up, I turn to look at him confused, like what I'm looking at is fake and we didn't just save a woman from an abusive relationship. "I should have checked your American accent first. It's terrible." He laughs, a belly laughs too. I can't help but join in, even I know it sounded ridiculous.

"I should have just used my normal accent, surely that would have worked better?" I mock him. He nods, laughing once again.

"You did good today, we also found a stash of cocaine, looks like he was a dealer too."

I nod my head, I knew that the powder on the coffee table had to be cocaine, or some sort of drug.

"All I want to know is how you didn't know it was just baking powder that had spilt on the coffee table." He says calmly, looking down the street and avoiding my stare.

"Because that is logical Detective." I joke. He begins to laugh probably coming to the conf Even he knows how ridiculous that sounds. "The reason you probably don't know is because you've not asked." I tell him honestly.

"You're right." He's quick to admit which causes me to look in his direction. "I feel like today has been a success, do you?" He asks.

"Oh! One hundred percent."

The silence takes over once more as Melissa begins to walk towards us both. A light smile on her face. Her walk is telling, for the first time in God knows how long, this is a walk of freedom for her.

"I have to thank you both." She says with a small smile. "You both just saved my life."

"It is our job." Detective Gomez is quick to respond. I watch as she shakes her head, laughing ever so lightly underneath her breath.

"It is yours Detective, but what about you?" She asks looking to me. "Where do you stand in all of this?"

I feel myself pause, not knowing how to respond to her. Although Detective Gomez forced me into the situation itself, I can't help but feel relief for knowing that woman will be able to be free of him.

"Just someone wanting to do some good in the world." I say with a smile. She smiles too, like my answer really did give her something she needed.

"Well, I have to thank you, he could have hurt you." She admits. "So, thank you both." She says with a smile.

Suddenly we both hear her name being called and she turns around to a woman, taller than

Melissa running frantically through the street towards her. "Oh! Thank God!" She exclaims while tightly holding Melissa who welcomes the hug gratefully, clutches onto the woman like she is her lifeline.

"I told you." She whispers, loud enough for us to hear. "I told you, you could." She praises her.

Melissa pulls away from the embrace and shakes her head. "I went to the police station last week and was told there was nothing they could do." She explains, practically gripping onto this woman for dear life. "But then this girl turned up today and well-".

I watch as she turns herself towards me, a smile almost plastered on her face like a mask. "She and her partner saved my life." She praises.

"Well, thank you." The woman says before extending her hand out to Detective Gomez which he shakes with a smile, something I've not seen him do much today.

She extends her hand out to me also, which I take gratefully.

Melissa waves goodbye while walking away with her friend who holds onto her tightly, like she's worried she Melissa might disappear.

"I see today as a success," Detective Gomez praises and he leans into me lightly. "Sorry I was a bit of a pain earlier."

I can't help but laugh. "A bit?" I joke.

He laughs with me, a much deeper laugh this time. "Okay, I was a dick. Is that better for you?" He admits,

I nod, a smile appearing on my face. "Much better, Detective."

We watch as the car taking Francis leaves the scene, probably to head to the police station. He glares at us both the car passes, neither one of us frightened by his look.

"She called me your partner."

He turns to me quickly, no expression on his face. "Well, you are for the next few weeks are you not?"

I can't help but laugh at the realisation, after all. I will be working closely with Detective Gomez.

"I think I need to earn the partner title, how about you just call me your volunteer?" I ask sweetly.

"Deal. So, would you like me to take you to your uncles?" Detective Gomez offers, causing me to look in his direction.

"I think there is still a stack of statements that have my name on. Then I'll go home."

He only nods to my answer, before turning his head and his eyebrows raise like he's just had an idea. "Ice cream sound good?" He asks.

"That sounds very good."

CHAPTER TEN

Juliette Sanders

Michigan, USA

I follow the security guard through the door of the Quinten home, and I can't help but exhale as I lean back on the door to close it.

What a day.

I close my eyes and run through the events of today, the first meeting with Detective Gomez and the Lieutenant, the woman who we managed to get away from her husband, who I am hoping finds closure and safety in her friends. Not to mention the exhausting task of having to use an American accent.

"Look what the cat dragged in." A voice from the top of the stairs speaks and I look up to find Clarissa standing there, a glass of wine in her hand. *Oh dear,* this is the last thing I needed.

"Not tonight, Clarissa, I've had a long day." I pull my bag up onto my shoulders and begin to walk through to the kitchen. I hear footsteps quickly follow me and I can't help but roll my eyes.

"I have something to say." She practically slurs. I turn around and find her inches away from my face, the stench on the wine coming into contact with my nose and I back off. The vinegar smell makes my eyes water. She's drunk and she's the last person I wanted to see.

"You've ruined all of our lives you know." She slurs and I exhale, loudly.

"So, you keep saying. Yet, I haven't seen any indication as to when I've put this family at risk?" I state. She doesn't like that, and I watch her eyes go dark, like she's been possessed by the devil within her.

She lets out a cackle. Which catches me off guard and I become unsettled.

"Juliette, is it? Or is it, Julianna?" She mocks me. Suddenly the slurs are almost non-existent as she closes off the space between us. "Let me make one thing clear, cause Oliver, Rodger and I are on the same page here. Your very existence is a risk to all of our lives. You being here ruined any chance our family had of signing off that deal with the other mafia family-" She begins to say before I cut her off.

"Oh! I was under the assumption Oliver killed them all?" I state to her. She laughs in my face and shakes her head.

"You know nothing." She says as the smile drops from her face.

"Don't I?" I taunt her. "Because I am one hundred percent certain I saw the crime scene photos today when I was working with a Detective at the police station who wanted to pursue a case against Oliver and the entire family." I say, my eyes never breaking contact with hers. The look she gives me is cold, but also anger is beginning to reside on her face and the joy that is bringing me shows she knows nothing.

"Let's be real here Clarissa, the only reason I am standing here is because Rodger wanted me to know that I was adopted. Whether he did it in a malicious manor or not in the attempt to ruin my life, all it did was build curiosity."

She's furious now, she doesn't like being told the truth. Her brows are frowned and the look on her face is murderous.

"Now correct me if I'm wrong, Robert invited me here; did he not? Because I swear if I was such a danger then why would he want to have a relationship with me, and invite me to his house?" I state to her, my voice is slightly raised, as the annoyance and the audacity of her is becoming a tiny bit unbearable.

"He only invited you because he thought it would be good for you. But we all know you'd never hack it in this family. The sight of blood made you collapse. It is pathetic." She spits in my face.

I can't help but laugh at her. "Just because I don't come from a family that has seen a fair share of blood and murder, sometimes caused by some of its members, doesn't mean I haven't seen a fair share of horror. We aren't so different you and I Clarissa, both of us were adopted, both of us have a good education not to mention both of us know when the other one is doing something to try and beat or bully the other. I've had to avoid girls like you my entire life, because your nothing more than a bully, who gets a rise out of ruining someone else's life."

She remains quiet, clearly the frustration and anger has become unbearable for her to deal with, and she now stands shaking with anger. Do I feel bad, no. It's probably because she has made my life a living hell since arriving.

"One day your fairy-tale to become a reality, Juliette. I can't wait to watch your world burn to the ground." She seethes through her teeth, getting so close to my face once again I can smell the alcohol. "You don't belong in this family. They will see it one day and when they do," she says quietly while a psychotic grin creeps over her face.

"The only thing you'll be able to hear for miles is my laughter, so you know that I've won." Her laugh is evil, never breaking eye contact as the smile grips onto her skin like a mask. "I always win."

CHAPTER ELEVEN

Juliette Sanders

Michigan, USA

I lie back on my bed and exhale, why does she have to be so difficult? It's not like I asked for this life or to be involved into the family.

After my little confrontation with Clarissa, I decided that after today I need a nap, or I need a will to live. I think she needs to grip into her skull that I'm not here to ruin her life or any of the others and this is a made-up fantasy in her head.

She doesn't scare me, which surprises a lot of people. Her actions and her words only showcase the amount of anger and jealousy she's radiating and to myself and everyone else, it's getting kind of boring.

I stare at my ceiling in the hopes that eventually, my eyes will just close, and I can forget, even for a little while that today went on.

Suddenly the peace is broken when I hear the bedroom door open and close, hinting that someone is now in my room. *If it's Clarissa with a knife, you need to get up...*

The thought made my hair stand up on my neck and I turn to find Robert, leaning against the door, his brown hair slicked back, and his black suit fitted tightly to his body.

"How did it go?" He asks, placing his hands in his pockets.

"I can ask you the same question." I joke. He laughs with me, still standing against the door. I get the sense he is hesitant to move into my personal space, and even more so to get the reaction from me after he met Arielle.

"You go first." He instructs, shifting ever so slightly. I sit up on my elbows.

"I helped a woman get out of a domestic relationship; her husband is now in jail."

He doesn't say anything, only stares blankly at me, and I can get the hint I know what is coming. "Were you involved in it at all?" He asks calmly. *There it is...*

"Yes, I was." I say quietly. He doesn't shift or move his eyes from mine for a brief moment, the only thing he does is exhale very loudly, to which I'm assuming is calming the fire that is within.

"Did you get hurt?" He asks calmly once more.

I don't lie, I'm not a liar. But showing him the bruise that is probably brewing on my arm from Francis Wilson grabbing me earlier, is only going to cause him to go off the rails.

"No. It was fine." I say with a hopefully reassuring smile.

I can tell he doesn't believe me, the expression on his face shows it. "Is the woman alright?" He asks changing the subject slightly.

"Yeah, she's okay. Someone she knew came for her, and it seems like she will be okay, eventually." I say with a small smile which he joins in.

"That's good." He says softly. He pulls one hand out of his pocket and gently strokes his chin, he seems stressed, or more like worried about what he has to tell me.

"How did it go with Arielle?" I ask in the moments silence that was becoming unbearable. Being in Roberts presence can be incredibly unsettling at times, and this has to be one of them.

"Well, she's not what I remembered, that is for sure." He says slowly standing up and walking round to my side of the bed. "She's different, more mature, which is good." He says while taking a seat next to me, causing me to sit up.

"Well Robert, she was only 16." I say as joke. He joins in with a small laugh. But the sound of it makes me nervous. "Were you disappointed?" I ask him softly.

"I don't know how I'm feeling honestly." He admits. The reaction and the pain in his voice is so raw that it is hard to look at. "I think, in my mind she was still the wild and wonderful Arielle who never understood the world. But never did I expect for her to stand in front of me, Queen of a country." He says quietly.

I don't think that Arielle's new life sunk in yet. "Did you talk?" I ask wanting to get him mind off his heartbreak.

"Yeah," He pauses for a moment, shaking his head. "She was incredibly selfish is some parts of the conversation, I don't know if it is because she never really connected with the fact that she had a child or she is completely—" He stops speaking and I turn to him. His head is hanging down and he's sitting in silence which is unsettling.

"Robert, whatever you have to say won't change anything, she made up her mind." We can't change how our lives planned out. He turns to me, the hurt in his eyes are clear to see and it makes my heart ache. I don't know this man properly, nor do I know any of the people I'm staying with, but I think it's apparent that he loved her and whatever happened today; it has upset him.

"She's completely selfish and she only sees you as something she can use in the long run."

The admission doesn't catch me off guard, if anything I expected it.

"Well, I'm not shocked in all honesty." I say to him quickly, so he knows my feelings aren't hurt. "But what exactly happened?" I ask once more. "I don't want you to sugar coat things Robert, you can tell me the truth."

He exhales loudly, not sure if it is because he knows what he is about to say is going to upset me more, if talking about what happened will only make him angry.

He rubs the palms of his hands together and rubs them on his tailored pants. "She never asked for your name." He says a moment later. He looks to me, the hurt in his eyes is clearer than before and I feel my heart ache once again. "I told her your name, she never asked."

I shake my head slightly. "Why would that matter?" I ask him slightly confused.

He laughs.

"Juliette, the first thing that I would want to know about my daughter, or a child I gave up is their name." He says, clearing his throat. "She never asked, which to me meant she didn't really care."

I sit, unsure on how to take Robert's admission. "What else?" I urge.

"Well, she wanted to know a little about you. I told her about your family, and she went on a little side tangent on how you could attend the school in the palace—" He begins, clearly getting quite angry.

"What!" I exclaim. He puts his hands up quickly to pause me from continuing.

"Juliette, I can assure you. That would never happen." He reassures me. "I think she was under the impression maybe you'd move over to Haroux or something ridiculous like that. Again, I think she sees you as something she can use to get the council to favour her." He whispers, the pain in his voice clear as day now.

"Council? What are you talking about?" I press, a little annoyed that Arielle thought she could take me from my own family.

"She said something about how she will be frowned upon by the country for having a child out of wedlock."

I roll my eyes, "Let me guess, men run the council?" He shrugs his shoulders.

"I can only guess; however, she told Edward, her husband about you before they got married." He admits. Now that takes me by surprise. Why would she tell her soon to be husband that she had a baby before they got married? Surely that would make her, not worthy of marrying into the family? *Unless they were in love...*

"So, where does that stand for me, what is your take on meeting her?" I ask curiously.

To me, the meeting didn't go how Robert wanted. Whichever way it went, or the conversation that happened has upset him.

"I'm leaving that up to you. If you would like to meet her, I can arrange it. But I would like to do more of a background check on her if that is alright with you?" He asks softly and I can't help but laugh.

"Wouldn't you anyway whether I gave you permission or not?"

He laughs with me, the light wrinkles on his eyes lifting up. He knows I'm right.

"Very true. I'm only asking as a curtesy. I'd do it anyway." He laughs harder, causing me to join in.

"I'm not sure yet." I admit in the laugher. He looks to me, his eyes filled with hope. I think this is the first time I've ever seen Robert unsure on anyone. Granted I haven't known him long, but even still you can see how he doesn't know how this is going to play out. He's always one step ahead.

"Well, maybe this can help stir you in the direction you want to take." He says softly before reaching into his pocket and pulling out an envelope. "I never opened it, so I don't know what it says. At the end of the day this is your decision. No one can judge you for what you decide."

He hands me the envelope slowly and I take it, looking up into his eyes. "You may want to ring your Mom." I meet his eyes confused and he smiles. "I told her, I don't want for her to think that I'm keeping anything from her. I told her you were here with the boys and the rest of the family. That I went to Spain. She was understanding, and if I'm honest, she checked on me and what Arielle said. It's safe to say, she's not her biggest fan." He laughs lightly.

I smile, I feel like this whole thing is really upsetting all party's involved. Especially the parents. "I don't want to be a problem." I say quietly. Before I can even try to get upset, he lifts my chin, so I make direct eye contact with him.

"Never." He reassures me before grabbing my face gently. "You're never the problem. You will always be the solution."

He places his forehead on mine, the gesture giving me some sort of comfort I was craving. "That makes me feel better."

He releases me from his embrace and moves my hair out of my face, tucking it lightly into my hair.

"Good, now you going to tell me if the way you're feeling something has to do with the devil herself?" Robert asks curiously.

I laugh, knowing exactly who he is talking about. "I know she's not right, and I'm not scared of her. But she likes to get under my skin."

"I can't even use the excuse that she doesn't like change anymore, she just likes to cause problems."

"Well, isn't that the truth." I laugh. He joins in.

"I don't know what kind of life she came from do I?" I ask him honestly.

"You more certainly do not. Tommy decided to leave and joined the Army to deal with his demons." He stands up and turns to look to me. "You'll meet him eventually, but only when he decides to come home."

I can only nod, not knowing what else to say. I know Tommy left not long after being adopted. But I wasn't told much else.

"I will let you relax. Are you wanting to go back to the police station tomorrow?" Robert asks while making his way towards the door slowly.

"Please, I think I need a break from the chaos that is the Quinten family." I joke, which he laughs at.

"Trust me, all of us need a break from being ourselves once in a while. I'll have the security guard drop you tomorrow at 9." He says walking towards the door, opening it even so gently. "Can you see yourself doing it as a job?" He asks, I smile at him.

"I couldn't see myself doing anything else for a while."

CHAPTER TWELVE

Juliette Sanders

Michigan, USA

I walk into the station to the stench of coffee and the sweetness of donuts. I thought it was just a joke, but these people really like their donuts.

I make my way towards Detective Gomez's desk only to find him not there. I stop in my tracks, uncertain on where to go from here.

"That isn't good enough Gomez!" A shout echoes through the station, and I see a lot of the officer's scurry to get away. I look into the Lieutenants office and notice him standing over his desk, screaming at Lieutenant Gomez.

"She could have been killed!" He shouts once more, and I decide enough is enough and place my bag on the ground. I storm into the Lieutenants office, not sure what I'll say, but hopefully he can give me some light as to why the Detective is being shouted at.

"Sir." I greet him and he exhales loudly.

"Miss Sanders, I was just about to call your uncle to let him know that your volunteering will be coming to an end, effective immediately."

I am stumped as to the sudden change. What has happened for him to decide I am no longer able to volunteer.

"May I ask why sir?"

"Let's just say that Detective Gomez, didn't understand the risks of putting you in danger yesterday. The man you arrested was wanted for murder in Florida, from about 20 years ago." He exclaims looking furious at Detective Gomez. "Something you'd know if you did a background check, before running to the hills and putting a volunteer who has no training in working a case, undercover!"

"Actually sir, I have worked a case." I say quickly in my defence. I earn a surprised look from both men. "I closed a drug ring case that was going on in my school and assisted in closing a murder case as well." I state.

Both men look at me baffled, not one of them saying anything as they just stare at me, shocked.

"I can provide you with a reference if you'd like to speak to Officer Bradley in Scotland Yard." I say while going into my bag and pulling out Officer Bradley's card he gave me the last time I saw him. "He can explain everything to you and give you a summary of my involvement in the case."

"How about you give me a light summary. I don't really feel like calling England for a reference." The Lieutenant says sarcastically, and it takes all of my power not to pull a face at him.

"Well, I was asked to go undercover to work out which students were selling, making and getting the shipment of the chemicals and contents of the drugs." I say, glancing over at Detective Gomez who sits quietly his mouth slightly open. "Linking in with this, a girl from my school, Georgia, died from a suspected overdose which then ended up with there being an investigation into the school." I continue.

I make my way over to the spare seat at the Lieutenants desk and take a seat. Avoiding his harsh stares. "From there, I worked with Officer Bradley in uncovering the culprits. We knew it had to be someone in the school who was selling the drugs, and one by one we narrowed it down to some of the students, the headteacher and a few other teachers. The local freak, as you would call him, was the one who was having shipments from the black market delivered to his dad's address, a pharmaceutical company and he was also the one who killed Georgia for revenge." I explain, finally taking a breath.

The men exchange a look with each other. A one filled with confusion and complete dismay.

"So, Miss Sanders, you're telling me you closed down a drug ring to the most elite in London and helped solve a murder?" The Lieutenant asks while sitting back in his chair clearly baffled.

"What? Like it's hard?" I joke, lightly laughing at myself for the *Legally Blonde* joke.

Neither of the men laugh. They just exchange a look between each other that only has them confused more and I roll my eyes. "Sir, whatever you were shouting at Detective Gomez for, I can assure you I consented to everything and if anything, some of it was my idea. He prepped me before going in, I was more than capable of doing what he asked."

The Lieutenant turns his gaze to Detective Gomez, who meets it. The look he is giving him is uncertainty, not to mention, anger.

"Miss Sanders, I would like for you to sign this form that states that in the event of anything happening, you, or your family can not sue the station." The Lieutenant explains while going into his desk draw and pulling out a piece of paper, placing it gently on the desk. He takes a pen from a pot and places in down firmly.

"Sign, if you would like to stay here for the next two weeks." He instructs me. I pick up the pen eagerly, but make sure to read through all of the terms and conditions. Last thing I want is to sign my life away to the police, only for them to use me in the future.

I sign my life away, just wanting to be out of this room and the tension that is building within. I look up to the Lieutenant, giving him a warm smile and turning my head to look at the Detective who gives me a slight smile almost.

The Lieutenant ushers us away and we get up, not wanting to say another word.

We both quickly leave the Lieutenants office, closing the door behind us and giving each other a look of 'well I'm pleased that's over.'

"I'm a big boy I can take care of myself Jules." Detective Gomez says as he walks towards his desk. I can sense annoyance in his voice.

"Not saying you can't Detective, I agreed to going in there, you didn't have a gun to my head." I say jokingly.

A small smile creeps up on his face which he quickly shakes off, not wanting to condone anything. "Well Miss Sanders, we have a fun filled day of filling out the paperwork from yesterday."

He says sarcastically taking a seat at his desk.

"I can sense the sarcasm, Detective. Let's just get on with it." I say, taking a seat next to him and pulling a pen from his pen pot.

CHAPTER THIRTEEN

Juliette Sanders

Michigan, USA

We finish up the paperwork and the Detective stands up and stretches, a yawn following his stretch. He slouches slightly and looks to me and laughs. "Long day."

"Detective, it's not even 11am yet."

"Oh, so that means more coffee?" He says while walking over to the table that's got a fresh pot of coffee.

"I'm going to assume so." I laugh as he waltzes over, a smile on his face. This man really does love his coffee.

"Jules, there is water in the fridge in the conference room if you'd like one." He says while pouring himself a cup of sludge.

"Okay."

I get up and walk towards the conference room, passing some empty desks and ones that have officers and Detectives doing tasks or taking statements. Passing one of the desks, I notice a few files and some small bits of evidence in bags. It catches my attention for a moment when I notice a small layer of dust on the desk.

My curiosity is only fuelled further by the fact there are 3 cases sat on a desk that clearly hasn't been sat at for weeks.

I decide to ask questions later and go and get my bottle of water from the fridge in the conference room.

I open the fridge and gently take out a bottle, grabbing one for Tracey as well, just in case she needed one. She hasn't moved from her desk or had a cup of coffee.

The sound of raised voices and an officer trying to calm someone down catches my attention and I am quick to walk outside of the conference room to see what is going on.

"No! You're all liars!" The tall man shouts at an officer. A woman stands with him, she's in tears, clearly distressed and heartbroken as she clutches her chest tightly. It breaks my heart seeing her like this and I quickly go over, offering her the water bottle and leading her gently to the seat behind her.

She's inconsolable, but so is who I'm assuming is her husband. He's swearing at the officers who are trying to calm him down, begging for them to do something.

"You should be ashamed, our daughter was murdered three weeks ago, and no one has contacted us for anything! We haven't been told anything and when we do all you say is an investigation is underway. I don't see anyone interviewing her school friends, her family, nothing!" He shouts louder. The officer in front slightly moves his hand to his gun and I notice this immediately.

"Excuse me!" I shout, moving quickly towards the man standing in front of him. He moves his hand away from his holster placing his hands in front of him, almost as if he was to shut me up. "The man is clearly distressed; he is looking for answers. He isn't harming anyone, so how about instead of pulling a gun on a man who is grieving, you sit with the family and discuss what's happened and the next steps."

I move back towards the woman, who is so visibly upset. I take her hand and hold it tightly. Giving her a reassuring look.

"Miss Sanders, this doesn't concern you." An officer warns me. I still hold on tight to the grieving woman, she grips my hand so tight I think she might break it.

"It concerns me officer, if I'm having to tell you how to do your job, clearly the American educational system is floored." I snap back.

His face fills with rage and he looks beside me, causing me to turn my head. There stands a very frustrated Detective Gomez. His face is red with anger as he stares down at me, like I've disappointed him.

"All we want is answers as so why no one is finding our daughters killer? There was another girl found wasn't there? Last week? What have you done for those parents?" He asks, his voice raised and booming through the station. Not one person has moved since the man began raising his voice. He's tall, stocky, bald and filled with so many emotions I can't even begin to understand. Two murders in a few weeks? I thought Detective Gomez said there was no open cases.

"The Detective will call you when he is back at his desk, please just give him time." The officer tries to calm down the man who shakes his head.

"Officer, that man has been on vacation for the last three weeks! He isn't coming back for another three!" He exclaims harshly. "That Detective hasn't got a clue about the case, so please stop wasting our time and find our daughters killer so we can lay her to rest." He pleads to him. The officers shake their heads as I watch the man gently pick up his broken wife, who hasn't stopped crying since she walked into the station.

She grips onto my hand tighter, and I look up to her, her mascara falling into the cracks of her wrinkles and her eyes puffy filled with heartache and answers.

"Please, please find her killer." She begs me before pulling me into a hug. "Please, please."

I nod ever so slightly, not wanting to get myself in anymore trouble until I know more on the case, and why it is being pawned off to a Detective that isn't here.

We exit our embrace, and she holds my face tightly in her hand. "You look like her." She says, catching me off guard. "You have her hair colour, her cheeks, her eyes." She says with a small smile that's filled with pain. "Please, find her killer. I need to bring my baby home." She pleads softly before taking her husband's hand and he leads her out of the station.

I look to Detective Gomez, who only shakes his head at me. I think he knows where I'm going with this.

"Miss Sanders, I suggest if you know what's good for you, you stay out of things that have nothing to do with you." The officer warns me.

Suddenly I feel rage flow through my veins.

Before I can speak, Detective Gomez is quick to come to my defence. "Don't threaten her like that." He warns the officer, who puts his hands up in his defence.

"Maybe get your pet under control, she's only ever gonna' do damage." The Officer jokes. Detective Gomez's glares at the Officer and makes his way towards the Officer.

I stand in front of him, pleading with him not to do anything stupid. "Please Detective, I can fight my own battles." I say to him.

He doesn't look in my direction, he only keeps glaring at the Officer. I really hope this doesn't turn into a fight, because the last thing I need is to get caught up in a brawl between two men battling it out to see who's the most dominant.

"You're a kid. He should know better." The Detective finally speaks, and I roll my eyes.

"Jesus, Detective! It's a man's club in here, put your dominance away." I joke to him. He doesn't budge, glaring at the Officer who at this point finds the whole thing hilarious. "Walk away, please it is fine." I reassure him.

He looks down on me, my eyes pleading with him that doesn't start something over something as silly as a comment.

He moves away, walking towards his desk and I feel myself take a long deep breath. *Thank God.*

"Officer, Jackson, is it? Let me put it this way in maybe a way you'll understand. You and I have very different outlooks on the criminal justice system here. Now, from a British person's perspective, you pull your gun on anyone who could so much as look at you funny. But for us, we talk about it. All those parents needed was closure, answers. And all you did is ruin any relationship they might have with the police in the future." I say coldly.

His face is furious, I don't know whether it's because I offended his intelligence or I gave him the biggest reality check. I'd like to think it was both because I don't know the man, yet he is getting on my nerves.

"You know nothing about the case, or how the world works." He barks in his defence, and I can't help but laugh.

"Clearly no one knows anything because you've left a murder case, or several should I say, to a Detective who's on holiday! So much for finding justice for the families." I laugh at him.

I watch as the vein on his forehead begins to show through, I'm clearly hitting a nerve, and if I'm honest I don't care. "Back down, Miss Sanders." He says as calmly as he can breaking the space between us. "That's an order."

"I don't take orders from mediocre men who refuse to do their jobs." I snap back before walking away. That man being in my person space sent chills up my spine. It's very evident that the man sees this as a job as a filler and not to do justice or do his job properly.

I walk round to the Detectives desk, ignoring the stares from the men and woman of the station. "Please tell me you're not just going to sit here and let the cases catch dust?" I plead with him. He looks up from his computer at me, startled. You'd think with the way he looked at me, I'd asked him to murder a cat.

"Juliette, that case has been left to that Detective, I can't go around stealing cases. He says quickly, his hand reaching out, trying to pull me to my seat but I make a stand.

"Detective, you don't have any active cases, all you would be doing is sitting here watching the minutes go by." I point out to him. He rolls his eyes, before getting to his feet standing over me slightly.

"Please Jules, I can't have you ask me to look into this case." He pleads with me. His voice isn't annoyed it is more hurt. I decide to take a step back from what I'm asking him to do.

"Detective is this case hitting too close to home?" I ask quickly. His face frowns, and the look of hurt gives me all the answers I need. He goes to speak, and I put my hand up. "You don't need to answer, your face said it all." I say walking towards that Detectives desk and picking up the three files and the evidence.

"Jules what are you doing?" He asks, now clearly frustrated with me.

"That family is looking for answers, and none of you are going to look for it. I will." I say while walking into the Lieutenants office.

"Sir, may I please have a word?" I ask nicely while placing all of the evidence and the case files on the desk. His hands go up and his eyes go wide.

"What's this?" He asks quickly, clearly annoyed.

"Sir, I'm here to ask permission to look into the current murders of what looks like three girls in this area. The family have come in demanding answers but don't currently have any as the man who has been assigned to the case is probably on a beach somewhere, catching some rays." I say frustratingly.

The Lieutenant looks up to me, in between going through the case files, and looking at the pile of evidence. "Miss Sanders, these are child murder cases, I can't in good faith ask you to look into these." He says, sitting back in his chair.

"Sir, surely you wouldn't let cases of children

sit catching dust on a desk?" I ask.

"Not at all –"

"So, why are these ones?" I interrupt him. "Let me volunteer to investigate the cases myself. Give me two weeks." I plead with him. He shakes his head throughout, clearly ignoring what I'm saying. "Sir, please. You didn't see that family today; they have to bury their child. No one should have to bury a child. But why are you allowing a murderer to go free?" I ask him once more.

This one seems to hit a nerve and he stands up from his desk elegantly, like he is about to give me the biggest telling off I've ever seen.

"Miss Sanders, you are here on a voluntary basis, you overstepping that means I can end it at —"

"I'll take the case." I hear a voice say beside me cutting him off. I turn to see Detective Gomez standing there, I stand there, too stunned to speak. "We can work on the case together." He says leaning against the doorframe.

I turn to look at the Lieutenant, who's just as shocked as me. "You sure, Mike?" He asks softly.

My attention is once again turned to the Detective, who only gives him a light nod. "I can't hide from it forever. I came back to this job. It's time to finally face the demons."

"Well then," The Lieutenant speaks clearly as

he slams the cases back down on his desk in front of me. "Miss Sanders, I present you your first case."

CHAPTER FOURTEEN

Juliette Sanders

Michigan, USA

I walk out of the Lieutenants office once more and turn to look at Detective Gomez, who gives me a smile slightly before grabbing his coat and heading towards the door of the station. Clearly him offering to take up this case has hit close to home.

I place down the cases and the evidence on the chair. I quickly grab my cardigan and head towards the door, following him.

"Detective!" I call after him. He stops in his track, and I watch even from a distance he takes a long deep breath as I make my way towards him. "Detective, I would rather talk about this than make you feel uncomfortable in taking this case." I explain to him. He places his hands on his hips, trying to contain his rage that I can see clear as day is on his face.

"Juliette, there are things I don't want to have to explain to you as a kid. You shouldn't be looking into cases regarding children." He says coldly. His intention is to get a rise out of me, to cause an argument.

"Detective, I asked for it. This wasn't handed, I asked—"

"I don't care!" He cuts me off. "Child deaths or child murders are something you can never get over." He shouts at me. Rather than his voice be filled with rage, you can hear the hurt.

"Detective, I'm not saying it's easy. But what I'm saying is that although these cases are hard, you can't expect them to catch dust? Can you?" I ask.

He shakes his head at me. "You don't get it Juliette; this will open up wounds I've only just healed." He says sadly.

I stop everything. Everything I wanted to say and look at the man in front of me. The broken man, who gives off this touch persona and loves his coffee. The man who when he seen a woman had been left to defend for herself, he jumped in and became her saviour in a way.

He opens up his car and takes a seat, placing his head in his hands. "I don't know why I agreed to it. Maybe because she would want me to." He says quietly.

That catches me off guard and I find myself placing a hand on his shoulder in comfort. "Detective, if it would help, I'd like to hear about your daughter." I say softly causing him to look into my eyes, his filled with pain and frustration. "I'm assuming that's who you're upset about is your daughter?" I ask.

He doesn't say anything for a moment while he grasps what I ask, but then nods slowly, closing his eyes to try and hide the pain.

"Detective I'd like to hear about her if you're okay to talk about her." I say softly once more, so he knows that he doesn't have to, but the option is there.

"I don't know." He hesitates.

"That's okay." I reassure him. "Whenever you're ready, I'm here."

He doesn't say anything he just places his hand on my shoulder accepting the gesture of comfort for a moment. He clears his throat.

"Give me some words of wisdom to stop me from driving to a bar and drowning my sorrows." He pleads with me. I lean against the car and take a deep breath.

"Imagine if it was your daughter, Detective Gomez, you wouldn't want her case to be sat in a pile. You would want people out there searching for the answers." I say softly. I know I probably hit a nerve with mentioning his daughter, but in the moment, I couldn't think of any way I was going to get him out of the car.

He hesitates for a moment, looking at me dead on. "Cold, Sanders. That was cold!" He shouts getting up from the seat and shutting the car door. "But I needed that. Now, let's go and find a killer." He says patting me on the back.

CHAPTER FIFTEEN

Juliette Sanders

Michigan, USA

I thank the security guard for dropping me home as I enter the palace once again. What catches my eye is the blood all over the door as well as leading up to the house.

I run to the door opening it gently only to reveal blood everywhere. The sound of chaos causing my ears to go up and I immediately drop my bag and head in the way of the screams.

This place is like a maze and trying to find the source of the screams, I keep getting lost and I can't tell if this is some sort of game.

"Robert!" I call out hoping that someone will hear me and tell me what is going on. I run pass one of the rooms and notice, what could possibly be a murder scene.

I feel my heart sink when I notice the blood, but most importantly when I notice Spencer and Damian curled up screaming in pain on two of the beds. *Oh my god...*

"Jules! You need to leave now." Robert instructs me placing his hands on my shoulders. I can't move, I'm completely frozen at the sight of two of the people who are my friends, screaming in pain. "Jules!" He shakes causing me to turn my attention to him. His white shirt dripping in blood.

"No way." I say quietly, fear taking over in my body. "How..." I trail off. I notice Alexis, Peter and Marcus tending to Damian whereas Felicity, Nathaniel, Ezekiel, and Serena deal with Spencer.

"I sent the boys on a task they were ambushed." He explains, every now and again looking over his shoulder to the boys who are hurled up in pain. "They were shot Juliette; they will be in pain but it's nothing to fatal thank god." He explains.

I begin to grasp at what is happening. Two people who I care about have been attacked while on a mission. I feel myself become angry and look up at Robert, tears still in my eyes. I'm not just angry at the people who attacked them, but at myself for standing here like an idiot.

"How can I help?" I ask quickly, glancing

between Robert and the boys.

"Huh?"

"How can I help!" I shout at him, and he still stands there, shocked by my offer. But internally so am I.

"I could use you over here Jules!" I hear Alexis shout from the far end and I immediately rush over to Damian's side. He takes my hand instantly, his eyes wide like he's surprised to see me.

"I'm here, I'm here." I coo at him, holding his face gently. "Shhh... it's okay." I reassure him and he begins to quiet down ever so slightly. "What do you need me to do?" I ask her.

She doesn't answer for a few moments, before looking at me deeply. "I'm gonna need you to keep him calm, I need to pull the bullet out." She explains looking down at Damian, who doesn't look at her, he's muttering something and none of us by the looks of it can make out what he's saying.

"I'll go the other side, Jules." Marcus says moving to the other side of me and taking Damian's other hand. "He may break your hand, it's gonna' hurt like a bitch."

The scream that leaves Damian almost shatters my ear drums. Robert is quick to run to check on me, and I shake him off saying I'm fine. I feel my heart ache for the boys. They are in so much pain.

Alexis pulls the bullet from Damian, and he tries to curl up in pain. "Does anyone know what he's saying?" I ask Robert who only shakes his head as does the rest of the room. I lean down to look at Damian, trying to understand what the hell he is murmuring.

"He's dead. He's dead..."

"Who's dead, Damian?" I ask him quietly, hoping he will tell me. He only screams, the cries follow soon after and I look over to Spencer, who is knocked out cold. The screams I had heard earlier must have been the ones where they had pulled the bullet out.

"Anyone have any idea?" I ask the room who shake their head. Suddenly I feel my heart sink when I realise who isn't in this room. "Where's Rodger?" I ask quickly, concern filling my voice.

I watch as looks are exchanged once again, this time filled with worry. "No one knows, he was meant to be on the task with them, but they turned up alone." Robert explains while gently wiping a cold towel over Damian's forehead.

"Please tell me you have someone out there —" I begin to ask before I get a look from Robert.

"No what kind of father would I be if I didn't? I've sent Oliver to look for him as well as some of the security team. I'm sure he's fine. It's nothing to worry about." He reassures me.

I find myself only being able to nod.

I look down at both boys. These boys have made me feel safe in the small time I've known them, not to mention they put their life on the line after their own brother tried to ruin my life. Although I feel the adrenaline rush through my veins, I'm very grateful for them both and place my hand on both of their faces. They both sleep peacefully. Whatever Alexis and Felicity gave them seems to be working and I stand there grateful that I'm not standing here saying goodbye.

CHAPTER SIXTEEN

Juliette Sanders

Michigan, USA

I wake up slightly to a blanket being thrown over me. Since both boys are sleeping peacefully, I decided not to move just in case something was to happen. I turn around and notice Robert, carefully leaving the room, not wanting to wake either boy. He's changed, he's in a black shirt and pyjama bottoms.

"I'm awake." I whisper causing him to stop in his tracks and turn around. A small smile creeps on his face and even in the light, you can still see his wrinkles.

"Well, that's not good." He jokingly whispers. I can't help but chuckle, wrapping the blanket around me. Looking down on both boys who sleep peacefully while I walk to go and meet Robert. "I wanted you to sleep, I never wanted to wake you." He admits as I come closer.

Shaking my head, I can't help but smile. The gesture is very sweet since I offered to stay with the boys, so they had a friendly face to wake up to. I still intent on keeping that promise. "That's okay, don't worry." I say softly to him.

"You were really brave today." He says to me which causes my heart to warm. "You did very well. It was a stressful environment." He explains sweetly before opening the door and I follow him out. "I was hoping that you'd be a few more hours. But I thought if I told you you'd have to stay later you'd get suspicious, and I couldn't be bothered to have an argument." He says jokingly while walking slowly down the corridor.

"Do you think that they will be okay?" I ask Robert softly causing us to both stop in our path. He turns to me and places his hand on my shoulder. "I can't lose anyone else." I plead to him. He pulls me into a hug.

"You won't. They are going to be fine." He reassures me in the embrace that I didn't know I needed.

"Do you know what happened today?" I ask him, pulling away to get a look at him to see whether or not he will tell me the truth.

His face gives me nothing as he placcs his hands down by his sides and moves towards the wall and leans against it. "We won't know till the boys wake up, or we find Rodger."

The thought of Rodger injured admittedly, makes me panic, I may not like the man, but he doesn't deserve to be stuck and in pain if he is. I do hope for his safe return.

"What's your theory?" I ask him, hoping he may have one.

"Well, I think maybe someone from the family we dealt with a few weeks ago may have people watching us, which is why I keep sending you into the police station." He says with a smirk. I immediately catch on to why.

"You're making them think I'm the rat if they are watching?"

He nods, a smile plastered on his face. *Very good Robert... Very good.*

"Sneaky." I smile back and he laughs hard.

"Of course, except I don't think they care about you. They don't know you exist and if they do, they will probably think you're Clarissa." He admits. I pull a face, which makes him laugh harder. "Sorry, but you do look very alike in each other. Height, weight, hair colour. You look very alike in that aspect."

"Well, I take that very personally, and I think you should apologise again because that is uncalled for." I joke and he continues to laugh.

"I'm sorry." He apologises once again and smile at him, knowing that he means it. "For not giving you better answers as to why I adopted kids after I gave you up." He explains softly, his eyes filled with worry, like I'm going to be upset.

I give him a small smile, one to reassure him that it is okay.

We are both broken from our moment when a scream comes from the boy's room and we both immediately run in. Damian is screaming, crying. There is blood all over sheets. It's like another murder scene except there is one executioner, one murderer and one suspect.

Damian.

"Please son, put the scalpel down. Please." Robert tries pleading with him. He has the scalpel on his neck, clearly something has happened today.

"He killed him." He screams once more. "He's dead." He cries and I begin to walk just that little bit closer. He's clearly hurting, not knowing how to manage his emotions or feelings.

"Damian, who?" Robert asks, slowly approaching him. It seems to trigger him and becomes incredibly distressed and presses the blade to his throat once more.

Spencer wakes up and Robert is quick to help him to his feet and hold him tightly. "What's going on?" Spencer asks, clearly confused.

"We don't know." I hear Robert say quietly to Spencer. This causes Damian to flip and press the knife so hard to his throat that he begins to bleed.

"Damian, hey!" I shout causing him to look at me quickly. His eyes soften once he sees me, like he doesn't see me as a threat.

"Jules..." He cries to me, and I place my hands up to show him I have nothing. "He's dead." He cries once more, and I place my hands down wanting him to know that I am here to help him.

"I know, Damian," I say softly, slowly walking towards him. He doesn't move, he just stares at me, the blade still to his throat but not as severe. "Damian please, let me help you." I say calmly approaching him ever so slightly.

I watch the scalpel loosen in his grip as I approach. "He's dead." He cries again as the scalpel drops to the floor as does he. I run to him, falling in the process quickly throwing the scalpel to the other end of the room and pulling Damian into my arms.

He bawls, breaking down for what seems like hours, murmuring the same things repeatedly. I can hear conversations go on behind me between family members that have now joined, but Damian has a hold of me so tight I can't move to see who it is, or what the plan is.

Suddenly, I feel someone place their hand on my shoulder and I find Spencer standing over me, his eyes tears as he looks down on me. "Robert has settled for him to go to a mental health facility." He whispers to me. I feel my heart break, but I know that this will be the best thing for Damian till we can work out what's happened. I nod to Spencer hinting I'm going to talk to Damian.

"Hey." I say softly in Damian's ear, and he lifts slowly. His eyes are puffy, and he looks so incredibly broken. I feel my heart shatter into tiny little pieces. This isn't the same boy who defended me. He's a shadow of that. He is a ghost. "Can I take you somewhere to make you feel better?" I ask. He nods ever so slightly and releases me from his grip.

We stand up together, my legs feel like jelly, and I watch as he looks around, his once frail and broken eyes are now filled with anger, and he grabs my hand hard. "Liars." He says under his breath, and I look to my family.

There stand the entire Quinten family, apart from Clarissa, Oliver, and Rodger. "How? Tell me Damian?" I plead with him, his grip on my hand getting tighter and I try not to wince with the pain. "Tell me." I plead in front of him once more.

"He killed him." He says looking down at me, his eyes filled with hurt. "They will let him get away with it." He says anger fuelling him as he grabs my hand so tight, I know now he's going to break a bone.

"Damian, I will make you this promise." I say to him causing him to move his eyes to me once more. With my other hand I place it gently, on his right cheek. "He will get what he deserves. I promise you." I reassure him.

His eyes seem to calm down and he releases my hand and I feel myself take a deep breath. "Do you trust me?" I ask him quietly. It takes him a second to nod.

"I always trust you."

I lead him out of the room in front of the family who follow behind, the atmosphere in the house is cold and sad. Damian's the light of this family, and suddenly our light has been taken out. Slowly we tackle the stairs, only a few hours ago the boys came in here with bullet wounds, and now I'm leading him out the same door that he came through.

The thought of leaving him in a facility that I know will help him get back to some sort of normal, makes my heart ache.

We climb into the car, a few swear words are exchanged from both Spencer and Damian as they climb into the car. Spencer was told to stay and rest, but his response was he would rather take another bullet than let Damian do this alone. We knew it wasn't best to fight with him, so we let him come. Robert decides so sit in the front of the car, in the hopes that Damian doesn't have another break.

The driver makes his way out of the gates, and we begin our journey in the dark. I don't even know what time it is, all I know is that I will be tired for my first proper day with Detective Gomez.

I look over at Damian, who seems so far in his own trance, he doesn't even know what's going on. He just keeps repeating 'he's dead.'

I would like to know who 'he' is, and the only person I'm thinking of is Rodger, except Spencer doesn't seem that shook up. But it doesn't seem that Spencer has explained what happened yet to anyone. I'm going to have a guess and say that conversation is coming later.

It feels like forever, but I think I had daydreamed for the majority of the drive. We reach the gates of a very fancy facility that I just hope is going to help Damian.

The driver pulls up and I notice a few people, all in nurses' uniforms and a doctor standing there to greet us. "Mr Quinten." The man greets Robert, his hand extended as he gives him a small smile.

"Thank you, Doc." Robert greets the man, giving him a small smile in return. "We're still establishing what happened, but Damian needs severe attention." He says softly to him. The man nods to Robert, giving me a gentle smile.

"And who might this be?" He asks Robert, who I see flusters slightly.

"I'm Jules, I'm a friend of Damian's." I say softly extending my hand out to the Doctor before helping Damian out of the car.

"Where are we?" He asks softly.

"You know how I promised you that I'd take you somewhere to make you feel better?" I ask him and he nods. "This is it. These people are going to take very good care of you Damian." I say holding his hand gently.

He turns to me, his eyes sad once again and I feel my heart shatter into one million pieces. "Promise?" He asks sadly.

"Do you trust me?" I ask him with a smile, a reassuring one. He smiles back, a one filled with hurt.

"I always trust you."

"Good. These people are going to make you feel better." I say giving a warm smile to the nurse as she approaches us.

"Hi Damian, I'm Jill. Are you hungry? Would you like something to eat?" She asks softly. He nods slightly, giving me a smile reassuring me that he's going to be okay, and I feel my heart hurt.

He follows her towards the door, and she asks him if certain things are okay, as well as if he would like some chocolate pudding. I look to Spencer who for the first time ever I see cry. I walk over slowly and wrap my arm lightly around his waist trying not to hurt him. I put my head slightly on his chest and he welcomes my embrace.

"I'm going to miss him." He says quietly, only loud enough for me to hear.

"Me too."

We watch Damian walk in with Jill the nurse, never looking back and if I'm honest I'm pleased, as I will be more upset that he looked back and see us here.

Robert shakes the hand of the Doctor and begins to walk towards the car. Still locked in our embrace, I don't move as Robert approaches. "He's gonna be fine, this is the best mental health facility in the area." He says, placing his hands in the pockets of his pyjamas.

"I'm going to assume a place like this has a waiting list, any reason why you would have got him in no questions asked?" I ask Robert curiously.

He looks at me funny while looking at Spencer who I feel chuckle. "I have them on speed dial, I drop Oliver off at least once a month."

He says before getting into the car. I look up to Spencer who only nods. I can't help but laugh in the moment. Why do I get the sense he's not joking.

CHAPTER SEVENTEEN

Juliette Sanders

Michigan, USA

I walk into the station like a zombie. I'm exhausted. By the time we got back from the facility it was almost 5am. Spencer didn't want to speak about what happened and went straight back up to bed after Alexis had put a new dressing on his wound.

There were a few questions asked but I couldn't really say anything, only because I knew I was going to cry. I hated seeing him like that, seeing either of them in pain. Something happened to Damian yesterday and Spencer is the only person who may know something and right now he's not explaining anything.

As I walk round to Detective Gomez' desk I notice a gigantic board behind him as he begins to put up evidence photos and photos of the victims.

"Morning." I say placing a coffee down on the table that I got for him at Starbucks. He looks and me and then down at the coffee and back up.

"Rough night?" He asks with a grin, and I nod taking a sip of my coffee, a white chocolate mocha.

"You don't know the half of it." I say jokingly while handing him his coffee. "I got you an Americano, is that okay?" I ask softly looking at his attire for the day. He's dressed in his usual, shirt, suit pants and suspenders. Whereas today I've opted for something more comfortable. Jeans, t-shirt and vans. It is still a ridiculous heat outside; however, I needed something practical today, and comfy and this is very comfy.

"Perfect." He says taking it gratefully and taking a swig. "So, I decided to get a head start so we can discuss the case further today." He says walking up to the board.

"You've been busy." I say with a smile, and he shrugs his shoulder at the praise.

"Better than drowning my sorrows."

The admission catches me off guard for a moment and I look deep into his eyes. "Detective, you don't have to—"

"I want to." He interrupts me. I decide not to

take it any further and give him a small smile once again. "So, are you ready for my briefing?" He asks pulling out a long stick from the side of his desk and smacking it against the board. I can't help but chuckle and I nod.

"Go ahead." I encourage.

"So, victim number one. Kassidy Simmons, she was 15, top of her class, honour roll, played multiple sports." He explains while pointing out different areas on the board that he's noted down. "She was murdered eight weeks ago about two miles from her home. She was walking back from her friend's house, something that wasn't out of the ordinary and she was strangled with what was found to be rope." He says, pulling the evidence bag from his chair and lifting it to show me the rope in the bag. I nod slightly, taking a sip of my coffee once again.

"So, any reason as to why she was found in the woods? Did she normally walk through that way?" I ask him and he shakes his head, pulling up a piece of paper from his desk and handing me it.

"I mapped out where she would normally walk and also the route she took the night she died. She would have ended up at a dead end.

"So maybe she was lured out? Or forced into the woods?"

"There is a possibility. She wasn't assaulted." He states, before pausing. Not saying anything for a moment, I give him a stare, unsure on what he is hinting here.

"Continue." I encourage and he nods to me.

"I think today we should go and speak to the family and the friends of Kassidy." He says, handing me the case file and I open it to find his notes.

"Sounds like a plan." I say, flicking through his notes whole taking yet another sip of my sweet coffee.

"Onto murder number two." He says moving my attention back to the board and not at the notes. "Sandy Green. She was killed in the exact way of the first victim, and she was the daughter of the parents that came in yesterday." He says handing me the file with a photo of Sandy. Her mother wasn't wrong, she does look like me, except she had glasses and braces. "She was killed in a park about two miles from her home. There is no connection between either child, Sandy was home schooled within the last year after she was severely bullied, but there is no link between Kassidy and Sandy."

I sit looking through Sandy's case for a moment, she was like me, hard worker, kept to herself, had a handful of friends.

"Why was she in a park?"

"She had gone to meet one of her friends

Olive who she normally chats with on an online messaging app. But it turns out that Olive had her phone taken off her that week for getting a B- in her test at school. Not sure how Sandy got the notification from Olive to meet her in a park. We haven't managed to crack that one yet." He says while I look through the messages between Olive and Sandy.

I begin to look at the messages, seeing if there are any noticeable differences between the messages, but there is nothing that is sticking out. Then I look between the usernames, and I see it.

"She was lured out." I say while looking between the messages once more just to make sure I'm correct in my theory.

"Well done, Detective." He mocks me and I roll my eyes.

"No, look." I say turning the messages to him and highlighting the usernames. "Olive's username normally is *OLIV3FRAN776* this one here is *OLIVE3FRAN778*. She wasn't speaking to Olive that night." I grab my coffee and walk up to the board and look between the two cases.

Although the way they were killed and the type of girls they are, are the same; there is no identifying factor that ties these girls together.

"When you speak to Kassidy's parents, will you ask if maybe she had befriended someone new recently, or maybe ask her friends. I know some people who wouldn't want their parents to know things, so they just tell their friends."

His facial expression confuses me as he walks closely towards me. "Jules this is your case, you can ask the parents, and the friends. I have full faith in you." He encourages me which makes my heart swell as little. I feel very welcomed by Detective Gomez and some of the other officers.

"Well, thank you." I say with a smile before turning back to the board not wanting to sit in the moment too long.

"Lastly, the third girl. She is the recent case." I say while moving back and looking at that side of the board.

"Yes, Hannah Robson." He says standing back. "Same cause of death, with the same rope. No prints have come up on any of the ropes that were found at the scene, only the victims. Hannah was a very bright girl, she went to a private school, got okay grades I guess you could say. She was a bit of a party girl, not to mention she's the oldest of all the girls killed." He says handing me Hannah's file.

I take a quick look in, and that is all it is, quick. "This is very thin; I'm assuming evidence is being gathered?" I ask him. I watch as he takes a long gulp of his coffee.

"That is all we have on Hannah's case right now. Her parents have asked us not to investigate her case further. In fact, they threatened legal action." He says quietly.

I begin to look around, surely this is a joke. I noticed that he is staring off into the distance and I catch what he is looking at.

Vote for Philip Robson as Mayor! You'll not regret it.

"Her dad is running for Mayor?" I practically whisper and he nods to me.

"I was told that he didn't want any press on this whatsoever, he wants to keep this hush hush, as if it never happened."

"His daughter was murdered, and he wants an open and shut case, so they don't find her killer? Doesn't that seem sketchy to you Detective?" I ask, clearly annoyed now, but still having to keep my voice down.

"Oh, one hundred percent Jules." He takes another long swig of his coffee before looking back up at the board. "Shame I can't interview the parents; I'm a police officer and he wants no cops coming to his door." He narrows his eyes. I know exactly what he is hinting at.

"Detective don't get smart. I know what you're doing." I say sarcastically and he begins to chuckle. "You want me to go to their house and ask the questions you've been told you can't." I state, my eyebrows raised as I stand tall, waiting for him to stop playing games.

"Fabulous! I'll even drive but stay in the car." He turns to me with a smile. I can't help but roll my eyes at him, I don't even hide it. It's a rude gesture, but I knew what his game was the second I noticed the expression on his face. "So, all we have is three different girls who come from three different backgrounds, never went to the same school. Don't look anything alike, are three different ages. Don't come across each other in any way whatsoever. So how did they end up dead?" He asks curiously.

"Detective, where was Hannah found?" I ask him quickly looking on the board.

"She was found in a cemetery."

"Detective, the only thing that is linking these cases is that they are all girls within the same age. Also, that their cause of death was the same." I say standing stumped. This killer is seriously making it harder for us. But I'm hoping we establish a pattern before this killer decides to strike again.

"What are you thinking?" He asks me after a while.

"I just know that if it was me up on this wall, my mother would stop at nothing to find my killer." I say to him, turning my head in his direction. "I think we should go and speak to the families."

CHAPTER EIGHTEEN

Juliette Sanders

Michigan, USA

The drive to the Simmons home doesn't take us long. It is hot today, and I applaud myself at wearing something comfortable. The wind blows in my hair as we drive through the streets of Michigan.

"So have you got any idea on what to ask the families?" Detective Gomez asks, breaking me from my thoughts.

"I have a few questions I've noted down. What did she do the day she died? Did she have any new friends? Did she have a boyfriend, girlfriend? Did they notice anyone following her? So, we get a better understanding of her."

He doesn't say anything, and the car falls back into silence as I see him approach a street and he begins to slow the car down.

To me, this case seems to have one link, but what that is I can't be sure. All the victims are of different race, not to mention come from different backgrounds and wealth. They are all different in ways of personality. Either these are just crimes of opportunity, or they are targeted. I do believe that Sandy was targeted, the fact that the killer went out of their way to create a fake username to communicate with the victim is very unsettling.

"We're here." He says while putting the car in park and getting out of the car. "I'm gonna state that you're my partner if that's okay with you." He asks nicely while waiting for me at the side of the car.

"Fine by me, I'll be happy to answer any of the questions the family have."

We walk up the path towards the house and Detective Gomez knocks on the outer door and pulls his badge from his pocket.

Suddenly a woman just a little taller than me comes to the door and looks to both of us, her eyes filled with confusion and worry, and I give her a warm smile as I'm not sure what else to do.

"Mrs. Simmons?" Detective Gomez asks and the woman nods ever so slightly. "My name is

Detective Gomez, and this is my partner, Miss Sanders. We are looking into your daughter, Kassidy's death." He explains while also showing her his badge.

I watch as a wave of relief fall over her, and she almost falls to the floor. "Oh! Thank Jesus! Thank the lord." She praises while pulling me in for a hug. "Thank you." She says in my ear while also pulling the Detective in for a hug and saying the same. "Please come in." She encourages and we thank her kindly.

"Mrs Simmons is your husband and other children home?" Detective Gomes asks and the woman runs into the kitchen and practically drags her husband out before calling down for the kids.

"What is going on?" The man asks startled and confused.

"Baby, these Detectives are looking into Kassie's death." She says enthusiastically and I see the same wave of relief as I did on Mrs Simmons only moments ago.

"It's about damn time!" He exclaims and he hints for us to take a seat into the living room. I watch as three children come down the stairs, all different ages but all older than ten. "So, what have you found out?" He says taking a seat with his wife.

"Well Mr and Mrs Simmons, Kassidy's

murder seems to be the first in a string of murders that we have connected together." Detective Gomez explains to the family. "Now we have only just been understanding each case. We are wanting to apologize for the delay in not coming and speaking to you earlier." He says sympathetically.

Mrs Simmons shakes her head, gripping her husband's hand tightly. "I'm just pleased that someone is going to do something. So, thank you." She praises us both. I give her a warm smile. "Gosh, you're just a baby. How you got wrapped up in this?" She asks me and as I'm about to answer Detective Gomez quickly chimes in.

"Miss Sanders was the one who fought for the case itself, she will be taking lead on this case while she is here for the next few weeks." He reassures them and they look to me and smile.

"No case should be sitting catching dust unless it's a one that's solved." I say with a warm smile, which almost has Mrs Simmons in tears. "I'd like to ask some questions about Kassidy if that is okay with you?" I ask softly and they both nod.

"Ask away." She encourages me as I pull out a notepad. I decided to get one if I was going to be working a case and I am patting myself on the back for deciding to do so.

"What was Kassidy like?" I ask them sweetly.

"Oh honey. She was the best. She was such a good girl, good grades, good friends. She worked hard for everything she wanted, surrounded herself with people who would lift her up rather than bring her down. Not to mention that she went to church, she was very into the choir. She also was very big on reading." Mrs Simmons explains, and I smile at her.

"What sort of books did she like?" I ask her curiously and she laughs lightly.

"Cheesy romance ones. The one thing you needed to know about Kassidy is she is a sucker for love. She was a hopeless romantic, she loved love." She laughs once more. I laugh with her as I know two people like that myself. "Yet the girl never had a boyfriend, she was too afraid to talk to boys."

"So, she didn't have a boyfriend before she died?" I ask and she shakes her head.

"No honey, she didn't. Kassidy didn't have time, as much as she loved reading about it, she never wanted to find it."

"I told her no boyfriends till she's 30." Mr Simmons jokes, and I smile to him, I remember when my dad had the same conversation with me.

"Did she have any new friends, whether they be online or in person?" I ask them and they both shake their heads.

"She surrounded herself with people who she

could see, and get a sense of their aura, if you get what I'm saying." Mrs Simmons explains, and I nod turning my head to Detective Gomez who looks like the woman has just spoke in a different language.

"So Detective, if they are someone positive, they will give off a great vibe, or their aura will be good. If they are bad... well then you get the gist." I say to him, and he nods along like he's understanding. But I can see he hasn't got a clue.

"She wouldn't surround herself with the negative people." Mr Simmons pipes up and I turn to him, making a quick note in my notebook.

"What did Kassidy do the day she died?" I ask them and I watch as suddenly the colour is drained from their face. They grip each other's hand tightly. "Mr and Mrs Simmons, I can understand this is going to be painful to talk about, but whether it be good or bad, I can assure you we have your daughters' best interests at heart."

Their eyes flash with a little glimmer of hope as I turn to Detective Gomez who gives me an encouraging nod.

"We had an argument with her. She got a B on her science test and that wasn't like her at all. It seems to us like she was distracted, but we couldn't tell from what, she has never gotten a B or anything lower than a A. It seems so silly now, but she got upset with us and stormed out of the house. That was the last time we saw her." Mrs Simmons begins to cry, and I can't help but immediately extend my hand for her to hold and she takes it gratefully.

"Mrs Simmons, I didn't know your daughter, but I would like to think that she knows that you loved her no matter what she got on a test. She knows she was loved." I reassure her and her cries only get louder as Mr Simmons hugs her tighter.

"Can I get you a water?" I ask her softly and she shakes her head.

"Please just find who did this to my baby. Please." She pleads to us both and I turn my attention to Detective Gomez who gives a reassuring smile.

As we say goodbye to the Simmons family, I look to Detective Gomez who looks more stumped than before as to why Kassidy Simmons was the first as well as the motive.

"I can't work out why she would end up in the woods." He says while walking down the path towards the car. "It makes no sense, unless it was a crime of opportunity." He says opening the car door and leaning on top of it, looking down to me. "Jules…" He trails off while looking behind me.

I turn around and notice one of the children running towards me with something in her hand. "Please don't leave yet." She pleads with us both. I hear the car door slam and within a second, I feel Detective Gomez stand beside me. "She had a boyfriend; someone she was speaking to online. Our parents didn't know, and she had a secret phone that she spoke to him on." She says while handing the Detective the phone and he takes it, glove immediately on his hand as he pops it into an evidence bag.

"Did she say his name?" I ask her and she looks down at the phone in the Detective's hand.

"Troy. Apparently, he was older." She says sadly. "I told her that he was trouble!"

Detective Gomez places his hand on her shoulder, and she looks to him, like she's going to get told off. "Thank you for telling us." He says sweetly and she gives us both a nod before heading back into the house.

I turn to look at Detective Gomez who looks at the phone. "She had a secret life."

"Doesn't every teenager?" I tease him and he raises his eyebrow.

"Do you?" He jokes and I laugh.

"Oh yes Detective, and it will stay a secret

forever." I mock and he laughs at me.

"Funny, now get in the car."

CHAPTER NINETEEN

Juliette Sanders

Michigan, USA

The rest of the day was filled with interviewing and talking to Kassidy's friends and by the time that was over it was almost 6pm. I didn't mind the late night, because in all honesty, the thought of going back to the Quinten family home is making me feel sick as I know I have all of that to deal with.

I say goodnight to Detective Gomez, who has given me homework to do today which I'm grateful for as I don't really feel like dealing with my family much tonight until I've wrapped my head around last night. I've not thought about it all day since I've been able to keep myself busy with the case and speaking to the family and the friends of the first victim, Kassidy Simmons.

As I approach the car, I suddenly slow down when I notice that someone is sitting in the passenger seat with him. I feel my heart begin to beat out of my chest as I approach the car slowly.

The car window comes down as I see a tatted neck, the 'W' clear as day as I roll my eyes.

"If you thought I was going to kidnap you, do you not think I'd do it somewhere… I don't know, maybe nowhere near law enforcement?" Spencer mocks and I roll my eyes again, this time so he can see.

"I don't find you funny." I say while getting into the car and putting my seatbelt on.

"Busy day?" He asks while turning around in his chair slightly and I see him wince with the pain. "You're an hour late home. Thought I would come and see what was taking you so long." He says with a smile which I return.

"Aren't you mean to be on bed rest?" I ask him and his smile only grows wider.

"I am. But like I said you're an hour late and I'd like to know why. Are you avoiding coming home?" He asks curiously and I look him dead in the eye. Unsure on how he could tell. The driver starts the car, and we pull away from the police station.

"I wouldn't say it's home; but yes. I am avoiding it. However, that's not why I'm late."

"Why are you?"

"Because I was interviewing the friends and family of the first murder victim." I say sitting back in my chair. He raises his eyebrows at me.

"What are you talking about? You're meant to be studying the Detectives, not taking on another case?" He asks me seriously and I roll my eyes again.

"I asked for a case. I'm currently looking into the series of murders that are happening to teenagers in Michigan." I say to him. He noticeably becomes frustrated and annoyed at me causing me to frown my brows. "What?"

"Are you trying to get yourself killed?!" He shouts at me, and I'm taken back at his tone of voice.

"Sorry?"

He scoffs at me and looks to the driver who just continues to drive. "Juliette, you could get yourself killed. This isn't England, this is America, where guns are the next iPhones and the criminal justice system is a complete joke. You can't be playing Detective; you will get yourself killed." He repeats. I find myself getting angry at his line of questioning. "I'm serious Juliette, drop the case, that's an order." He instructs and I narrow my eyes.

"I understand you're wanting to protect me Spencer and I find it flattering, but I asked for the case, I know the risk and right now I'm just gathering a better understanding on the victims. Spence they are my age or a little bit older. If I hadn't asked for it, then their cases would have been sat on the desk of a Detective who is on holiday for weeks. By then, evidence would have been lost, not to mention statements and people will forget the victims' names. There have been three in 8 weeks, same cause of death. I'm sorry but I've made promises to too many families to back down now. I'm giving the victims and the families a voice when all that has happened is they've been silenced for wanting answers. I may only be here for another two weeks, but I'm not going to sit around and take notes of how to make a pot of coffee when there is a serial killer who is luring young girls to their death. You might be able to sleep at night, but I'm not going to be able to." I shout back at him.

He's stunned at me. And I feel the tightness that has been causing me so much pain today is released, and I take a long deep breath. I needed to get that off my chest because between the situation with Arielle, Robert, Damian and Spencer, I feel like I've been bottling in all of my anger, and I've just thrown every bit of frustration at Spencer who sits in complete silence not being able to find the words.

A look is exchanged between driver and Spencer, and he looks back at me, wanting to find something to say but they sit in silence. I really did let all of my frustrations out at a man who almost died yesterday, one brother had to be put into a mental asylum, and the other brother is missing.

"I'm sorry Spence—" I begin to say before he puts his hand up.

"I'm sorry for telling you what to do." He says quickly cutting me off. "But you bet your ass I'm being a tattletale and telling Robert." He says with a cheeky grin and turning around. I groan in annoyance, knowing fine well that internally, Spencer isn't a twenty-one-year-old, he's a 13-year-old who has a ton of tattoos, some stupid, some meaningful and has the kind nature of a 40-year-old man.

"Who's the teenager?" I tease, causing him to turn around with that stupid grin. "Cause it's not me." I say with a sarcastic grin back to him.

I notice we come back up to the gates of the Quinten lair and I watch the grin on Spencer's face only get bigger.

"So, what do you think your dear old dad will say when he finds out his good little girl didn't listen to instructions?" He mocks as the car comes into park.

"I am pretty sure he will be fine with it. I mean, he knows I dealt with a domestic abuse case the other day." I say while getting out of the car. "So, I think he will be fine with it." I tease him and he lightly shoves me.

"Don't think so, Princess." He mocks further and I scowl at him causing him to laugh and clutch his side where he was shot.

"I hope you rip open your stitches with that comment you twit." I laugh and he places his hand hard on his chest as if I've just shot him.

"Who knew you were such a savage!" He laughs at me, and I can't help but laugh with him as we walk through the door. As we both enter, I feel a chill come over me and I notice Spencer feels it too. Because in a flash he's in front of me, gun raised as he begins to look around.

"Stay close, somethings wrong." He says hinting to the driver to go upstairs. I stick close to Spencer who runs moves slowly with the gun noting every bit of his surroundings. We move through towards the kitchen, and he clears the dining room as well as the kitchen, hinting for me to stay close. "No one's here." He whispers to me, and I feel myself become unsettled once again. *Where is everyone?*

We make our way down towards Robert's office as quietly as we can. Suddenly, Spencer pauses in his tracks as he hears movement from the office. His gun still raised, he looks to me and I give him an encouraging nod to continue.

He makes his way closer to the door, gun still raised, he tries the door and I'm going to assume it's unlocked as he moves quickly pointing his gun to the direction of the seat. I watch as he slowly lowers the gun, started by whoever he's seen. "Spence?" I call after him, walking quickly to go and see whoever has Spencer so rattled.

I feel my heart drop when I notice a pompous, smug git sitting in Robert's chair, grinning from ear to ear as he stares at us both. He's unharmed, not a scratch on him as he swivels in the chair.

"So much for a welcome home party?" Rodger mocks us both.

I have no time to respond before Spencer is over the desk faster than the speed of light and is choking his brother so hard. "Spencer stops it!" I plead with him, running round to pull him off Rodger. "Spencer it's not worth it please!"

"Enough!" A booming voice speaks from behind us, and I notice Robert, Oliver and Peter standing there, stunned as the rest of us to find Rodger alive, unharmed. "Spencer, stop choking him, he's going blue." Robert instructs calmly and he lets go almost instantly. The rage still fuelling in his eyes.

"Where the hell were you!" He screams at Rodger who is still trying to get his breath back for a moment. "I've been worried sick! Do you even know what's happened? Do you care?" He continues to question.

"What do you mean what happened?" He manages to ask in between his gasps for breath. "I came back, and the car was gone." He says leaning back in the chair. Spencer looks to Robert who shakes his head. My guess he was asking to choke him again.

"Where the fuck did you go!" He shouts once more in his face and Rodger stands out shoving both of us aside as he moves away from Spencer, probably so he doesn't choke him again.

"I had things to do, people to see. I couldn't care less about a stakeout task where it meant I had to sit with you, dimwit." He mocks lightly. I quickly stand in front of Spencer who tries to launch himself at Rodger again who only starts to laugh once more.

"Stop, you're going to hurt yourself." I say moving Spencer to the seat and force him to take it. I know he won't try and move past me in the risk of hurting me in the process.

"What the hell have I missed?" Rodger jokes, looking to the Quinten brothers who stand their unfazed by Rodger's attitude, although their faces tell a different story.

I wouldn't want to be Rodger right now, and if he lives through the night, that will be a miracle.

"If you had been with your brothers, you would know they were ambushed last night." Robert says calmly. His tone is calm and collected considering the man has a short fuse, I'm waiting for him to lose it.

"What?" Rodger turns to Spencer, his face filled with what could be seen as concern to everyone else, but I see right through him. It's a show, he couldn't care less.

"Now, Spencer since your already sat down how about you explain the events of the other evening." Robert says while taking a seat in front of the desk. Normally it's the other way round, but now it's Spencer in the hot seat, and all day I've wondered what happened and I feel like I'm finally going to get some answers.

"You have to leave." Spencer instructs me and my face drops.

"What!" I exclaim and he looks to Robert for support. "I'm not leaving Spencer, Damian is my friend, I'd like a better understanding as to what happened please."

"What happened to Damian?" Rodger pipes up while I stare down at Spencer. Our eyes not breaking for what seems like forever. He knows I won't back down no matter what, whether this breaks my heart.

"Damian had to be taken to a mental health facility, he had a breakdown." I hear Peter explain.

I continue to stare into Spencer's soul, searching for that little bit of him that will see that me being in the room is needed so I can understand what happened.

"Jules." He pleads once more, and I only take a long exhale while moving past Rodger and the rest of the family. I leave the office, Oliver giving me a slight nod as I leave and the gesture makes me uncertain as to what is going on, and what happened on their task.

I know fine well the Quinten's know something, and eventually I feel as though they will tell me. But I'm not going to kick up a fuss, because if anything it won't bring me any closure, it will only make me ask more questions.

I make my way up the staircase and along to my room, in the hopes that researching some stuff for the case will take my mind off everything that has happened, or what is about to erupt.

CHAPTER TWENTY

Juliette Sanders

Michigan, USA

Placing my head down on the bed, I let out the loudest groan. I can't concentrate on the task I've been given by the Detective because all I can think about is what they are talking about downstairs.

It doesn't concern me, but it might make me feel better since I don't know why Damian snapped or why Rodger decided to go rogue. Spencer clearly knows more than what he is letting on as to the Quinten brothers.

I keep replaying it in my head hoping that maybe one of them hinted with a clue or anything that I might have missed. The only thing that was unusual was that Oliver nodded to me, and I think that has to be the most communication we've had since I arrived.

I haven't heard from Alexis, Felicity, Serena or Nathaniel since they found out my mother was a royal. I mean we were together when the boys were shot, but in terms of a sentence or any communication, that's non-existent. I feel as though in some respects I'm being punished for being born.

Marcus had been sent on a task straight after we took Damian to the facility and I'm not sure when he is returning. I feel as though I've been completely isolated for being different and sent away so they don't have to deal with me.

When Robert wants to speak to me or make an effort, he is lovely. On my arrival, everyone wanted to get to know me, but since they found out that I am part royal, the sense of having a good relationship with any of my family has gone down the drain and I feel quite broken by that.

I don't have the one person I can talk to; he's currently seeking treatment, my entire family look at me like I'm scum, not to mention my so-called sister threatened me the other day. If anyone needs to be a facility, it is her, and she is to never be let out.

My mind is running fast, and I feel myself becoming overwhelmed. Now I'm sat in a room with my thoughts it has become quite dangerous, I feel as though I might be having a nervous breakdown myself, not to mention the fact I'm completely isolated.

I get up and begin to pace the room, I'm not one to have an anxiety attack or panic over something like this, but I'm regretting my decision to come here and have a relationship with these people, who I barely know.

My thoughts are quickly broken when I hear my phone go off on the bedside table. My breathing is erratic, and I look over, noticing the warm and friendly smile of my mother, Amy. *Nice timing mum.*

I take a deep breath and answer the phone, praying to the gods that when I speak, my voice doesn't sound how I feel.

"Hi Sweetheart." She greets me warmly and I feel that warmth radiates though the phone. Oh, how I miss her.

"Hi Mum. You, okay?" I ask her softly. She pauses for a moment, and I begin to think that the connection between us has gone.

"Juliette Sanders, why is your voice so sad? What is wrong? Are you crying?" She asks concerned and I can't help but laugh. I've never been able to get away with hiding my emotions from my mother.

"It's been a long day." I say to her, hoping that she sees my lie and doesn't ask any more questions.

"Well, what have you done today?" She asks me curiously as I hear her take a sip of something, probably tea.

"I've been helping solve a case with a Detective." I say with a smile trying to mask my inner pain.

"That sounds intriguing, can you tell me about the case?" She asks sweetly, and I feel my heart ache.

"Erm—" I pause for a moment, unsure on whether or not I can. "I think I can, I just can't give you the details if you know what I mean."

"Yep, gotcha." She says chipper and I can't help but laugh. "Tell me what you can darling." She encourages.

"Well, first you have to promise not to ground me, or tell Robert to put me on a flight home." I say quickly and I feel her go quiet.

"Juliette. What have you done?" She asks sternly and I feel my stomach drop. I would have broken out into hives if I had lied to her, but also telling the truth seems to be a harder option.

"I'm currently solving a serial killer case with a Detective and the victims are three girls around my age." I say quickly once again, and I feel her almost choke on the other end of the phone.

"Oh, you better be joking." She says sternly

and I cower away on the phone. She's thousands of miles away but I am fully expecting her to climb through the phone and spank me as though I was a child.

"Before you go mental Mum—" I begin before she cuts me off.

"Don't you dare try and explain, young lady. The whole part of you going to America was to get a better understanding of your family and the business. I agreed with Robert for you to understand the American justice system, never did I send you there to solve a case! You're home in less than two weeks. What are you going to do then!" She shouts once more and I fall silent, knowing that this isn't the end of her rant.

"Romeo, I think your mother's vein is about to pop through her head, can you please not add any more stress." Grandad Norman pops up on the phone and I have to try and stop myself from laughing.

"Dad, this is not funny." My Mums shouts back at him.

"Course it is love; you know your stress vein is very cute that is why we point it out." He mocks her. She groans loudly on the phone, and I hear her let out a large exhale. "What did we name the vein again Romeo?"

"Victor." I laugh and he begins to cackle immediately.

"That's it! Victor the vein. He's very cute." I hear him reassure my mum who only mocks his laugh.

"You'll look cute in a care home if you don't behave Dad." She warns him and I can imagine his face which causes me to start laughing.

"How wrude!" He exclaims harshly. The poor man added a 'w' on the front of the word rude when wanted to annoy the person more. To me it reminds me of *Jar Jar Binks* from *Star Wars.*

"Juliette, I am giving you one minute to explain the case and how it came into your peripheral. GO!" She shouts at me.

I begin to stutter, not knowing where to start. I tell her everything, from the parents coming into the officer reaching his gun, the fact that I begged for the case otherwise it is going to catch dust. I explain to her about the case in little to no detail, so she doesn't understand how dark it is. I don't even dream to tell her it's a cyber stalking case in two of them because then I will be banned from having electronics.

Not only does she not whine, nor does she butt in. She remains calm as I explain everything to her. It was over one minute but now she knows everything about the case, I haven't even began explaining what's happened here because they she will be straight on the phone to Robert, and I will be out of here.

"Sounds like your busy there, love." Grandad Norman says after a few moments of silence. "However, I think your mother has had a stroke." *Oh god.*

"Juliette, how dangerous on a scale of one to am I going to have to get on a plane and drag you home is this case?" She asks as calmly as she can.

"You want my honest answer, or the one that will make you sleep at night?" I ask her. The groan of annoyance returns as I hear her slam something against the table, more than likely her head.

"You choose, I'm not sleeping either way." She says almost muffled which confirms that she's placed her head on the table.

"Probably a 6, because right now I'm just wanting a better understanding of the victims, their families and who they are. I'm not doing any harm, am I?" I question her.

She is silent for a moment, before a long deep exhale comes through the speak and I hear a muffled conversation.

"I will not drag you home, however, I would like to speak to Robert and ask him why he allowed you to do this, I'll call him tomorrow. I know its late there." She explains and I feel myself cower away from the phone once more.

"Okay, so maybe let me tell him first Mum,

he hasn't got a clue." I say quickly and I hear her exhale loudly, this time full of annoyance.

"Why!"

"Because I haven't really seen him in all honesty and there has been other stuff happening that has taken priority." I say to her, and I feel her go quiet once again.

"You going to tell me what's happened? Will I lose my hair?" She asks.

"Oh, you'd be bald by the end of this phone call." I say honestly.

"Good god, Juliette!" She exclaims. "Is Damian with you? He promised he would take good care of you."

I feel my heart sink to the bottom of the ocean. She's asked about him, and my sudden silence will not help if I try to lie. I'm caught off guard when I notice Peter standing in the doorway of my room and I clutch my chest, clearly startled. "Jules are you there?" Mum asks once more.

Peter shakes his head at me, and I immediately know what he's referring to. "Yes Mum, sorry signal cut out. Damian is fine, he had an early night." I say to her as convincingly as I can.

"Hello Mrs Sanders, I don't think I've had the pleasure, it's been a very long time. I'm Peter Quinten, Juliette's Uncle." Peter introduces himself and for that I'm grateful.

"Oh! Hello. My god you're almost as posh as Juliette and me. How are you, Peter?" She asks sweetly and I watch him smile. He has the most dazzling teeth I've ever seen and he's in comfortable clothes, something I've never seen him in before.

"I'm well, thank you how are you?" he asks politely.

"I'm good, thank you!"

"I do hate to cut this short, but we are just about to have a family meeting, just about the new week and things like that. I'll make sure Jules calls you back very soon." He reassures her.

"Oh! No problem. Jules, just call me tomorrow! Bye both."

Both Peter and I say our goodbyes to my Mum, and I place the phone on the bedside table before gathering up all my notes and photos trying hard to avoid the stare from Peter.

"You going to tell me what you're looking into?" He asks and I shake my head, not wanting to start yet another argument with another family member. "Are you looking into the teenage murders that have been happening over the last eight weeks?" He asks me, his voice is stern, and it causes me to pause what I'm doing.

"How did you—" I begin before he cuts me

off."

"Juliette. I know everything. You should know this by now." He jokes with a mischievous grin on his face. "Doesn't help I had to find out myself rather than hear if from you directly." He says disappointed and I raise my eyebrows.

"In my defence I got the case yesterday and between the situation with Damian and me feeling completely iced out, don't sit and blame me for not telling you what I've been doing, because effort goes both ways, Peter. I'm the only one who's been banished, if you regret inviting me to stay, please let me know. I wouldn't want to be a burden." I snap at him.

He doesn't flinch, nor does his demeanour change. He remains calm and collected. Granted he has other nieces and nephews who have snapped at him before, so he knows how to deal with them.

"Juliette, I can assure you, you are not a burden. Robert asked you here because he wants a better relationship with you although it doesn't seem it right now." He begins to explain while taking a seat next to me. "The situation with Arielle caught him off guard. Did we ever think she could be a royal? Course not. But granted technology has advanced in so many years that now that I was able to track her down it gives him something he has always craved from her.

Closure."

"I just can't help but feel like coming here might have been a mistake. I am only upsetting him." I admit, looking down at my thighs, avoiding the stares from Peter.

Gently, a hand grips my chin, and I'm forced to look at him. "None of us know how to manage this. But we want you in our lives, Juliette. We just need to be able to protect you." He says softly while giving me a small smile. The gesture itself gives me comfort, but deep down I still feel anger inside and hurt that instead of properly getting to know me he sent me away to be someone else's problem.

"I understand you only ever want to protect me, and I get that with this being your job. But I can't help how I'm feeling. It is like since everyone found out that my mother is a Queen it's like they want nothing to do with me. The stares I get, they hurt. Because not even two weeks ago those stares were filled with excitement and love and now all they are filled with is questions and uncertainty."

He takes a long deep breath. I get the sense he understands where I'm coming from. But to him, he has been so busy doing damage control with what happened with Damian, and what happened with Oliver murdering all those people that he probably doesn't need me piling on my feelings to him. He has enough on his plate.

"Your siblings are just trying to understand

it all. That is, it. They don't love you any less because of who your mother is. They just need to get their head around it." He reassures me before lightly shoving me with his shoulder causing me to laugh. "We might be hard and tough to understand but we all love you. And we have since the day you were born." He says with a smile which causes mine to grow wider.

"That's good to know. So, are we going down for that family meeting?" I ask him. He shakes his head at me before turning around and picking up the case file behind.

"Nope, that's tomorrow. I just really wanted to speak to you, I had noticed you were upset." He says before lightly handing me the case file and I take it gratefully. "I do have another question." He asks softly causing me to look directly at him, hinting for him to continue. "Did you really see the crime scene photos of what Oliver did?" He asks.

Suddenly I have a small flashback to the photos, the blood, and the carnage they contained. "Yes." I say quietly, not adverting my eyes.

He does however, looking towards the door and taking a long deep breath.

"I wanted to avoid you seeing one of Oliver's tantrums for as long as possible. I'm sorry you had to see that." He says softly before turning back and looking at me, his eyes filled with worry and his face looking so sad.

"I wouldn't worry about it; you can't hide me from him forever. Speaking of him, where is he and why is he the way he is?" I ask curiously and it causes him to smile.

"Oliver has issues, especially with woman and kids. He hates all of his nieces and nephews, except Clarissa, but I guess you can understand why." He laughs and I can't help but join in. "I say this as nicely as I can, but he was always awful about you after Robert put you up for adoption. Leaving little notes to Robert, taunting him like he wanted to make the pain even worse. But then it stopped." He says, staring into space.

"Stopped? Why?" I ask curiously to which he shrugs his shoulders.

"No one knows. All of a sudden, he became almost bearable to deal with, he worked hard in the business, did his tasks Robert set him without question. All of us thought he may have a girlfriend." He says, his eyebrows raised, still staring into the wall. "But then it all came crashing down and the monster returned." He says taking a long deep breath.

"Do you know what might have happened?"

"I do not think any of us will know what happened. But when Robert brought home Nathaniel, Oliver left for six months." He explains and my interest immediately is peaked.

"Six months? What made him come back?" I ask and Peter looks to me and smiles.

"Oliver will never give you the answers to the questions that you want to ask. He has always been closed off, rude, and belligerent. But he is my brother which means I have to love him. He's your uncle, you don't have to if you don't want to. He hasn't been very kind."

"Does he know how to be kind?" I ask and he moves a bit of hair that has fallen in front of my face and gently tucks it behind my ear.

"He used to. But the man has been so hurt, he will never know how to love anyone, not even himself."

The admission makes my heart hurt for Oliver. Like Peter said, he has been nothing but unkind to me and extremely rude and awful. But by blood we are family, and I will have to put up with him if I'm to see him more.

"Enough of talking about him. I want to hear about the case and what leads you have with it." Peter says, snatching the case files out of my hands and looking through. Pausing when he notices the crime scene photos on one of the girls. "Juliette, these girls must be your age of just older." He says quietly, skimming through the cases, growing scarily quiet are he picks up another page.

"They are fifteen, sixteen and seventeen." I

explain to him. He doesn't look up, only stops to read the case report.

"Juliette, are you sure you want to be looking into this?" He questions me.

"Yes. I fought for the case. No one cares about the victims. The case was left to catch dust. The families were heartbroken, I just want to help them find some closure."

He nods to me before closing the case files. "Well, I have full faith in you. Find their killer Juliette." He says looking deep into my eyes. "Just be careful."

CHAPTER
TWENTY-ONE

Detective Gomez

Michigan, USA

I look over the board one more time. I can't understand a pattern between any of the victims, they are different ages, races, and they are all from different socially economic backgrounds.

The only thing that seems to be a connection is that one of the girls was targeted out of her home whereas there is a possibility that Kassidy Simmons was also targeted as was talking to a guy who never even existed.

With the crime lab still looking into the phone and the texts from her older boyfriend, I keep staring at the board. I spent most of the hours that I couldn't sleep looking through the statements and the notes from the family. The rest of the Simmons girl's family and friends seem to think that this was a wrong place wrong time situation, however I know that sitting next to Juliette yesterday, she really had to bite her tongue about what she could and couldn't say.

As a rookie, I screwed up so bad. I just wanted to do good in the force and by my peers. Some people used to think I was a people pleaser and to some extent, I would agree.

But they I came to the realization that the force and the system don't really care. I look at Juliette and not only do I see her as the female version of me at her age, but I see the determination that I once had and the trust in the force.

The system is floored, especially the criminal justice system. Unfortunately, Juliette looks at this case like it will come so easy, when in reality it will be the most challenging case.

Her determination, her work ethic and compassion for the families is something I envy so much. Her heart is a good one and she is so clearly a likeable person.

I know nothing about her, only that her uncle got her this gig and that she leaves next Friday back to London. I took this case because of her sheer determination not to back down. She stood up in front of that officer and in front of the family.

I pick up the photo of Sandy and look at her. She's a good kid, everyone said so. I feel for those poor parents. No one should have to bury a child; it's not how the world is meant to go.

I don't even need to look up from the photo and I can tell that the ray of sunshine and determination that is Juliette Sanders stands in front of me. I meet her eyes and find her standing, smiling with a coffee in her hand once again. Oh kid, you are too good to me.

"Good morning, Miss smiley. What has got you all chipper?" I ask gratefully taking the coffee and giving her a nod.

"I had a new outlook on the case last night, and I did my homework." She says placing her coffee down and pulling out the case files from her bag. "I think we should speak to Hannah's parents today if you're feeling up to it?" She asks inquisitively.

"Sure thing. You wanna tell me what your new sudden outlook is on this case or you gonna make me guess?"

"Sorry yes, okay." She says putting the case files down and taking the photo of Sandy out of my hand and putting it back on the board. "So, clearly this case makes no sense. They all come from diverse backgrounds, different parts of the city. They don't cross paths in school."

"You're telling me things I already know." I mock and she rolls her eyes.

"I'm getting to my point, chillax." She jokes in that terrible American accent. "The only thing that would tie this case together is if the third victim was lured out of her home. Now, whoever the killer is chose these girls. But why?" She asks me, I shrug my shoulders. "Okay, look at it this way. Something connects all these victims. Maybe it is something that their families are involved in, we are looking to heavy into the girls and with the first two victims, we aren't going to get anywhere apart from what her sister said was an older boyfriend."

"You're saying this has something to do with the families themselves?" I ask her curiously, granted we needed to investigate the families deeper, but I didn't think we would need to pull out all of the skeletons in the closet.

"I'm saying that instead of giving them the sweep over, we should look into them properly because I think that's where the real connection lies."

Following Juliette's hunch, we decided to do a deep dive into their families, their financial records and a background check on them all.

This is the part of the job I hate. The deep diving into someone's whole life. It is part of the job, I do understand that, however this section is so intrusive, and it makes me feel bad as a Detective pulling up people's private information. But what you've gotta' do for justice…

"Want a drink?" I ask her and she shakes her head, deep into a stack of papers that I had to check were okay for her to read and go through. I keep forgetting she's a kid, she's so mature for her age and incredibly smart that I keep forgetting the conversation I'm having is with a teenager.

"Detective, does Mr Robson have any children that are adopted?" She asks me as I begin to get up for my coffee. I stare at her, puzzled, my brows frowned as I try to understand her question.

"Yeah, their daughter Cecille is adopted I believe, that's one of his campaigns. He's trying to match parents with foster children which will hopefully lead to adoption. Cecille is practically the face of his campaign." I say while walking over grabbing my coffee and sitting back down, curious as to why she's suddenly asked that particular question. "Why do you ask?"

"Because the Simmons also adopted a daughter, Kiara. The girl who gave us the phone." She explains, a stumped look on her face.

"So?"

"Before I explain my theory, have you got the Sandy Green case file? Information about her parents and siblings?" She asks and I hand her the pile.

She begins scour through, looking at everything and everything while also putting them into piles. I watch her face drop when she gets to a set of papers and she pulls it up, her eyes wide. She turns the piece of paper to me, pointing out two names on the adoption certificate.

"The youngest Green child is adopted. Her name is Poppy." She explains and I feel my stomach drop. There is no way, it has to be a coincidence.

"Juliette, there is no way—" I begin to say before she cuts me off.

"Detective, please." She says while pulling up three different adoption records. "All children were born within the same year, making them younger than the child that was murdered."

I fall back into my chair, how in god's name did she manage to see that. "Shit." I manage to breathe out and she frowns to me.

"Detective, language please." She mocks and I

look up completely stunned in direction the case has taken. Granted it isn't a solid theory, but it is a very good one. All the kids that were adopted were born within the same year, not to mention that all the children that were murdered, were murdered closer to their house.

"This is possibly the most out there theory there is on this Jules…" I begin to explain, and she nods her head.

"I agree, it is just a theory. But a one that does make sense if you look at it. I don't believe for one second that Kassidy had an older boyfriend—"

"Neither did I."

"Exactly, so clearly she was targeted and if that's the case, the killer was having contact with her for a while, whereas with Sandy, they started messaging that day and went ahead with the kill that night." She stands next to the board, pointing out both child's crime scene photos. "I'm going to guess that Hannah was going to meet someone, possibly to attend a party or whatever she liked to do. These were targeted Detective; these aren't crimes of opportunity."

I sit forward in my chair, rubbing my head in my hands as I look into the Lieutenants office. I might lose my job after this. "Juliette, I believe we need to talk to the families again, but first we are going to need to start with the Robson family, and we will need to do this as careful as possible."

CHAPTER TWENTY-TWO

Detective Gomez

Michigan, USA

We stand together on the doorstep of the fanciest estate I've ever had to visit. Guarded with gates, security, and landscapers. How the other half get to live.

"Let me do all the talking for this one Jules." I explain and she nods her head while I ring the doorbell.

"I'll be as quiet as a mouse." She jokes, causing me to laugh. Sometimes her maturity shows through, and I get a little laugh out of it. The door swings open and we come face to face with a man who looks like he might be knocking on deaths door very soon. He's pale, tale frail looking.

"May I help you?" He speaks slowly, sounding like *Professor Snape* from the *Harry Potter* movies.

"My name is Detective Gomez, this is my partner, Miss Sanders. We were wondering if we could talk to Mr Robson?" I ask and he looks both of us up and down.

"Mr Robson is busy, make an appointment." He says while trying to close the door. I place my hand on the door instantly, causing him to look at me furiously while opening the door once more.

"Sorry, but we really have to speak to the Robson family." I insist once more, and he looks down at Juliette causing her to pull a face. I try my hardest not to laugh.

"The Robson's don't have anything to add to the death of their daughter, it was a tragic accident and would like for it to be forgotten about." He says trying to slam the door on us once more, this time Jules steps in.

"Sorry sir, but I don't believe for one second, they would want a killer going out and doing it to another child. This wasn't a tragic accident; it was a murder. So, the Detective and I would just like some time with the family while we try and understand what happened to their daughter that they publicly state they love so much. Think you can convince them?" I stare down at her, she might have just screwed with the investigation, and I feel my eyes roll. Teenagers.

After a long moment of staring each other down, he moves aside and takes a long deep breath. "Come in." He instructs. I feel my eyes almost pop out of my head. She turns to me, a smug look on her face and this time I roll my eyes in front of her. "Wait here." He instructs once he closes the door and walks towards one of the rooms.

"You trying to get me fired?" I whisper to her, and she looks at me in horror.

"Not at all Detective, but with smug, rich people you have to lay the facts out in front of them or they won't see why it's a problem. Even if it is just for the butler." She says with a smile, before looking around the entry way.

"You'd know this how?" I ask her curiously and she looks at me and raises her eyebrows.

"I live in London Detective." She says with a smile causing me to chuckle underneath my breath. I've never left the states, but I'm assuming the United Kingdom is another level of crazy.

"Can I help you?" A woman appears from the room.

"Mrs Robson, I'm Detective Gomez, this is Miss Sanders. We are looking into your daughter's death as well as similar deaths in the area." I explain to her. She quickly puts her hand up, annoyed.

"Detective, I do not mean to be frank. But our daughter's death was an accident, that is what my husband said. She'd overdosed. Since when did our hard-earned money mean you investigate overdoses?" She practically laughs.

I exchange a look with Juliette who just as much as me, can't believe what I'm hearing. "Ma'am, I can assure you, your daughter didn't die of an overdose." I explain to her, and she laughs once more.

"So, you're calling my husband a liar now?" She asks frustrated and I begin to stutter, trying to find my words before I screw the whole case up.

"He isn't but I might." Juliette speaks and I turn and glare at her giving her warning signs that she clearly ignores. "Mrs Robson, your daughter didn't die of a drug overdose. She was murdered on Friday." She explains and I watch the colour drain from Mrs Robson's face ever so slowly.

"Oh my god." She says before leaning against the wall, the butler quickly beside her leading her into a room. I lightly jab Juliette in the arms, and she gives me a surprised stare, like her outburst didn't just almost put the case in jeopardy.

"Mrs Robson, I apologise for coming over so harshly." She speaks as she takes a seat opposite the woman who is so quiet and shaken. "We would just like to find your daughter's killer." She explains and Mrs Robson nods slightly.

"Of course." She says wheeping ever so slightly. "Oh, my baby." She cries again. "How did she die?" She asks after a moment.

"That is still being determined ma'am, however we would like to know if we have your permission to perform an autopsy on your daughter. It would help with our investigation." I ask her calmly to which she nods quickly.

"Of course, do what you need to." She says dabbing the tears that fall from her eyes quickly. "I can't believe he would lie to me..." She places her head in her hands, looking for some kind of comfort while she lets the new information sink in.

"Mrs Robson, I'd like to ask some questions about your daughter." I ask her calmly, taking out my notepad. She nods, lightly dabbing her eyes again. "When was the last time you seen her?"

"That morning. They got in a fight, her father and her. A massive row that had her pack a bag. This wasn't unusual. They had been arguing so much with Hannah's changes in grades, not to mention her partying, her drug use and she had started drinking heavily too. She was mixing in with the wrong crowds. It just was going downhill, and it was all public because Hannah couldn't keep her mouth shut. She was hellbent on ruining her father's campaign." She explains frustratingly.

"Was there a reason for her sudden change in behaviour, or is it because she started to mix in with the wrong crowds?" I ask her and she nods.

"A bit of both. There was a girl she had met at a concert about a year ago. Odd girl, she used to bring her around a lot but then I noticed how she started to change Hannah and I told her she couldn't come over anymore. That was when the behavioural changes started, the drinking the drugs. That girl got her into them." She continues and I exchange a look with Jules.

"Do you remember this girls name?" She asks Mrs Robson.

"Alicia, I think. I'm not sure if Hannah still hung out with her or was around her. I think Alicia did the damage she wanted to do and then left the group. Although that's how I seen it. She never ever mentioned her around me." She says softly.

"Did Hannah mention anyone else new in her life? A boyfriend, girlfriend maybe?" Juliette continues to ask, and Mrs Robson shakes her head.

"We weren't even on speaking terms. She tortured her sister daily, ruining things that were hers, used to try and cause problems in school for her. They had grown up together and were the best of friends. Then all of a sudden, she developed a hatred for her." She explains while picking up a photo of the girls and handing it to us both.

The photo is of Hannah and Cecille, laughing while giving each other the tightest hug. They seemed so close. Addiction can ruin the best of people.

"Mrs Robson, if you don't mind me asking, when did you adopt Cecille again?" I ask her, getting my notepad out that I had just placed down to look at the photo.

"Twelve years ago. She was one when we adopted her." She explains softly. I nod softly while noting it down and giving her a smile.

"Thank you and thank you for your time." I say to her pulling out my card from my jacket. "If you can think of anything else, let me know." I say while handing her the card and she takes it.

"How did you get wrapped up in this then?" She almost laughs before lifting her head and looking directly at Juliette. "Are you some kind of journalist?"

She shakes her head as she tucks her hair behind her ear. "I'm someone who is curious about the American system and would like to learn more about it. But even with that being said, I want to help bring closure to the families. And that is why I'm here." She explains softly to the woman who raises her eyebrows to me.

"I think you've got some competition Detective." She laughs and I can't help but smile.

"Just do me a favour, make sure you find their killer."

CHAPTER TWENTY-THREE

Juliette Sanders

Michigan, USA

A S I arrive home, I feel a wave of dread come over me. Peter had mentioned there was a family meeting today. And as I walk through the door, and I immediately scream when coming face to face with Oliver.

"Jesus!" I shout at him, and he can't help but hysterically laugh. "That isn't funny, you could have given me a heart attack." I say to him and as he finishes manically laughing, he takes a deep breath.

"Family meeting. Robert's office. I was told to collect you." He says while grabbing me on my arm and leading me towards the office.

"I can walk myself." I say pulling myself from his grip.

"Oh, I know." He smiles creepily at me before entering the room. I take a deep breath; he is someone I will never understand no matter how hard I try.

"Hi Jules." Robert greets me as he hints for me to take a seat in front of his desk.

"This about Damian?" Alexis asks from behind me, and I turn to her and give her a small smile. She doesn't return it; she focuses ahead and ignores me.

I turn back around and focus on Robert who gives the room a nod.

"As we are all aware, Damian had to be checked into the local mental health facility after an episode once he got back from his task with both Spencer and Rodger." Robert begins to explain. "So, to no one's surprise Rodger didn't do what was ask and instead did everything but leaving Spencer and Damian. However, something went wrong. One night after Damian had went out, he came back to the camp covered in blood having a manic episode, he had clearly seen something that had distressed him, yet we are still trying to understand exactly what that is. Finally, when Spencer was trying to calm Damian down, both boys were ambushed, and they were both shot. Thankfully not doing too much damage.

Spencer managed to drive them here, and well you know the rest."

The whole room sits in silence, stunned by this. Why had Damian gone out so late? The whole room begins to look around at each other no one knowing what to say.

"So, how is Damian doing?" I ask, the only one who seems to think of the most logical answer.

Robert and the rest of the Quinten's smile at me. "He is doing very well; he is in recovery. We should be able to see him soon, hopefully before you leave back to London, but let's not rush things." He explains with a smile, looking to his other children who seem to not want to be here. Especially Clarissa who lurks in the corner.

"What was the task?" I ask them again ignoring the stares from the rest of my family. Spencer and Robert exchange a look and Spencer gives him a nod.

"They were to follow a family who we are to be doing business within the future, however there had been talk they were talking badly about our business, and I sent the boys in to look into it. No matter what it took." He explains calmly. I look to Spencer who gives me a glare to not ask any more questions and I take that as a hint that I don't want to know any more.

"Why do you care about what the case is?"

Clarissa pipes up, wanting to cause an argument.

"It was just a question." I say to her, and she laughs hysterically. But in the most chaotic way, her smile almost joker like.

"You never just ask questions. You have to know everything about everyone."

"You're right I do." I laugh back her causing a smug look on her face. "So, you going to tell us where your baby is then?" I ask her and I feel the rest of the family stop, they are all waiting for this answer, an answer that baffles the entire family.

She laughs psychotically while never breaking eye contact. "Never."

I roll my eyes and look at Robert who gives me a nod, hinting that he liked my attempt. I know Peter is still looking into the whole situation, but it does go cold.

"So, what is the next steps for Damian, or will we just see how it goes?" I ask Robert and he nods, ignoring Clarissa's outburst.

"We will, until we can establish who exactly he is he is referring to, we can't rule anything out. But once he is feeling a little better, we will visit him." He says giving me a wink. I give him a small smile before looking around at the room.

"Next part of the family meeting. Marcus." Robert says with a smile. "You leave today." I turn around quickly, my heart falling so hard I feel it shatter on the floor. I thought it was in a few weeks?

"They pulled my date up, which means I have to leave today. It's a shock, but it's now or never I guess." He says with a smile. Alexis places her head on his shoulder and Nathaniel gives him a pat on the back.

"We're proud of you."

"Very proud." I say with a smile which he returns.

"I'm sorry for being so shit with you recently." Marcus speaks up, looking directly at me. "I started to resent you a little bit for who your mother is and I'm sorry, and I'm sorry you've felt so iced out since finding out." Marcus apologizes which takes me by surprise.

"Oh, give me a break. I'm done." Clarissa shouts out again, leaving the room and slamming the door. I ignore her, which as always in the best tactic.

"Thank you. But it's okay." I reassure looking around the room. "I never expected everyone to be okay with it. Having me here and finding out who she is puts all of you at a lot of risk, I'm grateful you let me stay as long as you have." I say with a smile to Robert who gives me a gentle nod. "But, I would have rather you had said, I'm digesting it, give me some time rather than give me the cold shoulder." I say turning back at my siblings who all share the same look.

"Sorry Jules." They say in unison. I can't help but laugh, as does the rest of the room.

"I have a confession to make." Felicity speaks up finally and tucks her hair behind her ear. "I felt the same way as the kids. You could have the life all of us have ever wanted. Your birth mother is a queen, your father, the leader of the American mafia, and lastly your mum, Amy who gives you that normality. I guess we could say we are jealous in a way, or that is how I felt. I would love it if for just one day I could be like you. Fly back to a different country and forget the rest of us exist while you cope with home life." She laughs. No one else does, and I get the feeling like me, they noticed the little dig in the middle of her apology.

"Felicity, I'm not Arielle." I say coldly. I watch as the smile drops from her face as she realises what she had said. She looks around the room, looking at the other glares from the rest of the family.

"Oh Jules, I'm sorry I never meant to imply it." She says softly.

"Whether you did or not Felicity, please don't compare her to Arielle." Robert warns her, and Felicity goes quiet. Serena rolls her eyes at her sister and walks up to my chair and embraces me tightly.

The hug is needed, but a big surprise. She

exists it after a few moments and looks at her brothers. I have needed help for so long, I needed someone to say it's okay, I don't judge you. Yet no one in this room did, till your daughter came around. She seen me for the person I am, and she treat me with kindness and showed me compassion when that is all I have ever wanted from you." Serena almost cries. I look up at her, feeling so proud that she is finally being able to get this off her chest.

"Serena, we understand you have your own issues—" Robert begins to explain before she cuts him off.

"You know nothing. You don't know how many demons I deal with on a daily basis. I don't want to explain my trauma to you, because you wouldn't listen, nor would you care. Both Oliver and I get painted as the worst in this business, but we are the most understood. We are the youngest, the ones who have seen so much yet can never explain it. Where were you when we had to battle our demons, Robert? You promised to protect us? Oh, that's right, you were too busy adopting kids and forgetting about the people who were struggling. I adore all of your children as if they were my own, but I will never in a million years forgive you for giving Juliette away." She shouts at him.

The whole room is completely quiet, apart from Felicity's silent cries. I can't help but feel emotional, Serena has had this building up for so long that to her this is a weight off her chest and something she's been needing to shout about for so long.

"Serena, I'm sorry." He apologises sheepishly. "I knew you were struggling after I gave up Juliette, and I never did anything to help. I'm sorry to you Oliver for not being there and just sending you off to other people so they can deal with you during a psychotic break."

I think Robert's intention with this family meeting was to discuss Marcus and Damian, but in the end has spiralled into a therapy session for us all. Getting off everything on our chest that has upset us for no matter how long.

"Apology not accepted." Oliver says eventually and we all turn to look at him, his face is serious, and he isn't joking. He's angry, and understandably rightly so. Although Robert's apology was sincere, I believe that that apology hasn't even touched the surface as to what Oliver has had to deal with or witness over the years. He probably still needs time to process it, or maybe in the future find a way to forgive him brother and his siblings.

"I know you're angry Oliver—"

"You don't know what I am. So don't try and show that you care in front of your devil's spawn. Because I will make sure she sees you for the monster that you truly are." Oliver snaps before storming out of the room. I sit there, baffled by Oliver's name for me to start but also with the way he acted, I understand he has outbursts, not to mention severe anger issues. But that was on another level.

"I'll speak to him; however, I don't forgive you either Robert. One day I might but not yet." Serena says before also leaving the room, giving my shoulder s squeeze as she passed.

The air in the room is now thick from all of the confessions and the apologies. I don't think any of us have anything more to say, not to mention if I hear one more, I'm sorry, I might actually scream.

"I have to go." Marcus says before standing up, giving me a warm smile. "I will miss you all. I'm sad not everyone is here but they know I think they are okay." He says jokingly. Alexis shoves him, before pulling him into the longest hug ever. We all stand and wait our turn to say goodbye.

"I'm going to miss you brother." Nathaniel says while pulling Marcus into the best brotherly hug you can imagine.

"I think I'll miss him more." Ezekiel pipes up from the corner and embracing his brother. "Remember, be on your best behaviour." He jokes to him, and Marcus rolls his eyes.

"Like I'd be trouble... please." He laughs as

does the rest of the room. One by one he hugs everyone who is left. Felicity, Peter, a very long one with Robert who told him how proud he was of him. Then lastly it is my turn. I can't help but become emotional. He was one of my last connections to London that I had here.

"I think getting to know you has been the most adventurous and stressful months of my life." He jokes causing me to laugh through the tears. "But I'm so pleased I built up the courage to get out of the car and confront that headteacher, because I don't know where I would be now if I hadn't." He says, clearly getting emotional.

"You sound like your dying can you please just give me a hug already." I practically beg and he pulls me in for one of the longest hugs I think I've ever had. He holds me tightly, lightly crying on my shoulder as I feel someone place their hand on my back and I get the feeling it's time for Marcus to go.

"I love you sis." He says pulling away from me. "Just solve this case as soon as you can and go back to being the goody-goody girl that I know you are." He says playfully punching me in the arm causing me to laugh once more.

"I love you too. Just be safe and don't be an idiot." I laugh, he clutches his chest. "That hurt my heart, I'm wounded." He jokes around while pulling Alexis in for a hug who is hysterically crying.

"You'll get over it."

The whole room laughs and for the first time since I arrived, I feel a part of this family. We watch as Marcus grabs his things and heads to the car, waving us goodbye as we all stand at the door, heartbroken it has come so quick.

"He'll be okay, won't he?" Alexis asks and I turn my head to Robert who smiles down at us both.

"He will be just fine."

CHAPTER TWENTY-FOUR

Juliette Sanders

Michigan, USA

As we head back inside the house, the rest of the family depart to do their own thing. Alexis goes to study, Nathaniel is going to work late in the security room, Peter is doing whatever Peter is doing and he has decided to take up residency in the parlour. Felicity decided to go and check on Serena, whereas Ezekiel had something due for a client he had.

I stand finding myself unsettled and not sure what to do for the rest of the evening. I watch my family set on their ways and I decide until dinner, I will just stay in my room, or I will go to the library.

Detective Gomez decided that tonight I can have a night off as he has noticed how tired I am.

"What are your plans, Jules?" I hear someone ask beside me. I turn to find Robert, also watching his family go in separate areas of the house. He turns to me and looks down with a smile.

"I don't know yet." I say softly, to which he nods and begins to open his pocket.

"I believe this might be a good idea." He says while handing me the letter Arielle left for me. I hadn't read it yet, and I wasn't sure if I was ready to.

I carefully take the letter out of his hand and look at it gently. A letter. She decided that this would be good as a form of explanation. I don't hate Arielle; I do understand that she did what she had to do. However, I think the way she went about it really did a number on so many of the Quinten's that some of them have severe trust issues.

"You think it's the right time?" I ask looking up from staring at the letter. He nods, ever so slightly while giving me a reassuring smile.

"It's better to get it over and done with now, rather than wait and find out it was something disappointing." He explains to me. I have to agree with him on this, Arielle is someone none of us can figure out. This letter might say absolutely nothing at all, and it might be filled with a lot of lies. "If you feel like it, I would like to know what it says." He says with a smile before heading in the direction of his office.

"Robert?" I ask him softly causing him to stop in his tracks and turn around. "Can I stay with you while I read it? If you're not busy."

He smiles wide at me, as he extends his hand out. "Never too busy." I walk towards him and take his hand as we head towards the office. I take a seat on the sofa, and he joins me, getting comfortable. "Take your time." He encourages me while giving me a warm smile yet again.

I open up the envelope, not wanting to waste any more time for this woman and her answers. The paper itself is incredibly thick with the Haroux crest on the top of the paper. I look up at Robert, who gives me a very encouraging nod as he leans back in the chair.

My dearest daughter,

Oh, how grown up you will be. Fourteen, now that in itself is a scary revelation.

I do hope you're happy and healthy. That you have surrounded yourself with great people and a great family who love you. That is all I ever wanted, for you to find a family that loved you.

I don't think a day has gone by where I haven't thought about you, what you were doing, what you were growing up to be. My husband, Edward, begged for me to come and find you. But what I did not want is to face that side of myself once more. Although I had been honest with him, I didn't want to come looking and potentially rip you from someone I know who would love you and care for you more than I ever could. I am sorry for that. I always wanted to be able to be the mother you needed but I just couldn't.

You reminded me so much of your father, a segment in my life that I had chosen to forget for so long. When he did call, I felt as though my reality was shaken. He wanted to talk about you, and my worry was that it was nothing good. So, I do hope when you're reading this, that you are happy, and you are loved like a commoner should be.

I had decided to not mention you to your sister Robyn. But she will be Queen of Haroux one day, and I don't think I could see you standing by her. She's built for this life, to take over from my reign. Where you wouldn't be.

The council will not be nice to either of us! They will be harsh labelling me publicly, however you will be known as the abomination. Children born out of wedlock are shunned upon in Haroux, so for the both of us. Since they found out it's been nothing but awful for me. As much as I tell myself that I deserve this, I can't help but feel like if I hadn't had you and you hadn't found Robert, my life could have remained perfect.

I hope that one day I can meet you, tell you stories about your father and who he really is as a person. By blood, you are a royal. But you were never given an official title, as much as I would like to give you one; I know he would never let me.

Safe love and light,

Queen Arielle of Haroux

I sit there, in complete and utter shock, not to mention anger. That gave me no answers, only more questions. I begin to get upset and Robert notices, placing his hand on my thigh looking at me concerned.

"She is a very selfish woman." I breathe out while looking away from him. "How you ever stood her for that long I will never understand." I say while handing him the letter and getting up from the seat trying to control my emotions.

I pace as I watch Robert read the letter, his face growing more and more angry the more he reads it. She never mentions why she did it, only that she would be shunned if the council were to find out. Her husband tried to get her to look for me, but she didn't want any part of it.

"Jesus Christ, I could kill her." He says placing the letter down and rubbing his head in his hands. "Juliette, if I knew the contents of the letter,

I would have never let you read it. That was completely selfish of her, she is trying to blame you and you are not to be blamed for any of her problems. Her being shunned by the council. That is her problem. Not to mention the fact that she brought in what they might think about you just to make you feel even worse. I can't—"

He stops immediately not wanting to say anything else. This man to a lot of people may seem cold, heartless, conniving, when I look at him, I see a man who has to protect his family no matter what happens. And he knows that by giving me that letter it has only opened wounds that might never be closed.

"Why does she blame me so much? Is it a coping mechanism?" I ask him and he shakes his head, standing up to meet me. I can't stop the tears from flowing because of how hurt I feel. He pulls me in for a hug, a one that clearly both of us needed. He holds me tight, never letting me go for a while.

"I don't know darling. I feel like she may point blame in order to make herself feel better." He explains in the embrace. Not one of us let go, and I doubt he would let me with how much I'm crying.

"I don't want to meet her Robert, please don't make me. I don't want a title." I plead with him; he shushes me gently while holding me gently.

"I promise you Juliette, we will only meet her when you're ready if that ever happens. But I can assure you, you will never get that title. Because that is so cruel and unfair to give you something you never wanted." He says while pulling me out of the hug to look at him. He wipes my tears away before kissing me gently on the forehead. "You're always safe with me. That I can promise you."

CHAPTER TWENTY-FIVE

Juliette Sanders

Michigan, USA

I sit at the Detectives desk, coffee on the table for both of us. I think I spent the majority of the night crying, not to mention I phoned my mum in tears too and told her about the letter.

She was as furious as Robert was and found the letter completely selfish and cold towards me. I think that is what is upsetting me the most, the fact that she blamed me for a lot of things that might happen. But then again am I surprised? Probably not.

I had in my head that this woman was lovely, she was kind, thoughtful and gave me up because she knew because of Robert's occupation, she could never keep me safe if she was to stay. But how wrong I was.

Robert had mentioned that he will speak to my mum today. He said he will call her later on in the hopes that they can talk and discuss something in regard to Arielle and the Haroux family, also probably because they want to vent to each other. He was going to tell the other Quinten's about it too and asked that I leave the letter and home, to which I responded with "Burn it, I don't care."

That woman and her letter made me angry, and what is worse is that Robyn is having to deal with her, so I dread to thing what she is like to a child she loves. I'd like to think she was better, but I don't have high hopes.

"Jules." I hear the Detective shout and I snap out of my angry stare at the wall and look at him. "You okay? Your eyes are puffy, and you look like you're losing sleep." He says to me while sitting down, pushing my coffee right in my face.

"I'm fine Detective but thank you." I say while giving my coffee a sip and nodding to him. I know he doesn't believe me; I can see it over his face. But I can't tell him about me properly or my family because then my own would kill me, and the Detective will quite possibly never speak to me again.

"So, I managed to get the crime lab to pull off all of the texts from Kassidy Simmons so called boyfriend and it is a dead end. The phone itself is a burner phone which can't be traced which is kind of what I expected." He says while handing me a case file that contains the texts. "The photos that have been sent are from an Instagram user called Kian Powell, he's an Irish model and it seemed that whoever was speaking to Kassidy, had ever intention on luring her out of the house. Look at the last sheet of paper." He instructs and I do just that.

The texts are something that you would read in a soppy romance book or that of a cheesy movie. A lot of I miss you, I can't wait to meet you... And that is where I notice it.

'Come to the woods near your house. I have a surprise for you.'

So, she was lured out, and now that we have confirmation on that, I would like to put money on that Hannah left willingly as well. Maybe in the hopes for drugs or a party or even to meet this new friend.

"Do you remember how the friend that was last to see Kassidy said she couldn't sit still throughout the whole night; it was like she was waiting to go home? What if she never told her friends about the boyfriend, only her sister? Because I doubt my friends would let me go alone." I explain and he nods his head picking up the statement from the girl Kassidy was last seen with.

"She said, 'it's like she had ants in her pants. She wanted to leave; I could tell. I just don't know why.'" He says looking up and turning his attention to the board.

"All of these girls were lured out Detective, and not one of them came home. With Kassidy it was planned, they pretended to be her boyfriend whereas with Sandy it was quick, and Sandy never noticed the changes and that she wasn't speaking to her friend. Then we have Hannah..." I say while looking at the board.

"The Medical Examiner is doing her autopsy now, it was signed off by both parents and we can really find out what's happening, hopefully we can find something that can lead us to a killer." He says while standing looking at the board as well.

"Have you managed to find that Alicia girl?" I ask him curiously and he shakes his head.

"Nope, I'm going to assume it's a nickname of some kind and that she really is good at hiding." He says while placing his hands on his hips. "You got any theories?"

"What about local sex offenders, any that may have a background in IT possibly or may have come in contact with all three girls. A bus driver or something? Maybe." I explain and his eyes go wide.

"Look at you, little miss Detective. Hell, what do you need me for? You're looking at this in all the right directions." He jokes and I can't help but laugh at him.

"You out of your mind!" A man screams at the other end of the precinct. I turn around to see Mr Robson storming towards us both and I turn to the Detective who places his hand up, hinting that I don't speak.

"You told my wife how my daughter died! What if this got out to the press, that she was murdered, it could ruin my chances of winning. Are you stupid?" He screams at Detective Gomez' face. The man is as cool as a cucumber while places his hands up in front of Mr Robson.

"Sir, I can assure you, I only want to find your daughter's killer. She was murdered so brutally with two other girls dying in the same way. Please tell me that you understand that this can't just be swept under the rug." The Detective says so calmly causing Mr Robson to become more irritated.

"I don't care how she died or that there are other girls who died in the same way. They were probably the same as Hannah, druggies and low lives. They would have amounted to nothing, just as much as my daughter. Jesus, even in death she is trying to ruin my campaign." He laughs and I look to the Detective, annoyance clearly in both of our faces.

But as I scour the room, it looks like the rest of the station agrees with us. Everyone is angry that a man could speak so little about his daughter as well as the other girls on the board.

I look at the Lieutenant who stands in the doorway of his office watching the whole thing unfold. "Drop this case immediately, that is an order if you would like to keep your job Detective." Mr Robson warns him, getting so close to his face he is breathing the same air as him.

"I'm not doing that, Sir. I have a serial killer on my hands that is running around your town killing young girls in the area. I hate to be so forward sir, but the way you speak so confidently about giving children new homes whether it be fostering the child or even adopting, I would like to think you would have had the same determination to find your daughter's killer." The Detective speaks calmly, and my mouth drops open. "But I couldn't be more wrong, could I? You demanding I drop the case shows that you don't really care about these kids at all. You put on a front, when to all of us in the station you have just shown your true colours. All we want is to show justice to your daughter, the other murdered girls and the families that are grieving. This isn't about you Mr Robson, because once upon a time it was my little girl up on this board. And I stopped at nothing to assist the Detectives and officers who worked their ass off to find her killer." He says coldly. I feel the whole station stop in their tracks. *Oh my god, his daughter was murdered.*

"I care deeply about the system and finding justice—" Mr Robson tries to speak but the Detective cuts him off.

"Don't try and now paint yourself as the grieving father, because you've said not one nice thing about your daughter since you walked through the door." He snaps at him causing Mr Robson to move back ever so slightly. "So, what Miss Sanders and I intend on doing is finding your daughter's killer with your cooperation or not. But just note when it comes to the day of deciding you aren't getting my vote, whatsoever."

The station in eerily quiet as Mr Robson looks around to the disgusted looks on all of the officers' faces. He knows he has come in without any backup, yet we have tons. Not one person in this room looks like they would be up for voting for the man in the election. Their faces are horrified, angry and disgusted with the lack of respect he has shown his daughter and the other victims.

He straightens up his suit jacket and turns to me, glaring down at me. "Miss Sanders, is it? I hope I can secure you're vote in the election." He says with a creepy smile. I look him up and tilt my head.

"Sorry, I don't get a vote." I say sweetly. I

watch the smile fall from his face as he realises my accent. "But even if I did, you wouldn't get mine. Because I wouldn't dare vote for a man who just publicly bashed his daughter after she died." I say standing up to meet him. The bald man looks down on me, he's not that much taller as he looks around my face for any sign that I am joking.

"My mother always told me Mr Robson, if you have nothing nice to say, don't say anything at all. And this life lesson would apply to you if your mother had taught you any manors as a child. Instead of doing some good in the world, you became a politician and you got to lie for a living. You paint yourself as a man who wants to do good things for this city, to try and help the children find forever homes. So, if you're lying about caring about all of the children in this city, what else are you lying about? Because the truth is never far behind the lie Mr Robson. And if I have to, I will dig out every single skeleton in your wardrobe. Because to me, you are the perfect suspect. You had motive, you hated your daughter, and she was ruining your campaign with her drinking and drug addiction. But where were you as a father? Instead of being there for her and getting her the help she needed you ignored her and blamed her for everything." I say as calmly as I can. The man is so up his own behind he doesn't even know what is going on. He cares about one thing and one thing only. Himself.

"Miss Sanders, I don't like your tone!" He shouts and I stand up just that little bit taller.

"And I don't care."

He turns around and stares directly at the Lieutenant who I watch shrugs his shoulders, still leaning on the door frame. "Mr Robson, Miss Sanders and Detective Gomez are giving you that truth you needed. Either you cooperate with us to find your daughter's killer, or we go to the press and tell them about this little outburst." He threatens.

The vein on the top of Mr Robson's forehead is pulsing through and it looks as if it is about to burst. He closes his eyes, trying to compose himself. "Take what you need, find the killer." He says before storming out of the station. I turn around to Detective Gomez who smiles to me, holding out his fist.

"You really like burning bridges, don't you?" He asks jokingly and I laugh with him.

"Oh yes, I like to watch them burn."

"I think we should take a little trip to a Starbucks for yet another coffee since that man was here complaining for so long, ours have gotten cold. Come on." He ushers me out of the station, as he receives pats on the back as we walk through.

"Detective, I never knew that about your

family." I say softly as we begin to walk towards the car. He opens up the driver's side placing his hand on the car door and looking over at me.

"Well kid, I think you've earned yourself an explanation as to why I didn't want to take this case."

CHAPTER TWENTY–SIX

Juliette Sanders

Michigan, USA

He sits at the booth fiddling with his coffee for what seems like the one hundredth time. I can tell he is nervous to talk about it, it is opening up wounds that may have healed.

He puts one more sugar in his coffee and I notice how much he is fidgeting. I place my hand gently on his causing him to look up at me, like I've just released him from his own little world.

"Take your time." I reassure him and he nods to me. I lift my hand away and take a sip from my coffee, hoping it will calm my nerves. The whole time we were in the car, I reassured him he doesn't need to tell me, but he insisted that it would help him deal with the case better.

I don't like the thought of the Detective hurting or in any pain whether it be caused by past trauma, because there is nothing worse than talking about something you try and forget.

"Okay, so. The main reason why I didn't want to take this case is because it involved children. I've only ever had to do one case involving children and it was the most painful situation. The family and their grief was exactly how I felt not that long ago, and I never wanted to feel like that again." He says before taking a swig of his coffee and pulling a face. Probably because he added in that extra sugar.

"The Green family that came in about Sandy, did that give you flashbacks to what happened with that case?" I ask softly and he nods slightly.

"I can't deal with the pain they go through, because it reminds me of my own." He admits, trying to compose his feelings. "It was three years ago, and I had been on a double shift. It was my daughter Riley's birthday the next weekend and I wanted to get her a bike she wanted. Between my wife and I, we needed to scrape together to get her this bike she kept asking for." He explains. He takes a deep breath for a moment, trying to compose himself. "I came home, and I walked into carnage, blood was all up the walls and it was cold. The whole house was freezing cold." He says taking another swig and pulling that same face. "I screamed out for them, but no one answered. I went into the living room and found my son Steven first. He was on the floor, he wasn't responding. He was… cold." He begins to become so upset he can't say anything else. I gently place my hand on his arm as he cries lightly reliving the events.

"I found Riley and my wife next." He cries softly trying to contain himself. It's quiet today in the Starbucks and he sits, lightly rubbing his hand down his face. "It was awful. They were all so innocent." He explains quietly.

"I'm so sorry Detective." I say softly still holding on to his arm. Seeing him so raw and honest about his family makes me cry. And we sit in a booth, crying. I think in theory we both needed it.

"I had sent a gang member to jail on a case I was working on about a month prior. It was revenge for sending him to jail. He was bragging about it." He says, his whole tone changing from sad to angry. "I wasn't allowed near him, because I would have killed him."

"But then you would be no better than he is. And it wouldn't have brought your family back. It would have just caused another fight."

"That gang caused us so many problems, but

thankfully we managed to arrest and charge every single one on multiple counts of murder, drug trafficking, and prostitution." He explains taking another swig from his coffee before moving it away. "I regret putting that sugar in there that was terrible." He coughs up causing me to smile. I watch as he wipes the tears that have sat on his face for a moment.

"Thank you for telling me, I'm so sorry Detective." I say sincerely and give him a warm smile which he returns.

"You're a good kid. I think Riley would have liked you." He says with a smile before grabbing my coffee and taking a swig. His face turns sour, and he places it down gagging and coughing. "What the hell is that!" He shouts and I can't help but laugh.

"White Chocolate Mocha." I laugh at him; he looks at me horrified.

"Come on, before I arrest you for ruining coffee. That is disgusting Jules." He says before taking a swig of his sweet coffee. "This is just as bad." He says almost coughing up a lung.

I am to the point where I am in tears while laughing. He does know how to make a sad situation better.

"I think we should go and speak to the local adoption agency here. These guys are the ones that dealt with the adoptions of the three families." He says leading me out of the Starbucks and towards the car.

"That's a good idea, what if they were hacked?" I ask him as he opens the car.

"I'm thinking the same thing. Let's hope they can give us some answers that we are looking for." He says opening the door. "First, we need to stop off at a gas station so I can get some gum. I need to get taste of sugar out of my mouth."

CHAPTER TWENTY-SEVEN

Detective Gomez

Michigan, USA

As we arrive at the adoption agency I begin to look around while waiting for the receptionist to return back off her break. It is one of the fanciest reception area's I've ever seen, yet I know behind closed doors the number of cases each social worker will have is unbearable.

The theory that is going round in my brain is that the killer is a social worker who is going off a list and killing the birth children of adoptive kids so they can have a better life. The killer is adopted themselves or has witnessed something to cause this change is behaviour and resolve to killing. But then this is just a theory, but a one that makes the most sense.

The theory Jules is looking into is that it could be a sex offender, granted all the children don't come in contact at any point but they might have said something to someone in a street that has made the killer interested in them.

Different theories with one end motive – devastation to the families. This is something that the families will never recover from, not to mention the fact that they will have to deal with it being public once an arrest is made.

"Can I help you?" I woman with a sweet voice rushes back and places a coffee cup on her desk.

"Yes, my name is Detective Gomez, and this is Miss Sanders we were just wanting to ask some questions to whoever is in charge if they are available, please?" I ask her kindly and she looks between us both.

"Are you looking for someone in the system?" She asks curiously and I shake my head.

"Not at all, we would just like to speak to whoever is in charge please." I say one more time with a smile. The sweetness in her voice turns bitter as she stands looking down on Juliette and myself.

"I'm afraid I can't he's busy today." She says sternly while giving Juliette a rude look, which she ignores.

"I would like to think he would be cooperative when I tell him it's about a murder investigation." I say to her sternly. Her eyes go wide, and she looks at me in horror for a moment. She quickly reaches for the phone and clicks a button. I watch as she quietly explains the situation before giving us a small smile.

"You can head in, he's expecting you." She says with a smile before opening the door for us.

"Thank you so much." I say with a smile as both Jules and I walk through the door to the absolute carnage that is the adoption agency. It is packed with people, phones ringing, some children crying as well as stacks and stacks of cases as tall as me. The poor work these people are going through only makes it so much worse.

We head straight through the hall and towards the door at the bottom the sign reading 'Randy Pickett. CEO.'

I knock loudly and faintly hear a 'come in' before opening the door slightly, and peeking my head in. "Mr Pickett?" I ask him nicely and he gets up from his chair buttoning his suit.

"Yes, please come in." He says encouragingly making his way round the desk to welcome us in. "Please call me Randy, Mr Pickett was my father." He says with a smile extending his hand out to me which I take. He smiles sweetly at Jules before extending his hand out to the seats hinting for us to take one.

Jules and I sit down in unison as the man gets comfortable in his chair. He's mid to late fifty's, tall and in a very expensive suit.

"Randy, my name is Detective Gomez, this is Miss Sanders. We are looking into some recent murders of young girls in the area." I explain to him, and he looks at both of us concerned.

"Oh my god. And you think it could be someone from my agency?" He asks shocked.

"We aren't sure yet, we just thought we would come down and have a chat. We don't have any solid leads at this moment in time, however, doesn't say that something might come up." I explain to him, and he nods and moves forward in his seat.

"How can I help?"

"How many people have worked here for more than ten years would you say?" I ask him and he freezes for a moment trying to think.

"The majority of my staff Detective. They have been loyal since I started this agency more than 30 years ago." He explains leaning back in his chair ever so slightly.

"Have you ever had any problems with hacking at all? Potentially within the last two years?" I question and he looks at us both confused.

"I'm sorry, hacking? Did you see the stack of papers are you walked through; we haven't yet ventured into the digital age yet. We are trying but we are all people who have done this for years, and quite frankly, technology can be a pain. The most we have is a website." He explains and I feel the hacked theory go out of the window.

"The reason we ask Randy is because three girls have been killed in the space of two months. They were all the birth children of children that were adopted through this agency. The killer is killing the birth siblings." I explain as calmly as I can, but he begins to freak out.

"Jesus Christ..." He mutters underneath his breath. "That is insane. And you think it has something to do with one of my workers?" He asks.

"Not necessarily, however we have to rule it out. Now have you noticed anyone who has changed their shift pattern. Anyone who has had anything dramatic changed in his life?" I ask curiously.

I watch as a lightbulb goes off in his head. "The only person I can think of that has changed in the last year is Tony. Tony Cardeo. His wife left him just over a year ago. One of his children was adopted, Samantha. He had a daughter, Janie who died of a rare lung disease before he adopted

Samantha." He explains and I exchange a look with Jules, which Randy notices. "You have to understand, Tony is a great guy, he cares so much for the kids. He wouldn't do this. Janie's death devastated him. It took the majority of my team and his wife to get him off the deep edge. That was when they adopted Samantha about three years later." He explains and I still exchange a look with Jules.

"Did Tony help with these adoptions?" I ask pulling out the adoptions of the Simmons family, Green family as well as the Robson family.

The expression on his face drops as he looks up at both of us. "Yes. Tony helped these adoptions go through." He explains, his face as white as a ghost and I exchange one more look with Jules.

"Is he in today?" I ask him and he nods his head. "I'll need to speak to him if that is alright with you?"

He nods once again and I get up from my chair, Juliette joining me. For some reason she's been super quiet since we arrived in the building, and I can't tell if it a good thing or a bad thing. "I'll call him in here, saves us trying to find a free room." Randy explains before opening the door and calling out for Tony.

I watch as a man's head bobs up from his desk and he makes his way over towards the office. He's not very tall maybe 5ft 3, I believe Jules is taller than him. He's a man who clearly likes his beer just as much as me as a little beer belly hangs over his trouser belt. He waddles in, the man a sweating mess as he takes a seat.

"What's going on?" He asks looking around the room and looking over at Jules. "Is she a new case?" He asks Randy who shakes his head.

"These Detectives have some questions to ask you Tony. I need you to be honest with them." He asks and Tony frows, looking between myself and Jules.

"Detectives, what for? Oh my god! Did something happen to Samantha?" He shouts concerned and I put my hands up, trying to calm him down.

"Your daughter is fine sir; we just want to ask you about some adoptions that you settled a few years ago." I ask calmly, watching him frown and look to Randy.

"They were all legal!" He shouts in his defence.

"Tony, no one is saying they aren't just hear them out." Randy pleads with him, and Tony takes a long deep breath. I can already tell this guy isn't our killer, he's sweating like a pig, he can't stop twitching, besides the person who killed the girls is patient whereas this guy is completely on the edge.

"Do you remember settling these adoptions?" I ask handing him the file and he begins to look through the records. He eagerly nods before handing them back to me.

"Yes, I settled these adoptions, why?" He asks, his voice cracking from the nerves.

"Tony, I am gonna need you to take a deep breath please. You are not under arrest; we just have some questions that are routine as you are the only person linking to the victims and their families." I explain to him, and he shoots a look at Randy who only gives him a nod.

"Ask away." He says as calmly as he can.

"Where were you eight weeks ago? It was a Saturday?" I ask him and he thinks long and hard for a moment before shaking his head.

"I don't know I'd have to check my diary. More than likely, I was here, I am most days and nights." He explains while taking a tissue from Randy's desk and whipping it over his face.

"Okay, what about 3 weeks ago? It was a Friday?" I ask him and he turns back to me.

"I've been in Florida over a month, I only got back on Saturday, I was visiting my daughter." He explains. And I watch as Randy lets out a long exhale. Now he definitely isn't our guy.

"Can you provide me with evidence of this just so I can rule you out?" I ask him nicely and he nods very quickly.

"Take my entire calendar. I was not here; I didn't do anything." He panics and I place my hand firmly on his shoulder.

"No one is saying you are I just have to rule you out, okay?"

He nods quickly as he rubs the drenched tissue over his face once again.

"Tony, within the last year have you noticed anything go off your desk? A file maybe, a one that was filled with documents and records of the adoptions you finalized?" Jules asks him softly and he begins to think for a moment, before looking at Randy, I watch as two lightbulbs go off in the room as they both realize something.

"About a year ago, a girl came in she was about seven months pregnant and asked to talk to someone about potentially putting the child up for adoption..." He begins to explain before Randy buts in.

"The girl was about twenty or twenty-one. She went by the name Alicia Hayward." He explains and I immediately look over at Jules who has already clocked what he's said. That must be Hannah's mystery friend.

"She went to the bathroom and then her boyfriend came in to speak to me, he was about the same age, tall, dark hair. He didn't seem like he was all there, in my opinion. He had a colder response to everything it was very blunt. Yet the woman seemed quite happy, excited that she was having the baby and to be giving it away." He continues. "After a while I went looking for the woman, who was long gone, I even sent in a female social worker because she had been in there such a long time, but she was gone. And when I had returned so had her boyfriend. It was only when I went back to my desk, I noticed it had been ransacked, my filing cabinets were open, and everything was everywhere. They stole so many details from me on so many of my closed cases. It took weeks for me to understand exactly what they had stolen." Tony comes in his defence all flustered.

"We had to do a thorough investigation into it, contacted the police and gave a statement. The names they gave us were fakes, but the girl was defiantly pregnant." Randy says to defend Tony who looks between the both of us.

"Are there security cameras?" I ask to which Randy nods.

"Everything was sent to the police, but nothing was ever found." Tony explains.

I exchange a look with Jules who looks like she has just won the lottery. We never thought about this being a duo. And if it is, we have our hands full and we are going to need some help.

CHAPTER TWENTY-EIGHT

Juliette Sanders

Michigan, USA

As the car comes to collect me from the station, I hear my name being called behind me and I turn to find Detective Gomez calling out after me.

"You forgot your notepad." He says handing me it carefully before taking a look at the car. "Well, isn't this a fancy car." He jokes while looking it over. "What exactly does your uncle do?"

"He has a lot of businesses in the area, I'm not sure what. This is my first time meeting him." I explain sheepishly while he still continues to look over the car.

"It seems to me like you haven't really had a lot of time to get to know him, it seems like you spend more time looking into the case than you do with spending time with your family." He says observing my behaviour.

"They are very busy, and besides, I am not one to do touristy activities, this is my way of spending my summer before going back to school." I say to him while placing the notebook in my bag.

"Well, I hope you have a good night, I'll let you know once I've found something, I'm about to speak to the officers now who dealt with the case." He says while walking into the building.

"Okay." I say sweetly before getting into the car and greeting the driver.

"This he suspects something ma'am?" He asks curiously as I put my seatbelt on.

"Oh god, I hope not."

As we pull up to the house, I see that Robert is standing there waiting for my arrival. The car comes to a stop, and I almost leap out, wondering if something else has happened.

"How was your day?" He asks curiously as I walk to meet him.

"It was fine, what is going on?" I ask curiously noting down what he's wearing. "Why are you in your gym outfit?" I ask curiously while he takes my bag off my shoulder and takes my hand in his.

"I believe that we need a bit of a therapy session. I thought of a few different ones, we could smash up a room with a hammer, that can be very therapeutic. Or we can talk, but that seems pretty boring but then I had the greatest idea and I thought why don't we do some boxing while expressing how we are feeling? That sounds fun right?" He jokes as we walk through the door, he keeps tight a hold of my hand.

"I guess. Maybe your idea of fun, but I am okay with bottling up my feelings for this one." I say with a smile which he returns. I can sense the sarcasm on him, like an odour and I can't shake the unsettled feeling he is putting me in.

"Nonsense, we will get out all of our frustrations and I will teach you a few self-defence tactics as well." He says, stopping me at my bedroom door. "Besides, you can explain to me why you were at an adoption agency today with a Detective and why you haven't bothered to tell me you've been studying a case that relates to a serial killer." He says with a creepy grin, that also tells me I have no choice no matter how far I try and run. "Get changed into something comfortable. I will wait here. You're not getting out of this." He jokes with me pushing me into the bedroom door and closing it behind me. "Hurry up!" He shouts behind the door, and I exhale loudly. This is my idea of hell, I hate P.E in school so why he think's I'll be any good at this I will never know.

I get changed in my comfy jogging bottoms, a pair of socks, t-shirt and hoodie. My comfy attire for the majority of my time away. I open the door to reveal Robert and Spencer standing there, both of them grinning from ear to ear as they notice me.

"Don't smile at me." I warn Spencer who begins to chuckle very lightly. "Have you not bled out yet?" I joke with him causing him to clutch his heart as if he's been struck.

"Oh! I'm hurting!" He mocks as I lightly punch him in the arm. "You'd miss me if I was dead." He says with a smile causing me to join in.

"You know what? I would." I admit looking up at him. "Who would I bully then?" I taunt. Scrunching me nose causing him to do a fake laugh as he punches me in the arm this time harder.

"Funny, Sanders." He laughs with me. Robert exhales and rolls his eyes as he begins to walk in the opposite direction from the stairs.

"Where are you going?" I ask him curiously as he turns a corner.

"The gym." He shouts back and I look at Spencer shocked more than anything.

"This place has a gym?!" I practically shout and he rolls his eyes before taking my hand in his and leading me towards to what I'm assuming is a room I was yet to discover.

For about twenty minutes, Robert has been trying to get me to express my anger in a way where if I really put my mind to it, I might try and break his hand.

We've been sparring for what seems like forever and I can hear Spencer laugh with every punch I try and go for. "Harder!" I can hear his shout through his giggles and if he doesn't shut his mouth, I may go ahead and punch him.

"Don't you have something better to do?" I ask him after I can't stand to hear one more giggle from him.

"I'm still in recovery, this is paid time off. I get paid to see you hit like a girl, do you not understand how great this is?" He laughs again and I turn to Robert who is secretly trying not to join in.

"You don't hit like a girl, ignore him." He reassures me before hinting for me to hit the pad again. "So how are you feeling about the letter?"

He asks as I keep hitting the pad.

"Angry." I say not wanting to talk about it further, although I know he is going to press into it.

"Rightly so, the letter wasn't very fair to you." He says while I continue to hit the pads, hoping that he will stop this conversation. "You know when I met her, she said the exact same thing, the only thing she could ever do is talk about herself. She never used to be like that, it might be the way she's became but she never used to be the way she is." He explains, ignoring the expression on my face. I'm filled with rage about what she said, and the letter just made me angry that instead of owning up to her mistake, she blames everyone else for it and what is to come if it ever to go public.

"Well, she's made her bed she has to lie in it." I say punching just that little bit harder. Silence falls between us for a brief moment, while I try and gather my emotions still hitting the pads.

"So, tell me about the case." He instructs. I turn to Spencer who pretends to be on his phone scrolling when I look at him.

"Did you tell him?" I ask frustratingly. And Spencer chuckles, not looking up from his phone.

"I told you to. You didn't so I did." He laughs before looking at Robert. "He doesn't like secrets Jules."

I turn my eyes and glare at Robert, who smiles sweetly at me, waiting for my response. "What was it you told me on the day I arrived Robert? 'The lies we tell are to protect the ones we love and adore from harm. But the secrets we keep are the reasons we fight off our demons in our nightmares.'" I quote him and he never stops grinning at me like he expected me to say something.

"And the betrayal that follows hurts more than a secret ever could." He says coldly to me. "Don't lie to me Juliette, it doesn't look good on you." He whispers and I feel the rage fuel within me once again.

"I never lied, you I just never told you, there's a difference." I state and he begins to laugh.

"It's all the same, you never told me that you, a fourteen-year-old girl is trying to solve a case involving a serial killer. Do you know how crazy that sounds!" He shouts, throwing the pads to the floor.

"I apologise for doing something with my time while I'm here. I've been too busy getting iced out by the entire family so I couldn't exactly go to Alexis and say let's watch a movie. No one has bothered with me since they found out about Arielle. You've not tried to bond with me you've not tried to get an understanding of who I am and why I decided to go into this head first—"

"You're a kid, Juliette! You shouldn't be looking into a case that involve kids almost your age!"

"You never had a problem with it when you sent me in to uncover a drug den or to find Georgia's killer." I state and he stops in his tracks.

I believe that he genuinely forgot about everything and how we initially met. He sent me on a task to uncover a drug den that eventually led to a killer being caught. He had no idea what he was getting me into, but did he try and stop it. No, he handed off the responsibility to his soldiers or my mother.

"That is different." He says quietly in a defence, and I can't help but laugh.

"How? How is that different Robert? Because from where I'm standing; I'm helping a family find closure for losing their loved one yet you're the man who more often than not pulls the trigger." He stands there, taken back by my statement and the tension is so thick in the room you can cut it with a knife. "Robert, since the second I was born you've handed me off to someone else. Whether it be my parents, the boys, or Detective Gomez. You don't want to deal with me, and that's fine. But I would rather you own up to the fact that you will never take responsibility for something you created. You just hand that responsibility for someone who is more equipped." I say slamming the gloves on the floor and storming out of the gym.

I'm seeing red and I have now found out why I've been angry since I've arrived. It's because the person who was meant to protect me and love me, has only showed me heartbreak and agony since the minute I walked through the door of his palace.

CHAPTER TWENTY-NINE

Robert Quinten

Michigan, USA

After my argument with Jules, I had decided to take a walk. No matter how angry I felt I couldn't point the blame at her because everything she had said was the truth. I did hand her off to someone else and refuse responsibility. And for her at fourteen years old to give me a reality check, I think it's safe to say she's more of a Quinten than she'd like to think.

To only add to my rage that I feel within, I receive a call while on my walk from the Queen herself, Arielle. I wanted to ignore the call for as long as I could, but she called twice; probably knowing I wouldn't pick up since I now knew the number off by heart.

"You're ignoring me, Robert." She says while I answer the phone.

"Oh! So, you noticed? What can I help with, Your Majesty? Or are you calling to stick the knife in even further?" I ask her and I hear her scoff on the end of the phone.

"What are you talking about?" She asks and I roll my eyes.

"Jesus Christ woman you are so far up your own ass you can't even tell what is wrong. Well let me tell you. Your daughter, the one you claimed to love and adore, she read your letter." I say sarcastically and I hear her gasp on the other end of the phone.

"Oh! Fabulous. What did she think?" She asks enthusiastically.

"I swear if you are smiling at the other end of this phone, I may fly over and attack you." I say placing my thumb and my forefinger on my nose trying to reduce the headache that I can feel brewing.

"What! What was wrong with the letter?" She wines and I groan in annoyance.

"Everything was wrong with it! You know when I met you, you asked if she hated you? Well, I can confirm. Yes. Yes, she does!" I shout down the phone. "Because not only does hate you, but she also hates me too. So, I guess we can go in for the parents of the year award. Because our daughter that neither one of us wanted to take responsibility for, she hates us."

"Why does she hate me! I thought my letter was heartfelt and thoughtful!"

"It was the most selfish bastard letter I've ever fucking read Arielle! Not once do you say I'm sorry, not once did you say that you loved her. You called her an abomination in a letter that was meant to give her some answers to a part of a life she was curious about!" I scream down the phone. I hear her take a long exhale down the phone.

"She should know how her birth can complicate my life here, it won't be easy welcoming her in. I've already be shunned by the council, not to mention my country. She should know how that can ruin my life." She explains and I debate throwing the phone into the water.

"No! This is your problem. You decided to keep her, you knew what would happen. You don't bring my daughter into your fucking royal problems! She's a kid Arielle, she should be going out with friends and not worrying about the both of us and surely not sitting in her room hating us both." I say harshly and I feel the phone go silent, hoping that maybe she's ended it.

"She needs to understand where she came from." She eventually says and I roll my eyes.

"Arielle, I've never known you to be this impossible to deal with. You wanted nothing to do with her, you said you wanted to meet her, but only if she was to stand and learn the ways of a royal. Well guess what! She isn't a royal, she isn't a princess, and she most certainly isn't your daughter. I won't have you make a joke out of her. She's a kid and she can decide at eighteen whether or not she wants a relationship with you. That is her decision. You cannot force her." I say coldly and I feel her mutter something to someone before coming back to the phone.

"Well, she's going to have to make a decision quick." She says sternly and I feel my anger build ever further.

"And why is that?"

"Because in light of my recent news to the council, we have planned a ball in preparation for her to be welcomed into the country. She will need to be available this Friday night through to Sunday." She says calmly. My eye begins to twitch, and I want to scream bloody murder. It's Tuesday.

"You're fucking joking." I state harshly and she gasps.

"I can assure you I'm not."

"You are otherwise I may commit murder. Arielle, you cannot force her to attend! This is ridiculous!" I shout and she laughs at me.

"Oh Robert, don't be so dramatic. A girl her age has always wanted to be a princess!" She says enthusiastically and I feel myself become so angry I begin to see red. "She will have a date—" She begins to say before I quickly cut her off.

"Like hell she will Arielle she's fourteen!"

"And she will need the full princess experience. Robyn will have a date also!" She says enthusiastically down the phone while makes me want to rip out my eardrums if I hear her go that high pitched one more time.

"Arielle, this kid wants to be a Detective and solve crimes, you hold a ball for her, and you will never have a relationship with her whatsoever. I can assure you of that."

"Robert, she has to attend. She has no choice." She says coldly to me, and I feel a shiver go down my spine. I'm no longer talking to Arielle; I'm talking to the Queen. And no matter how hard I shake it, I feel as though she has put a spell on me that I can't be released from.

"Not making any promises." I say as I hang up the phone and place it in my pocket, so I don't throw it into the lake. She has to the most unbearable woman and how her husband deals with her, I will have to owe him a beer. Because if I had decided to marry that, I would have left a hell of a long time ago.

CHAPTER THIRTY

Robert Quinten
Michigan, USA

I feel myself go insane as I walk up towards Juliette's room. How I could have ever loved something so ridiculous as Arielle is making me question myself.

I want the feeling of how we once were, the love we both shared for each other while we brought a new life onto this earth. But instead, she has become a monster that is so wrapped up in her own little world she can't remember how the real world works.

I walk into Juliette's room to find her packing and I immediately stop in my tracks. What in god's name is she doing?

"Don't worry I'm getting out of your hair." She says as she walks out from the bathroom and begins to pack up her toiletries. "If you could just let your little minions know I may need to use your plane to get home. That would be great." She says sarcastically, once again turning her back on me.

"Juliette, I know your angry." I say to her, in the hope to reason with her. "But I will not let you get on that plane." I say harshly. She whips her head around.

"Why not! I'm going back to someone who will take responsibility for me, so you don't have to. I thought you would be thrilled!"

"Well, I'm not and that is not happening over my dead body. So, I suggest you stop packing, you sit on the chair, and you listen to me for a minute!" I shout at her.

She's taken back by my tone but does what I ask and sits in the chair without question. I feel a wave of relief over me that she may actually listen to me.

"I'm sorry. For everything I have put you through. You're right. You gave me the reality check I needed and although I may sound annoyed and angry, I can assure you it isn't directed at you. I'm proud of you. I just want you to be careful." I say softly sitting on the window ledge. "Do you forgive me?" I ask her nicely giving my best impression of puppy dog eyes.

"I might eventually, but I'm still mad at you."

She says trying not to smile.

"Besides, you promised three families you were going to find their killer. You aren't letting them down, are you?" I ask her curiously and I watch her become slightly annoyed.

"God no." She states and I can't help but laugh at how she reacted.

"See, I told you you're a good kid. But I keep forgetting that's what you are. A kid. You're so mature for your age, but that isn't an excuse. I haven't made much of an effort since your arrival, with little conversations here and there. I am sorry." I repeat once more and this time she gives me a small smile.

"Okay, I forgive you a little bit more. But you have to tell me what has got you so worked up." She asks curiously and I feel my heart fall from my chest. I've just got her to like me again, now I'm going to have to tell her the monster she calls a birth mother has decided to hold a ball to welcome Jules into the family.

"I've just spoken to Arielle." I say quickly waiting for her to begin shouting at me. She doesn't do that her eyes go wide however she sits there; calm as can be while gripping the arms of the chair.

"And?" She asks calmly, her voice slightly shaking as I can feel the eruption from the anger volcano begin and I watch as she grips the chair tight anticipating my next sentence.

"She's said that you have to be available on Friday to Sunday for a ball she is holding in your honour." I say quickly and I watch as she stands up from the chair and begins packing.

"Nope! Not a chance. I'm not a Princess, she's not ruining my future for her own personal gain." She shouts while aggressively packing. Not even bothering to fold things she is just packing everything as can as quickly as I can to get as far from this conversation as possible.

"Juliette, listen to me." I say while putting some of the clothes on the bed and turning her to face me. "I told her no; I told her we aren't doing that. She can't force you into anything." I say calmly but I watch as she narrows her eyes.

"You told her yes, didn't you?" She questions coldly and I feel my heart stop as I try and conjure up the words.

"Juliette, I dread to think what would happen to us if we didn't go." I say quickly and she exhales loudly through her nose while her eyes are wide. She moves to quickly pack up her things.

"There is no way that the head of the Quinten family is scared of a woman who is probably about my height who runs a country. Surely you can keep your masculinity in check or are you sure she doesn't wear the pants even after all these years?" She mocks me and I glare down at her.

"Don't start, young lady," I warn her, and she glares right back at me. Jesus she really is my daughter.

"Or what Robert? Cause I remember you telling me I have a choice. And my choice is the woman can get lost. I want no relationship with her, her husband, or her daughter." She says seriously and I watch as the anger in her eyes turn to pain. "I thought you'd be the person to understand that. But clearly not." She says before moving past me and back into the bathroom and slamming the door.

I think it is fair to say she is right on this, and I am quite possibly the worst father in the world.

CHAPTER THIRTY-ONE

Juliette Sanders

Michigan, USA

I keep staring into space while waiting for the Detective to arrive at his desk. I've been here thirty minutes early. But I don't mind, anything to get out of that house. I avoided the rest of the family for the rest of the night as I didn't want to bring my problems to anyone else. This is between Robert and me. I just hope he sees why I won't want to meet Arielle or attend anything she'd decided to have without talking to either Robert or me first.

I know Robert is trying to do right by me, by having me establish a good relationship with Arielle, but how can there be any trust when all she has done is everything to make herself feel better.

I don't even believe that she's doing this to interest me, she's doing it to show how amazing I've turned out, no thanks to her. She's upset me, not to mention she would humiliate me. I know nothing about her country, it's rules and its values. She married into that. I didn't.

"Earth to Jules, you good?" Detective Gomez waves his hand in my face breaking my trance.

"Of course, how are you feeling today?" I ask and he shakes his head.

"Not good. You can't really see the faces of the two that stole the documents. We would have to go off the sketch from Tony and Randy." He says turning the sketches towards me, hinting a take a look.

I suddenly feel unsettled as I look at the sketches. It isn't a very detailed sketch; however, it does give me an unsettled feeling and I can't understand why.

"What's wrong?" He asks. While taking a seat at his desk.

"Oh, nothing. I just can't help but wonder, why they would want a list containing children that were adopted? I don't understand." I say while rubbing my temple. This whole case is baffling to the point where we keep hitting dead ends.

"Hey. We will work it out!" He says enthusiastically while gripping my arm. "You not been sleeping?" He asks kindly while examining my face and I'm taken back by his question.

"Why?" I ask, lightly narrowing my eyes.

"Because you look exhausted. Are you sure you want to continue looking into this case?" He asks softly, a look of concern coming over him and I nod my head.

"I do, unfortunately, I do leave on Friday." I say quietly causing the expression on his face to drop.

"Why?" He asks quietly looking around the room. "Jules you can talk to me—" He begins to say before I cut him off.

"Oh! Nothing's happened just I'm having to cut my trip a little short is all. My Mum wants me back home." I lie and I feel terrible about it. The truth is, I plan on speaking to Peter tonight in order to get their plane ready for Friday morning. I don't want to be put onto a plane and forced to go to a country that I have no intention on visiting, not to mention a family member I loathe for the simple fact she is so selfish.

It makes me grateful for the Mum that I do have, how sweet she is and how understanding she can be. She would never force me to do something I wouldn't want to do or be placed in a situation where I felt uncomfortable.

"That sucks." He says sitting back in his chair and sighing. "So, I guess I might as well use you to my full advantage today before you leave, and this becomes my case." He says with a grin and a wink.

He does make me laugh and for that I'm grateful. Today I need the distraction from the chaos that is what some would call a family, or a cult. Depends on who you ask.

"So, with regards to the suspects, I feel as though we should focus our attention on the girl, Alicia. Now she's been mentioned multiple times since we spoke to Mrs Robson at the house. Now we know she got Hannah into drugs and alcohol and its possibly she lured out both of the girls too. But why?" I say trying to distract myself from my own thoughts, I need to keep busy and focus on the case rather than my family, or Arielle.

"Jules', you do know you're implying that the killer is a female, right? They are incredibly rare?"

"But they aren't that rare. Think about it this way, everything so far has pointed to Alicia, the only thing we can't link her to right now is the messages to Kassidy and to Sandy, but if she has the list surely, she's making her way down it?"

My thought couldn't of came at a worst time, when I notice a few officers, begin to run towards the exit of the station. "Banks? What's going on?

"They found a fourth victim."

CHAPTER THIRTY-TWO

Detective Gomez

Michigan, USA

Jules stands well away from the body while I go over and talk to the officers who found the girl. "What's her name?" I ask while taking my notepad, approaching them.

"Sophie Cutter, sixteen." Officer Torres says while walking in my direction. "She was killed the same as the others." He says handing me over the girl's school ID in an evidence bag.

"So young." I say while placing the ID in my pocket. "What do we know so far?" I ask him and he begins to look at his partner.

"Well sir, Sophie was reported missing four

days go. Her killing was different, but the killer left a message." He says, gulping hard. I look between the men, their faces almost green while they stay down at the body.

"What do you mean?" I ask them and they exchange one last glance before his partner, I think is name is Patterson, reaches over with a glove on and lifts up the sheet that is placed over the body.

I am almost sick at the sight, and I feel my stomach churning as I look at the poor girl's forehead. The word *'traitor'* carved into her head with a knife. "That's enough." I say turning away and gulping. That sight is something that I know will haunt me for the rest of my life and I'll be damned if I will let Juliette see it.

"There is something else sir, there was a note left." Patterson says while going over to one of the forensic guys and collecting a bit of evidence. "The killer left a note for Miss Sanders."

I look him dead in the eye, unsure on if he is joking. But sure enough, he hands me a note that is addressed to Juliette. Well shit. I look up at them both and turn to look at Juliette who stands there, her talking to one of the officers who begins to ask her some questions. "Move over here." I instruct the men and we begin to move away from the body. "Jules!" I call after her. She is quick to end the conversation with the officer and begins to walk in our direction. She's almost hugging herself, but at the same time avoiding looking at the body all together.

I forget this is her first crime scene. This must be so surreal for her, and so unsettling. I'm about to make this only ten times worse for her.

"Yeah?" She asks as she approaches us, I look to the men before looking down at the note and handing it to her slowly. She takes it looking around at the facial expression between us all. I watch her soul leave her body and her face go as white as a ghost. "Oh my god." She almost cries and I place my hand gently on her back.

"You going to be sick?" I ask her and she shakes her head, swallowing hard.

"Was this left by the killer?" She asks looking around and we all nod causing her to take a long deep breath. She looks over at a man in the forensic team. "Are you okay if I open this?" She asks and the man nods while giving her some gloves. She takes and hands me back the note so she can put them on properly.

She carefully takes it out of the evidence bag, handing it to me. She lifts the note up and I lean in curious as to what it says.

Miss Sanders,

I thought I'd introduce myself since we haven't been formally introduced and you've taken an interest in my recent hobby. My name is Alicia, obviously that isn't my real name. You'll not find that out unless your smart enough to catch me, and I find it adorable that you think you can.

You'll be chasing me for years to come, and when you think I've stopped, I'll come back out of hiding and ruin your life all over again. Because there is something that you need to know about me, I never lose.

Catch me if you can, bitch.

Xoxo

THE TEENAGE DREAM KILLER AKA: YOUR WORST NIGHTMARE.

I watch the colour slowly fade from Juliette's face once again as she rereads the letter repeatedly.

"Jules?" I ask her softly, causing her to look up at me, her eyes teary.

"This girl was killed because of me." She says quietly before gently taking the evidence bag from my hand and placing the note gently in the bag and handing it back to the forensic guy. Giving a teary smile before taking off her gloves. "I'm going to go for a walk and clear my head." She says before disposing of her gloves and taking off as quickly as she can.

"Well shit." I say looking down at the body.

"That isn't what we needed." I say avoiding the stares from the two officers.

"What will happen to her?" One of them asks and I shrug my shoulders.

"Either she will come back more determined than ever to find this killer or she will let it consume her. I'm praying it's the first one." I say quietly while looking at the men. I'm praying it's the first one, because I don't believe for one second, she will let a killer take over her life.

But then I remind myself that not only is this her first crime scene, but it is her first case and her first taunt. The killer has taken as interest in her, and this is overwhelming for anyone. You think you're responsible for the death that is caused that the hands of the maniac, when in reality you're trying to understand how they think, how they are more and how they choose their victims. That last one we've managed to crack.

"Want us to go look for her?" Patterson asks and I shake my head.

"Give her some time to clear her head, she will be back." I say as calmly as I can. "If she isn't then we will send out a search party." I say while patting them on the shoulder. "Take me to the man who found her."

CHAPTER THIRTY-THREE

Juliette Sanders
Michigan, USA

I walk around completely numb, unsure on how to process the information. A taunt, left for me on the body of a girl who was innocent in all of this. I only have two days left, today is Wednesday and I had every intention of leaving on Friday, but can I? A killer left me a message. They are aware I'm looking into their killings, and they want to play a game.

The more I walk around in these woods, it makes me question why was the victim in the woods? More than likely being lured out, but why... and how?

Clearly this Alicia girl is good with computers

or hacking or her partner is, the boy in the video who helped her steal the documents. They must be working together yet she likes all of the attention, she likes the chase whereas he has only been linked to that one crime.

The one thing I don't understand is that Tony and Randy from the adoption agency both said she was pregnant when she came in about putting the baby up for adoption. But if she was adopted herself, why would she want to subject her baby to being put into the system the same way...

Suddenly I begin to feel sick, remembering I had the same conversation only months ago with the boys at my dining room table about Clarissa.

As I continue to walk around, I try and match up the timeline, the boys said she had a baby six months prior to us sitting around the table, which wouldn't match up with the timeline unless she was faking it.

I decide to shake off the thought, I know Clarissa is unhinged, but is she so unhinged to become a killer? I doubt it. The girls on the surveillance photo had brown hair, not blonde and they were certain that she wasn't wearing a wig, and that she was older. Now granted, she could have had makeup on, and dyed her hair. But surely the family would have noticed. She was pregnant at the time this happened and according to the boys Peter was keeping a very close eye on her.

I really am starting to think like a crazy person. Pointing fingers at one of my own family members because I can't seem to comprehend that a killer has taking a liking to me and wants to mess me up mentally.

I come to a standstill while in circle full of trees. I look up and taking a deep breath of the air and I'm immediately regret it and I almost gag.

The air is thick with an awful smell that I can't seem to place. I begin to look around, look for anything that can lead to that stench.

I look around the trees and notice a carving on one of the trees. I slowly approach it, curiosity getting the best of me. *Oh my god...*

I feel my heart grow tight as I read the names.

Damian <3 Carter

I suddenly begin having flashbacks to the night Damian went into the hospital. That was four days ago.

'*Sophie went missing four days ago.*'

'*He's dead. He's dead.*'

The tears begin to stream down my face as I slowly look around for the something that can link everything that is buzzing around in my head. That is when I notice it. A pallet covered in blood. The timelines match, Damian went into the facility four days ago, the same night that Sophie was murdered. Whoever 'he' was, I'm going to now assume is Carter, someone Damian was dating.

I begin to look around the way I came and from afar, I can see a police car, and some officers.

The night that Damian was taken into the facility, Robert had said he had gone out for the night, my guess to meet Carter. That same night, Sophie was being murdered not that far away, and to avoid any witnesses, Carter must have been killed with the amount of blood, my guess is that he was shot.

I'm struggling to breathe, because no matter how hard I try and think I'm being crazy, I keep coming back to the same conclusion.

Somehow, my family is involved in this, and something I am absolutely certain of is that I've just walked in on a crime scene.

CHAPTER THIRTY-FOUR

Juliette Sanders

Michigan, USA

After discovering Carter's crime scene, I located the nearest officer and asked if he could take me back to the station to wait for Detective Gomez as I was feeling unwell.

I quickly went round to his desk and turned on the computer. I tried my hardest to calm myself down. I had been hysterically crying after finding the carving in the tree and I needed to compose myself otherwise I'd be sent straight home.

This case now involves my family members, and I fully believe that after witnessing Carter's death that he had a break down. My theory is that he was also followed by Alicia's partner is crime.

Alicia likes the fact she can strangle her victims, using a gun is really not her style.

I begin to search the missing persons database for anyone named Carter who could be between sixteen and twenty years old. I don't see Damian going for an older guy.

I'm not even upset he never told me he was gay or bisexual; I think he knows deep down that I would accept him no matter what. He did however give me a hint the first time I came over to revise. *'They have always teased me about girls, and how I'll never have a girlfriend or be able to talk to a girl when in reality I just didn't want to.'* That there should have been a telling sign, but I guess I missed it.

A name pops up instantly on the screen and I feel my heart shatter into a million pieces. There in front of me is the face that is Carter Edrington. A senior, who's birthday was right next to Damian. I feel myself begin to get teary and I quickly wipe my eyes hoping no one saw and delete the search.

The Detective will be back in any minute and the last thing I need it to explain why I'm looking up a mystery boy who is missing.

Unfortunately, because this is a in house situation, I do want to speak to Robert and the rest of the Quinten siblings first before I run in with my theory.

I do however believe that the killer I'm dealing with might quite possibly be Clarissa, or someone maybe just as evil. I can't help but point the finger when so many things tie it to her and her level of chaos.

"You okay?" Detective Gomez says as he comes towards me quickly taking a seat on my normal chair, concern filling his voice. "A uniform told me he brought you here. I know this morning was a lot with the note and if you want to go home and let me deal with the case, I completely understand." He says sincerely.

I smile at him and before I can say another word, Tracey a woman who works closely with Detective Gomez appears from nowhere. She has a smile on her face like she's just got the juiciest bit of gossip and she needs to tell someone of she will scream.

"What's up?" Detective Gomez questions and she looks to both of us.

"Okay, so I decided to give some adoption agencies in the nearby cities a call because to me, something didn't seem right on how well they pulled this off, surely, they had to of tried it before. And they had, well the girl had." She says while handing Detective Gomez a case file and he opens it, giving me a look of intrigue and begins to read through. "Six weeks before the situation at the adoption agency here, twenty miles away, the girl attempted the same thing, except she was on her own, there was no partner. She came in expressing that she would like for the baby to be put into the system as she doesn't feel she can cope for the baby. When she asked to use the bathroom, she went on the hunt for the woman's desk, except she stumbled across someone else's, and the woman came back. She was escorted straight out by security. And I got a new alias." She says handing us the other case file in her hand.

"Brady Williams."

CHAPTER THIRTY-FIVE

Juliette Sanders

Michigan, USA

On my way home in the car, I had sent a message to Robert asking if we could talk once I arrived home. He was quick to respond with a yes and a 'I'm sorry' followed on, but I decide to ignore that. I message him back asking if Spencer, Peter, Felicity, Serena, and Oliver can be around too and if we can meet in the outhouse where we had my party on the day I arrived. He responded yes, no questions asked.

I don't want to talk about Arielle or the ball or the fact that Robert would like for me to go, I don't care about that. What I care about is finding justice for Carter's killer.

I'm starting to see this family in a whole new light, secrets so strong that they will break even the strongest of families. Especially secrets such as sexuality, or better yet about becoming a serial killer.

I get out of the car and make my way to the outhouse round the back, if Clarissa has decided to come home, I don't want to come face to face with her just yet till I get a better understanding as to what I'm dealing with.

The walk takes me about five minutes, but as I begin to grow closer, I notice everyone there and I instantly feel sick knowing that I'm about to out my friend and his sexuality not to mention his secret boyfriend.

I open the door, all eyes on me and close it gently. "Thank you for meeting me out here. I didn't trust the house and I wanted this to be as confidential as possibly. I say taking a seat asking everyone else to do the same.

My stomach is in knots trying to work out how to approach the topic. I can sense the tension in the air because of my silence and I decide to just rip the band aid off rather than letting it settle.

"Why didn't you tell me Damian was gay?" I ask the room. I watch as stares are exchanged between them all and the look back at me, stunned.

"How they hell..." Spencer begins to say before I go into my bag and grab my phone. Getting up the photo of the carving on the tree.

"I went for a walk in the woods." I say almost as a whisper. "I got to a little section where the trees were in a perfect circle, and I decided not to go any further in case I got lost. But then I could smell something, and it made me so sick to my stomach and I was looking around for the source of the smell." I begin to explain, the tears falling down face and I can feel them hit my jeans. "But instead, I saw the carving in the tree and my heart sank so far. It read Damian loves Carter." I pass the phone to Oliver first who looks at it and the rest of the room. "I tried to wrap my head around it. The smell, the carving on the tree. The longer I looked that the carving that was when I noticed the blood. It has dried up because of heat, but it was most definitely blood. I thought I was going insane until I noticed the pallet against the tree. Unless you were standing where I was standing you couldn't see it. But it was soaked. Completely soaked in blood." I begin to whisper while crying.

My heart is aching even at the thought of Damian dealing with this alone; to see what he witnessed.

"Jules, why were you in woods?" Felicity says gently pressing on my leg. I don't bother looking at her, I just take a deep breath and trying the courage to continue talking without having a complete breakdown.

"There was another girl murdered, a few minutes' walk from where I was standing, I could see some Detectives and some officers as they looking over the body." I cry. "She was sixteen and had been missing for four days. The same night Damian came in hysterically crying saying that someone had died." I breathe heavy.

The silence in the room is eerie, but you can feel the tension radiating from Robert in the corner.

"The killer left me a note today." I say trying not to bawl. "They left me a taunt on the body of a girl who had died because they were jealous. But what surprised me, is how they said that they found it adorable that I'd think I'd ever catch them, yet they made one great mistake and that was underestimating the police department." I say taking my phone from Robert and pulling up the sketches of the two suspects from the robbery. "Over a year ago, about twenty miles away, a girl walked into an adoption agency to have a meeting with a social worker about putting her baby up for adoption. The woman they met with said she was young; slightly manic and kept laughing at certain things, serious things that she shouldn't have found funny. She asked to use the bathroom, to which the social worker gave her directions, and the girl went in the opposite way looking for an empty desk. When she eventually found the desk, she began rummaging through only to get caught and was banned from the agency. She gave one alias." I explain while handing the phone to Oliver for him to look at the sketches of the two people.

"I'm confused." Serena sits looking around everyone's faces who shrug their shoulders also.

"A few weeks later the same thing happened in a different agency, this time she brought a partner. They successfully took a list of names of children that were adopted in the same year, amongst other things. There was an investigation, but no one was caught." I explain receiving my phone back before closing it. "The woman doing this is killing the blood daughters of the families that adopted children on that list. Sophie Cutter, Kassidy Simmons, Sandy Green, and Hannah Robson were all sisters of the girls that were adopted. Do you see where I'm going with this?" I ask looking around the room. I notice a few confused faces, Serena, Felicity's. Yet Robert stares at me or more like stares through me. He knows what I'm hinting, and I can tell he doesn't like the direction. "Maybe this can help. The alias she gave in the first adoption agency robbing, was Brady Williams." I watch as their faces drop in unison and they begin to look at each other, questioning whether or not to believe me, and if I'm honest with the day I've had I wouldn't have believed me either.

"Wasn't Brady Williams the name Clarissa used to give herself when she jokingly used to say she would marry Rodger?" Serena speaks and Peter is the only one to nod at her. The rest stunned.

"Rodger had nothing to do with this." Spencer is quick to come to his defence. I try to speak and no matter how hard he tries, he shuts me up. "No! Rodger wouldn't do any of this! He's unhinged, yes. But Jesus he isn't a killer!" He shouts standing up and pacing the room.

"Spencer, I don't want to believe it either." I'm finally able to say. "But there was three people who weren't in the room the night you were shot. Oliver, who couldn't have shot you because he was here at the time of the shooting and Clarissa and Rodger. Now, I have a feeling I know what Clarissa was doing but think about what Damian said. 'You will protect him.' He was talking to you Spence. You'd protect Rodger to the ends of the earth no matter what he did. And rightly so he is your brother but in the middle of a psychotic episode, your brother, someone who you love and someone you would call a son or a nephew." I say towards the entire room. "He called you liars."

"Juliette, this is all speculation now. Stop it." Robert speaks up frustrated and I get up out of my chair.

"You're right it is. But I know damn well you

knew exactly who he was talking about which is why you sent Oliver and you didn't go after him yourself." I say harshly causing his eyes to widen. "The betrayal that follows hurts more than a secret ever could." I say, quoting Robert once more and I see his chest rise, his nostrils flared, and he is angry at me. But I don't care.

"Every time I even think I'm getting close to trusting you, you betray me yet again. You say you love me Robert, but I find that very hard to believe when you want to fly me off to Haroux to attend some ball so you can get in Arielle's good books." I say coldly. "I'm not being your messenger. You wanna see her, you go. But I will not be made a fool out of. I know my worth and I'm worth more than a family who can't tell each other the truth." I say harshly while leaving the house and slamming the door.

I want them to do their own research, come up with their own conclusions. I left my bag in there for a reason, it has all of my evidence, all of my theories. They can look at it all they want.

I know I'm right. I just have to make sure they see it too.

CHAPTER THIRTY-SIX

Juliette Sanders

Michigan, USA

I lie down on my bed hoping to just go to sleep and forget all about today. I feel like I have overstepped with Robert and the family today and I feel like if they have taught me anything, it's how to go crazy.

I know I'm right in my theory, whether Rodger is involved or not, but a lot of the evidence points to Clarissa as well as her behaviour towards me since I arrived, to me it just adds up.

But then I can't help but think I'm going insane. The taunt today, although I might not admit it to my family, really did a number on me. Clarissa knew I would blame myself for all of this and knew exactly how to get under my skin.

I hear the door creak open ever so slightly but I don't bother to turn around. The amount of guilt I'm feeling about Sophie's death and how brutal it was, if Clarissa was standing there with a knife, I wouldn't be surprised.

But then I realise something, what was the reason that they decided to write traitor on Sophie Cutter's forehead? What changed within the last four days? The killer had never used a knife before in the killings, always rope. So why the sudden burst of anger?

"You going to turn around?" I hear Robert speak after a moment and I can't help but roll my eyes.

"Do I have to?"

"Yes." I hear him say as his footsteps begin to come closer to the bed. When I do eventually turn around, I notice Spencer standing there, looking just as exhausted as me, if not worse. He doesn't move from the door frame; he just leans against it.

"We are just trying to understand your theory, but we get why you're upset." Robert says sitting on the bottom of the bed looking to Spencer. "Deep down, we may have thought it was him. Clarissa and Rodger got too close about two years ago, then all of a sudden, they go everywhere together, and they may be good for each other if you look at it from afar, but because we know them so well, it always ends in tears with them." Robert admits looking back at Spencer.

"Now, I'm not saying I don't believe you, but I'm doing a *you*. You want to wait until evidence is found rather just go around and accuse people." Spencer speaks calmly. I begin to pick my fingers, a nasty habit that I've developed since I arrived here in America.

"I think this week has been a lot for you. With what happened with Damian, you witnessed something so heart breaking, not to mention you're solving something that could break even a grown man. You got a letter from a killer Jules, whether it be Clarissa or not, and you walked in on a crime scene. That was probably one of the most traumatic things that anyone could have experienced. But I couldn't be prouder of how you've handled it." He says reaching out and placing a hand on where my legs are crossed causing me to meet his eyes.

"I feel like I'm going mad." I whisper to Robert who gives me a weak smile while grabbing my leg harder.

"Jules, a bit of madness is key to uncovering the truth, especially in this case." He reassures me before looking over at Spencer.

"Robert's right, you wouldn't be you if you didn't lose your hat like the *mad hatter*." He speaks sweetly while sitting on the other side of me.

"*Everyone is mad here.*" He says with a *Cheshire cat* like grin. Robert is the first to break into laughter and I follow not long after.

The creepy smile that Spencer sits with makes me slightly unsettled and I elbow him to stop him from doing it. It's the grin of my nightmares.

"Never do that again." Robert laughs and Spencer clutches onto the side of his stomach breathing heavy.

"Don't make me laugh please, it hurts." He pleads causing me to laugh a little harder. Robert lets go of my leg and I stand, turning around so I can see them both clearly. Both exhausted and annoyed although the feeling in the room is a lot better than what it has been.

"I sent a team of my guys to go and look for Carter's body." Robert speaks after a moment, killing the mood immediately. I raise one eyebrows, curious as to how he managed to know where to send them since I never said anything. "I track you." He openly admits causing my mouth to fall open. But the more the news settles in, I can understand why.

I can't help but feel joy because finally, Carter will be going home to his family who have been searching for answers. I nod at him, processing the news while I feel a hand on my back comforting me.

"You've always wanted to do good by so many people. And I've watched you over the last few weeks become someone unrecognizable. You've threw yourself into this case headfirst having one thing on your mind and that was justice, you checked on everyone else, but Jules when was someone gonna check on you? The light behind your eyes is gone, and you're so angry all of the time and so sad." Robert speaks sweetly and softly while tucking a strand of my hair behind my ear that had fell out of my bun.

"I think I just let it pile on without doing a check on myself first. I've been building up a lot of anger since I found out about Arielle, and I feel like in some ways I've had no support. People only ever came to me when they were doing their moral duties as an uncle, aunt or friend. But I could tell it was just to get information, and that in the end they would stop caring." I say quietly, picking up that bad habit of my nails. This time Spencer pulls my hands away and holds them tightly.

"We care about you; we don't want this to get to you. We know that no matter what, whether it is Clarissa or not, that you did this because you had to tell us. We know you probably couldn't but because you knew you couldn't speak to the Detective you came to us and for that we are so grateful, because we can't lose you too Jules." Spencer speaks softly to me, however the tone of is voice is motivational. That he wants me to see that

I'm doing good. I've lost my way with this case; I've let it blind me and he's reminding me of that.

"Can I get something off my chest?" I ask them both, to which they nod eagerly. I look over at the door and decide that just in case Clarissa comes back I close it. I don't want her to really hear about what we've been speaking about, yet I can't be sure she didn't bug this room. "On the fourth victim, the word traitor was carved into her forehead. But why the change in the weapon and why the taunt on the top of her head? It makes no sense. I get it's a message but why traitor, what have I done that had caused me to be a traitor?" I ask them and they exchange a look of worry between themselves. I notice that there is something missing here, and they know more than what they are leading on.

"When Clarissa found out that you were royal, not that long after, she burst into my office labelling you as a traitor and a freak and demanded I cut any ties with you. She went on a forty-minute rant about how you could ruin this family and how Clarissa has done everything to be the perfect child and why wasn't she enough." He begins to explain, and I feel the last bits of the puzzle come together. "She went on and on about how she hated you, hated who you were, how she's jealous of you. That you get to be my blood daughter and wouldn't stop calling you a traitor to this family."

I look to Spencer who takes a long deep breath. "I feel like the more I sit here, more red flags about her are going to appear that we missed for so long. We could have stopped this Robert, we just didn't see it, nor did we bother to look." Spencer admits and Robert nods to him.

"Any murders, they are my fault. I should have seen the warning signs, but I didn't so don't you blame yourself for your sisters' mistakes and choices. You're not responsible for her, I am. Just like I'm responsible for you." He admits causing me to raise an eyebrow curiously. *He's now going to take responsibility for me? How thoughtful.* "Don't give me that look, you were right when you went on your rant these past few days. I don't take responsibility for you. I said this to Arielle that neither one of us can take responsibility because we are both still immature. When you were born, we were so young, yet I believe that if I had raised you or if we had raised you together, that responsibility would have been shared. But I lack that and I'm sorry." He apologizes.

I give him a light smile, because for the first time this entire trip I can see how sincere he is and that he is telling the truth. He knows he didn't do right by me since the minute I arrived. There were some instances on the trip where I thought maybe he was going to be able to properly get to know me, but every single time I was let down.

"I forgive you. A little." I tease causing him to chuckle a little bit. "But I may take that back with how bad the ball is on Friday." I tease at him, and I watch his expression drop.

"You mean you're gonna go?" He says with a grin, and I nod.

"On two conditions, we collect my mum from London. I need to see her." I say to him sternly, causing him to grin from ear to ear and kiss Spencer on the cheek. The man looks absolutely disgusted got a few moments before he wipes it away.

"You can have whatever you want. Thank you, I thought she may kill me if you didn't go." He says running up and swinging me around.

"The second one being that if I so much as sense her blaming me, I leave and I never want anything to do with her whatsoever. I will find a way to have her permanently removed if I have to." I warn him and he shoots me a look.

"Jules, if you're wanting to escalate to murder; you need to speak to Oliver." He jokes and I lightly smack him on the arm.

"This is going to be hell." I whine causing him to chuckle.

"Nope, this ball is going to be great!"

"What do we do about Clarissa? And what are you going to do about the case?" Spencer asks.

Robert turns to me, the smile no longer on his face as he presses down hard on my shoulders.

"If you chase her, she will run and she will make sure to leave carnage everywhere she goes." He tells me honestly and I feel myself gulp before looking between the men.

"It's a good thing I like the chase, but I'd like to see her try."

CHAPTER THIRTY-SEVEN

Juliette Sanders

Michigan, USA

I enter the police station with a pep in my step. Not because this is my last day working on the case, but because I know who the killer is most likely, I just have to prove it in an eight-hour shift. As I walk round the corner, I'm met with balloons, a cake and a banner on the Detectives desk. The balloon read's *We will miss you!* and in more likely sharpie and underneath it reads '*maybe.*'

I laugh as I walk towards the officers and Detective's smiling like an idiot. This is one of the nicest things anyone has done for me. And it makes me grateful that I've been able to call this place home for the last two weeks. They have been so welcoming, they never questioned anything, and they have always made me feel included no matter how hard I was to deal with.

"Surprise!" They shout in unison as I approach them and for the first time in weeks, I feel myself smile but properly. And not a fake one either. This one is filled with so much love and warmth.

"What is this for?" I question looking on the Detectives desk. The cake says the same as the balloon. Tracey is first to bring me in for a tight hug almost suffocating me.

"Because we are going to miss you, even Gomez. He will miss you terribly." Tracey teases and I can't help but chuckle at the admission. The Detective goes bright red, rubbing his forehead trying to find the words to argue with her, but he can't come up with anything.

"Don't worry, I'll miss you too." I say reaching over and giving him a hug which he accepts eventually.

In the midst of all the talking of my next steps after I leave, I look behind Tracey and notice Mrs Green, the mother of Sandy Green, the second victim; standing, clutching her bag.

"Hold on." I say to the circle and begin to make my way over to her, a warm smile on my face. "Mrs Green?" I question and she meets my smile.

"Sorry, I didn't want to ruin the party." She says quietly giving me a small smile causing me to frown and shake my head.

"Don't worry, is everything okay?" I ask her and I notice that she is staring behind me, not looking at me one bit.

"You're leaving?" She asks sadly and I turn back at her giving her a warm smile.

"I leave tomorrow morning." I admit causing her to take a deep breath.

"You know, as sad that is, I do have to thank you. Because without you, we wouldn't be getting any answers as to what happened. So, we are grateful for you." She says sweetly, but you can hear the pain in her voice.

"Mrs Green, although the case is being left to Detective Gomez, who is a very hardworking and caring Detective, I have also said that I don't mind assisting and keeping up with the case from when I get back in London." I explain to her. I watch her eyes widen at what I've said, and she begins to lightly cry.

"You know, you've been nothing but amazing with all of us, thank you. Thank you." She praises gripping my hand tightly. "Miss Sanders, can I ask you one thing?" She says softly while wiping the tears away with her other hand.

"Of course." I encourage. Her face after a few moments becomes almost emotionless as she looks up at me, tears ever so slightly still falling on to her cheeks.

"Once you find my daughter's killer, just pull the trigger." She says almost as a whisper, and I feel a shiver go down my spine. "I don't want to see her as much as the rest of the parents."

I suddenly feel my stomach drop when I realise what she's just said. "Sorry, Mrs Green, how do you know the killer is a female?" I ask her curiously.

"The other mothers of the children that died, we met up to talk about how we are feeling, and Hannah Robson's mother had said that she believes that it was a girl called Alicia who killed her daughter. Both Mrs Simmons and I were trying to think of instances when a girl has said anything to either girls. That's why I came here. About six months ago, Sandy was in the mall with her friends and apparently this girl who looked about her age approached her and started asking her personal questions. Sandy was spooked, she was completely freaked out because this girl was asking about her sister and how did she feel about the adoption, and it completely freaked her out. I had just assumed it was someone on the campaign for Mr Robson and put in a complaint about it with him, but I don't think it was." She begins to cry again, and I feel sick. This was so planned that she went out and spoke to the kids that she killed. She's even worse than I thought.

"Mrs Green?" I hear a voice speak sweetly. In the middle of her cries, I turn to find Mr and Mrs Simmons standing there, hands interlocked so tight you can see they are losing circulation. "Have you told her?" She asks extending her hand and gently placing it on Mrs Green's shoulder. She welcomes the gesture, holding tightly as the stand beside her.

"I've just mentioned it." She cries, turning to me. "Our daughters all have met the killer, or at least we think so."

I stare wide eyed at the parents before turning around signalling Detective Gomez who immediately walks to be beside me. "How about we go into the conference room. We can make notes." I say with a smile signalling them to the room behind. They follow, one after each other with the Detective being the last one to come through the door.

"What is going on?" He asks while standing against the door.

"Mrs Green, can you repeat what you've just told me, please." I ask with a smile, and she gives me a nod. She repeats what she told me about the situation with Sandy in the shopping centre.

"Kassidy had a similar experience." Mr

Simmons speaks clearly causing us to look in his direction. "She was coming home from school just over a three months ago and some girl came out of nowhere and started asking her the same questions. Apparently, she was incredibly aggressive and kept trying to grab Kassidy a few times, but she ran away. She came home in tears and for a while she refused to walk home."

I look at Detective Gomez and take a long exhale. She went from provoking the two girls she lured out but pretended to be the friend of Hannah Robson. My only explanation to that is because in a way she thought she could relate to Hannah, she was becoming the outcast, silenced by her family for her addiction. But I can't be sure on that theory.

"So, what happens now that Miss Sanders is leaving?" Mrs Green asks the Detective who gives her a warm smile.

"Wait, you're leaving! You can't leave." Mrs Simmons pleads with me extending her hand and taking mine in hers tightly.

"Miss Sanders will still be working on the case just from London. I will be taking over the case here and we will work together. Nothing will change other than she will be based over the water." He explains calmly and they nod ever so slightly.

"Promise you won't give up on us?" Mr

Simmons asks. The tone in his voice gives me the hint that this wasn't a question it was more of demand.

Giving him a warm smile. I lean forward on the table, taking Mrs Simmons hand in mine. "I promise. But I would recommend that you keep in contact with Detective Gomez, he will have all the updated information." I say with a smile.

"I think our daughters would have been forgotten about if it wasn't for you two." Mr Simmons says returning the smile.

When the parents leave, I feel a wave of relief. I feel like such a hypocrite especially to Detective Gomez. I know eventually he will work out that more than likely the killer is Clarissa. But I can't help but feel guilty for playing dumb or not saying anything at all.

"So," Detective Gomez says while placing a bottle of water on the desk and sliding it over. "I think we should try and trace Sophie's last steps. She was quite secluded and was only noticed when the dog walker found her." He begins to explain while taking a sip of the sludge he calls coffee.

"You notified her parents yesterday?" I ask while opening my water.

"Yeah, were you okay yesterday? You seemed funny after you came out of the woods. I know reading the note must be a shock. None of us expected that." He says leaning in towards me. I back away ever so slightly.

"Yeah, I'm fine it was just a shock." I say while getting up and looking at the board. "Shall we go over everything we know so far?" I ask avoiding his stares.

"Sure. Let's start with victim number one." He instructs and I stand next to the board. "Kassidy Simmons was led out of her house with the promise of a date with a boy she had been dating for over a year, that has since been proved as false. The photo is of a model and the phone of the killer is a lost cause as it was a burner phone." He says while picking up Kassidy phone in the evidence bag.

"She had a separate phone to talk to him or should I say her. I find that incredibly intriguing." I say taking the phone from him and looking the phone over. "Why did she have a separate phone?" I ask.

"What do you mean?"

"Kassidy Simmons parents weren't that overbearing, they didn't go through their kids' phone, not to mention they are very loving to their children's. So, why did she lie? She could have easily had the number on her own phone. Why have a new one?" I ask curiously looking over the phone again.

"I honestly don't know, maybe she felt as though she couldn't trust her parents?" He suggests but that doesn't sit right with me.

"Am I okay to open this?" I ask him nicely holding up Kassidy's spare phone. The fact that Kassidy had a separate phone meant that she was hiding something much worse from her parents or that's the feeling I'm getting.

"Sure." He says with a nod while watching me carefully. "What are you thinking?"

"I don't know, I just have a feeling we are missing something." I say while inspecting the phone. It is covered in fake gems and even has something attached to it. At the end it has a pompom. For a phone that was meant to be a secret it doesn't look like it.

"What exactly did the team look at on the phone?" I ask looking it over inquisitively.

"Well, they opened the phone, it had a password, but it was pretty simple to crack. They looked at the messages but other than that because the phone was in the possession of the family, they didn't feel the need to look over it with a fine-tooth comb. What are you thinking, Jules?" He asks once again, and I look over the pompom.

"It's just a thought, but do you have Kassidy Simmons phone, the one from the crime scene?" I ask him and he turns his head looking over at the boxes in the corner.

"It should be in one of those. Nothing was found in the phone Jules. The phone was cleared of any bugs or anything." He says opening the box labelled 'Kassidy'.

I shake my head, unsure on this unsettled feeling that's in my stomach.

"I don't doubt for a second that the forensic team did do a thorough check of the actual phone but what about the contents?" I ask curiously.

A puzzled look grows on the Detective's face. "What about the contents? Jules' that thing has been cleared."

I sit in dead silence wondering if my theory is too farfetched. Why would she have a phone that was meant to be a secret but is so in your face? I begin to fiddle around with the pompom, thinking all of this Detective work is getting to my head.

"Jules, I can promise you. It is just a phone she was keeping from her parents. There is no hidden back story too it. It is just a phone." He says calmly while trying to get my attention which is currently fixated on the pompom.

"You're right." I speak eventually. My voice is slightly deflated. "I'm jumping to conclusions." I say while placing the phone back in the forensic bag and back on the table. "Where were we?"

The Detective gives me a reassuring smile before handing me the next case. "Now, this is the case of Kassidy Simmons, assumed to have been talking to an older boyfriend on a burner phone, she has an adopted sister Kiara, who is on the same list as the rest of the adopted children. Cause of death, strangulation." He says while pointing over to Kassidy's section on the board. "Next, we have Sandy Green, she was a year older, same cause of death. She was lured out by someone pretending to be her friend Olive online, yet Olive didn't have her phone." He continues.

"What was her sister called?"

"Poppy Green." He says putting a photo of Poppy and Sandy on the board. A photo of happier times, them both on holiday laughing and smiling. "Next, we have Hannah Robson. She was lured out by our good friend Alicia who seems to be causing a lot of stirs recently. This means that your right in your theory, that the killer is more than likely female, and she has a vendetta against siblings, especially blood siblings."

No kidding.

"Lastly, we have our most recent victim, Sophie Cutter. She had the word traitor carved into her head and the cause of death was the same. I had some uniforms canvas the area this morning for any sign of any evidence, but apparently there was none." He says, placing Sophie's photo on the board. It is such a shame, this could have been prevented, but Clarissa went on a tantrum, and it caused another innocent life to be lost.

"Does Sophie Cutter have a sibling that was adopted?"

"Yeah, Tallulah Cutter, she's the same age as the other girls. I'm still waiting for the full list from Randy at the adoption agency." He explains placing his hands on his hips. "You know what has me stumped?" He questions. I look over in his direction as he heads over to the board pointing out the CCTV footage of the adoption agency, "This. This girl said she was seven month pregnant, but I think it was a lie, that bump was clearly a fake."

Yeah, I wish it was Detective.

"Any ideas?" He asks me, breaking me from my thoughts.

"I mean, we still haven't been able to place the guy she's with, the guy pretending to be her boyfriend for example."

Rodger.

"It's a dead end. No doubt they are partners, however I feel like she's the mastermind behind this whole thing." He explains before looking behind me. I feel the room suddenly go cold as every around me stands, stunned as if they have been frozen in time.

The Detective stands tall, I mixture of anger and disbelief filling his face.

I finally turn around to see what everyone is so stunned about and find myself just as shocked as the rest of the room.

There stands, the Quinten five. Robert, Peter, Felicity, Serena and Oliver. All of them dressed in over their top outfits, looking like a million dollars. I feel like this is the start of a joke - Fiver murderers walk into a police station...

My jaw is on the floor, why and *what* are they doing here? I can't blow my cover, because all that will do is ruin the relationship I have with the Detective.

"Detective Gomez?" Peter speaks in the silence of the room. Mike stands taller, glaring at the entire family. "We have a person in mind for those murders."

CHAPTER THIRTY-EIGHT

Juliette Sanders

Michigan, USA

The tension in the entire station is so cold and hard you could cut it with a knife. I feel sick, why are they are? And the number of questions about their sudden appearance have me on edge.

"You came to hand yourselves in?" Detective Gomez says sarcastically looking directly at Oliver who grins the grin of nightmares while looking down on the Detective who begins to take a seat.

I really want to be the one to tell him not to aggravate Oliver. But I decide to keep my mouth shut till I know what is going on.

"We have nothing to admit to Detective, however we would like to give you a helping hand in this case. We believe we know who you are looking for." Felicity speaks clearly, and suddenly I feel like I am not looking at my family, I am looking at the Quinten five, a family who so many in this city fear.

This is what they mean by business, and this is what they mean by dealing with this as a family.

"Please enlighten me." The Detective taunts, earning a groan from Oliver who moves from the back of the seat and stands next to the door. The Detective watches his every move, probably to see that Oliver doesn't do something erratic.

"The person you're looking for is Clarissa Brady Quinten." Robert says clearly, the coldness in his voice chilling as it flows through my vein. *Is he actually serious?*

My eyes widen as I feel my jaw slightly drop. I look over at my family who sit at the meeting table, calm, cold and collected. There is no way he's just handed over his own daughter as a suspect.

"And who is she to you?" The Detective asks while making a note of Clarissa's name in his notebook.

"She's my daughter." Robert answers calmly causing the Detective to look up at him in disbelief.

"You believe your own daughter is the murderer Mr Quinten? I hate to be frank, but are you sure it wasn't the psychopath is the corner who decided to go on a teenage killing spree?" He asks through his teeth, and I have to bite my tongue and not get involved.

Oliver begins to laugh while leaning up against the door. "Murdering kids isn't my style."

The Detective begins the chuckle while looking around the room and the five siblings. "Funnily enough I find that very hard to believe."

A glare is exchanged between Oliver and Detective Gomez that is one of warning, Oliver can snap so easily, but with how he is standing against the door, my guess is he has been told he has to be on his best behaviour, so instead of entertaining it, Oliver simply shrugs his shoulders and looks over at the other four sitting at the table.

"Detective, if we didn't think this was serious, do you honestly think we would spend our time sitting in a police station? We have multiple businesses to run." Peter states and the Detective begins to laugh.

"Which ones? The legitimate ones or the illegal?"

The look on Robert's face grows annoyed and I know I am finally looking at the head of the American mafia. The look sends a chill through me that I am now no longer looking at my father, more of a man who is a murderer, an executioner and the jury himself.

I believe the Detective is getting the hint too, because I find him shift in his seat as he presses down on the pen and placing it to the paper. "What do I need to know?"

A sudden smirk falls upon Serena's face and for a slight second, she catches my glare before quickly looking away. I look forward towards Robert as he tilts his head to look at Felicity.

"On the days of the murders of the children, we cannot seem to track Clarissa on any of the devices and we cannot seem to locate her on a few other occasions." Robert says while Felicity leans over and elegantly slides a file over to the Detective who takes it curiously.

In a few moments of silence, he seems to pull the file apart, looking at dates and locations and some CCTV footage stills that we have never even seen before.

"Where is this from?" Mike asks and I slowly walk over and peek over his shoulder. I begin to look around the photo and to my surprise there is a clear photo of Clarissa with her hand clearly on Sandy Green's arm.

"Six months ago, Detective. This is a still from what the Green family were talking about earlier."

His head shoots up and fury is on his face. "How did you know about this? We only found out about the altercation this morning from the Green family?"

"We were enjoying a coffee other day when the grieving mothers of the teenagers came in for their meeting, we couldn't help but overhear." Serena says sincerely, but I can tell she is lying. Her red stained lips have a slight twinge on her face, and I know fine well she's gotten that information somewhere and they have paid for it.

"And how did you manage to get this?" Detective Gomez asks curiously.

"Let's just say the owner of the mall will give you whatever you want if you ask nice enough. And we made a very large charitable donation to their fundraiser for this year's Christmas Tree Ceremony." Felicity says sweetly but there is a hint of sneakiness in her voice, and I can't help but smile. If they want something, they know how to get it, no questions asked that is for sure.

"How grateful of Mr Ross to hand this over." He says sarcastically before taking a deep breath, looking over all of the new evidence. "Anything else I need to know?" He asks, his eyes slowly looking up at Robert whose whole demeanour remains unchanged.

"A birdy told us you believe that on one occasion, my daughter had an accomplice in a theft of a document retaining to the adopted children, is that correct?" He asks.

The Detective's mouth falls open, as does mine. I know deep down they wouldn't through Rodger under the bus, but my guess is with the way they are looking at the Detective, they are going to put someone else in the hotseat.

"Yes, that is correct." His eyes dart to each member of the family, unsure on what else is going to come from their mouths.

"We recently located the body of a boy called Carter Edrington who we know was close with Clarissa and who we believe is another victim of hers." Peter states and my heart falls out of my chest. I knew it.

They will protect him, even if Damian is currently in a mental facility because of Rodger's actions. I turn away and bite my cheek holding in the amount of anger that is bubbling within.

"Well, this is news. I never heard of a male victim."

"That's because the murder came past one of our team and we decided to conduct an out of city autopsy with a medical examiner we can trust. Carter was shot with a 9mm not far from where the fourth victim Sophie Cutter was found." Robert explains before handing over what looks like a medical examiners report, and I roll my eyes. Unbelievable.

"Carter died from a shot through the heart, and from what they determined, he died within minutes. The body has since been sent to the family who have wished to cremate him." Felicity explains, sitting tall and unbothered while steam comes from my ears.

"Now, hate to break it to you, but the killer doesn't use guns. Her choice in murder is strangulation." Detective sits back in his chair waiting for them to spew up some new lies.

"Clarissa was gifted a 9mm handgun for her fifteenth birthday by my brother Oliver. Here is the licence and certificate." Felicity speaks while handing over a new set of documents.

There it is, clear as day. Clarissa Brady Quinten's gun licence.

"Well, you must feel like you've won uncle of the year." The Detective exchanges a look of annoyance with Oliver before taking a long deep breath. "The other thing I have to ask is has your daughter Clarissa had any life changes recently, a new sibling perhaps or anything that would be the reason she would go for the kids in the city?"

A long pause enters the room and I look around my family to see which one will conjure up the lie. They can't exactly say, It's me, because that would ruin me, and I watch Peter lean forward very slowly, shaking his head in disbelief.

"Clarissa has always been troubled. The girl witnessed her father murder her mother at such a young age, not to mention her brother went into the Navy and left her with us the second he was adopted. She struggles with bipolar disorder and psychopathic tendencies, but also, she is a pathological liar who will manipulate you into think you drove her to do this." Peter explains calmly and I can't help but grow cold. I know Clarissa is slightly unhinged, but to know the ins and outs of why she can be the way she is.

The Detective notes all of this down as he slowly stands up from hid chair. "I'm going to look into this Carter Edrington kid, before I let you go, would you mind staying a few minutes?" The Detective asks as nicely as he can.

"Of course, take your time." Serena says sweetly looking Mike up and down while he leaves the room.

"Miss Sanders, would you get them a bottle of water?" He asks before leaving and the door shuts quickly behind him.

Instead of speaking to them just yet I decide to do what I'm instructed and not give any one any reason to suspect I'm a Quinten. I get five bottles of water from the fridge and in complete silence hand them one while also noticing the looks that are exchanged around the room.

"You know Robert, she has your controlled

anger and I hate to say it, but she's scarier than you." Serena says in the silence, and I lean back against the wall.

"I just was waiting for the moment you defended Rodger. I knew it was coming, but never did I think you would accuse Carter, the boy he probably killed as an accomplice. That is what has me shocked to say the least." I say leaning back against the wall.

"Juliette, until we have some actual evidence on Rodger, I can't go throwing him under the bus." Robert defends himself and my eyes widen.

"Well, you're quite happy to throw one child under the bus."

His eyes narrow, annoyed with my accusation. "You defending her?"

"Now we both know that I would never do that, however I do find it suspicious how you turn up day before we leave for Haroux to try and close this case."

A devious smile creeps upon his lips as he leans forward across the table. "Juliette, I have every intention on you not continuing this case and keeping you safe. There is mountains of evidence against Clarissa, some of it, admittedly, we have chosen to ignore."

"What a surprise." I say sarcastically. He leans back in his chair, realising that no matter what he says he knows I'm not backing down from this case. "What you going to do when first, Detective Gomez works out that Carter had nothing to do with any of this and they work out it's Rodger and he lives with you or second when Clarissa works out that the one person, she has tried to prove herself to, has handed her into the police. Because I'm sure you said that no matter where she goes, she's going to leave a trail of bodies." I frustratingly state. The man sits there, as cool as a cucumber as he looks over at Oliver briefly.

"She will be handled."

Suddenly Detective Gomez walks through the door, a file in hand and begins to look around the room. My face tells a story I'm sure of it, I feel completely defeated. They had every intention on coming in and closing the case. There was probably a family meeting this morning after I left the house.

"Everything okay?" The Detective asks and I give a reassuring nod and fake smile. Mikki and Katy always said I've never been able to hide my emotions, and with how I'm feeling right now, I'm sure I'll have a severe resting bitch face.

"Find what you needed Detective?" Peter chipperly asks as the Detective sits down, making a groan of a mixture of annoyance and frustration.

"Yes. It turns out you are correct, Carter Edrington had been arrested for theft a year prior. Thank you for the information. I'll get in contact with the District Attorney to inform them of the recent progress on the case." He says calmly while extending his hand towards Robert who surprisingly shakes it. "Thank you for the information, Mr Quinten, I'll be in touch regarding more information on your daughter." The Detective says before getting up.

"Just to note Detective, my family and I will be away on a business in Spain for the next four days, if you are to need to get in touch regarding a statement of any information, I'll leave my sister Serena's, just in case. She will be able to get in touch with me." Robert grins and I watch a nod come from the Detective.

"Just out of curiosity Mr Quinten, is Clarissa included in this trip?" The Detective asks and I watch the smile on Robert's face only grow wider.

"Not at all, in fact, we haven't seen Clarissa since her other brother left for the Army." Robert admits.

The Detective looks around at my family, waiting for someone else to say something, however they all give off the same emotion: cold and heartless.

"Well then, I'll be in touch." The Detective nods and the family begin the rise from their seats.

"One more thing before we leave," Robert begins before looking over at Felicity who begins to get something out of her bag. "For Miss Sanders. We hear it's your last day on the case, and we want to wish you the best in the future." He says while walking round slowly and handing me a box with a cake. "You never know, one day we might be working with you on future cases." He grins and I feel the anger only boil within me more.

"I wouldn't count on it." I say through my teeth.

The Quinten's all leave in silence one by one, all giving me a small look before the door is closed and it is just the Detective and I in the room.

"Well shit, never did I think I would have to arrest Robert Quinten's kid." The Detective says almost laughing at the admission while gathering the different evidence files and looking over at me. "You seem to have a hatred towards the Quinten's, the same as me." He jokes and I begin to giggle.

"Let's just say they haven't been too kind to my family is all." I say going over and putting the bottles of water back in the fridge which they didn't touch, more than likely not wanting to leave any fingerprints in case they can be linked with any other cases they more than likely are involved in. "Don't you find it suspicious how Robert was quick to hand over his daughter?"

The Detective shrugs, "I don't care, he probably got sick of defending her. The kids got quite a rap sheet." He says while handing me a stack of papers that could equivalent to an essay I would write at school.

I look through them quickly and notice a pattern - stalking, harassment, arson.

I find myself feeling surprised, because this seems fake. Surely if Clarissa did all those things, they would have everything expunged from her record, not just sitting there for the whole police department to find.

"You seem stumped, kid." The Detective says while I look up at him. "I don't like the fact I'll be looking into a Quinten, but just know you don't have to. I'll take it from here." He says reassuringly, placing his hand gently on my shoulder. "I've got this covered."

Looking into the Detectives eyes, I have no doubt in my mind that he is capable of closing this case. But what I do doubt is him coping with the amount of carnage Clarissa is going to leave behind.

"I know Detective." I say with a slight smile, hopefully enough to convince him to drop this, and he does. He decides to walk out of the room leaving me in the emptiness alone.

I decide instead of sulking over my family's

ambush, I should help him, in some ways, try and prove that Carter wasn't a part of this. I owe that to him, but also to Damian.

Suddenly something at the door catches my eye. I bend down and lift up what looks like a licence. Flipping it over I feel the blood in my body go cold.

Brady Alicia Williams.

Clarissa's alias.

Suddenly my mind starts going back to Clarissa and her troubled past. Her Mum and dad, Tommy who I am still yet to meet. She was practically left with Robert. She grew a connection, or some would call it is fascination with him and the family.

But what about Sapphire? And why can't anyone find her? There was multiple witnesses said that Clarissa had a baby girl called Sapphire, yet the only one who has seen her is the nurses and the Doctor.

My mind begins to start asking questions about Clarissa. I can understand her lack of trust for the rest of the family, but why would she hide Sapphire from Robert? She trusted him, and she loves him. No matter what anyone says.

"Miss Sanders?" A voice interrupts my thoughts and I look up to find Oliver. My brows frown as he slowly closes the door and takes the licence out of my hand. "Now this is going to be the only time I ever help you; do you understand?" He says harshly, almost as if I'm doing him a favour.

I decide to just nod and hear what he has to say, because I always knew he knew more than he was letting on. Like Serena said, they are the youngest and they see so much.

"Clarissa has multiple aliases. But what Robert failed to mention is that the one she mostly uses is her birth one. She never legally changed her name; she just changed it for Robert." He explains holding up the licence.

"So, Clarissa isn't legally Clarissa? She still goes by her birth name?" I ask him and he nods.

"Her birth name is Alicia Brady Allington. And I think you should look up the name Jade Allington."

"Why?"

"Because that's the name she legally put down as Sapphire's in the state of Michigan."

"How do you know that?"

He looks down, fighting with himself for a moment before looking back up and his eyes meet mine. They are filled with a mixture of excitement and betrayal.

"Because I was the one who helped her do it."

CHAPTER THIRTY-NINE

Juliette Sanders
Michigan, USA

As I leave the room and watch Oliver give a warning glare to Detective Gomez, I begin to find myself unsettled. Why would he help me? He doesn't like me, and he has made that very clear.

But better yet, why would he help Clarissa? It makes no sense to me that he would help her get rid of Sapphire, or at least help hide her.

After a moment in my own thoughts, I watch as Detective Gomez walks closer, a look of concern filling his face as he reads mine, which from what I can tell is only puzzled.

"You alright? What did he want?" He asks curiously, while still examining my face.

"Just to make me ask more questions. They had forgotten to give us one of her aliases." I say walking towards his desk, and he begins to walk alongside me. "Do you want to take half and I'll take half and we can look up each alias and see what comes up?" I ask him, wanting to quickly get off the subject of Oliver.

"Sure, that would help. But if you see anything relating to a death, don't open it. I don't want the Lieutenant on my ass." He jokes while leaning over and turning on the computer. "You know, I think that entire family had a soft spot for you." He admits looking back at my surprised expression. "They are the most dangerous family in America. The FBI are after them, so is Interpol, you name it. Yet here you stand, and they looked absolutely terrified of you in that meeting room. Like you were their biggest fear."

I don't think the Detective understands how right he is. Not that he would ever think I was Robert Quinten's daughter. I look nothing like him, I look more like Arielle, thankfully. I am the one piece of the puzzle that any of Robert Quinten's enemies would love to crack. But they can't, because they will probably never know that I'm his daughter. Unless you did a DNA test, then... well you will have your answer.

"I do have a really good RBF." I say sarcastically and I watch as the confusion only grows on the Detective's face.

"What does RBF mean?" He asks, the look of disgust lingers as he stands tall.

"Means resting bitch face, Detective. You have a very good one as well." I compliment. I watch his eyes widen as he looks around to see if anyone heard me.

"Who told you, you could swear?"

"I wasn't aware there was a rule book." I joke and he only leans in closer so I can smell the stench of coffee on his breath.

"There is always a rule book." He says with a wink before turning back and pulling the chair out. "How about you get a start on looking up those aliases, while I go down to the morgue. They have just finished Sophie Cutter's autopsy." He says moving the files to the side of the computer and looking over at Tracy who sits just opposite. "Tracy is here if you need anything, just run the names through CODIS and if anything comes up, write it down." He instructs before leaving quickly, grabbing his tanned coat on the way and a coffee.

I open the file and notice eight names on the list. Nine if you count her birth name.

My one question is why? Why would she go

out of her way to kill four teenagers just because I existed then hid her child from the rest of the family?

Clarissa has issues, clearly. But there are a lot of holes in her story, some of which I am itching to find out more.

I decide to get started in the hopes of finding something out hopefully something about Sapphire, or Jade.

Three hours later, I still sit here; baffled by my lack of evidence. Nothing on any of the other aliases, as far as I can see anyway.

"Any luck?" Tracy asks after a moment of me just staring at the screen. "You seem like you're getting nowhere."

"Stating the obvious Tracy." I say, exhaling loudly before closing yet another file. "The aliases are a dead end; they haven't been picked up by any other agency."

"Meaning more than likely the Quinten's gave you fake aliases, so they can hide the one she really uses." She explains clearly, not wasting a breath before looking back over at her computer screen.

The idea is plausible. Because of course, they would want both the Detective and I to waste time on looking at the other aliases, ones that are likely fake, in order to try and hide the main one. All possibilities. Especially with the Quinten's.

"All the ones you looked up, have they gave you dead ends?" She asks again and I nod at her.

"I have one more to try, so let's hope that they've given me something." I type in Alicia Brady Allington, praying something comes up.

Access Denied.

What?

I try again, the same message. What have I missed?

"Tracy, I'm getting an access denied message when looking up this alias." I tell her and watch her brows from as she rises from her seat.

She stands behind me, looking at the message on the screen. "I get the feeling we aren't the only people looking into her." She says coldly looking down on me as I meet her, my expression is confused. "Either they are looking into that alias, or we aren't meant to know about it. Other agencies clearly have an interest in her." She explains, her tone flat and slightly harsh. But it's giving me the warning I need it to.

I hear a buzzing sound come from behind me and notice it's my phone. I lean over to grab it and notice that it's an unknown number.

I hesitate, and Tracy notices before giving me

an encouraging nod.

"Hello?"

"Why am I not surprised it's you out looking for trouble." A British accent greets me on the other end of the phone, and I feel myself relax immediately as I recognise the voice.

"Well, hello to you to." I sarcastically reply and I hear him chuckle at the other end of the phone. "How can I help you, Officer Bradley?"

Tracy tilts her head slightly and I mouthed to her that everything is fine, and she proceeds to go back to her desk, not asking another question.

"Why are you looking into Alicia Allington?" He asks curiously and I feel a wave of adrenaline flow through me.

"The question that stands merit Officer Bradley is why are you looking into it?" I ask him and a sigh of annoyance greets me on the other end of the phone.

"I asked you first."

"How mature."

I hear him pause after a moment and some shuffling going around. "Juliette, I need you to answer me honestly. Is there cases in Michigan that currently involve her?" He asks me and I pause for a second, why is he looking into Clarissa?

"Yes." I say to him quietly and get up from

my seat and begin to walk towards the meeting room. I'm limited to what I can say in a room full of police officers and Detectives, especially when talking to an Officer who is well known to the Quinten's.

"Juliette, do you understand how dangerous she is?" He asks me harshly. "I can't say much at the moment, but when do you arrive back in London; I'd like to meet you and your Mother."

"I get back into London next week." I say to him, and I can hear a door close on the other end.

"I will arrange to come over if that is alright. I'm hoping your Mother knows about this case, I really don't want you to land yourself in trouble which you are very good at doing may I add." He replies sarcastically and I pull a face, a one only I can see.

"Very funny. But you're not giving me the answers I need." I state harshly and he groans once more on the other end of the phone.

"Juliette, Alicia... she's dangerous."

"I'm well aware, I've seen the state of what she has done to four girls over here." I reply which suddenly catches him off guard and he goes quiet. "Not to mention I've been living with her for over two weeks, and I've had to sleep with one eye open." I whisper away from Tracy.

"How long do you need access for?" He asks

quickly and his question takes me back.

"What?"

"How long do you need access for? Some things I will need to send you privately. But I can give you access to some of her information."

"How kind of you. Is five minutes too much to ask?"

"I can give you that, but you have to be quick. Is it still the same email address as last time? There are some documents I can show you, that I think your gonna wanna see." He says and the curiosity in me only grows. Why is he looking into Clarissa and her background, and why is he trying to get himself in trouble?

"Yes, it is, and are you sure you can do that?"

"No, I can't but I know this is something that you've been looking for."

My phone starts to buzz, and I watch an email come through from Officer Bradley. "You've got five minutes Juliette. Make it count." He says before hanging up and I look over at the Detectives desk.

Finally. Let's hope I get some answers.

CHAPTER FORTY

Juliette Sanders

Michigan, USA

My goodbye to the Detective, Tracy and the other officers was a hearty one. Lots of hugs and tears, however Detective Gomez just said see you soon, and no other goodbye after that.

I wasn't hurt by it, I can understand that it might be hard, however we will still be working together on the case just I will be in London.

Keeping my composure for the rest of the day, that was the challenging part.

Officer Bradley gave me minimal access, but it gave me a good idea into what he has been looking into and from what I gathered, it's Clarissa and Clarissa alone. She has quite a history with police all over the world and they have managed to link her to a few petty crimes, which means more than likely she's linked with something much darker, that I will no doubt find out when I get back to London.

I've found that what Officer Bradley emailed me, that was the topping on the cake. It gave me the answer to a question I've been searching for since finding out I was adopted a few months ago. But it begs my question on how many Quinten's know Clarissa's big secret.

If Robert never knew that Oliver was the one to hide Clarissa's baby, then how is he going to know about this? She has always been one step ahead of everyone this entire time, and now that I'm starting to get a better understanding of her, I feel that soon I will be able to play her at her own game and get justice, but also answers.

I'll happily ruin her life, because in my eyes she's ruined so many. All those families that have to bury their children because she couldn't control her hatred towards me, she of course will blame me for every single thing that has happened. I know she will. Cause that is all she is good for, never admitting her mistakes and never taking the blame.

I don't know what I'm about to walk in to. They know that they are in the wrong by handing over Damian's boyfriend to the police. They are out of line. And I feel like I'm walking into yet another intervention.

"Home sweet home, Miss Sanders." The driver says as we pull up to the gates. "It has been a pleasure." He says sweetly while looking up in the rear-view mirror.

I smile to him, he has always been so sweet, never saying a word while driving me to and from the police station. However, I made sure to get him a Starbucks, as he does drive me everywhere.

"Thank you for taking me every day. I know it was probably quite frustrating having to take a teenager to the police station." I joke to him, and he joins in with me.

"Funnily enough, I really enjoyed all of it. I loved being able to leave this place even if it was just for an hour a day."

I only smile because I find myself speechless. I don't doubt that he probably hated the fact that he had to drive round a fourteen-year-old. But knowing that in the end, he didn't mind it as much does make my heart happy.

I do feel like the men and woman that work for the Quinten's have probably seen so much yet are bound by NDA's and contracts.

I thank the driver again and get out of the car, shutting the door behind me. I feel like I'm about to walk into another intervention, however I feel I have one up on them. Which excites me a little bit.

Opening the door, I am met with Robert, Felicity, Serena and Peter and to no surprise, there is no Oliver. The one person I actually need to see.

"Juliette," Robert greets me as I shut the door. "We will be leaving early in the morning, I've had someone pack your suitcase for you, all you need to do is put your clothes from today in, and I bought you a new pair of pyjamas for tonight." He says while walking away from me, the rest of the family watching him.

"Where's Oliver?" I ask, ignoring what he says.

The whole family turns to me, a look of confusion is on their face. I can understand why. I never ask to see Oliver and it has probably piqued their interest as to why I need to see him.

"Why?" Robert asks curiously, placing his hands on his hips. "You never ask to see him." He states clearly and I shrug my shoulders.

"Why do you care? Anything I say now could be used against me since you were happy to throw one child into hot water." I say pulling my bag up onto my shoulder as it started to slide down.

"You're not defending her, are you?" He repeats himself.

"We both know I wouldn't. She's been nothing but awful to me. But that doesn't mean

I trust you enough to tell you why I need to see my uncle." I say coldly and watch as looks are exchanged with the other members of my family. They know I'm right deep down.

"The study." Robert says after a while, and I turn right and head in that direction while ignoring their curious stares.

They lost all right to ask me questions and quiz me on anything when they walked in here and made themselves the centre of attention.

Clarissa, or Alicia, I don't even know what to call her, she has a lot of secrets and a lot of lies. Some of which I know Robert hasn't got a clue about, or the rest of the family.

I enter the office, making sure to shut the door behind me.

Oliver looks up and meets my gaze. He's emotionless, as usual. He made himself vulnerable today by handing me the licence. But also, it makes me question why would he do that for me? He hates me. Or so he says so.

"I thought I had seen enough of your face." He remarks harshly. I decide to ignore him, because although he says it, he knows that I would have found what I have and that I will have questions. "I like my peace and quiet Juliette, and you are not peace, or quiet. So, ask your question and get out." He snaps at me quickly, and I instantly become annoyed.

"Why did you help me today?" I ask him and he rolls his eyes, groaning at the question.

"Because Juliette, sometimes you need a little push in the right direction to find the right answers. Is that hard to understand?" He mocks slightly before looking at his screen and I take a seat in front of him, indicating I am not leaving, and I have no intention to.

"You don't like me, so why help me?"

"Because although I am an unhinged psychopath - as you point out quite often Juliette, I do actually have a heart. And I might be okay stabbing people that deserve it, but I draw the line at hurting kids."

His admission catches me of guard slightly and I find myself struggling to ask another question. Even for Oliver, honestly isn't in his mind at all, he lies all the time and when he is honest, he's painfully honest that in the end does more harm than good.

I sit back in my chair, thinking for a moment on how to respond to that. "Why did you help Clarissa hide Sapphire?" I ask him calmly. The frustration growing on his face but instead he turns to me.

"Because at the time, she was the only one who understood me. Now that I know what she's been doing. I feel stupid, so I gave you the ID to do some digging which I'm assuming you've done, and you've found something." He slightly taunts causing me to place the file down in front of him.

"You know I'd find out who Sapphire's father is." I say to him calmly and I watch as his face doesn't change shape one bit. That same face that shows no emotion unless its frustration or annoyance.

"I know it wouldn't be hard once you found the birth certificate." He mocks slightly, and I can tell by the tone of his voice.

"So, you knew that Rodger is Sapphire's father?" I ask him and his face stays the same.

"Of course, I knew. It was clear as day to me, but to everyone else, they decided to ignore it. Rodger is completely manipulated by Clarissa. When she first announced she was pregnant, she told everyone it was someone she met when she was in Alaska. That's why Peter has been looking since Sapphire was born. But he couldn't in the end, even place her there."

"You think that's because she never even went there?"

"We both know that's what I think." He says leaning closer to me. "Both you and I know that Clarissa is a compulsive liar, and if we add up everything, I know where she was and what she was doing." He says while turning the computer around and showing me a mug shot alongside a report. "Brady Williams got arrested in Mexico." He says smugly and I feel my eyes widen.

Why didn't that come up on my initial search? But more importantly, how did he find it? "What was she arrested for?" I ask him, trying to read down the report before he moves the computer back.

"Fraud. But she managed to get off lightly. She had another fake ID with a fake age and because she was a child, the Mexican authorities decided to let her off as they actually had no physical evidence to tie her to it. They still don't and the charges were dropped."

"How did you get it?"

"I know people."

I roll my eyes at his answer, but I also know that is the best I'm going to get from him.

"I'm going to assume you didn't know about Clarissa's other secret?" I ask him curiously and I watch his brows raise, waiting for me to continue. "Prior to being adopted by Robert, did you know that Clarissa had another baby?"

He watches my face carefully, waiting for me to explain in the hopes I'm joking. I don't let my face budge, my guess is no one knew about this baby, probably because it took me forever to find him.

Opening the file placed on the desk earlier, I

show him a birth certificate for a Dracov Chase Hayward. He was born about a year prior to Robert adopting both Clarissa and Tommy and my guess is Tommy knew about the baby as there was a photo, I had managed to find from some adoption agency site where I had assumed Dracov, if that is even still his name, where he's been sent."

"Where did you find this?" He asks coldly, picking up the birth certificate and reading over it a few times.

"I looked into the name you gave me, and I had Tracy from the station get me the number of some adoption agencies in the area where she lived with Tommy before moving in with Robert. One lady said she remembers her, saying she was slightly cold and off about the whole pregnancy thing, she seemed more 'mentally disturbed' she said. Anyway, she had come in with a guy called Chase Hayward who, by the looks of it is the father of Dracov." I say pulling out an incident report from the agency that she was kind enough to send over. "I recognised the name Hayward. Because that is the name she gave Hannah Robson's parents. Alicia Hayward."

He goes quiet while going over the report. I wait patiently, watching his every move.

He stands up tall before rubbing his hands over his face and groaning in frustration. "So, you're telling me Clarissa has two kids?" He says, placing his hands on his hips.

"Exactly."

"And who is Chase Hayward?" He asks, the tone of his voice annoyed.

"I don't know. I couldn't find that information out without raising eyebrows." He groans and places his hand firmly on the desk and lowering his head. "I'm assuming you're going to tell Robert."

He sighs before lifting his head slowly. "Not yet. But I have an idea on when we tell him. And you little Miss Detective, need to gather up your own case file to show the rest of the family. Because we need something to show them, and if I know Robert, he will not be happy about a birth certificate. He is going to need more evidence than that." He says sarcastically and I can't help but roll my eyes.

I know he is right about Robert; he needs more evidence.

"You need to find something on Chase Hayward, and I am going to find the kid." He says while sitting down and pulling the keyboard towards him. "Hopefully." He mutters under his breath.

CHAPTER FORTY-ONE

Robert Quinten

Michigan, USA

I sit, waiting outside of the office on the entry chair for Juliette and Oliver to finish their little chat. I have no idea why Juliette would need to even speak to him. They don't get along, purely because Oliver wants nothing to do with her. And has made it very clear since day one.

My mind is racing, what could she possibly need to speak to him about, that she couldn't have sat down and told me?

My mind goes back to the time I was debating putting cameras in the office just for safety. And I am deeply regretting my decision to decide against it now.

"That's wrong." I mutter under my breath and raise from the seat. I place my hands on my hips, walking the length of the hallway and back as I wait for their meeting to end.

I've sent the rest of the family to finish packing their things. Serena will be staying here along with Nathaniel, Ezekiel, and Rodger. The last thing I need is for him to try and ruin Juliette's meet up with Arielle. Although it seems Arielle is trying to do that on her own. Clarissa hasn't been seen for days which isn't a good thing and no matter how much we try and locate her, she seems to of disappeared of the face of the earth. Until I can actually link Rodger to the shooting of Carter and the boys, I've sent him on a task far away.

I hear the click of the door open, and I stand to meet Juliette who stares at me blankly. I can understand why she is being cold towards me. She told me not to intervene in the investigation and I did. Not to mention I handed them a prime suspect on a silver platter like I would some of my enemies.

"Why did you need to speak to Oliver?" I ask her calmly in the hopes of a response that doesn't reek of attitude.

"You'll find out soon." She says, ignoring my pleading stare as she walks up the stairs.

"Juliette-"

"You said you wouldn't interfere. And you did." She says coldly, staring down on me her face a state of calm but in her eyes, you can see the hurt. "You said you wouldn't get in the way, yet you stood in front of Detective Gomez and handed Clarissa as a prime suspect. You are aware that is going to give him more reason to look into you and the entire family. No doubt finding a private adoption that held place fourteen years ago that he will probably go and unseal and find that you had a daughter. Did you think of any of this? Because I did. And I'm the child." She says so softly. He voice filled with pain and the more she speaks the more my heart is aching. "So much for keeping me a secret. Because you've just given the police department every reason to start looking into your family. And in no time at all, you'll all be in handcuffs. Whether it be Oliver for that family murder, or you for your dark and mysterious businesses. They aren't going to look into Clarissa, the Detective wants the whole family arrested and that is what I was trying to avoid."

I stand speechless as I look at her. Here is where the Sanders comes out in her. This sense of family and loyalty I had seen so much of. Although I've broken her trust, I can see her trying to repair it with her heart.

"I now have something else to deal with. I'll tell you, don't worry. I won't ambush you. But I need more evidence and I'm not exactly sure on how I'm going to get it." She says her hands placed firmly on the staircase as she lowers her head. "A heads up would have been nice, Dad. That's all." She says almost as a whisper before running up the stairs, a file in her hand and she disappears down the hallway.

She just called me Dad.

My heart bursts with both excitement and heartbreak. It's something I have wanted her to say for so long, yet she said it with so much hurt in her voice that I know I can't enjoy and that I shouldn't.

I exhale, not sure on what to do next. I know I have to trust her, but the person I don't trust is my brother.

"Dad, huh?" I hear Peter speak beside me. I knew he was in the kitchen and undoubtedly heard the whole thing. He's been my biggest supporter in all of this, he has helped me through so much and I owe everything to him.

"It was out of anger. She didn't really mean it." I say walking through to the kitchen. I open the cabinet and grab two glasses and a bottle of scotch from the cabinet below. "I'd hope one day she'll say it out of love. But I can't ever force her to." I say pouring out two glasses and pushing one over to him. "She lost her real dad. Paul was everything to her." I say quietly before throwing back the scotch in one and placing the glass down.

"You know she's right. If we had just left her to it, it would have been handled better. She's very selfless and would have found a way for Clarissa to be handed safely, but you've now put a target on Clarissa's back and as you've said before if she feels as though she's been targeted – she will cause carnage everywhere she goes." Peter explains harshly and I feel my blood begin to boil. Although the harsh reality he is giving me is making me angry, it is a wake-up call.

"Think she'll forgive me?" I ask him honestly. I watch him exhale loudly and shake his head.

"I don't know. But I think you should listen to what she has to say, and you have to trust her. Just like we need to trust Oliver."

I had forgotten about Oliver and their conversation, and I begin to let the curiosity crawl through me. I can't help but begin to fill irritated on why she would need to talk to him. I love my brother, however the thought of him conjuring up a plan with my daughter does boil my blood. Considering he has been nothing but vocal about how much he hates Juliette and wants nothing to do with her.

"Stop." Peter instructs harshly cutting me off from the running thoughts in my mind. He looks at me irritated. "I know what you're thinking. You have to trust him, Robert. Trust that he has her best intentions. Ours too."

I lean off the counter and place the bottle away, ignoring Peter's comments. I go to collect his glass and he grips his hand on the other side causing me to look at him. "He'll never have her best intentions. He'll watch her die before he thinks to save her." I state bluntly, gritting my teeth slightly before I hear someone clear their voice behind me.

"You're wrong Robert." Oliver speaks clearly, annoyance in his voice as he goes to the cupboard to get the bottle I only just put away and grab another glass in silence. It unsettles me. I know I shouldn't have spoken about him behind his back, but the man can be so unhinged I worry what he might do. "You were in the wrong today. And I came to her honestly and I gave her something she needed in that moment." He states while pouring us all a glass and I watch him carefully. His face is expressionless, yet his voice tells a tale.

"And what did you give her?"

"I gave her trust. Something you've just torn away from your relationship with her." I says looking up at me while swallowing his drink whole. "I didn't have to give her anything, but you were out of line today with how you treat her. You all were."

"You were there too." Peter says bluntly stating the obvious.

A slight grin grows on Oliver's face as he

pours himself another glass. "You're right. But she needed to know someone thought she could solve this case. And I just pointed her in the right direction." He says smugly.

My blood begins to boil even more every time I look at him. The grin on his face tells me he knows more than he's telling us. I know Peter expects me to trust him. But I don't and I don't think I will when it comes to Juliette.

"You better not put her in trouble." I warn between my teeth, and he laughs slightly taking another drink while making direct eye contact with me.

"Don't worry brother." He says sarcastically placing his hand on my shoulder and looking deep into my eyes. "You did that on your own."

CHAPTER FORTY-TWO

Juliette Sanders
Michigan, USA

I've paced around my room for the last thirty minutes. I can't seem to work out how I'm going to find information on Chase Hayward. Out of all the tasks Oliver could have given me, he gave me one of the hardest ones.

I lay down on my bed in the hopes that I'll have some sort of epiphany and I'll be able to find information no problem. A google search turned up nothing, not to mention I couldn't find anything about him on Facebook. There were quite a few Chase Haywards and none that I could say, yeah that looks like him.

I think about how much Clarissa has

manipulated and lied to everyone. Although there isn't physical proof yet to tie her to the murders, there is too much evidence, granted at this moment in time it's circumstantial that leads everything to her.

At first, I was just thinking I was being harsh, but now that she's sent me a letter in the middle of an investigation to taunt me into dropping the case. Well, that I think was incredibly foolish.

Surely, she would know I would link it back to her. Not to mention, why would she kill Damian's boyfriend? What did that prove? That she's dangerous, unhinged? Psychotic is the only word that comes to mind.

I need to come up with something convincing by the time I get on that plane to see Arielle tomorrow. Thankfully we are stopping off in London to pick up my Mum beforehand.

I honestly don't think I could do this without her, and I need to explain to her what's happened with Damian.

"Come on Sanders." I whisper in encouragement while tapping the side on my brain. My mind is coming up empty on ways I can try and find Chase Hayward.

Just as I think I'm about to admit defeat and ask for help from Oliver, my phone begins to ring. I lean over and pull it from my bag to notice a familiar name and I can't help but smile.

"Hello, Officer." I say, my grin getting wider as I hear him chuckle on the other end.

"Hello, Miss Sanders. I heard through the grape vine; you're looking for a certain person." He asks nicely. I put his number in my phone in case I needed anything before the school incident goes to trial next year.

"Well, you know me. I can't help but get myself in trouble. I'm looking for information on Chase Hayward." I say calmly and I hear him exhale loudly.

"What do you need to know about him? Also, dare I ask how you came across that name?"

"I did some digging, while you gave me access. Are you surprised?" He chuckles on the other end of the phone.

"Not in the slightest, Miss Sanders."

"You know something Officer Bradley, you're just holding off telling me." I state bluntly. He exhales, long and deep on the other end of the phone.

"You know I shouldn't be telling you this..." He pauses. "but you need to know who you are dealing with. Only on the promise, you don't tell Robert I was the one that gave you the information." He pleads, his voice getting slightly quiet giving me the indication he's in a space where he can't talk for long.

"Deal." I say quickly.

He chuckles on the other end, and it causes me to laugh a little. He knows how demanding I can be, and he helped me massively earlier on today with letting me get into the records. "I can't tell you much, and it's not because I can't, it's because we don't know anything. At this moment, Chase Elliot Hayward only turned up on the FBI's radar about two years ago. He and a bunch of others were trying to sell guns to an organised crime group in Illinois. Instead of infiltrating them, they've been keeping an eye on them. Purely because they came into the game with so many weapons just out of nowhere, so obviously it was something intriguing." He explains as I grab paper and a pen and note them down.

"Have you got photos of him? Also, any other information?" I ask lifting my head up to notice Spencer standing in the doorway.

"I can send you a few over. He can't be older than eighteen, and his group shouldn't be older than twenty or twenty-one. However, we can't find anything on them either. It is like they are ghosts before this." He explains as I watch Spencer take a seat on my bed. I watch him carefully as he takes my notebook out from underneath me and begins reading what I've jotted down so far. "He's covered head to toe in tattoos, most of them look like gang related and he has a woman's name tattooed on his arm, but we can't seem to find her anywhere."

My stomach drops. "What's the name?"

"Err…" He pauses while I hear some papers get moved around on the other end of the call. I take my notebook from Spencer giving him a warning look and he puts his hands up in defence before leaning back on the bed. "Alicia."

My heart stops. *Oh god.* "Alicia?"

"Yeah." He says slowly. "That same Alicia we are looking into."

I take a note of the name and write something and show Spencer. He reads it slowly, but once I see him grasp what it says, his eyes widen as he looks up at me hoping I'm joking.

"Juliette, why do you need to know about Chase Hayward?" He asks me honestly and I put my pen down on my notepad.

"Chase Hayward must be the ex-boyfriend of Alicia, because they had a child together. I found the birth certificate you tried to hide." I explain and I hear him chuckle on the other end of the phone.

"You know you are a nightmare for me." He laughs before taking a break. The silence is only temporary before I hear some people in the background. "However, I would still like to meet you and your Mum to talk about this when you get back?" He asks nicely and I can't help but smile. Officer Bradley has been great with us since the investigation, and I see myself looking up to him for a while on future cases once I officially get into the police force.

"Of course."

"Great. Send Damian my best. I'll send over what I can, but please be careful. I'll organise something for next week." He says sweetly.

We exchange goodbyes. I dare to tell him anything about Damian, because every time I think about it I want to cry.

"So, what was that about?" Spencer says after a moment of silence and I look up to him, his eyes searching for the answers that I don't want to give just yet.

"You can find out tomorrow." I say picking up my notepad and placing it back in my bag.

"We both know that's not fair. Why has Clarissa got another alias?" He asks again and I go and stand beside the door.

"Out." I instruct and he rolls his eyes before lying back on the bed in protest. "Spencer, get out. I've had quite a day and the last thing I need is for you to be a toddler." I state annoyed and he grins.

"I heard what happened at the police station." He says smiling wider. "Juliette, I'd be so fucking pissed if I was you. Robert is a dick for doing what he did!" He exclaims and take a deep breath. I know he's right.

"Your language is disgusting, you know." I state while leaning against the door.

"Sorry, *Mom*." He mocks, still while refusing to move. "Spill, Princess. Who was on the phone?"

"I'm not a Princess." I say walking back over to my bed and sitting down. He isn't going to leave how much I try.

"I believe you are. I mean by blood." He teases earning a slap from me. I'm not a Princess, nor will I ever be, and I don't want to be. That comes with too much drama, damage and destruction. I bit like the rest of my family.

"I'm going to ignore you till you leave." I say leaning back and folding my arms.

"Not happening." He states bluntly while sitting up. "Spill. What happened today? I've heard it through the grape vine, but I want the gossip from the actual source." He states.

"Is it because you need to know everything?" I ask bluntly and a hearty laugh explodes from him as he clutches his heart. I can't help but slightly giggle with him.

"We both know I do. Spill."

I take a long breath and decide rather than just keeping this to myself, I might as well tell someone I trust. But it needs to be in secret.

I get up and shut the door quickly, not before checking the corridor is clear and I can speak freely without someone lurking in the shadows.

"All of them showed up at the police station today and handed Clarissa in as a person of interest." I say while taking a seat back on my bed and I watch his eyes widen. "They labelled Carter as her partner in crime and didn't mention Rodger at all. If Damian found out it would crush him. He warned us. He warned us that they would protect him." I say to Spencer, and I watch his face go from a state of shock to anger within a millisecond.

He gets up from the bed and begins to march towards the door. I knew this would happen, but the last thing I need is for him to cause a fuss and by the look he might commit a murder.

"You going down there and making a scene is ridiculous. And if you think you're doing it on the plane… think again Spencer." I warn him standing firmly in front of the door.

He is seeing red; I know he is. I can't begin to understand what he is going through, his brother warned us that Robert and the rest of the family would protect Rodger and they did just that. They threw Carter into the firing line and I'm hoping and praying that the Detective sees right through them.

Detective Gomez has his own history with the Quinten's. My hope for the future of the case is that he sees that Carter didn't know Clarissa and more so that Carter has nothing to do with any of this and he is the victim, just as much as those other girls.

"I owe it to Damian-"

"We owe it to him. And to Carter. We will make sure Carter gets justice, and Damian gets closure." I say gripping onto his arm tightly forcing him to look down on me. His eyes are becoming blood shot, I don't even want to imagine how this would feel. But I know that if this was to happen to Ava, I would do the same thing. "I need you to trust me, Spencer. Please." I plead with him.

"What will happen to Rodger?" He asks as calm as he can be. It almost comes out as a whisper as a tear begins to fall down his cheek.

I shake my head. My voice breaking as I scramble to find the words. "I don't know." I whisper back.

He doesn't say anything, only holds my gaze for a few moments before making his way back to the bed. I notice as he takes his jacket off his gun in his back pocket. It's dangerous to give a man like Spencer a gun at the moment. He's going through so much, I would dread to think what he did if he was in the room with Robert, or any of the Quinten family.

He suddenly gets up from the bed and grabs his jacket and makes his way towards the door. "Come on." He instructs while opening the door and taking my hand, leading me down the corridor.

"Spencer where are we going?" I whisper as we begin to go down the stairs towards the garage.

"We're going to see Damian."

CHAPTER FORTY-THREE

Juliette Sanders

Michigan, USA

I get a strange and eery feeling while pulling up to the hospital. It has been a few days since I was last here. The same night that traumatised me.

I have been having flashbacks to the screaming, the amount of blood and the way Damian was. No doubting he is still hurting, but I'm hoping that they have managed to take some of the pain away.

Spencer gets out of the car first, making sure to come round to my side and place his gun in the glove box. "Robert will kill me but fuck it."

I roll my eyes; his language is worse when he's here. "Language, Spencer."

"Yes, Princess." He mocks as we walk up the stairs. The air is slightly cooler tonight. I pull my coat closer to me as we walk into the hospital.

Spencer greets with receptionist with a smile as the door shuts behind me. The walls are white and it's clean, like squeaky clean.

"Spencer Williams. Here to see Damian Williams." He announces as we approach the desk. The receptionist gives us a smile before pushing the visitors book towards us.

"Sign in Mr Williams. Your friend won't need to." She says warmly before going back to her computer and typing. I look over to Spencer while he signs his name and pushes the book back gently to the receptionist.

She hands us both lanyards and we place them round our necks and look at her for the next step. "He's upstairs in room 225. He's just had his medication, so he is stable and coherent. But the Doctor says please don't ask him anything to do with what might trigger him." She speaks calmly before raising a hand hinting for us to go right.

I look up at Spencer who only gives her a smile and begins to walk in the direction we were instructed. "Spencer, why wasn't I allowed to sign in? Surely that's against hospital rules."

As we reach the end of the hall and to the sign that says stairs, he opens the door for me, looking beyond me making sure no one can hear him. "Because if that Detective friend ever worked out that Damian and Carter were dating, they would come to speak to him. And no doubt will want to see who has come to see him and I don't think you would want your name to be on there would you?" He questions smugly.

I can only nod, as I walk through the door and make my way up the stairs. Spencer is very right. The last thing I need is for Detective to find out I'm friends with the Williams or that I am a Quinten. That would seriously put a spanner in the mix.

The corridor is cold, quiet. If this was a scene in a horror or paranormal movie something would pop out with how eery it feels.

To no surprise as we approach number 225, the room is at the end of the hall. The best of course. Robert wouldn't have anything less. Spencer takes a moment to compose himself. I can't understand how hard this is for him. His youngest brother in a place like this. None of us seen this coming.

"Remember what she said. Don't mention you know who." He mutters quietly before opening the door with the fakest smile, I have ever seen.

As we enter the room it feels warmer than

the corridor and I feel somewhat grateful for the heat. Damian smiles as we approach him, and I put on a fake smile too in the hopes he is so drugged up he can't tell that I'm faking.

"Hi." He greets us warmly while looking between both Spencer and I. Spencer's smile can only be described as demonic. I can't be sure if in the space of five minutes a ghost has taken over his body and possessed him.

"Hi back." I say trying to ignore Spencer as I take a seat at the bottom of the bed. "How are you doing?" I ask nicely as he takes my hand in his and squeezes tight.

"Better. Although I feel lonely." He whines a little and I hear Spencer clear his throat from beside me.

"Are you forgetting I have been sat here all day beating your ass at cards or have you suddenly got amnesia?" He teases causing Damian to laugh slightly.

He holds on tightly to his side, the one he was shot at before glaring at his brother. "You know you aren't meant to make me laugh. It still hurts, no matter how much medication they give me." He teases slightly while squeezing my hand. The smile he gives me gives me a flashback to the other night of him inconsolable on the floor. I try to shake the feeling of sadness from me while he looks at me, but by the drop in his smile, I know that he knows somethings wrong.

"Stop." He pleads and I narrow my brows slightly. "I know what you're thinking about and I'm sorry." He apologises. I look over at Spencer, slightly confused about what Damian is referring to. But by the look on Spencer's face, he hasn't got a clue either. "I know you would have my best interests which is why you asked Robert to put me here." He says honestly. "I needed a break I was feeling overwhelmed, used and I was heartbroken. I-" He pauses before taking a breath and continuing. "I just can't remember why I was so sad... or angry." He smiles between Spencer and me.

A wave of dread comes over me as I realise that Damian has no clue what happened in the woods. He doesn't remember probably because it's much too painful to talk about or even think about.

This man watched his boyfriend die in front of him. Then was ambushed with his brother in the place they were staying while on a what they call stakeout to keep an eye on another family. When really it was their own family, they needed to watch out for.

"I wouldn't worry about it, Damian." I express while gripping his hand tighter. "Everything is fine. You're safe." I say calmly while I watch his eyes flicker between mine. He's searching, or more so remembering.

"Dam?" Spencer asks while reaching over and shaking him. "You okay?" He says lightly shaking him.

"What did I say?" I say to Spencer who only looks at me with the same questionable look.

"Where's Rodger?" Damian asks after a moment. My heart is pounding out of my chest and with the dead silence in the room from Damian's question, I'm sure you can hear it.

"What?" Spencer asks him. This time Damian turns to him, his face filled with rage as he stares onto his brother.

"Where. Is. Rodger?" He says clearly. His eyes dark and filled with hate while I stare at Damian trying to work out what he possibly could remember that could have triggered this kind of response. "Did they protect him!" He shouts while still maintaining eye contact with Spencer. Something tells me that the bond between both of the brothers is sacred because with the was Spencer is almost leaning back in his chair frightened gives me the indication that Damian can tell when Spencer is lying.

"Yes." Spencer announces after a moment of silence. My jaw hits the floor as I look over to him. My eyes writing questions while I'm searching for the answers.

"And you let him?" Damian speaks clearly. Slowly turning his head towards me. "You said you wouldn't!" He screams at me, and I grip his hand tighter.

"And I won't." I say calmly while looking into his anger filled eyes. Behind the anger you can see the anguish of trying to remember. But you can also see the pain it would make him feel if he was to open up that wound. "I need to find evidence on him Damian and there is nothing." I state.

He doesn't move a muscle; he only takes a long deep breath through his nose while he closes his eyes. "I want to help." He pleads after a moment, but it comes out as a whisper. "I don't want more people to get hurt."

I raise my hands to place them gently on his face. A tear falls down his cheek. This man is hurting, and it pains me too.

Damian is my friend, and all I want to do is take that pain away. I'm sure Spencer wants the same.

He closes his eyes once again and in a brief moment I look over at Spencer whose eyes are fixated on Damian's face. He breaks from his worried stare to meet my eyes, agreeing with me that this is probably for the best and if Damian can remember and or bring himself to say it, we need him to say who shot Carter if he can remember.

"He wasn't wearing his ring." He speaks after a moment of silence and I turn to Damian, my brows frowned as I pray, he explains what he's talking about. "I noticed Rodger first. Carter—" He begins before dropping his head and placing them into his hands. "he had his back turned."

I lower my hands to hold his as he grips mine so tight his knuckles go white. "What happened after that?" Spencer asks.

"I shouted out for Rodger to stop." He begins to bawl. "But he pulled the trigger anyway and Carter fell to the floor. I couldn't take my eyes off Rodger, and I can remember he didn't have his ring on his middle finger." He explains softly and I grip his hand tighter.

"He might wear it on the other hand—"

"He is left-handed, and the gun was in his left-hand Jules." He says sternly, his voice clouded with annoyance. He takes a long deep breath closing his eyes once more. "Rodger shot Carter. But Clarissa was right behind him."

Spencer looks over to me and I catch his look, both of us stunned that Damian could remember clearly that Clarissa was there, the same night that Sophie Cutter was murdered and placed near where Carter was shot.

"Do you know why?" Spencer asks him eventually. The curiosity in his voice makes me wonder too.

"Something to do with loose ends. But I just ran back to you but then everything went black." Damian explains, suddenly he starts to shake as I grip one hand and Spencer takes the other one in his. "Did they shoot us?"

"More than likely. But what's worse is that the bullet is currently being processed and my guess it is going to match the gun that Clarissa got for her birthday off Oliver." Spencer explains.

Damian's eyes become saucers as he looks between us both, clearly confused. "What else aren't you telling me? Do you know why Clarissa and Rodger were there? Am I in danger?" He exclaims, his voice frantic.

"Dam, I promise you. You're safe. Rodger is on the list of people that can't come into the hospital, his photo is everywhere in the office so is Clarissa's. Besides, you will need to say to everyone that you don't remember anything?" Spencer explains, a determined look on his face as he leans into Damian a little.

"Why?"

I can't help but smile. Spencer is thinking like me. More than likely Robert is too. "Because when we eventually have enough evidence on him, we can bring you in as a witness. And he won't have a clue."

Damian nods as he slightly moves back in his bed. "So, what now?"

"Tell me about this ring. So, I know what I'm to listen in or look for."

Spencer takes a ring off his finger; one I've always noticed yet never asked about. "We all have one. It has our initials on."

"I wear mine around my neck on a chain. It's a little big and I can't be bothered to take it to be tightened. But Robert got us one when he took us in."

"So, Rodger will more than likely know it's missing?"

"Oh absolutely. He cherished that ring when we got it, we all did." Spencer explains while looking over at Damian. "How you feeling now?"

"Better." Damian answers honestly. "I don't know why I bottled it all."

"You were scared. I would be too." I say softly, gripping his hand again.

"I never get scared." He jokes a little before looking at me. "I wanted to tell you. I just didn't know how." He says sheepishly before looking down.

"Damian, you did tell me." I explain softly and I watch him slowly lift his head, his dark brows frowning as he looks back up at me.

"When?"

"When Spencer took me back to school and you got out of the car to talk to me. You said, and I quote – "'They have always teased me about girls and how I'll never be able to have a girlfriend or be able to talk to a girl. When in reality I didn't want to.'"

Damian begins to laugh, tilting his head back as he clutches onto his chest. "Wow," He says between the chuckles. "I did didn't I."

Laughter fills the room, and it makes my heart jump for joy. A few days ago, I didn't think that we would see Damian this awake, aware or even alive. He was so upset and broken about Carter and the betrayal of his older brother that I couldn't even imagine how he must have been feeling.

We decide this is the best time to say goodbye. Damian says he will come see me as soon as he is allowed, but he does want to see what kind of monstrosity of a dress they put me in when I arrive in Haroux.

As we leave down the steps of the hospital I am greeted with a wave of dread as I notice another car parked right next to Spencer's. Black tinted windows, a big, large SUV; it is definitely a Quinten car.

My heart begins to pound as I watch the door

open, and Robert's face appears in front of me. A few seconds later, so does Peter's. "If you wanted to see him, you should have just asked. I would have taken you." He speaks calmly while placing his hands tightly together in front of him.

"Don't you trust me, Robert?" Spencer questions and rightly so.

"Of course, I do Spencer. However, I do know Juliette and she would have told you about what happened today at the police station, and I could understand if the anger you felt towards me might cause you to do something... irrational." He teases a little. I feel my blood begin to boil as I roll my eyes away from Robert.

"What kind of irrational thing would I apparently do? Put her on the next flight to London, away from your crazy ass? Maybe." Spencer mocks back to get a rise out of Robert but his face is stone cold. "How dare you do what you did today. Damian said you would protect him, and I thought you wouldn't. But I was once again proven wrong." He bites back at him.

The Quinten brothers exchange a look and then focus their attention back on Spencer. "We need evidence in order to prove it was him. There was too much against Clarissa, and besides I have every intention on keeping Juliette safe."

"Well, I bet she sure feels safe when you raised a serial killer. Four girls dead and you—"

Spencer stops before I decide to stop their little bicker.

"Stop. I'm getting tired of the bickering." I say walking towards Spencer's car. I quickly decide to turn back around, seeing clearly that they are all looking at me. "Were you just following us?"

"Well, I went up to your room and couldn't find you. But your phone wouldn't stop ringing." He says while pulling my phone out of his jacket pocket. "You might want to call the Detective before he decides to track your phone." He says walking in my direction and handing me the phone.

I quickly turn around from them and click the Detective's contact on my phone. I listen for the rings, but none come as he answers almost immediately. "Hey kid, you okay? I've tried calling a few times." He says his voice I can tell is filled with worry.

"Sorry, I was packing." I lie. God that feels wrong. "Is everything okay?"

"Well, I thought I would tell you some news I have. This first bit is a bit gruesome so I'm sorry. But the word traitor on Sophie Cutter's head was carved after she died. More than likely, it was done at the crime scene." He explains and I place my hand over my mouth.

Sophie Cutter's death is eating me up inside because there was a taunt left purposefully on her body. What Clarissa left for me. She knew it would torture the parents who probably wouldn't want to see their daughter like that or have that lasting memory.

"You okay kid?" He asks softly when I realise, I wasn't answering.

"I guess. I just feel guilty." I explain quietly, not wanting the Quinten's to hear too much. But the area is so quiet you can hear a pin drop.

"Nothing you could have done would have prevented this, Jules. You're doing great." He encourages which does put a small smile on my face.

"What else did you find?" I ask wanting to wrap this call up as quickly as possible.

"Some of the crime scene techs found something in a puddle. Now it has some initials on it, but we can't seem to place who it would belong too, however unless she wore it on her thumb, it is too big to fit her fingers." He explains and I feel my brows frown.

"What would be too big?"

"The ring they found." He explains and I feel my heart drop but also loop back round with joy. I turn my attention immediately to Spencer who meets my eyes with confused ones. He begins to search my face for any answer's as to why I'm looking at him like a crazy person.

"What are the initials?" I ask in the hopes that Spencer will catch on, and after a few moments and a few confused exchanges with Peter and Robert; he does and relief washes over his face.

'They found it?' He mouthed to me, and I nod before turning back around to focus on the conversation.

"RW, WR. We aren't exactly sure. We can probably guess it is some boyfriends, but we also threw out the possibility that she would have had help to carry Sophie Cutter's body to where she was left. Like we said the other day, we don't think she did it alone." He explains calmly.

My heart is pounding out of my chest, and I begin to feel sick. Because there is evidence that can now link Rodger to Sophie Cutter's murder. I don't believe he killed her; however, I do believe he helped Clarissa. And that shows with the team now finding Rodger's ring.

"More than likely." I say after a moment. On the other end of the phone, I hear the rustling of papers.

"I'll speak to the Quinten family when they get back from their trip and let you know. Maybe they will know the boyfriend." He questions and I look over at them. They haven't stopped staring at me, waiting for me to hang up.

"Let me know what they say." Only because I'm beginning to trust them less and less the more, I'm here.

"Hey kid –" He begins before stopping momentarily. "I just wanted to say thank you. Because over the past few weeks, er, it's been great having another set of eyes on this." He says nearly as a whisper, probably not wanting the other Detective's to hear. "It's not going to be the same without you here." He admits.

My heart shatters into a tiny million pieces. The Detective has his struggles, like many people do. One of which he trusted me with, and I will keep that so close to me and cherish the trust he has in me. Yet I can't help feeling like a hypocrite. Right now, I want to tell him everything. That I'm the secret love child of a mafia leader and a Queen yet that would leave him in anguish and that is not what I want.

"I'm going to miss you too." I admit with a smile. "You know, for someone who was extremely against the idea of having a kid be their assistant you seem to have warmed up to me Detective grumpy." I mock, slightly chuckling.

My laughter only escalates when I hear him laugh on the other end. "Yeah, well what can I say. I have a great partner."

The gesture makes me smile and I quickly look back on the Quinten's who are finally looking annoyed with me and are clearly wanting to end this conversation.

"See you soon Detective."

I can feel the warmth on the other end of the phone as I feel the conversation come to a close. "See you around, kid."

I smile before hanging up and putting my phone into my coat pocket.

"Are they sure?" Spencer asks as I walk towards his car. I give him a nod, not wanting to speak to the Quinten's right now about the find in the police department. I know I'm going to have to mention it. Yet, I know I'll have to on the plane.

"I'm going to trust you'll tell me what they've found Juliette?" Robert asks. The smugness in his voice gets right under my skin as I turn around to face him while opening the car door.

"Yes. I'll tell you. But when I want to. And don't think to go and sabotage the investigation. Because it won't be worth it." I warn before getting in Spencer's car.

He's not far behind me, before he gets in the car. Shuts the door and begins driving, leaving both Robert and Peter standing there. Because they are both stone cold, I can't tell if I what I said bothered them or not, but I couldn't care less.

"They found it?" Spencer asks again and I turn my head towards him.

"Yep. Only one problem—" I say while getting comfortable in my seat. "It was found in a rock pool and had been there for a few days. Meaning…"

"No DNA. Shit."

"Language."

"Sorry. So, what now?"

I think for a second. I know there is two options here. One being I tell the Detective everything which deep down I know that isn't the option I'm going to do. "We're going to have to trust that when we get back from Haroux, that Robert does the right thing."

CHAPTER FORTY-FOUR

Juliette Sanders

Michigan, USA

The next morning is as busy as to be expected. Robert wasn't joking when he said we were leaving early. I got woken up at 3AM from Spencer shaking me like a crazy person screaming "WAKE UP PRINCESS! IT'S TIME TO GO!"

I've never thought about laying my hands on another human being until that moment. But I decided not to give Spencer a black eye.

He's very excited to see Haroux and meet Arielle, as is the rest of the family. Robert more so than anybody.

He has ordered ten new suits this past week. From Hugo Boss, Armani and god knows who else. I've not been one for designer items, however he decided to have some kind of fashion show last night past my room in the attempt to build a better bridge than the one that was broken.

Ignored every single one, but made sure to make a face when it was one that I thought he looked good in. I owe him that. He's seeing Arielle after all.

Yet, I'm unsure on what it will prove. He knows she's married, but I seem to think that if she sees him again, she will leave her life in Haroux for him. I don't know her at all, so I can't comment on whether or not she would do that.

I mean I'd hope not.

She has a family, a life, a country to think about. I highly doubt she would decide to put that all in jeopardy for the Quinten's.

All she did in the letter was say how perfect her life is. I mean I see it as prison, but then again, I'm the abomination.

The drive to the airport goes by so quickly considering I slept through most of the journey. I'm gently shaken awake by Felicity who gives me a warm smile while I adapt to my surroundings. "You can sleep on the plane sweety."

I pull myself together and get out of the car

and make my way up to the private terminal. Of course, they are going through their own security who don't even bother checking anything, just wish all of us a safe flight for London.

Boarding the plane, I make sure to get a window seat, in the hopes that no one sits next to me. My attire for this plane is comfy and I have a change of clothes in my bag for when we are getting close to Haroux. It had to fit within the guidelines of their code of conduct. A dress, long and flat shoes. Something that covered my shoulders and my hair had to be up in a bun. So many rules for someone who is only coming to greet the Queen as a courtesy. I don't want to go, and I'm debating fleeing the plane as soon as we get back into London.

My hope for a peaceful trip is cut short when Oliver sits next to me. He's dressed in black, of course. His hair slightly gelled, probably from yesterday still. He doesn't say anything to me as I look over at him. Only holds up a folder and a smug look on his face.

My guess? He found Dracov Hayward. Of course, he did.

As the rest of the family get settled and I watch them board the last few suitcases onto the plane, I think of how quickly these few weeks have gone. It doesn't seem two minutes since I left for Michigan with all three Williams brothers and I'm returning back to London with only one.

My Mum is going to freak when she realises that Damian isn't here. And what happened to him.

Clarissa still hasn't been located; however, Serena is still at the house waiting for someone to spot her. More than likely, they will find her. But, my guess, is they probably won't. She knows how to hide. And better yet. She's hidden a daughter.

Rodger disappeared the other night while he was meant to be on his task, no doubt to follow Clarissa and he probably thought that he was suspected in Carter's death and the shooting of both the Williams brothers. Spencer, however, was not cleared to fly by the doctor they hired. They assured he needed to be on more rest. Spencer told him to shove it.

The plane takes off and I clutch on for dear life. Spencer laughing at me while seated across from me. For someone who was the grumpiest person around a few months ago. He really is a teddy bear.

As people get comfortable in their seats, coffees and a bunch of different breakfast options start filling the tables. Its 4:30am. The last thing I can think about is food. I want sleep. But I also want to know where Dracov Hayward has been hiding and how the world Oliver found him, when Sapphire still hasn't been found after all this time.

A bunch of conversations begin as people fill their plates and drink their coffee. That sweet smell that I remember from my first day at the police station.

I'm going to miss Detective Gomez. But I'm also going to miss Damian. Alexis didn't really want to say goodbye, however my goodbye from Nathaniel was another big bear hug as he spun me round this morning. Told me to take no rubbish from the Queen and to make him proud. From a far I watched Robert roll his eyes and that made me laugh even more.

"So, Juliette," Robert begins while finishing his coffee. "anything you'd like to share with the group?" He asks curiously but I watch him also glance over at Oliver who suddenly smirks.

I decide to start with the more shocking news. I go into my bag and pull out my own file and my notebook. "When you gave me a list of aliases yesterday, I eventually worked out that the ones you gave me, or some of them at least, were fake. I begin to say looking up at Robert directly. He puts his lips together and I can see him try not to laugh. "But someone gave me the truth, and that I greatly appreciated." I say looking over at Oliver who glares down at me to just continue. "Alicia Brady Allington." I say confidently and I watch Robert's eyes widen, turning his direction over to Oliver, who grins from ear to ear. "Thanks for creating a really thorough and fake rap sheet for Clarissa's alias though, I saw right through it, and I think the Detective will too."

Robert's face is a picture as he sits, taking long deep breaths trying to control his anger. "Go on," He encourages while getting comfortable in his seat.

"Now, I got stonewalled when I put Alicia Brady Allington to the database. I didn't have access. But it turns out that we weren't the only ones looking into her." I explain while pulling out the birth certificate and keeping it close to my chest. "Did you know that Officer Bradley and the team over in London were looking into her too?" I question. I kept thinking last night that Robert probably knew about the investigation into Clarissa over in London. But by the look on his face, that is filled with fury, he hadn't a clue about it and his face tells me the whole picture.

"I didn't." He answers as calmly as he can. His chest is rising, and he is clearly annoyed. I can't tell who the feeling is towards – me, Oliver, Clarissa or Officer Bradley. I can put my money on that it's all of us.

Looking over at Spencer, I feel guilty for just dropping this on him the way I am. But between Oliver and I we are the only ones on this plane that knows who Sapphire's father is. I look over at Oliver, hoping he will just explain. Afterall, he has completely lied to his family for months about Sapphire.

"So, you're going to hate me. However," He begins sitting forward leaning onto his thighs with his forearms. "I may have been the one to help Clarissa hide Sapphire."

The only sound that can be heard is Spencer choking on a croissant. Felicity pats his back hard as his signals to her that he's alright. "You?" He slightly chokes as he opens a bottle of water next to him and takes a drink.

"What can I say? Uncle of the year." Oliver jokes and I can't help but roll my eyes.

"So, you helped hide an innocent baby with our now presumed serial killer niece. That's great of you." Felicity says sarcastically, the frustration clearly plastered on her face.

"If I knew she was a killer, do you really think I'd help her?" Oliver says in his defence, and I hear Peter scoff from beside him on the other isle.

"But you still helped her hide the child. I have been searching for Sapphire—"

"Jade." Oliver buts in looking over at me.

"Sorry, what?" Peter asks, stunned by Oliver's interruption.

"Her name is legally Jade Allington. Which is why you couldn't find her." I say looking down at the birth certificate in my hand. This piece of paper is going to shatter Spencer's heart.

I watch Peter place his head in his hands and sit there for a few moments. "What is in your hands Juliette?" He groans pursing his lips looking over at me.

"The name of Jade or Sapphire's dad is on the birth certificate, that was filed." I say slowly looking over at both Peter and Robert.

Robert's breathing only gets heavier with frustration as he continues to glare over at Oliver. If we weren't on a plane and I wasn't here; he would be screaming at Oliver or doing something worse than that.

"Who is it?" He asks after a few moments then turning his attention to me. I decide to turn my eyes to Spencer who is taking yet another sip of his water. He places his water down and I hand over the birth certificate to Spencer.

"Rodger is listed as the father." I say softly and I watch as Spencer's eyes widen, reading the certificate. The whole plane is completely silent. I expected outrage, however by the silence we have fell into, I'm going to assume that some of the presumed that he was.

"I said it." Felicity is the first one to speak. The whole family turning to her. "I said that they were too close." She explains, taking a sip elegantly from her coffee.

"It was always a possibility." Robert explains looking over at Spencer who is sitting in silence, staring at the certificate. "Spencer," He says softly to him. "we all knew that he might have been, we all had a conversation about it."

Spencer hands me back the certificate and sits back in his chair. The pain on his face is so hard to see. "Doesn't make it any easier." He says, clearing his throat. "So, Rodger has something to do with Sapphire—I mean Jade's disappearance?" He asks curiously, looking more over to Oliver than myself.

"I think he helped her, but that can't be proven." Oliver explains to him. His voice is softer this time and I look over to see him scouring Spencer's face, his eyes filled with concern. No matter how Oliver reacts around the kids there is no point in denying he has a soft spot for every single one of them. But a severe hatred for me. Which, considering he helped me find evidence against Clarissa, I'm not too bothered about. I don't see the need in trying to get him to like me, not that I had already started.

"Is that what you two were discussing in the study?" Robert asks, his eyes darting between us both.

"Amongst other things." Oliver says before sitting back and giving me a signal to continue.

"How much did you know about Clarissa

and Tommy before you adopted them?" I ask him honestly.

By the look on his face, he is taken back by my question, as is Peter. "What are you implying?" He questions, his tone harsh. "That I adopted two kids that I knew absolutely nothing about. I know what I was told, and they were old enough to tell me if need be. But they were very damaged." He practically shouts. The rest of the plane just listens to him. "Juliette, what is in that file for gods' sake. I'm sick of the games." He shouts to me.

I practically launch the folder over to him and he catches it in a scramble. "Alicia Allington had a son just before you adopted her." I say sitting back in my chair.

"No, she didn't." He quickly answers, looking over at Peter. "I would have known."

"But you didn't." I snap back, my tone annoyed. I don't like how Robert is speaking to me as if I'd lie. "Open the folder." I instruct.

I watch as he hesitates and then opens the folder to reveal the very birth certificate I found yesterday when Officer Bradley let me look into Alicia's background. "She had a son called Dracov Chase Hayward. The father, Chase Hayward is on every single government watch list there is. He's someone Scotland Yard, and MI6 have been dying to get on something, yet they know it's going to lead to something so much bigger." I say while opening my bottle of water and taking a drink.

The plane is silent for the better half of ten minutes. Robert is completely stunned that this missed his radar, or if he knew about it – he's doing a very good job at acting like this is news.

"I just have one question," Spencer speaks in the silence. We all turn to look at him, there is a slight smile on his face causing a wave of dread to fall upon me. Oh god. "Why did she name him Dracov?" He asks.

I look around the plane and see a slight smile grow on Oliver's lips. "You know who her favourite character from *Harry Potter* is right?" He tries not to laugh.

It takes me a moment, but then the realisation hits me and the rest of the plane.

"Oh, dear god." Robert says under his breath, placing his head in his hand.

"She named her child after Draco Malfoy?" I ask pressing my lips together. I have to admit, she has some interesting names for her children.

Spencer begins to hysterically laugh as does the rest of the plane. I feel like I'm missing some sort of inside joke, yet I can't deny – her naming her child after the misunderstood character in the biggest franchise in the world really isn't surprising to me.

The laughter begins to die down, and it does

create a warmer atmosphere on the plane rather than tension you can cut with a knife. "So where is the child?" Peter asks looking over at Oliver. "Did you help hide this one too?"

I press my lips together holding in the laughter that desperately wants to escape my lips.

"No," He says sarcastically before opening his own file. "From what I can find, the kid was put into the system in Boston. He's never been adopted." He says while handing over the file to Robert.

Both Oliver and I lock eyes. He knows that if I was old enough, I'd be on the first flight to Boston to take that child home. I don't doubt for a second that once Clarissa has been caught and convicted, the same with Chase Hayward. I have full faith in both the Detective and Officer Bradley.

"He's in a group home for boys. I'll have one of my men from standby to go out and keep an eye on him in case Clarissa or Chase go to collect him or even visit him. They might lead us to Sapphire." Robert explains placing the file down in front of Oliver. "Good work. Both of you." He applauds. Oliver and I exchange a look of confusion before looking back over at Robert. Rolling his eyes, he picks up his water bottle and takes a drink. "Don't make me regret praising you both." He says annoyed.

Oliver and I chuckle together. Looking out

the window, I reflect on the strange few weeks I've had. Never did I think I'd be investigating another case; I just hope that justice is served soon and Clarissa is caught for what she's done. Even Rodger needs to be held accountable for what he did to Damian, and Spencer, his own brothers. But also, Carter. He was innocent in this. So were the girls.

A shiver goes down my spine. That could have been me. Clarissa has so much hatred towards me, I don't doubt for a second that she's plotting something against me. I just hope she's caught before that happens.

Fourteen and I'm related and being targeted by a serial killer. What a way to sum up the summer holidays.

CHAPTER FORTY-FIVE

Robert Quinten

London, United Kingdom

I'm nervous.

And I don't get nervous often.

For the first time in fourteen years, I'm about to come face to face with a woman I owe so much too.

I'm absolutely terrified, and I know I shouldn't be. She's a tiny little thing who I've spoken to a few times before Juliette arrived in Michigan. I remember her being so sweet and so kind that I know this is all in my head.

The one thing I do worry about is how she's

about to find out about everything. Juliette said that she wants to be honest and not lie to her Mum. Therefore, Amy is about to find out about Clarissa, Damian and Rodger and I think deep down that is what I'm most nervous about.

I finish off my bottle of water before placing it into the bin next to me. We should be in London in no more than five minutes and the lower we get to the ground, the more I want to jump out of the plane than deal with the situation. Looking over at her, I try to listen in as her and Oliver exchange theories as to where Chase Hayward could be.

Am I surprised my daughter has another child? Absolutely, yet; nothing she does surprises me anymore.

Tommy had never been close with any of us, nor had he ever tried. He's extremely distant, he didn't try to bond with me, or any of my siblings. The only people he seemed to get on with before he left was Clarissa and Marcus.

Yet, Marcus would never call him his brother. Whenever Tommy was mentioned, he would use his name. I'm grateful for my children as they all eventually made an effort and got to know one another. My whole intention when I adopted my children was to give them a better life than they would have had in the system.

Some would call me a hypocrite. Because I put my own daughter into the system then adopted others out of it. But I gave her to a loving home, with parents that adore her and a sister who looks up to her. I admire how close she is with her Grandparents, her Grandad especially.

"Jules, are you excited to see your Mom?" Felicity asks her and a grin appears on her face. Her smile is infectious, and in this moment, she looks like a young Arielle.

"Very. I think she will be excited to see me too." She says, still grinning as she looks over at Spencer. Her friendship with Spencer is something I don't think any of us saw coming. He's a stubborn mule, especially when it comes to opening up and being himself. He has always had a front on, and I know that one day he will want to help assist in the running of the business or possibly taking it over once I retire.

He's always proved he is capable of doing so, he's always been one of my choices for who I would want to handle the business. Oliver would burn it to the ground if he could, and Peter has always said he never wanted to run it. I could leave it to my sisters, yet I know that deep down Felicity is one day wanting to have a family of her own and Serena... it wouldn't be that I didn't trust her it would have been that I wouldn't know where it would stand after she took charge of it.

As the plane hits the tarmac, I feel my nervousness grow within. I know how fierce Amy

Sanders can be. She is raising two children on her own and she lost her husband, she is going to be my worst nightmare once she finds out Juliette has been working a case and the extent of it.

"Wait here." I tell Juliette as I release myself from my seat belt and head up to the front of the plane. My heart is pounding out of my chest. Undoubtedly, she is walking towards the plane with one of our security.

I watch the stairs fall down to the tarmac, and sure enough, walking towards me is Mrs Amy Sanders.

I walk down the stairs slowly to greet her and she meets me with a smile. I give the security detail a nod before looking down at Amy. She hasn't grown at all since I last saw her fully. She's still barely 5ft 5, yet her personality is bigger than she ever will be.

"Hello, Robert." She greets me. "You've grown since the last time I saw you." She teases causing me to chuckle slightly.

"I don't want to be rude Amy, but I cannot say the same for you." I say quietly. She's small, but hell, she frightens the life out of me. She's quiet for a few seconds and I feel as though I have overstepped my mark.

All of a sudden, she begins to laugh as she puts her bag on her shoulder as I notice it is falling off. "I can't say I disagree." She chuckles before opening her arms indicating I'm welcome to a hug.

I greatly accept it, the hug she gave me all those years ago stuck with me as one of the best hugs I could have ever had. And this one is no different. She's warm and she's welcoming. That is something I've always admired about her.

"It's good to see you." She expresses, exiting out of the embrace. "However, I feel as though I'm going to regret sending her to see you. I want to know everything." She says sternly and I feel my heart sink. I know I can't keep anything from her, after all – she is Juliette's mother.

"Of course." I say as I extend my arm for her to go up the stairs first. She doesn't say anything more only makes her way up the stairs, a small smile on her face.

I give a nod to the stewardess to close the plane door which she agrees as we make it onto the plane.

Juliette runs into Amy's arms, and I watch her grip her so tightly. That is something I know I would always envy her of her relationship with Juliette, the sense of unity that I knew I would never have with her. That I will always be jealous of.

"I've missed you!" Amy exclaims while looking Juliette over. "Are you okay?" She asks her, and I see Juliette look over at me, who stands behind Amy. I give her an encouraging nod.

First and foremost, Amy is Juliette's mother, and I would hate for Amy to feel like we never took care of her while she was in our care. I mean she might have worked a case that may or may not have caused her severe emotional distress, witnessed a blood bath when Spencer and Damian came in shot, witnessed Damian's break down and lastly walked in on a crime scene. I'm going to be paying for extensive therapy.

"I've missed you." Juliette repeats as her Mum looks around saying hello to everyone, including Oliver who greets her with a smile Once she notices Spencer her face settles as he gives her a warm hug.

The angle is awkward, and he winces ever so slightly, and she immediately pulls back and asses him. "Don't worry. I'm all good." He reassures her, yet her face just sway away from the state of panic.

"Amy, sit here." Oliver instructs moving away from the seat and taking a seat opposite Peter. I exchange a look with Peter, this isn't like Oliver to be this welcoming, let alone smile. No one says anything as Amy looks around the plane.

"Private jet?" She asks after a moment as I usher Oliver to move along one, he moves along, no fight, as I take a seat where he was. I exchange a look to Amy, raising my eyebrow, kind of hinting at anything else. "Of course." She mutters.

Suddenly her brows frown and she looks around the plane, undoubtedly searching for that one person. "Where is Damian?" She asks alarmed as she looks over at Spencer.

Looks are exchanged from all over the plane. We were hoping that she wouldn't have noticed as quickly, but then, she did assist Juliette in the case at her school.

"We have quite a bit to tell you." Juliette says as she looks softly over at her Mum. "Please don't be mad."

Amy takes a long exhale, turning her glare round at me. I have stared cold blooded killers in the face, and god knows what else. But Amy Sanders is a woman I am deeply afraid of.

She slowly turns back at Juliette, her eyes fuelled with fire and Juliette meets her with sorry eyes. "I can't make any promises. So, you better start talking."

CHAPTER FORTY-SIX

Robert Quinten

P lacing her head in her hands, Amy lets out a long groan "I need a glass of wine." She says almost as a mutter. I feel Oliver shift beside me, pressing his lips hard against each of them to stop the laugher from coming out.

Exchanging a glare, he turns to look out of the window, hopefully he will keep quiet and not make me bringing him turn into a mistake. "For god's sake, why would you keep all of this from me?" She exclaims to Juliette and me. "The rules were that you were to tell me anything that happened. You just so happened to not tell me that Clarissa, who is one of your daughters," She says while pointing at me. "is potentially the killer,

Rodger is the father to Clarissa's baby girl that you are yet to find, the one that you," She says pointing her finger over at Oliver. His eyes go wide as the small smile that was only on his face moments ago, turns into sheer panic. "helped hide, because you felt you could *relate* to her." She mocks him and he stares at us, his hands extended with a look that says, 'why is she picking on me?'

"She's also had another baby with a gun dealer. She sent you a tormenting letter that she left on a poor girl's body back in America." She begins to ramble while she looks over at Spencer. "You and Damian were shot by your brother, who may I say, is an unhinged little git," She expresses harshly. "Damian is gay, which I had a feeling he might have been and had a secret boyfriend who Rodger murdered, and you walked into the crime scene. Lastly, Damian is in a mental hospital while he recovers the traumatic ordeal. Is there *anything* I've missed?" She exclaims loudly, her pale pink face now flushed as she completes her rant. No one dares open their mouth, because if they did, she might bite our heads off.

The expressions on the plane are priceless. Juliette's eyes are going to pop out of her head at her mother's outburst, Spencer is holding his hand over his mouth I'm assuming to not laugh, Oliver is doing the same. Felicity has a smile on her face that she's thoroughly enjoying this. Peter has chin listening in intensely to Amy's meltdown. She takes a long deep breath looking over at Juliette. "And now we are going to meet your birth mother who just so happens to be the Queen of a small island." She says slumping back in her chair.

Felicity stands up ever so slowly as she gives everyone a smile. "I think I'm gonna get that wine now." She says walking towards the back of the plane.

"Thank god!" Amy exclaims, her head in her hands as she slowly moves down the chair. She's still processing everything, and in all honesty, I don't think any of us have processed it properly. Juliette being one of the main ones. She's fourteen yet has seen so much she shouldn't have.

"Juliette," I issue her. She breaks away her worried stare of her mother to look over in my direction. "we will be landing soon; do you want to go and get changed?" I ask her.

She nods slowly before hugging her mother slightly and picking up her bag and exiting the isle, making her way down to the back bedroom.

When I see that the door is closed and I'm sure she won't be able to hear me, I lean over and place my hand on Amy's leg. A sign of reassurance and I'm hoping she sees it that way. Her eyes peek out between her fingers while she looks down at my hand and then back up at my face.

"I will never let anything happen to her. None

of us will. You have my word she will be safe when she is in my care." I reassure her removing my hand from her leg while she sits up. "None of us expected Clarissa to be a killer, or did we expect her to torment and drag Rodger into her crimes." I explain to her.

She listens quietly, the tears beginning to form in her eyes. Peter is quick to hand her a tissue while like clockwork, Felicity hands her a small glass of wine. She takes it gratefully and takes quite a large sip, easing her nerves.

We sit quiet for a moment, I'm hoping she will express how she is feeling, because I would hate to have this dwell on her on the trip.

"It is just a lot to process." She says quietly, taking a sip of her wine. "A lot has happened in the last few months that wasn't meant to. You were meant to stay away from her." She says, her tone harsh and firm. "Yet, she was looking forward to this trip. And from the sounds of it, you handed her off to a Detective and allowed her to get involved in a murder case." She expresses while finishing her wine and placing the glass on the table. "I know deep down you thought you were doing her a favour, all of you." She says while looking around at the rest of us on the plane. "But all you did was fuel the energy in her that makes her think this is normal. It's not." She says harshly.

I shift in my seat uncomfortably. "Amy, I

know it seems that we didn't spend any time with her—"

"You didn't." She cuts me off. "However, I can't say I'm surprised. I wanted to believe that you were different Robert, that you hadn't subjected yourself to your criminal ways and you were going to actually get to know her." She says leaning forward on the table. "But the second you found out about Arielle being a Queen was the second the only person you cared about in your relationship with her was you. And your needs. She is here doing this, for you." She expresses.

My heart beating out of my chest, I feel a great sense of guilt and shame. She was the only person I have ever trusted to give me the truth. And she has. And it fucking hurts.

"I have to protect her Robert; you should understand that. You gave me her to protect, to love and to raise." She explains. "Please let me do that. Please don't put fantasies in her head that she can become a Detective over in America, or that she will be able to have a relationship with Arielle, because I've heard about the letter and how it is the most self-absorbed thing that woman could have wrote. So please. Please when we leave Haroux in three days, you leave her to live her life. I'll do the parenting, and you go back to doing whatever you do. All of you." She finishes and I feel as though my world has just shattered around me.

Amy is a generous woman, and even I know with her sat in front of us that she's at her end. She can't cope with anymore. She is a parent, a single parent to two beautiful girls. Both she has raised to be wonderful, compassionate and caring kids. And Juliette is the light of her life. And the life of mine. She is very much right. This whole trip is to feed my selfish needs of seeing Arielle again and hoping we will be a happy family, completely ignoring the fact that Juliette isn't a baby anymore, she is a teenager, a kind and generous one. But also, completely ignoring the fact she has a family. She has Amy, Ava, Grandad Norman and her Grandma. She has great friends around her that are the complete opposite of her in ways of thinking and ideals on the world.

Just as I'm about to apologise, the door opens and looking up, I see Juliette in the most beautiful dress I have ever seen. He blonde hair, in a half up, half down style. She's dressed in a blue dress that goes down to her knees. Almost like a shirt type of dress, it comes together with a golden sash around her stomach and into a bow. On her feet are gold pumps that she had brought from home. She is wearing a necklace I sent her for one of her birthdays with her initial on. In this moment, she looks like no one other than herself. The similarities are there the same as Arielle. But right now, she looks more like a Sanders than a Quinten.

"Oh, darling you look wonderful." Amy says

getting up and giving her a hug. Her baby face looking over at me and I feel a sense of sadness wave over me. Her standing her, dressed to meet her birth mother makes me emotional. Something I don't do.

"You look beautiful, Juliette." I say softly, trying hard for my voice not to break as I extend my arms, hoping she might give me a hug.

I feel my heart leap for joy when she enters my embrace. I hug her tight. I'm so proud of her, and grateful that she came to this. Although she really doesn't want to be here. And since Amy's harsh realization, I'm debating telling the pilot to turn around and let Arielle get on with her ball.

She releases herself from my hug and looks over to Spencer. "Surely you aren't going dressed in that?" She teases him and the smile that was plastered on his face drops.

"Don't start with your attitude Sanders." He warns her playfully, moving past Felicity with his bag. "I have a low tolerance. I've had three coffees. And I need a minimum of five to not kill a small child." He says as a warning. His demeanour is playful as laughter erupts from everyone on the plane as he lightly shoves past her.

"I'll go in the bathroom and get changed if that's okay?" Amy asks and Felicity leads her with her bag as they both make their way to the front of the plane to use each of the lavatories.

"Come on, Oliver." Peter instructs while getting his bag from overhead. "We will get changed too; we should be landing in under fifteen minutes." They both make their way back to the room next to Spencer.

Leaving Juliette and I alone, she places her bag underneath her seat, sits down and puts her seatbelt on. The silence between us isn't awkward, but mutual.

I think she's nervous. She hasn't met Arielle, and in her head, she has a vision of someone who is selfish and only has one person in mind, herself.

"Do you think I'll regret coming here?" She asks softly.

With my heart beating out of my chest I decide to sit in the chair next to her. "I think that's for you to decide. Arielle is... unusual to say the least. I just hope that she treats you with the same kindness that you will show her. If she starts assuming things or oversteps the mark. Just give me a look. And I'll know." I reassure her.

She looks at me deeply, unsure on whether or not to say anything more. She decides not to when the door to the back room opens, and Spencer walks out. For the first time I think ever, I see the man in something other than the colour black. My jaw drops as he walks towards me. Juliette turns around, her eyes widening as Spencer stands and leans on the side of the chair. "Not one word."

He instructs before putting his bag above his seat and sitting opposite Juliette. His tattoos are on full display. He stands in white pants and a light blue denim shirt. Not Spencer's normal style either and I'm sure when Oliver and Peter return from the other room, he will probably be subjected to a couple of teasing comments.

Juliette presses her lips together while Spencer gets comfortable in his seat. Undoubtedly this is to make a good first impression. But it's nice to see him in something other than the colour of my soul.

Amy is the next to exit, her jeans and top that she wore a few minutes ago have been changed into a beautiful pink and white flowered dress and some sandals. Paired with gold jewellery, the outfit is very fitting and suits her lovely.

"You finally found an excuse to wear the dress!" Juliette exclaims with Amy giving her a big grin.

"It was about time it got used. It was catching dust, and this seemed like the perfect occasion to wear it." She says sitting next to Juliette and giving her a slight nudge. Her eyes catch Spencer in the corner. His tanned face glistening as he glares down at Amy. "Spencer, you look very smart." She compliments him, no sarcasm in her voice as she says it with a genuine smile.

"Thank you." He says honestly almost

bowing his head at her. Oliver and Peter are next to follow with Oliver dressed in a black shirt and black suit pants. His hair is slicked back and while staring him down I notice a new tattoo peeking out from the side of his shirt.

"New tattoo?" I ask him. It's one I haven't seen before and by the looks of it, it's still healing.

"Yeah." He says quickly pulling his shirt, so I don't see it. From what I could see it looked like numbers and with Oliver's track record of tattoos, it's always something meaningful. Our birthdays, the day he killed someone for the first time, our parents' names. The sentimental kind of stuff.

Peter on the other hand is as fresh and lively looking as Spencer. He's dressed in navy suit pants and a crisp white shirt. His hair is a slicked back as usual paired with his gold jewellery. "I've seen the tattoo. It's cute." He mocks Oliver nudging him ever so slightly. Oliver scoffs, pulling his shirt to cover the tattoo that is on his chest.

I decide with everyone now ready that I should probably get myself dressed to impress the Queen. Opting for a pale cream shirt and black dress pants and brogues, I make my way towards the back room and decide to get ready. We should be landing very soon, and the more we come closer to Haroux, the more I feel my stomach in knots.

Just hours ago, we were boarding this plane

to leave America to collect Amy. The uncertainty of finding out what has been going on with Juliette and Oliver had me unable to sleep all night, anxious to find out what they had been doing.

I look at myself in the mirror. I'm almost thirty-one yet with everything that's going on at the moment – I feel as though I've aged ten years. I have a few grey hairs now, nothing that can't be fixed with hair dye.

Doing up the last button on my shirt I think back to June, when Juliette first contacted me and how far we've come. I can understand where Amy is coming from. I'm also a parent to five other kids and I would feel the same way. With how some of the kids grew up, I've had to take precautions to make sure that they could never be found in case their birth parent did want to look for them. They were old enough to know that what their parents were doing wasn't right, and I saved them from that.

Amy is a mother first and foremost and I have to respect her wishes, as much as it pains me. Hopefully once this is all over for the next few days, she might let me have calls with Juliette, but I want to be able to earn whatever visitation or communication I can get.

Giving my hair a quick brush through once over and placing some gel so it will stay in place,

I decide I'm going to look as good as I'm going to get. Placing my gun in the box and locking it with a key, I place they key back around my neck. One of Arielle's many rules of coming to Haroux? No guns. Which is fine, I will respect that. I just hope that they have enough of a good security system to protect everyone.

I hear a slight knock on the door, noticing Peter on the other side. "We will be landing in five." He explains before shutting the door behind him. "This visit will be fine." He reassures me. "Juliette is tough, and she won't stand for anything Arielle puts her though. She may be a Queen and I don't doubt that Juliette will respect that, yet I do think that she will be the first person to tell Arielle when she's in the wrong." He says, placing his hand firmly on my shoulder. "I mean she's done it this entire trip." He teases causing me to look back at him through the mirror. "You can't see it, but she has you wrapped around her little finger." He continues, nudging me slightly. "But she only has a tolerance for so much, and I think this is the extent of it."

I turn around and stare at him for a moment. "You think Amy's, right?" I ask him honestly.

"I do. This world isn't made for her." He explains. "What we do isn't something you want her involved in. And besides, she's too stung on the law, what is right and wrong, that she could never fully obey to what we would need for her to do.

And the rest of your kids want nothing to do with this business."

I sigh, tucking my shirt in fully and giving him a long hard stare. "It doesn't make any of this easier. I've enjoyed having her around." I say to him.

He takes a sorry look at me, "Robert, you and I know more than anyone that if you could see Juliette fully you would. But that kid has a life in London, a family who loves her and a dream and can't be crushed. She's a kid. Let her be one."

CHAPTER FORTY-SEVEN

Juliette Sanders

Haroux

Robert and Peter leave the back room of the plane just as Felicity comes out of the toilet. She's dressed in an emerald-coloured maxi dress with small white flowers and black sandals. Her blonde hair is out of their rollers and her make-up is flawless.

She sits down, putting her seatbelt on, giving everyone a smile. She is always so elegant and regal looking. I fully believe that she won the heart of the Prince that wanted her. She is always so radiant in the way she speaks and the way she moves.

I watch out of the window as the tiny little

island gets closer as we begin to land. It is so surreal. And in theory they weren't joking. It is like something you would picture out of a fantasy book or TV show. As we land closer you can see people waving as we land near the tarmac.

That is when I notice it, clear as day, the most beautiful castle I have ever seen. Its white and tan walls are tall, and it reminds me of a castle you would get in a toy set or better yet something you would imagine in your head.

Everyone is staring, especially Robert. He's sweating, and it isn't hot on this jet. It's his nerves dripping off him.

"That is one big castle..." Spencer says while making eye contact with everyone on the plane. "Think Edward is trying to compensate for something, Robert?"

The plane erupts into light chuckles and laughter from all parties apart from myself. I don't understand, yet I'm so nervous I might be sick, so I decide not to ask.

We hit the tarmac a few minutes later and we all sit in silence, everyone unsure on what to say. I rub my palms together, trying to calm my anxiety which is radiating off me. My mum takes my hand in hers and holds it tight.

"You don't have to do this. Say the word, and we will fly back to London. This is your choice, Juliette." She reassures me. My eyes break from hers to make direct eye contact with Robert.

Giving me a reassuring nod, he clears his throat. "Your mom is right Jules. This is your choice."

Taking a long deep breath, I look out the window one last time. I'm already here, and her letter to me not only caused me an unsettling amount of anger, but also feed my curiosity. Could she really be as bad and self-absorbed as she claims to be? Has the title of Queen messed with her head?

"We're here. We might as well get it over with." I reassure everyone giving them a smile. Mum squeezes my hand once more before exchanging a look with Robert.

One by one, we exit the jet. As I get to the front, the hit hits me. It is ridiculously hot.

"I don't have any cell service." Felicity says while I hear her click her phone behind me. Robert stands at the bottom, his hands in his pocket, sunglasses down and shaking his head.

"Felicity." He says as we reach the bottom. His voice sounds tired, and I turn my attention to face them both. "I don't think one person in this little country owns a cell phone. Whatever businesses you needed to do; it is going to have to wait till we get back on the jet in a few days." He explains.

Felicity starts to laugh before placing her

sunglasses on. "You would think she would have learned but whatever, she might have Wi-Fi at the palace." She states. Robert tilts his head forward, hoping that she will realise, more than likely Arielle will not have any access to the internet.

"Might I be right in thinking that you're the Quinten's?" A posh voice speaks from behind us. We turn to face a small bald man in a suit. How is he in a suit? I am dying from heat stoke just in this dress.

"Were you expecting other visitors?" Oliver asks sarcastically. The man doesn't budge, only clears his throat.

"The arrival of the first born of the Queen is something all royal families would like to be here to visit. So, the answer is yes. We are expecting other visitors." He answers Oliver. He raises his eyebrow, stunned at the man's sass.

"Your Highness." He greets me and begins to bow. I immediately become uncomfortable and begin shaking my head stuttering.

"Er- sorry. I'm—" I stutter while he stands from his bow. "I'm not royal. Just regular." I inform him with a slight smile.

"On the contrary Your Highness," He begins, fixing his tie. "you're the daughter of the Queen, who was before that a Princess in her own right. You may not have an *official* title. However, I would like to address you properly." He explains, returning the smile.

I begin to get really uncomfortable at the thought of him calling me 'your highness.' "You can just call me Jules. That will be fine." I explain with a slight nod.

He stands stunned, unsure on if that is appropriate let alone in his book of rules. "Very well... Jules." He practically chokes. I give him a reassuring smile as he looks over at the Quinten's. "Which one is the father?"

Peter tries to contain his composure while Oliver has a gleaming smile on his face. "That would be me." Robert speaks up next to me. The small man looks Robert up and down and gives him a slightly sarcastic grin.

"Welcome Mr Quinten... and" He pauses before looking directly at Spencer glaring him up and down. The man's eyes widen while slowly taking in every single tattoo that is on show. "friends."

"Family." Robert is quick to respond. "These are my siblings," he says pointing at Peter, Oliver and Felicity. "and this is my son." He says looking over at Spencer.

"Son?" He asks looking Spencer up and down. The small man looks frightened. Just like I did when I met Spencer for the first time, He can be very intimidating when he gives the glare of death.

"Adopted." Spencer says. His voice is cold, yet his expression is playful. The man moves back unsure on the vibe Spencer is radiating making me smile. He really knows how to make people feel uncomfortable.

"I see."

"I hate to be a pain," Mum speaks while the man turns his attention to her. "Jules and the Quinten's have been travelling for quite a few hours, and it is very hot. Would we be able to move this along to somewhere cooler?" She asks sweetly.

The man's expression is one of confusion. "I'm sorry, who are you?" He asks harshly, a look of disgust growing on his face.

I immediately turn my attention to my Mum who looks so defeated instantly and turn back to the small man, my tone filled with annoyance. "My Mum." I state harshly.

The colour drains from his face while he suddenly realises who stands with me. "My deepest apologies, Mrs Sanders. I wasn't told you'd be attending." He apologises while looking over his little clipboard. "I'm so sorry." He says again before looking round at us all, clear anger on our faces. "Let's get you some lunch. Follow me." He instructs making his way towards the cars.

I take my Mums hand in mine and give it a squeeze. "Amy," Robert says placing his hand on her shoulder. "I told her you were coming." He explains. Mum only nods, holding my hand tighter while we walk towards the car. With how apologetic Robert looked, I do believe he told Arielle, but she might have just forgot, or if it's what I'm really thinking, she did it to be spiteful.

We each break up. Robert, Mum, Spencer and I heading in one car with Felicity, Oliver and Peter in the other. The small man drives us as we leave the jet behind and make our way towards the castle. I'm grateful for the aircon in the car as it is melting outside. Only a few moments later we reach the town.

My mouth falls open while the streets are lined with people waving and cheering. I instantly feel sick and begin to sink back into my seat, regretting my decision to come here. Mum is very quick to grab my hand without look at me as she looks out at the hundreds or thousands of people.

I'm beginning to become overwhelmed. This is just the people; we haven't even attended the ball yet. I feel Spencer grab my other hand. Turning to him, he gives me a reassuring wink. Spencer and Mum are squeezing my hands so hard I can see the end of my fingers going white.

As I look out the side of the car and watch the buildings pass us by and the people, the only thing I can think of is how picturesque Haroux really is. It reminds me of the little village you would read about in the fantasy books.

I completely zone out for a while before noticing that we are coming up to golden gates. I thought Robert was over the top, but of course, Arielle has to outdo him.

The gates open immediately, and we are straight through leading up to the castle.

This whole thing is so surreal and looking over at my Mum, her mouth is wide open as she takes in the scenery. Spencer has the same expression, except his is slightly more dramatic. "The photos don't really do it justice." He compliments and a light chuckle escapes from the small man's lips.

"Just wait until you get inside. You will not believe your eyes." He says looking through the rear-view mirror directly at me. I turn away, unsure on what he is indicating towards me. I'm not one to be jealous, she created this life for herself, and I have my own life in London. But deep down, I feel as though she is up to something. It might just be because I can't place or understand her intentions just yet that I'm speculating and assuming she's up to something. But with how self-centred her letter was, surely it will be something to benefit her.

The car comes to a stop as we reach the front of the castle and one by one, we exit. I straighten up my dress and stand close to my Mum and

Spencer.

"We will deliver your bags to your individual rooms. First, I would like to give you a tour of the palace before you meet their Majesties. They have been in important meetings this morning." He explains before giving a nod to a bunch of men in old fashioned Victorian clothing who begin to get the bags out of the car.

"You know they have too much money when we each get our individual rooms." Spencer whispers to me. I press my lips together praying I can hold in the laugh that is desperately trying to escape.

"You afraid of being alone Spencer?" I taunt and a small smile appears on his lips.

"Terrified, Juliette. I'm afraid of the dark." He jokingly whispers.

"Do you need me to gold your hand Spencer?" Mum whispers to him and he looks over to her nodding.

"Please, I might need a hug." He whispers and we all begin to chuckle under our breaths.

Robert looks over, giving us a confused yet playful stare wanting to know what we are all laughing at. Spencer shakes his head pointing over at me.

Immediately I defend myself mouthing that it was Spencer that started it. He's quick to come to his own defence while signalling to the fake halo that is apparently on his head. Robert decides to ignore us and begins a conversation with Felicity.

"Welcome to Oxborne Castle." The small man says signalling us up the stairs.

CHAPTER FORTY-EIGHT

Juliette Sanders

Haroux

The entrance to the Castle is like something from your wildest dreams. The pale pink and gold colours complement each of the other paler colours of white and cream in between. It is breath taking and this seems to be something that happens quite a lot recently with my birth family, I seem to be quite speechless while taking in their wealth and their beauty when it comes to their houses.

"The palace was built in 1563. The first ruler of the country, King Sebastian, he wanted something that his daughter would be able to call home. The original palace was... small shall we say." The small man explains.

"Small?" Spencer asks curiously.

The petite man clears his throat. "It was a house in the middle of the village. Not exactly royalty." He states clearly. Spencer nods and looks over at me- his eyes widening a little at the audacity of the man's tone. I give him a humorous smile as we each begin to look around. "King Sebastian ruled until his daughter married a Lord from the town." He says walking around. Noticing a ton or portraits, I begin to take a look. Each dated at the previous royals on the throne.

"Her name was Celeste?" Robert asks while standing underneath her portrait. She was beautiful, blonde and had incredible blue eyes.

"As in the Latin word for heavenly, that is right, Sir." The small man indicates with a smile. "She went on to have two children, one of which died in its early days on this earth, but she had a son, Antonio. He unfortunately never took over as King." He says with sadness in his voice.

"Why is that?"

The man's face turns sour as he looks over at Peter. "Because American's infiltrated Haroux killing thousands of our people including the soon to be King." He explains harshly to Spencer.

Spencer shifts nervously. "You sound bitter..." He says under his breath and the man chuckles slightly.

"It's a touchy subject here in Haroux. So, when the council found out that Juliette is the daughter of an American. Let's just say, it didn't sit too well on the councils' stomachs." He explains.

Silence falls upon us for a few moments, I now realise why Arielle was so hesitant to tell the council about me. They have a history with American's. And by blood. I am one.

"Definitely still bitter..." Spencer murmurs and I feel my Mum let go of my hand and smacks Spencer on the arm.

"Ignore him." She says while giving him a warning look.

"Can I ask if us being here is upsetting the council?" Robert asks while placing his hands in his pockets.

"Do you want my honest answer, Mr Quinten?" The small man says.

Tilting his head to the side, clearly accepting the tone in which the man responded. "That's why I asked."

The man shifts uncomfortably. "Yes." He answers harshly. "The council aren't happy that currently they have four, five if you include Miss Sanders, American's standing within the walls of the castle. So yes, Mr Williams. They are still bitter." He speaks clearly. "Haroux lost over two hundred years of royalty and structure due to the American invasion. It was only in 1897 when they got it back. And that was because the Spanish and British government took charge of giving it back to the people of Haroux. People who wanted peace, structure and a break from the world that is filled with technology and likes on social media. They wanted old fashioned times and that is how it was wanted by the royals too." He explains.

"So, how did Haroux end up with a King if the last King was killed?" Felicity asks.

The man smiles, he clearly likes speaking about the history of Haroux and the royal family. And it is so fascinating. "Unbeknownst to Queen Celeste, Antonio had a son out of wedlock that wasn't killed in the invasion. Through the generations we managed to find a direct descendant of Antonio. Who was a Haroux citizen through and through. No American in his blood." He says with a grin. "Now the man they had their eyes on, he was too old. He was eighty. But he had a son and a grandson. Now, the grandson was an incredible young man. Very well educated, a businessman and a family man. The council discussed and he was named King of Haroux a year later. The people were delighted." He explains as I walk over to look at the portraits. Next to Antonio who they have a portrait of next to Queen Celeste is the next ruler of Haroux.

"King Ferdinand?" I ask curiously. Although

it had been generations, he distinctively looks like Antonio.

"He was a great King." He admires. "He made Haroux into the happy and thriving country it is now." He smiles. "Following on was his son, King Henry, then the late King Simon and his son now, King Edward." He says walking me through the final few portraits of the wall. "When Princess Robyn takes over as Queen then we will have our first Queen in three hundred years." He says, his voice excited as he looks at the empty space on the wall where her portrait will be put.

"What is she like?" I ask curiously while turning to the small man, who I am yet to know the name of. "Princess Robyn? What is she like?"

He looks almost taken back by my question. "She's kind." He says with a smile. "Head strong and courageous." He continues before the smile slowly drops off his face and a look of annoyance grows in its place. "But she's stubborn."

Robert let's out a laugh from behind the small man who turns around curiously to see what is so funny. "I don't doubt for a second I know where she got that from." He chuckles along with Peter and Felicity.

The man doesn't laugh, only looks at them with disgust before moving on into another room and we are all quick to follow.

He shows up around rooms that are just for

artifacts and show items. Items that have clearly been within the palace for generations but also paintings and sculptures that when you read the plaque next to them it says that they are from the time before the American's took over.

As we begin to walk up a set of stairs, I hear heavy footsteps run up behind me to find Spencer grinning as he leans down to get to my height. "Do you feel like Mia Thermopolis yet?" He asks, humour in his tone of voice and I press my lips together trying not to laugh in the silence.

"I'm concerned that you of all people knows what *Princess Diaries* is." I whisper back to him, looking around to see if the man heard me.

"Juliette, why do you think I'm not cultured on the classics? Anne Hathaway and Julie Andrews? Iconic duo." He says nudging me while we get up the stairs. I shake my head and look away from him. Why has he decided now to start making me laugh in the most serious moment.

"Mia's Grandmother was the Queen. It isn't the same thing." I whisper back, desperately looking in any other direction or I will burst into a fit of giggles.

"Ah! Ha! Yet it is the same because you were both teenagers." He explains catching my eye and giving me a wink. He's proud of himself and it's probably because he's making me feel less nervous by being an idiot.

We make our way to directly to another room where he pushes on the door hard, and it reveals what looks to be a ball room. "This is where this evening's event will be held." He explains while opening his arms for us to take in the beauty of the room. Its gold rimmed ceilings and hand painted drawings give off the same vibe as before. Old money. The palace never lost its beauty if it was infiltrated by the Americans yet, I can't be sure they had to put it back to its original beauty. "Just in time." The man announces while walking towards a gentleman who stands behind us and extends his hand. "It's great to see you, Sir." He welcomes the man.

"Likewise, Bertram." He gleams while shaking his hand. Never would have guessed the small man was called Bertram. The man who has just entered has an accent, yet I'm unsure on what it is. Dressed in black suit pants a white shirt and a badge of some sort, he begins to look around the room to each of us individually and stopping once he gets to me. He's almost taken back my appearance as he glares at me and starts to make me feel uncomfortable.

He notices my discomfort and shakes his head before walking in my direction. "My apologies, Princess." He says before bowing. He's Scottish and it's a very strong accent. I don't doubt some of the Americans are going to struggle and by some... I mean Spencer.

"Officer Fitzgerald—" Bertram tries to get his attention which the man ignores. I instantly become more uncomfortable and step away from him.

"I do have to say you look so much like Queen Arielle." He compliments me before looking around the room at the stunned faces. "What?" He asks dumbfounded.

"Officer Fitzgerald, may I introduce you to Juliette Sanders. She is the Queen's daughter, but she's not a Princess." Bertram comes to my defence and watch as Officer Fitzgerald's face turns whiter than a ghost.

"Miss Sanders, I'm so sorry. I was told to address you as Princess. I can only apologise. I'm Fredrick Meredith Fitzgerald. You can call me Freddie." He introduces himself while extending his hand out to shake mine.

I'm taken by surprise by his middle name. "Meredith?" I ask curiously. A wide grin appears on his face.

"Can you tell my mother was drunk when she named me?" He asks, his hand still extended and waiting for me not to leave him hanging.

Trying not to laugh, I shake his hand to try and get rid of the awkwardness that has appeared in the room. "Can I ask who asked you to address her as Princess?" Robert asks Freddie. Crossing his arms, I can see he is becoming uncomfortable with Robert's question and the longer the silence goes on, the certainty we all have that it was Arielle.

"Was it the Queen?" My Mum asks him. He's alarmed by her question but ultimately nods.

"I care and cherish the Queen deeply. Which is why I went with what she had instructed me." He says looks over at me with an apologetic look.

"I don't forgive him." Spencer speaks harshly behind me. I turn around giving him a warning stare to be nice.

"Why you've got some impressive tattoo's on ya there lad." Freddie compliments Spencer catching him off guard slightly. He won't tell you it has with his face but you can tell with his eyes.

"I've forgiven him. Let's move on." He instructs. I collection of eye rolls begin around the room to how quickly Spencer has forgiven Freddie.

"How do you know the King and Queen?" Mum asks Freddie. Slowly the rest of the Quinten's begin to walk closer almost crowding Freddie.

"I knew the Queen before I met His Majesty. She came to London a few years ago in search of a recruit to help her run the Security in Haroux. It was practically non-existent." He explains. I watch as Peter raises his eyebrow and whispers something to Oliver and Robert.

I raise my eyebrow looking over in their direction. Robert strays away from my glare before moving away from both of his brothers. They both give me a hard glare, one that I am struggling to understand the meaning of.

Out of the corner of my eye, I see Bertram talking to a young woman. She's probably mid-twenties, very well dressed and she's beautiful. "The King and Queen are expecting you. Please." Bertram instructs while signalling for us to leave the room.

I ever so quickly move to stand next to Peter. "What were you talking about?" I whisper to him, hoping Freddie doesn't hear me. He begins to walk ahead, and I am hoping Peter will just tell me. "The look you gave me. What was it for?"

"I got the list of everyone on Haroux's security list. Past and present. Freddie Fitzgerald wasn't on that list." He says quietly while exchanging a quick glance with Robert. "Your new friend isn't telling the truth." He says giving me that glare again before walking ahead leaving my dumbfounded as we make our way through the castle.

Why would Freddie lie about how he knows Arielle? He is younger than her although he has stubble on his chin. I reckon early to mid-twenties. But why wouldn't he tell us the truth?

The only logical explanation is that Arielle told him not to. Like she told him to address me as Princess and completely forgot to mention that my Mum was coming with me.

As I am about to meet her, I feel a sense of hostility towards her, more so than I already had. She seems to be doing a lot of lying and we have been here all of an hour. That seems to be one thing she thinks she's good at.

Being a liar.

As we approach a door at the end of the corridor. I notice how different this door is to the rest of them. It's all white, including the wall around it. It is pristine, not a speck of dirt in sight. Bertram knocks and a gentle and soft voice ushers for him to come in.

He opens the door and stands slightly to the side. "Your Majesties, may I present Miss Sanders, Mrs Sanders, The Quinten Family and Officer Fitzgerald." He says loudly before giving us a nod to enter the room. Freddie goes first then Felicity and Oliver. One by one we enter yet I stand still, so nervous to walk around that corner to see someone I have never been able to know. I have already made my mind up about her in my head but what if her actions have spoken louder than her words and I've jumped right in without even giving her a chance.

I won't get this chance again. Being

surrounded by people who care so deeply to meet the woman who abandoned me and her moral duties as a mother. But I get to experience it with my own mother.

Mum gives me a nudge and we begin to walk into the room. It all feels like slow motion as we walk into the room. She isn't in my peripheral just yet, but I can feel her presence and I can smell the sweet scent of the perfume she's wearing. Not Mums or Felicity's. Hers. It's smells floral and fruity.

As I come round the corner of the door, I see the outline of her skirt and as I move closer, I finally see her. Operation Red Head.

I'm almost blown away at her beauty and how graceful she stands near the desk where her husband, King Edward stands up slowly. I can't break my eye contact from hers. And she can't break hers either.

Fourteen years.

It has been fourteen years since I last saw her, yet she has not changed since I saw her wedding photo with Edward. She was so young, yet I don't see a wrinkle in sight or a frown line.

Her bright blue eyes become teary, and she is quick to pat her eyes with a tissue as she tries to compose herself. Edward is quick to come to her aid and offering her some comfort by placing his hand on her shoulder. "Hello, Juliette." She welcomes me with a smile as she grabs onto Edward's hand tightly and chuckles. "I promised myself I wouldn't get emotional." She laughs again lightly tapping the tears that have fallen onto her rosy, pink cheeks. "It's so lovely to finally meet you." She says with a smile.

I hesitate to say something back, unsure on whether or not I should bow or address her as her Majesty.

"You don't need to bow to me, Juliette." She speaks almost as though she read my mind. "You can call me Arielle." She says with a smile.

I manage to catch my breath after a few moments. "It's nice to meet you too."   I express finally, thankful that my voice doesn't crack or come out as a whisper. Her face and voice is so sweet that you wouldn't think that she was the same woman that wrote the letter. Yet looks can be deceiving.

She smiles as she begins walking in my direction, every step she takes is graceful and so light she looks like she is walking on clouds. "We would never expect any of you to bow or address us by anything but our names." She says softly looking around the room. "You're family to us."

As she comes closer, she extends her hand out to my Mum who takes hers nervously. Staring into her eyes for a moment, she smiles. "It is lovely to meet you, Arielle." Mum speaks nervously.

"I can assure you; I am most pleased to meet you." She squeezes her hand gently. "I have a lot to ask you, but I also have to thank you." She says very softly, her voice breaking. "You took on the role I never could at the time. I owe you a great debt." She speaks while holding Mums hands tightly.

Mum only seems to give her a reassuring smile. I know that will mean a great deal to her.

Looking over at Oliver, he is incredibly quiet and he's behaving, which is unusual. From what I had been told he hated Arielle for that time she was with them. But Robert's face is what surprises me the most.

He's looking at her like she is a completely different person. He's watching her every movement as if she's going to disappear.

Robert has never seen her like this, in her world where she plays this character. Because the woman he knew all those years ago was wild, reckless and foolish.

She finally looks over at the Quinten's and Spencer. Freddie goes over to greet Edward who is standing there, a smile on his face like this is something he's waited a long time for.

"You haven't changed. None of you." She compliments the Quinten's. Oliver scoffs before trying to making it come across as though he's clearing his throat.

"I have to say, you have." He speaks, his tone is harsh, yet honest and by the look on her face that doesn't surprise her.

"You know your brother said the same thing. I'm sorry I lied to you all." She apologises. This time Oliver begins to laugh, and he can't contain himself.

You can now cut the tension with a knife. "The sorry is about fourteen years too late, *Your Majesty*."

The silence becomes uncomfortable with both Arielle and Oliver having a stare off. I knew he didn't like her. But would he have accepted an apology if she was to give him one? I highly doubt that.

"I owe you all an explanation for the reason I left. I was young—"

"So were we." Felicity responds, cutting her off. "Yet you still did what all of us expected, but we were still disappointed because we hoped you would be different." She responds harshly.

Arielle begins to shift uncomfortably while holding her hands and squeezing them together. "Please." She begs them, tears in her eyes before she exchanges a look over at me. "Can we not do this in front of Juliette. I don't want for us to start this trip with hatred filling the air." She pleads.

Watching carefully, Felicity begins to relax, and Oliver seems to calm himself down for the most part. This is the most contained I've seen him.

"The last thing we want is for there to be tension in the air while you're here on your visit. We want you to enjoy the sights and smells that Haroux and what its people have to offer." Edward says, in a way of coming to his wife's defence. "We just want a good and stable relationship for all. I know it will take time to build those bridges that have burned. But my wife wants to repair them." He says while placing his hand on her shoulder once again.

"So why isn't she saying all this herself?" Robert asks, his arms crossed, and his brows frowned. Robert is right. Why isn't she saying all this?

Arielle gives a smile to Robert before relaxing her shoulders. "I struggle to say how I'm really feeling." She says in her defence, which only angers me more.

"But you didn't have a problem telling me how you were feeling while also calling me an abomination in the letter you gave to Robert." I state and I watch her head snap round and glare at me. Edward's face is horrified as he takes his hand off Arielle's shoulder.

"My love, what is she talking about?" He asks

as he stares at his wife, stunned by my words. She glares down at me, and right in this moment I know that I am staring at the real Arielle. The one who doesn't see the consequences to her actions and expects everyone to pick up her mess or lie for her. She suddenly switches to sad eyes before looking back at Edward.

"I had to warn her about the council and how they would be with her. There was no point in making it all sunshine and rainbows. I was simply giving her a reality check as to what it is like here when it comes to their power." She practically cries and I feel the anger bubble within. That's not the full story and she knows it.

"Arielle, we brought the letter. Please stop with the crocodile tears. There was nothing sentimental in that letter. You blamed Juliette for everything and everything that was about to happen. Please don't paint yourself as a victim." Robert is quick to defend me. She turns her head round to glare at him. She's warning him. "I will not have you paint yourself in a way that makes your own daughter look like the villain. You did that all on your own." He says tightening and straightening his stance, so he doesn't look intimidated by her. The whole room is eerily quiet while we watch Arielle scramble to save herself.

Edward is as stunned as the rest of us. Unsure on how or if to come to his wife's defence to save her from drowning in her own lies.

Arielle turns back to me and Mum who is now holding my hand and squeezing hard. Arielle's look shows an unstable woman who has been backed into a corner and is a ticking time bomb waiting to explode.

She loosens her shoulders and clears her throat. "Juliette you are to meet Robyn after you've ate. Since Officer Fitzgerald is your date for this evening, I expect for you to learn the traditional dance of the royals. That will be in one hour." She says coldly and I am trying hard not to roll my eyes.

"Is that a request or a command *Your Majesty?*" I answer back. A small smile creeps along her face.

"It is an order, Juliette. You're in my country, you play by my rules." She snaps at me before looking around at the room. "If you would excuse me. I have a ball to prepare for." She says coldly before walking out of the room.

The deafening silence fills the room. Mum takes a long deep exhale next to me while still tightly holding my hand.

Edward slowly moves back to his desk and sits on the end of it. Looking out to all of us who are just as stunned as each other. I never thought she would show her true colours so early on into the visit. She's got a role to play and a one-woman stage show starring herself and only her.

It's an act to her. Pretending to be noble, honest and kind. When deep down, if something doesn't benefit her, she will make sure to ruin anything and everything that gets in her way.

"I want to apologise for my wife." He speaks after a moment. "Juliette, I would never have let her send you a letter. This history between Americans and Haroux is something you don't need to worry about, nor do you need to worry about her reputation when it comes to the council." He expresses with a small smile.

"It's like she is a completely different person." Peter expresses to which the rest of the Quinten's nod. "Has she always been like that?"

Edward shakes his head.

"No. Only recently has she been like a loose cannon, as you people would say." He says a slight smile growing on his lips. "She's determined." He says before standing. "When she came back from London, she was different. But very obedient. When she eventually told me about Juliette," He begins to say before meeting me with sorry eyes, "all she said was that London was a big mistake." I feel my heart rip out of my chest. I know I'm not a mistake. "Juliette, in all honesty, I don't think you were the one she referred to." He says harshly breaking his eye contact to look directly over at Robert.

I think that hurts worse. Robert did so much

for her. All of the Quinten's did, so this admission from her own husband must be like someone ripping out their hearts from their chest.

Robert's face is incredibly pained and all I feel like doing is going and giving him a hug. He isn't a mistake. He was never a mistake to any of us. And hearing that must hurt so much.

"I don't want to speak badly about my wife. But she has a way of saying things that she may not have meant. When she's overwhelmed—"

"She has outbursts and says things she doesn't mean." Robert finishes Edward's sentence. "You're forgetting we were together just under a year. Hiding from the people who were determined to have our heads on a stick. We protected her throughout it all. The only decent thing she could have done before she left was be with me when I handed over our child to Mr and Mrs Sanders." Robert begins to shout. He's emotional and rightly so. I would hate to be told I was a mistake after everything I did for the other person.

Arielle had no right speaking about him like that, and because with how little I now trust her, I doubt we would ever get the truth if we were to ask for it.

"I want to introduce myself to you properly. And I have a lot to thank you for." Edward says, extending his hand.

Robert looks down at Edwards hand. The look on his face is as if he is hesitating shaking it. I know this is a lot for him, yet Edward showing his gratitude is something I hope he accepts. He's innocent in all of this, torn between two ex-lovers who brought a child into the world fourteen years ago.

Robert releases his hands and shakes Edward's and I feel a sense of relief in the air. Edward smile is gigantic, whereas Robert has a small smile, but he still looks angry. "If we are ever in the position where she needs saving, I hate to be cruel Your Majesty, but I will leave your wife to fend for herself." Robert speaks clearly. You can hear the strain of hurt in his voice as he speaks to Edward.

Edward only nods for a moment as I see him searching for the right thing to say. "I can't say I blame you, Robert. She's my wife, she is my responsibility." He professes.

Robert removes his hand and steps back. "I'm pleased you agree."

Edward bows his head as he looks around to all of us in the room. "You all must be hungry. You've had a long journey." He expresses. He isn't wrong. I'm starving, and with all this talk of dance lessons. I'm going to need all the energy I can get.

One by one, we exit the room. I hold back, hoping to maybe speak to Freddie but he cuts past me and down the corridor in the opposite direction.

CHAPTER FORTY-NINE

Serena Quinten

Michigan, USA

I sit, glaring at the front door... waiting. I know she will come home. She always done after her little benders. What the others in this house fail to notice is that Clarissa and I were more alike than her and Oliver. She may have trusted him, however she trusted me more.

Or so I thought. The text I got off Felicity when they were on the plane only spurred my anger. She lied to us all. From her background to her missing children, to her ex-boyfriend. She. Lied.

And I hate liars.

But deep down I know I didn't know her as well as I thought. Her little days away must have been when she was killing the first two people and needed somewhere to come down from her high.

I should have seen it. I thought I knew her though and through, only now do I know that I knew nothing about her. Or her past.

When she gave birth to Sapphire the only thing, she told me was that she was in a better place. Yet, when I asked if she was dead. She would say, 'don't be so silly I would never kill a child!'

How wrong I was.

Because that is exactly what she was doing.

She came to me when she found out about Juliette and ranted about how Juliette will ruin her life and the rest of ours. She labelled her as a traitor and a few other words I dread to even think about.

A teenager, speaking about her younger sister in such a horrific way. I'm not here to let her know what we know. Felicity told me to act like we know nothing, don't give her any reason that we are suspecting her, when I all I want to do is wrap my hands around her throat and ask where that poor baby is and why she was going around hurting innocent girls.

Clarissa has always been logic, and she has always had a plan. No doubt everything of her plan, from the killings, to shooting the Williams boys and dragging their brother into this is all part of her despicable act to get revenge on Juliette.

I was hurt when my brother decided to hand her off to the Sanders like she was a piece of meat. But as I've grown and aged, I've realized this world was not made for a baby. Our world would have caused her so much trouble.

Like it has me.

Checking my watch again I notice it's almost four o'clock. I've been waiting here for her since my siblings left for Haroux with Juliette and Spencer. And I plan on waiting here for days if it means that I get to speak to her.

Nathaniel has been told to keep an eye on any possible other routes into the house and if she appears on the security cameras.

The door suddenly flies open and there stands Alexis, who screams and jumps back, holding onto her chest.

"Jesus, Alexis, you gave me a fright!" I exclaim holding onto my chest trying to tame my beating heart.

"Er, you were the one that gave me the heart attack what the hell are you doing!" She shouts while placing her keys on the side table. "You're lurking in the shadows like a mad woman."

"I'm waiting for Clarissa." I express and she

scoffs in front of me while looking through her bag.

"Is the lunatic on her way back from the asylum is it that time of the month already?" She teases while walking into the kitchen. "I like the peace and quiet." She pouts.

Smiling at her, I move the dark shiny hair that's in front of her face and move it behind her ear. "You should be nice to her."

She lets out a laugh. "You're joking, aren't you? That girl has been nothing but awful to me since the minute I arrived. If you're expecting me to just forgive and forget Aunt Serena, I'm sorry but no can do. She's a bitch."

Trying not to laugh at her honesty, I take a seat on one of the stools at the end of the island. "Where do you think she goes?" I ask her and she turns around. "When she goes away for those few days, where do you think she goes?" I repeat.

Taking a seat at the other stool, she falls silent. I can see she's thinking, but if I know Alexis, it is only going to be a sarcastic response. "Maybe she's got another family? She reminds me of a cat." She answers harshly. "In all honesty I couldn't tell you, but also Aunt Serena… I don't care. She hasn't made a single effort with me while I've been here. She's been a bitch since the minute she walked in here. Acting like she owned the place and the rest of us were scum." She expresses before reaching into her bag and pulling out the cutest hipflask I've ever seen. Knowing Alexis, it's pink of course.

"You don't like her then?"

"Like her? Are you kidding? I like Juliette better than I like her." She answers honestly before taking a swig.

"I wouldn't say that if I was you…"

"Why not? It's the truth."

"It would upset her." I express quickly.

"Yes, it would." A voice from behind me speaks. My heart instantly sinks when I recognise the voice.

"Back from your bender then? Nice to see you care enough to come back." Alexis mocks her while placing the flask in her bag. "You're like a cat. Only coming home when you want feeding and the attention you think you deserve."

"Well at least I had fun. That's the main thing, right?" Clarissa mocks, walking round to the island, heading straight for the fridge. "And why are you suddenly caring about my whereabouts anyway? You leave soon Alexis. And I cannot wait for that day to come."

"Don't get too excited Clarissa, I might decide to take a year off and go and search for that baby you've been hiding from all of us." Alexis snaps back.

The temperature drops in the room by ten degrees. Clarissa slowly closes the fridge door and turns to face Alexis. "Why would you want to waste a year of your life?"

Alexis scoffs. "So, save us the trouble and tell us where she is."

Clarissa walks closer to Alexis from around the island that stands in the middle of the room. A smile begins to grow on her face as she inches closer to her, getting up into her face. "What fun would that be?"

I stand, getting ready to break up a fight. How could we not see this? The level of mental instability that Clarissa has been portraying for the time she's been here. "Clarissa, you're making it worse on all of us by not telling us where that baby is." I say in the hopes that Alexis will back off and let me deal with her.

But she doesn't. Alexis steps closer. Their breaths intertwining as one. "Do you know how much of a crazy bitch you are?" She says, her voice low. "What kind of mother hides her daughter from the rest of her family and thinks it's a game?"

Clarissa gleams. "The kind of woman who wouldn't want her child anywhere near the likes of *our* family. Do you know how cursed we are? We were adopted into a family of psychopaths! —"

"You fit right in then, don't you?" Alexis bites

back.

Clarissa decides to move away from Alexis, however we both watch her carefully, our eyes never breaking away from Clarissa's every move. "Watch it Alexis—" Clarissa says while moving away to leave the room.

"Is that a threat? Please spare me the emptiness of it. Also, how shallow do you have to be to leave in the middle of a family meeting?" Alexis barks back at her.

"Shallow? Speak for yourself Alexis."

"You're so full of shit, Clarissa. You made a scene the other day because you want to be the centre of everyone's attention. The centre of Robert's attention—" Alexis is quick to respond while Clarissa turns on her heels and marches towards Alexis breaking the space that was once between them.

"And I deserve that! Who the hell does Juliette think she is? Waltzing in here, taking Robert all for herself? She has no right to do that. She is *not* his daughter!" Clarissa screams.

"She is his daughter. Just because they are blood related, doesn't mean that you and Robert aren't related. It just happens to be that little bit different." I explain calmly to her.

Clarissa's eyes are wild and she's breathing so heavy you would think she was on the verge of a heart attack. "She is a waste of time, for all of you. She'll get what is coming to her."

"Don't threaten her Clarissa."

"I make promises, Aunt Serena." Clarissa speaks coldly. A chill runs through me and I look at her. She really has some sort of personal vendetta against Juliette, who is innocent in all of this.

"I'm done listening to this crazy bitches' ideologies." Alexis says, grabbing her bag off the island walking towards the staircase, leaving Clarissa and I alone. Or so she thinks. Out of the corner of my eye I catch Nathaniel watching carefully in the shadows. Robert informed him of the update on Clarissa so that while I'm here, Nathaniel and the security team can make sure that the rest of us are safe.

I think Robert is forgetting we live among murders on a daily basis. Each of us over the years have had to do our fair share of killing in order to send a message. I think his dad brain has clouded his leader brain.

"She just can't see my logic." Clarissa says going back over to the fridge and getting herself a can of soda.

"And what logic is that?" I ask her. I can't tell if she's in the middle of some psychotic episode.

"That she's the enemy, Aunt Serena. Can't you see that?" She says facing me.

"No one can see that." I admit honestly and the small smile that was residing on her face drops slowly. "Can't you see that you're the only person that feels this way towards her. You've never given her a chance…"

"She has ruined my life." She almost whispers. I can see tears forming in her eyes. I know that they are angry tears, Clarissa would never show that she is visibly upset. Turning on her heels and walking through to the entry way she opens up her arms and looks around. "Where is she? Is she listening?" She practically laughs.

"She's not here." I express and she is quick to turn around.

"Is she off pretending to save the world?" She laughs again and I begin to shake my head.

"She's left. She's gone." I repeat and she smile drops from her face.

"Back to London? She was meant to be here till the end of the week." She begins, I place my hand up stopping her from talking.

"She went to Haroux to meet Arielle, her birth mother." I explain and her expression turns from something of confusion to damn right anger in a split second.

"Why? Why would she do that? And why didn't anyone tell me she was leaving!" She screams to me. I'm taken back by her tone but also her audacity. Never has she raised her voice to me. We have always had an understanding, yet deep down I know that I'm looking at someone who is very clear going through some sort of psychotic episode, especially if she is killing kids.

"Why would we need to? You don't want anything to do with her!" I shout back at her. She begins to hyperventilate and pace backwards and forwards.

I've never seen her like this. Not much frightens me, but right now, she's beginning to scare me because she is being so unpredictable. "Why were you all at the police station yesterday?" She asks curiously, staring right at me. Her face is filled with anger.

"To get Oliver off the hook for that murder that happened the night Juliette arrived." I lie. I feel sick the second I say it. I hate lying. She must see right through me as she begins to laugh like a crazy woman, tears falling down her flushed cheeks.

"You're lying!" She says manically. "All you ever do is lie, all of you!" She cries. "You'll regret lying to me, Aunt Serena. That is my promise to you."

I can sense Nathaniel's presence get closer. He must be thinking the same as me, what the fuck is she going to do next.

"So, who is with her?" She says softly, this

time the tears that are falls clearly show that she is upset, and there is no doubt about that.

"Spencer, Peter, Oliver, Felicity and Robert." I explain and her face immediately fills with rage.

Without saying a word, she turns on her heels and runs out of the front door, slamming it behind her.

Hearing footsteps behind me I turn to stare back at Nathaniel who is just as stunned. "What the hell was that about?" He asks as he stands staring at the door.

"I haven't got a clue, but whatever is going on... that might have just made it ten times worse."

CHAPTER FIFTY

Robert Quinten

Haroux

I sit down while hearing Serena explain the exchange between Clarissa and Alexis. I'm in Arielle's office because this is the only phone line available.

"Are you all okay?" I ask Serena over the phone.

"Yeah, we are fine. I don't think it's us we have to worry about. She has a hatred for Juliette, Robert, we just thought was teenage jealously. It's so much deeper than that. She's on the verge of a breakdown."

Placing my head in my hands I hear the worry come through the phone from my younger sister. She's strong and defiant, but I never knew that Clarissa was this whatsoever. But I don't think I've paid attention to a lot of things recently.

"Do you know where she went?" I ask her and I hear someone clear their throat on the other end.

"We lost her. I've issued a warning to the police, and I called that Detective Juliette has been working with to let him know. They have placed an APB on her car and any of her aliases. They will find her, or we will first." Nathaniel explains.

"Let's hope so because I'm worried that there will be another dead child." I say placing my head in my hands. "Wait- Nathaniel, what did you tell Detective Gomez?"

My heart is pounding at an alarming rate. I don't doubt that Nathaniel used his brain and didn't mention that Juliette is a relation of Clarissa.

"That Clarissa came into the house and was spiralling out of control. She was clearly on the verge of a psychotic break but left before we could stop her." Nathaniel explains and I take a long deep breath. *"Dad, I know better not to tell anyone about Juliette. She's the hidden jewel for a reason."* He begins to laugh, Serena joining in.

"Do you need me home?" I ask then cutting off their little chuckle. Nathaniel clears his throat.

"No, we've got it handled. Just enjoy your time with Juliette." Nathaniel instructs.

Letting out a long exhale, silence falls on the

other end of the phone. "How did we not see this?" I say quietly. "She has more psychopathic qualities than Oliver and we know how unhinged he is sometimes."

"Look, no one could have predicted that she would be this way towards her. All we thought it was, was sibling jealousy. So, we need to find her. You, need to be there for Juliette. How are things going over there?" Serena asks.

I scoff. "It's worse than we thought. Arielle is completely out of touch." I explain and she groans.

"She was always out of touch Robert, she's so far up her own ass, you can see out the other side!" She laughs as do Nathaniel and me.

Serena tolerated Arielle all those years ago. It was Felicity she seemed to get along with better, and Peter.

"I'm going to have to go and speak to the rest of the family. You just call this phone, and someone will get back in touch with me. I want to know immediately." I instruct them.

"Of course, but you are aware we can take care of ourselves." Serena laughs.

I know both of them, and all of my children are capable of taking care of themselves.

We exchange goodbye and I sit in silence in Arielle's office to take in the surroundings.

She did well for herself.

She always would have done well for herself. By blood, she was a Princess of another small island. God knows what would have happened to that when the American invasion happened on Haroux, and I dare ask.

I place my head in my hands and let out a long exhale.

This is not how I thought Arielle meeting Juliette would go. I always thought about it in my head. That Arielle would want to know her, feel something, even compassion or love towards her. But with the look she gave her when she mentioned the letter... the only look on her face was hatred.

It was plain for everyone to see. Even Edward, who I think is so whipped into shape that he will always come to her defence.

Deep down I want to keep thinking that this is a façade, or that it's a game to her.

But deep down I know it isn't and I've had an idea of her in my head for so long that I'm denying any other way she could be than *my* Arielle.

I fell in love with someone who would never had loved me back. Or was she even capable of loving me the way I loved her? The Arielle I meet today only shows me there is one person she loves.

And that is herself. Plain and simple.

I get up and push the chair back in, leaving

everything in the same place as before.

Making my way out of the room, I almost get a shock when I realise Bertram is waiting for me at the door.

"Mr Quinten, Her Majesty would like your presence in the tearoom." He orders before turning on his heels and making his way down the hallway, hoping I'd follow.

I guess with how quickly he is walking I'm going to have to follow the small bastard. Anger begins to boil within me while I follow him. The last thing I need is to see her face more than I need to.

The less I see of her the better. But of course, Her Majesty would like to see my sorry face.

I don't doubt my face tells a picture. That I do not want to be here for in her presence. The way she spoke to my daughter was the work of a manipulative woman, and not a mother.

Bertram opens the door and just as I expected, Arielle sits there, like a lady sipping a cup of tea.

It's like I'm witnessing an entirely different human being to who I met fourteen years ago. Because clearly, I knew nothing about her before I decided to jump into bed with her.

"Robert are you just going to stand there or are you going to join me for a cup of tea?" She asks sarcastically, a playful grin emerging on her face that only boils the anger within me more.

"Is that a question or a command. I can't seem to tell the difference." I snap back. She tilts her head slowly with the smile dropping on her face giving me the hint, that wasn't a question.

Trying hard not to roll my eyes, I make my way over to the seat in front of her and watch as she places her teacup down next to her and picks up the teapot. "Tea, Robert?" She asks sweetly.

"No, thanks."

Placing the teapot down harshly, she lifts up her cup elegantly and takes another sip. "Robert, if you'd prefer. I did buy some coffee when I went over to Spain. It's not something we decide to have here. Although I do miss it." She admits with a smile.

"What I'd like to know is what you want?" I respond harshly, catching her off guard. Tilting her head away from me she places the teacup down and sits back in her chair slightly.

"How was your phone call?" She asks.

"Fine." I don't like this line of questioning, and the look on her face is telling me she knows more than she's playing out. "Spill whatever you have to say. Now, Arielle." I instruct.

Letting out a small giggle she turns to the right of her to lift up an unusual looking machine.

"Best invention I found." She says picking up the top to reveal a phone. *That sneaky...*

"You were listening in on my conversation?!" I shout at her, and she looks at me like my reaction is out of pocket.

"Hush now, Robert. Did you think I didn't have a right to know what you were talking about when you're in *my* country?" She says sweetly while placing the phone back in my place.

"Actually, it is in my country and has nothing to do with you, or Haroux!" I shout back.

She tuts while picking up that teacup again. "Robert, it concerns me because you're in my country and you have a little situation regarding another one of your children. It worries me... how many woman did you get pregnant?" She asks and my mouth falls open to the accusation.

"They are adopted." I manage to say eventually, trying hard not to snap right in front of her.

"That's interesting..." She says placing the teacup down and pouring herself another cup. "You give one child up for adoption and you adopt others. I believe you would qualify for worst father of the year."

That's what made me snap.

"And what about you?! Abandoning one daughter and raising another to take over a throne. Some mother you are!"

"I am doing what is expected of me! For the future of Haroux!" She is quick to come to her own defence.

"You know I feel sorry for Edward, he really has been given a life sentence if he is married to you for the rest of his life..."

And that's when I feel the burning.

She slapped me.

Placing my hand on my cheek, I turn back to her and look down at the woman who is filled with rage.

"It's so telling that the only person you love is yourself Arielle. Deep down, you may think you love Edward, because that is what you tell yourself. But you love him because he fits into the fantasy you've carved out. None of it that includes the daughter you abandoned fourteen years ago." I whisper harshly.

There is no change in her emotions. The sixteen-year-old I knew was determined to stand up for herself. Not let anyone speak over her and would defend herself until the day she died.

But she doesn't stand in front of me anymore. I see someone who is so cold blooded and so out of touch with reality that trying to reason with her would only cause me a headache.

"We will be back on the jet first thing in the

morning. As much as I would love to embarrass you by taking Juliette away right now, I know it is good for her to meet Robyn. So, we will stay for your ball. However, that Freddie kid you've brought to be Juliette's date and get lost for all I care." I say getting closer to her and breaking the space between us. "He touches her. I kill him, and we both know I make good with my threats Arielle. He stays away from her. That is my order."

CHAPTER FIFTY-ONE

Juliette Sanders

Haroux

I'm lost.

Normally I don't take wrong turns and I did follow the instructions Bertram told me to follow. But can I find the room I need? Absolutely not. This place is a maze.

I'm not sure on whether I'll be meeting Robyn or if it will just be me attending this dance class.

I understand that this is Arielle's country and what she says goes when it comes to a lot of things, but forcing me to dance with a stranger, not to mention that she is doing this for appearances and not because she actually would like to get to know me as a person.

So far, with how she's been acting with me, I have to admit that for the future, I don't want a relationship with her.

I'm happy sticking with my Mum, and my small family in London and forgetting that I'm the daughter of a Queen. Because I'm only a relation to her by blood.

I hear a door creak open behind me and I turn to see a woman, maybe mid-thirties with dark hair looking out into the hallway. "Juliette?" She asks smiling at me.

Giving her an encouraging nod, she walks towards me, and extends her hand. "I'm Celeste, I'll be teaching you the dance of the royals." She welcomes while shaking my hand.

"Celeste? As in..."

"One of our late Queen's? You're very right." She smiles before walking through the same door she came from, and I join her.

"So, are you just the dance teacher?" I ask her curiously causing her to laugh while she takes a seat.

"No, but I can see why you would think that." She laughs, hinting for me to sit next to her. I look around the room, there is mirrors instead of wallpaper on every wall and even has bars attached for probably ballet. I take a seat before turning back my attention to her. "I handle lots of personal affairs for the King and Queen, but I also studied in London at the school of Ballet. So, the Queen asked if I could teach both you and Princess Robyn, the traditional dance of the royal family." She explains before reaching down and handing me a bottle of water which I thank her for.

"So, the Princess will be joining us?"

She nods. "Yes." She speaks. "Princess Robyn is here to get to know you, however she does need to work on the positioning of her feet. They tend to move not in unison with the rest of her body when she dances." She chuckles and I join in.

"She has two left feet you mean?"

She begins to laugh, hard. "Exactly right, but she is lovely once you get to know her." She explains.

Why do I get the sense she is going to be a younger version of Arielle, just with that statement alone from Celeste.

The door opens up and stands there is a girl, only a few years younger with the curliest hair I think I've ever seen. She has red hair, just like Arielle and she looks more like her than I do, but then that is my opinion. "Hi Princess, come on in." Celeste welcomes as Robyn walks right towards me.

She glares up at me and narrows her eyes.

"Did you forget that when you're in the presence of a royal, you curtsy." She says coldly and I can't help but raise my eyebrow at the audacity.

I go to curtsy, but I feel Celeste place her hand on my shoulder, stopping me. "You don't need to do that Juliette. Robyn, you were told that when it comes to Juliette, she doesn't need to bow or curtsy."

Robyn scoffs. "But it is a sign of respect. She should know that."

Celeste lets out a long and frustrated sign and Robyn moves away from me and stands in the middle of the room. No introduction, yet I don't think I will properly need one. She is an Arielle 2.0.

"Juliette, meet Princess Robyn of Haroux. She's next in line to the throne and tends to forget that won't be for a while if she doesn't knock her audacity down a few notches and learns to treat her own sister with some respect." Celeste says harshly.

Robyn begins to slightly pout before a small smile begins to appear on her face. "Sorry, Juliette." She says looking over.

Giving her a reassuring smile, I walk to stand next to her. "It's nice to meet you, Robyn." I say sweetly and she tilts her head and frows her brows.

"You sound funny." She admits, which

catches me off guard.

"I sound funny?" I repeat to her, and she nods. Suddenly, a wave of giggles comes over me while I open my bottle of water and take a sip.

"What is it, Juliette?" Celeste asks.

I shake my head. "Nothing, I'm just getting some serious déjà vu." I say giggling again.

Celeste and Robyn exchange a look. She then heads over to what looks like a CD player and presses play. "Okay. Let's begin."

CHAPTER FIFTY-TWO

Juliette Sanders

Haroux

I turn around, my eyes still closed after being instructed to by the ladies who are getting me dressed for the ball.

The dance I had to learn was something quite easy, it is only 6 moves, so I'm sure I will get the hang of it, hoping that Freddie knows what he is doing.

"Okay, Miss. You can open your eyes!" The lady says enthusiastically. I hesitate. Because I know that underneath whatever I'm wearing I've had to subject myself to torture from a corset and I think I've lost my ribs.

I open one eye first and the other one follows before my jaw hits the floor.

I look...

Ridiculous.

"Oh, Miss, you look fantastic!" One of the other ladies celebrate.

I look like I belong in a toy shop. The dress is a sapphire blue with silver diamonds and sparkles along the dress. It reminds me of the one Arielle wore when we looked at photos in Robert's office. In fact, I think it could be that same dress. The sleeves are poofy and large. My hair has been placed into a bun and there is flowers in my hair.

"The Queen is going to be so happy the dress fit!" Another one exclaims. "Miss Sanders, you look beautiful." She says sweetly.

Giving her a smile, I thank her. After a few moments, they leave me, and I struggle to get off the podium they put me on.

"I have to say, you definitely look the part, blondie." I hear that Scottish man say while walking over and helping me down. "Arielle really knows how to make someone relatively normal, look like they belong in her world." He says while releasing his hand from mine.

He's dressed in his Navy uniform, however, it's not what I thought the United Kingdom's uniform looked like. He notices me looking and begins to chuckle.

"I know, I do look good." He compliments himself, making me laugh. "I wear Haroux's uniform. Queen's orders." He explains before sitting down on one of the seats opposite.

My room is bigger than my house in London and my room at the Quinten's combined. It's a peach colour on the wall with gold furniture and paintings of Haroux and its past monarchs. The bed is in the middle of the room with a dressing room opposite and a bathroom through a door near the one to the corridor.

"How about you tell me how you really know Arielle?" I say attempting to sit down without suffocating myself in this corset.

"I told you—"

"A lie. You told me a lie Freddie, and I hate liars. Peter said your name wasn't on the list of names given to him from Arielle on the security of Haroux. So don't lie, because I've already worked out your tell."

He raises his eyebrow. "My tell?"

"When you lie your raise your eyebrow slightly." I tell him. He automatically does it, this time out of curiosity before frowning at me.

"Arielle warned me that you can be quite the Detective. She said you would it out."

"So, why lie?" I ask him. He sits back in his

chair. "Why lie for her? What exactly does you owe her?"

He shifts uncomfortably before rubbing his hand on his legs. "I used to be an officer back in Scotland. I had decided that when I came back from one of my tours, I didn't want to continue it." He explains.

I feel death slowly creep upon me the longer I sit down. I have no idea how woman did this, and deep down I'm applauding them. Yet secretly torturing Arielle in my head for making me wear one. I stand up and decide to pace while listening to Freddie explain himself.

"I decided to travel. So, I did up a ship—"

"A boat?"

"Ah, no. This is my ship. She is my baby." He chuckles, leaning forward. "I'll introduce you to her." He taunts.

I roll my eyes. "So, you bought a boat and decided to come to Haroux?" I ask him wanting to move the conversation along.

He laughs. "No, blondie." *What is it with men and their nicknames?* "I went exploring like any normal man would." He explains. "I came across Haroux out of chance and thought that I would just be able to stay in hotel. But because the security thought I was infiltrating, they sent me to prison in the castle for a few nights."

My eyes widen. "So, because you were exploring, you got thrown in prison?"

"Exactly. A few days later, the Queen came down to visit me. She dropped all charges and said that my ship will be returned to me. Apparently, I reminded her of someone she once knew." He says standing up and fixing his uniform. "I know now, who she was referring to."

"Robert?" I ask him. He nods.

"Only when I saw how she was with him in Edward's office did I realise that was who she was referring to all those years ago. She had never mentioned you, Robert or any of the Quinten's. But when she told me about her past, I had to say I was shocked. She follows every rule, even the one she makes herself. But that was the one thing that shocked me. How cold she was when talking about you." He explains making my heart drop.

"Well, she hasn't been very kind if I'm honest. That letter I got... I should have listened to it. It was a hint to stay away." I explain.

He lifts my hand forcing me to look up at him. "Unlike Arielle, I find you fascinating. The daughter of the Queen of Haroux and an American mafia leader. That is the kind of stuff you read in fantasy books." He laughs.

I join in. "Tell me about it. I feel like my whole life is one big mess at the moment."

"I think, do this for Arielle, and get out of here as soon as you can. I'll be beside you for most of the evening, so if the council start with any of their rules and values, I'll be quick to come to your defence. They can be very misogynistic. Just a heads up." He says letting go of my hand and grabbing his hat that remained on the seat. "Please don't stand on my toes tonight." He pleads with a smile.

"I can't make any promises."

He exits out of the room leaving me alone with my thoughts.

I hate this dress.

But I think it's the sleeves. I unhook my arms from the dress and notice that the poof is added and can be taken off. *Thank god.*

Placing the spare fabric on the table, I try and move a little. This dress is so heavy. So unnecessarily heavy. But it is only for a few hours while I meet the people of Haroux.

I look out at the window and notice another plane on the verge of landing. I'm curious to know who is on that plane and the other three I have watched fly over in the space of two hours.

My room looks out onto the harbour, and I glance around looking for that boat that Freddie seems to have brought himself on, or so I thought.

And that is when I see it.

Freddie just forgot to mention... that his ship? It's an old-fashioned pirate ship.

CHAPTER FIFTY-THREE

Robert Quinten

Haroux

I'm standing at the bottom of the stairs tapping my foot. Amy decided to go up and escort Juliette down here, and rightly so.

Arielle and Edward are greeting guests while Robyn is standing over and greeting some other children.

I stand with my siblings, people watching to see who we may or may not know. And sure enough, The Queen of England walks through the door.

"Is that...?" Oliver whispers in my ear. Nodding slowly, I watch Arielle curtsy to the

Queen and to the King. Welcoming them with a gigantic smile as she shows off some of the work around the palace.

I take another swig of my water, hoping that soon they will issue something stronger. I'm nervous because I dread to think what Arielle has planned for Juliette at this ball. No doubt not taking on board what I said about Freddie, because Peter let me know he caught Freddie leaving Juliette's room earlier.

That is something I want to talk about with her, not him. Because he's a twenty something year old man and he's the date of a fourteen-year-old. It makes me feel sick.

"Robert—" Felicity says catching me off guard, hinting for me to look at the top of the stairs.

There she stands. My daughter, in possibly the biggest and most beautiful dress. It's a sapphire blue, that compliments her hair and eye colour, and she looks down on me, fear in her eyes before clutching tightly onto Amy's arm and the handle and making her way down the stairs.

She's afraid she will fall. I hand Felicity my water and make my way up a few stairs and take Juliette's other arm. "It's okay baby girl, we've got you." I say as she grips my arm tight trying hard to keep her composure.

We manage to make our way down the stairs

in one peace. And I watch as Juliette takes a long exhale. "Juliette, you look beautiful." Felicity says, placing her hand on her cheek and rubbing lightly.

"I'm with Felicity, you look like the part." Peter compliments her. She begins to blush while trying to move in her dress.

"Thank you. But I feel ridiculous." She says trying to move her skirt. "You know, I applaud the woman that have to do this every day, I feel too hot and I'm suffocating. I also think I've punctured my lung with one of my ribs that I think is broken." She says trying to breathe.

"Are you being dramatic?" I ask her curiously, unsure on where or not she's being serious.

"Robert, should I stick a corset on you and see how you survive?" She snaps sarcastically causing all of us to laugh.

"I'd rather not, I don't think I'd suit it, Juliette." I say back to her.

She takes another long and deep breath. "I feel like I smell, I'm so nervous. Do I smell Mum?" She asks turning to Amy.

"You smell disgusting, I can smell you from here." Oliver is quick to answer. All of us turn to him giving him the same look of 'are you being serious?' "Juliette, I'm kidding, you smell fine from here." He reassures her.

She narrows her eyes at him. I am pleased

that they are somewhat getting along, however, right now is not the time to play with her anxiety.

"Well if I do, I'm sure Freddie won't have a problem telling me." She says moving her skirt again.

"Speaking of Freddie..." I say before taking a glass of water off a server who is walking by and hand Juliette it, hoping she will take a drink and calm down. "Why was he in your room earlier?"

Amy had also grabbed a glass of water and was taking a sip when I asked the question. She almost spits it out in Oliver's face, but instead chokes on her water. "I'm sorry!" She exclaims quietly. "He was where?!"

"Okay, don't start jumper over a hundred hurdles. He came to see me earlier after my dress fitting." Juliette says taking a drink of her water. "I got the truth out of him about how he knows Arielle and Edward. Would you like to know, or should I keep it to myself?" She teases, grinning as she takes another sip.

"Stop being a brat." Spencer states before taking the water off Juliette and finishing it off.

"Are they having an affair?" Felicity whispers.

Juliette frowns, a disgusted look growing on her face. "No! Well, I don't know. But what I do know is that Freddie was exploring, came upon Haroux and got arrested as they thought he was infiltrating. Arielle dropped the charges and decided that he reminded her so much of Robert, she decided to hire him."

I narrow my eyes. "And you believe that?"

"I do." She admits.

"How's that?

"Because he wasn't lying when he told me. That's how I knew." She says looking up at Amy. "I don't want to dance, but I would much rather get this over and done with so we can leave." She says honestly fixing her dress again.

"It's a good thing I've told Arielle we are leaving in the morning then." I admit and watch everyone's eyes dart around looking at me.

"When did you decide that?" Peter asks and I take a long deep breath, taking my water from Felicity.

"When Arielle admitted she had listened in to my conversation with Serena and Nathaniel." I say finishing the rest of the water. "She knows about Clarissa."

"Well shit…" Spencer says placing his head in his hands.

"What? When did you speak to Serena?" Juliette asks placing her hand on my arm.

"She called the palace earlier; Clarissa came home and had a meltdown when she realised you had left with me. Detective Gomez has been told about the altercation obviously not knowing the reason for the meltdown was because of you leaving." I explain and I watch the worry grow on her face.

"Robert, if she's out there she might hurt another child. It feels wrong being here when she's the way she is…" She begins to ramble.

I place my hand on the top of her arm. "You are forgetting that Detective Gomez is involved in locating her. I know you trust him. So, for one night. Let him do his job. Please just be a kid." I plead with her.

She raises an eyebrow, that I can tell is filled with sarcasm. "Be a kid? Is a kid meant to be attending a ball dressed as a Disney Princess? That's your idea of me being a kid?"

"If it keeps you safe tonight, yes." I say quickly. "It's just for one night, we will deal with Clarissa tomorrow."

She moves out of my grasp and places her glass of water that's empty on one of the waiters passing by. "Can this night get any worse?"

"Juliette!" I hear Arielle call behind me. She glances over, giving Arielle a fake smile. "You must come meet the Queen of England." She exclaims and I turn to see fear flash in Juliette's eyes.

"I spoke to soon. Excuse me." She

sarcastically states, walking away from us and curtsying to the Queen, just not to Arielle.

I glance my eyes over and catch Freddie staring over at her. Juliette may think he's telling the truth but I sure as hell don't.

"We stick together tonight." I say to my family and to Amy.

"Do we have to? I'm here for the buffet." Oliver whines. Turning to him, I give him a look. "I want this night over, just as much as your devils spawn over there." He says pointing at Juliette.

"Your night will be a hell of a lot worse when I tell them to not serve you alcohol at any point." I snap and he immediately backs down.

I think we will probably all need liquid courage to get through tonight.

The night is going well without a problem in sight. Juliette is being introduced to every person in the room alongside Robyn and Edward who is introducing her his stepdaughter.

He has every right to do so, although the thought of it, does boil my blood. That should have been discussed prior to this ball if he can introduce her as that, but once again nothing is mentioned to me, or Amy, her mother.

She's standing with Spencer who was forced

against his will by the gentleman getting him ready that he had to wear a turtleneck to cover up as many tattoos as possible. They even offered to give him a top hat to try and hide some of them around his ears. His answer was a very Spencer-like answer.

I'm pleased they get along. I also know how much Spencer respects her. He's always had a soft spot with woman. He has always been kind even though he gives off a don't-fuck-with-me attitude.

"Are you Mr Quinten by chance?" A posh gentleman beside me asks.

"Depends on who is asking." I say taking a sip of my champagne. Not long after Juliette was escorted to meet every Tom, Dick and Harry, that may or may not have a royal title. They finally came round with the alcohol which put a smile on Oliver's face.

"My name is Raf. I'm one of the people on the council." The man explains and I feel the annoyance that was settled begin to grow.

"Oh, I've heard of the council. The same ones who listed my daughter as an abomination?" I sarcastically say with my face saying a different story. "I suggest you move away from me Raf; I have nothing I would like to say. None of which is pleasant talk for a ball such as elegant as this one." I say finishing off my drink and placing it on one of the trays with the waiter.

"We say how we feel Mr Quinten. Your daughter being the blood of a Princess of Donevia and the blood of an American causes great worry for the people of Haroux." He explains which is only causing my blood to boil faster.

"You seem to care more about the parents of the child rather than the actual child herself. Do you know what it says on her birth certificate Raf? On her nationality?" I question, while turning to face him. He turns to me, slightly backing off. "She's British. Born and raised." I explain before turning and pointing to Amy. "That is her mother. Not your beloved Queen, that is the woman who has raised and loved her for the past fourteen years and will continue to do so until the day she dies. The woman, I as the blood father of that beautiful girl over there, owe my life to." I explain harshly. I keep my voice low not trying to cause a scene and attract unwanted visitors to our interaction. "You have a problem with me and my people, that's fine. But don't start professing your values and hatred for us onto my fourteen-year-old daughter who is innocent in all of this." I say coldly looking down to him.

The man backs off and walks away from me, his eyes startled as I undoubtably have probably frightened him. *Good.*

"We would like to welcome Officer Fredrick Fitzgerald and his date Miss Juliette Sanders to the floor. They will be doing the dance of the royals alongside, Her Royal Highness Princess Robyn of Haroux and Prince Philip of Switzerland.

Robyn and Philip make their way towards the dance floor alongside Juliette and Freddie. I feel Amy and Spencer stand on one side with Felicity, Peter and Oliver on the other.

I don't know how Juliette is feeling, but I feel sick to my stomach.

They get into their positions, and I watch as Freddie gives her an encouraging nod and smile. She still looks over at us for encouragement which we are all happy to give her.

The music starts and gracefully, the couples begin to move almost effortlessly along the dance floor. Arielle and Edward sit at the top where their thrones are. All high and mighty, watching Juliette and Robyn carefully. Edward is smiling as I can see he watches Robyn move and smile while dancing with Prince Philip of Switzerland.

Arielle's focus is on Juliette. I can see from here she is glaring down at her, hoping she will make some sort of mistake.

But I watch as Freddie encourages her, as he glides them along.

The dance is over in a few minutes and just as everyone begins to applaud.

BOOM.

CHAPTER FIFTY-FOUR

Robert Quinten

Haroux

My ears are ringing as I try and open my eyes.

I can hear muffled screaming and someone lightly shaking me.

Slowly, I open my eyes to see Spencer screaming at me. "Get up! Robert! Get up!" I can hear him scream as I get my hearing back.

The room is filled with smoke and there is a fire in the far corner. I get lifted to my feet by my brothers and I see Felicity consoling Amy. "Juliette and Robyn have been taken." Spencer explains as he goes to grab Freddie who is holding his head. I begin to look around, glass is shattered all over the floor and there is bodies lying everywhere.

"Juliette's been taken?" I ask as I take in my surroundings. I knew something wasn't right, I knew she would have planned something. But there are so many people lying unconscious or dead that this doesn't make any sense.

"Robert, we need to come up with a plan." Peter explains grabbing me sternly as I try to come to my surroundings. "Arielle and Edward were both lead away while Juliette and Robyn were taken. They cared more about themselves than they did those kids." He says as he points over to the security that have now surrounded the ballroom trying to get people to safety.

"Which way did they take them?" I ask turning to my brother.

"They took them down a side door. Robert. Something isn't right. This is so out of the blue!" Peter exclaims.

"Why didn't you stop them?" I turn to Freddie, grabbing him by his collar. "You were next to her!"

"They knocked me out!" He shouts moving out of my grip. "Do you really think I would let them take her?!"

"We know nothing about you or your intentions!" I shout at him getting closer to him so there is inches between us. "How do we know that you and Arielle didn't conjure up this plan to kidnap Juliette and keep her here!" I scream before Peter and Oliver move me away.

"Robert, this has nothing to do with Arielle!" Peter shouts to me. "Arielle doesn't care about anyone but herself. She wouldn't put her people or Edwards people in jeopardy. This is something bigger!" He exclaims.

"We need to find Juliette…" I say holding my head. It is pounding.

"We will, but we need to work out a plan. So, think." Oliver slaps me in the attempt of waking me up.

I think for a few seconds and look around, trying to work out exit strategies, and the best way in order to locate Juliette.

"Which way did Arielle and Edward go?" I ask my brother and he turns to a side of the wall. Without looking at it properly, you would just think it's a normal wall. "Okay, we're going to split up." I say before grabbing one of the guards. "Sir, we want to help. We want some weapons in order to locate the Princess."

"We only use swords, sir."

"They will have to do." I instruct him and the guard heads off out of the room, hopefully to get us a few weapons to use.

"Robert, I'm not six." Oliver whines before pulling out a gun of his own. "I don't like listening to the rules."

I almost jump for joy. "For once, I'm pleased you didn't listen to me." I pat him on the back. "Okay, Amy you're with me. Peter and Felicity pair up. Spencer you're with Oliver." I instruct while watching the man come back with a handful of swords. We each thank him as we take one.

"What about me?" Freddie asks and I can't help but groan in annoyance. "I want to help find the Princess and Juliette. So, let me help." He pleads.

"Fine!" I shout turning to him. "You can join Spencer and Oliver." I say before turning to my psychotic brother. "If he is remotely out of place, shoot him." I instruct.

"Sir, we have a location on the Princesses." The guard informs us before leading us away and to a tiny room filled with monitors and hard drives. "Play it."

The guard at the computer desk plays something that is on one of the bridges, I can't be sure which one. We watch as Juliette is dragged kicking and screaming along the bridge by a few men in black hoods. She manages to kick the one dragging her in the crotch having him fall to his knees. She gets away, running from a bunch of men that chase after her.

"Where is that?" Peter asks and the man turns to a large 360 map of the castle.

"The south side of the castle. It's believed that is where they entered from before setting off the bomb near the ballroom."

"How long ago was that?" I ask.

"No more than five minutes. We don't have security cameras inside the castle. So, I can't see where she went after." The guard explains.

"Anything on Princess Robyn?" Felicity asks.

"Nothing, ma'am."

"Okay, so we know which area she could possibly be. Oliver, Spencer and Freddie, I want you to head in that direction. If they are coming in that way, you might be able to stop them." I instruct.

The three men dash in that direction. I turn my focus back to the man at the desk. "Any news on who might be behind this?" I ask and the man turns to his computer and begins looking around for something on one of the screens.

"A jet passed over Haroux about forty minutes ago, it had no identifying features however up to twenty-five men got off that plane and have since headed into the castle."

"So, the castle has been invaded?"

"Yes, sir. Can I ask something, sir?" The man

turns to me. "Why would you send your own people to come and attack our country after we welcomed you in?"

I frown down at him and look around at my siblings. "What are you talking about?"

"The attackers are American."

CHAPTER FIFTY- FIVE

Juliette Sanders

Haroux

I run as fast as I can away from the bridge. I'm not one for physical activity, yet I probably will never run this fast in my life. I can hear a few of the men run after me, screaming after me.

They're American.

And I am so confused. I can't work out if this is something Arielle has planned or Robert to try and get back at her. But also, why do they want me and Robyn?

Robyn.

She got lead away down another exit. She was

screaming for me, screaming for them to let her go.

I keep running as fast as I can, knowing that this dress is the one holding me back. It is ridiculously heavy, and I've been forced to wear heels, which deep down I'm thankful for, because I managed to do some damage to the man back on the bridge.

I cut down one corner and hide, hoping that they will just pass me, and I will be able to hide here until it's all over.

The men run past, one by one. Guns in their hands as they shout out for me. I place my hand over my mouth to cover my heavy breathing. I need to work out what is going on and why the palace is under attack.

Even with us being led away by those men, I still watched Arielle and Edward get whisked away by Bertram down a secret passageway.

I then hear a scream, an earth shattering one. But it sounds like a child. "Help me!" She screams again.

Robyn.

I have to stop myself from running out and attempting to rescue her in case I get caught again.

I slowly move down the corridor and listen carefully for any movements. The corridor is quiet, and I decide to step out and slowly make my way down to the next hallway, hoping that no one sees me.

"Let go of me!" I hear Robyn scream again. My heart is pounding so loud I think it might get me caught. I move down the hallway slowly, trying to control my breathing.

"I honestly don't know why I'm playing the saviour when I know the Quinten's are somewhere in this castle and Haroux has security. But also, how could this get slipped through the cracks?

I hear a door open in front of me and I dash to get to the nearest exit on the long corridor, next to a door.

"Find that Sanders girl. I don't care if she's dead or alive." An American man instructs.

"But I thought Mrs wanted us to keep her alive?" Another man asks before I hear him wince.

"Don't listen to her, listen to me. I want her dead. She's only gonna cause more problems, and I'm done hearing about her." The man says to the other. I can still hear him whining before he stops, and a door is shut.

In under a second, I hear a man scream saying they think they've found me. I hear that door open once again and a brief interaction happen with him and another man.

"Take the Princess to the next location. We need to find that brat, and then we can leave. Go!"

He shouts at the man.

Two sets of footprints run from that area in the hallway, and I watch them pass me by to the left and leave the way I came in.

The door never shuts, and I move slowly but quickly to look out and see what's going on. I look either way and notice a man, bald, pulling Robyn out from the room and standing her in the middle of the corridor. She's tied behind her back with rope and what looks to be like cloth in her mouth.

"Stay here." He instructs before going back into the room.

I make my move quickly, running up behind Robyn and pulling the door shut on the man and pulling down the shutter. It will hold him off for a few minutes while we try and get away. He is screaming to let him out. I ignore him, grab Robyn and we take off running as quick as we both can down the corridor.

Suddenly, I hear the door open, and I drag Robyn down into one of the rooms and slowly closing the door. She runs over to a cupboard and hints for me to open it.

It's open. Thank the lord, and both of us in our poofy dresses scramble inside before I close the door.

She's been crying and just as I'm about to remove the cloth from her mouth, I hear the door to the room we came in open. It creaks and I hear footsteps.

I place my finger to my lips telling Robyn to be quiet while also placing my hand over her mouth.

Frozen in fear, we listen for those footsteps. He's carefully looking around and begins to get closer to the door. She shuts her eyes and I turn my attention to the door handle, praying that it doesn't turn, and he doesn't find us.

"How did you lose her?!" A man shouts and I hear the footsteps fall back.

"It clearly wasn't what I was hoping to achieve, that other little bitch came and ran off with her."

The footsteps move away from the door, and I try hard not to let out a sign of relief. I'm terrified and I can feel the tears begin to run down my face.

Who are these people?

And what do they want?

"Well if it was Juliette, it means she is sneakier than we thought. Which way did they go?" The man asks.

"I don't know, my guess is in the main palace, I was just checking the other rooms."

"Let's hope she hasn't reunited with her Dad, because he'll be out for blood." The other man explains before we hear the door shut and silence fall upon us both.

I shake my head at her, telling her not to speak just in case.

I wait a few minutes until I fully believe that the room really is clear, and I remove the cloth from Robyn's mouth. "I'm really happy to see you." She says as she begins to cry. "Juliette, I'm scared. Why would your Papa do this?" She asks as I turn her around and untie her.

"This isn't Robert. He wouldn't do this." I defend him.

"Juliette, they are American, and he is the leader of the American mafia!"

"Okay, Robyn. He is cruel but he isn't that cruel." I say once again in Robert's defence. Unfortunately, I can't say for sure that this isn't Robert, only that whoever it is has a real vendetta against the family.

Deep down I think it's someone Oliver has annoyed.

"Robyn, did they say anything? Their names? Where they were from?" I ask her and she nods.

"The man who spoke last before they left the room, they said his name was H."

"H? Okay, that doesn't tell me anything. That could be anyone."

"Well, I don't know who he is!" She snaps. I place my hands on her shoulders.

"We need to work together, okay? We aren't gonna make it out of here if we don't listen to each other." I snap back at her.

She steps back, clearly frightened by my tone, but nods in agreement. "Where are we in the castle?"

She thinks for a moment, "We're on the south side. This hasn't been used since the American's had it. It was once used as cells for prisoners." She explains and I nod.

"How do we get to the main part of the castle from here? Where we were originally?"

She shakes her head quickly. "That is where they will be waiting for us. There is another exit that will lead us to another hallway. We need to go down the stairs, and there is a door at the bottom that will lead us to the great hall. We can exit out of there and head for the woods till this is over." She says holding tightly onto my hand.

I nod in agreement. "That's a good plan. How far is the great hall from here?"

"Not far, should only take us a few minutes to get to it normally, but because we are being hunted, we will have to be careful." She tells me.

"Okay, we will be. But we are going to need to be quiet. So, take your shoes off. They cause unnecessary sounds." I tell her.

She frowns. "Juliette, I object to having to run around in my socks."

"I'll let you get caught?" I say sarcastically. Fear flashes in her eyes as she takes off her heels in one swift motion.

"Please don't."

CHAPTER FIFTY-SIX

Robert Quinten

Haroux

I walk towards the rest of my siblings who stand in the room opposite the great hall. The great hall opens up with two French doors leading over into another smaller room where they are all standing. There is a door to the left of them that leads out into a wooded area. "Anything"? I ask them.

They shake their heads. Amy has been a wreck while we've been having to fight through the American's trying to find Juliette. Weirdly enough they all seem to know who I am, yet I can't get any information as to who any of them work for.

"The guard in the security room said the people who ran after Juliette have been spotted in the south side of the castle." Peter explains. "The only thing down there is old cells, all of them empty, so sign of Juliette."

"Oh god." Amy says coving her face in her hands. "Do you think they got a hold of her?"

"Let's hope not." Spencer says before pulling Amy in for a hug. "We will find her."

"I agree with Spencer." Felicity says. "Juliette is both a Sanders and a Quinten. I know she won't go down without a fight." She reassures her.

"So, what is the plan now?" Oliver asks.

I think long and hard. "We're gonna have to think like Juliette." I say to them. "Amy, what would Juliette do in this situation?"

Amy begins to stutter. "Er—" She pauses before I watch a lightbulb go off in her head. "She would go and find Robyn."

"Why? Why would she risk getting caught again?" Oliver asks and I watch a smile grow on Spencer's face.

"Because if anyone is going to know the ins and the outs of the castle..." Spencer begins looking over at me.

"It's going to be the Princess herself."

We hear door slam behind us, and we turn around to see two men, one bald and one with a beanie on looking over at us. "You must be the

Quinten's!" A man with a New York accent greets us.

"We've heard so much about you." The man with the hat says while pulling out his gun. "Anyone ever told you guys, not to bring a sword to a gun fight?" He laughs, along with the other man.

In a split second the man in the hat's brains are blown all over the room and I turn to see Oliver pointing his gun right at him.

In a split second, Freddie appears from the same door they did only a few seconds earlier and places a sword around the bald man's neck. "Put the gun, down." He instructs.

The bald man is hesitant at first, so Freddie presses his sword harder into the man's neck, drawing blood. He drops the gun and Freddie moves him over into the room across from the great hall and makes him get on his knees. "Where is Juliette Sanders?" I ask leaning down to his level. Freddie removed the knife and Oliver has now placcd the gun to his head.

"I don't know. The little bitch decided to lock me in one of the cells and run off with the Princess." He explains. Confused looks fill the room as we look down at the man.

"She was on the south side of the castle?"

"Yup." He says popping the P. "Boss wants her

found."

"Why? And what has this got to do with Juliette?"

Suddenly the man starts the laugh hysterically. "You know nothing. That's great!" He laughs harder.

Oliver steps forward pushing the gun further onto the man's skull. "I suggest if you want to keep your fingers, and your brain you're going to tell us everything."

The man continues to laugh. This time, its cut short and not because of Oliver. A bullet goes through the man's brain and explodes all over us before he hits the floor. Looking up we stand to see the King and Queen themselves, with Edward being the one to hold the gun.

"Sorry. Did I ruin your torture session?"

I begin to see red. "What the hell is your problem?"

"My problem? You're the one who decided to break our trust and order an invasion!" He shouts.

I frown my brows. "Actually, Your Highness, this has nothing to do with us!"

"Actually, it does." A voice from behind us says. We all turn to look in the direction of the door that leads out to the wooded area.

I feel betrayal swoop in and take over my

broken heart. Gasps fill the room as we look at someone who none of us expected.

Rodger.

CHAPTER FIFTY-SEVEN

Juliette Sanders

Haroux

Robyn leads me down the hallway and we enter the much warmer and prettier side of the castle. This hasn't been damaged yet, however there are muddy boot prints and down one corridor, I can see a body. We really need to make it to the great hall.

"This way." She whispers and we start to make our way down the hallway.

As we run through the palace, looking for any indication of our parents, we come face to face with one of the intruders.

His balaclava covers his face, so we only see

his eyes, and they are filled with humour. "Well, isn't this just too easy." He laughs to himself. Moving closer, his gun raising ever so slightly, pointing it towards us. "Two for the price of one. Now this will make me rich." He speaks clearly in an American accent. This has to have something to do with Robert.

My survival instincts kick in, and I pick up the sword that is left next to the dead body of a guard. I know not to bring a knife to a gun fight, on this case a sword but right now I have no choice.

"What's that gonna do Princess, huh?" He mocks me, and the chain next to me catches my attention.

"I'm not a Princess!" I scream before moving my sword and cutting down the light, quickly moving my sister out of the way.

The light comes crashing down, hitting the man on the head as he falls to the ground unconscious.

"Juliette!" She exclaims behind me. "You're not meant to know how to fight! That's the boy's job!" I roll my eyes.

"Says who? The boys?! The misogynistic things they teach you here are ridiculous!" I say while grabbing her hand and running away and down the stairs, sword still in my hand. I drag Robyn through every back corridor I can find in order to get us to some sort of safety.

She decides to stop, clutching onto her chest a little, how is she out of breath? We've barely been running more than a minute. "Princesses are meant to stand and look pretty." She says in between the deep breaths. I suddenly watch as two men in balaclavas stand at the other end of the corridor, discussing something with each other.

"Well, you'll look pretty dead if you don't move!" I whisper as loud as I can, giving her the hint that we are still being hunted. "Come on!" I usher her, and we run down the next corridor, hoping to find someone who doesn't want to kill us.

"In here!" She exclaims while opening the door. We run in and stand in the great hall.

I feel my heart get ripped out of my chest noticing Rodger with a gun in his hand.

I move Robyn to stand behind me, moving to protect her unlike her parents did. Spencer has to hold my Mum back who is pleading with Rodger just to leave me alone. Rodger places his hand up, hushing my Mum.

"Rodger, come on. She's innocent in all of this." Spencer pleads with his brother.

"Innocent?" He snaps his head back round. "None of this would have happened if she had just stayed away!" He shouts pointing the gun at Spencer. "Those kids that died? Their blood is on her hands." She says coldly turning around and pointing the gun at me.

"I knew you would regret coming to America. I wouldn't have had to shoot my own brothers if you had just stayed in England like you were instructed. But you had to be curious, you had to know where you came from. How selfish can you be?" He says walking just that little bit closer to me.

"And Carter? Was he my fault too?"

"Of course, he was! Did you really think I wanted to shoot my own brothers? I didn't!" He shouts.

"You only have yourself to blame Rodger, you pulled the trigger!" Felicity shouts over to him.

"No." He snaps his head back around. "I did it because it was what was needed. Juliette was the reason it happened."

I'm scared. I've never seen Rodger like this. He's always been cold, but cold enough to kill me?

"Was it my fault that Clarissa hid your baby?" I ask him.

Slowly, he lowers his gun and turns back around. "Sapphire deserves what is coming to her."

"She's a baby, Rodger. You don't mean that. Your cold, your isolated but you're not cruel." I practically whisper the tears falling down my face.

"She's the creation of two killers, just as much as Chase and Clarissa' son. They should be destroyed."

"Is she going to be killing babies now?"

He laughs slightly. "Something new for the books, I guess."

He begins to back off as I hear footsteps from behind him. "What is taking so long?" A blonde man says looking over at my family.

The colour drains from their face as does mine when the man turns around to face me.

Chase Hayward.

He's dressed in a black t-shirt, black jeans and a pair of trainers. His eyes are filled with curiosity as he sees the set up around him.

"H." I whisper, pulling Robyn behind me.

"So, you have heard of me?" He gleams as he walks towards me. Passing Rodger who walks towards my family, glaring at them. "Well, it is lovely to meet you Miss Sanders—" He says while getting too close for my liking.

I pull out the sword and put it to his neck. I can't stop the tears of fear running down my face, but I stand strong for Robyn who shakes and cries behind me. "That is far enough." I whisper, pressing the blade closer to his neck.

He begins to laugh lightly. "Well, you told me

she was feisty. I didn't think she would be this feisty." He laughs again moving away from me. "I have a message from Clarissa." He says walking towards my family.

"She's a bit out of reach to start demanding orders don't you think, Chase?" Robert replies.

He stands next to Rodger who is leaning against the wall between the two rooms. He begins to laugh. "Just listen up, *Dad*." Robert narrows his eyes. "Have the Detective in Michigan look somewhere else. If we feel as though we are being chased or followed, we will kill those kids." He warns.

"And if we follow that demand?" I ask. Surely, it's a two way street, and from the smile that is growing on his lips, I'd say that he's already thought of a counter offer.

"We'll give you those kids. On the basis that we don't get arrested."

I exchange a look with Robert. Neither one of us are wanting to back down from this, but we know with how unstable all three of them are that they would kill those babies just to prove a point.

"I can't make any promises." I say to Chase. He begins to chuckle and starts walking towards me slightly.

"Well, you better try." He instructs. He glares down at me, before a smile grows on his face and he turns his back. "Come on Rodger, before Juliette over there drives that sword through my heart."

"Don't tempt me."

The men laugh as they exit, leaving us all standing in disbelief as to what has just happened these past few minutes.

Robyn moves from behind me and pulls me in for a tight hug. I drop the sword, pulling her tighter as we cry together, both praying that for the moment, this is over.

She then runs over to Arielle and Edward who greet her with a hug, not as tight as ours but I'm sure in royalty, that's as good as its going to get.

Mum runs over first, pulling me into the biggest hug known to man and kisses my head repeatedly. "Oh, I'm so pleased you're okay." She says hugging me righter. "Did you use a sword?!" She exclaims which causes me to laugh.

"Yeah, I didn't want to be captured again." I say as I hug her tightly. I feel someone rub my back and I exit my embrace to find Robert greeting me with a smile.

"I'm so proud of you." He says as he opens his arm for a hug. I decide to take it.

Two hours ago, I didn't even know that they were alive.

I would even hug Oliver if he was to come

over and stop standing in the corner.

I immediately feel unsettled when I hear someone clear their throat from behind me. We all turn to see Arielle, Edward and Robyn, standing in a row like they are bouncers, stopping us from entering.

"We want you to leave Haroux as soon as possible. You are no longer welcome here." She announces and I feel anger rush within me.

"Not even a thank you." I say under my breath.

"Thank you? What for? For putting my daughter's life in danger?" She announces.

I move out of my Mum's grip and begin to walk closer to Arielle and Edward. "If it wasn't for me, your daughter could have been on her way to god knows where with three killers! Clarissa is not my fault."

"Everything is your fault, Juliette. The fact that my reputation is ruined because of your curiosity and Robert's lack of morals. That my country is now up in flames because of American's yet again!" She shouts at me.

"That is enough, Arielle." Robert stands in front of me, but I shove past him.

"How about you take some accountability, Arielle." I say harshly. Her eyes widen at the accusation but I'm too angry to stop. "You decided to have me, yet you didn't want the responsibility of raising me, so you handed that to someone else. You are very good at playing the victim Arielle." I say to her.

She begins to say something, but I cut her off. "Actually, there is two things your good at." Her eyes become dark with anger as she stares down at me. "Playing the victim," I say while looking down at Robyn who holds Edward's hand. "and abandoning your daughters. Because not once, when we were being dragged away by those men did you try and save Robyn."

"I love Robyn—"

"But you didn't try and save her. The only person you saved was yourself. Oh! And your husband."

She takes a long deep exhale but doesn't say anything, probably because she knows I'm right.

"Whatever you wanted from me? From me being here or for the future? I want no part of it, Arielle. I don't want you to contact me, I want you to stay away from me. I don't have time to deal with your royal ways, and..." I say going back over and hugging my Mum. "I don't care. You're not my mother. My parents are Amy and Paul Sanders. And my other dad is Robert Quinten. But you? You're nothing to me. Just because you made me Arielle – doesn't mean you get to try and own me."

CHAPTER FIFTY-EIGHT

Juliette Sanders

Haroux

I walk along the harbour, there is a breeze in the air although it is still early morning.

Instead of getting any sort of sleep we all decided to pack and get out of Haroux as quickly as possible. Robert managed to get in touch with the pilot who set off from Madrid where they had decided to stay while we were here. The plane landed not that long ago, and they have been making sure that people it is ready for when we need it, which is soon.

Thankfully all the royal families were fine who attended the ball. A few guards were killed and Arielle didn't seem to upset when Bertram told her.

Robyn came to my room earlier and said that from now on, American's are officially going to be banned from Haroux. Not that I think Robert would mind, he is very excited to get out of here and go home. She had also thanked me again for saving her from the American's and said that she is going to demand a sword fighting class, so if she would ever need it – she's ready.

The thought of Princess Robyn trying to fight someone with a sword brings a smile to my face.

I manage to get to that dusty old pirate ship that belongs to a fake officer. He's up on the top, sorting out one of the sails when he notices me and slides down, like a fireman on a pole.

"I thought you had already headed back to London." He exclaims before making his way off the boat.

"Just leaving, thought I would say goodbye."

He walks to meet me and extends his hand. "It's been nice knowing you, Miss Sanders." He tells me sweetly.

I extend my hand to shake his. "Feeling is mutual Meredith." I tease.

He gasps, letting go of my hand. "Don't upset me. That better not be my new nickname."

I laugh. "Well, I think you suit the name Meredith."

"Don't lie to me, blondie."

"I don't lie."

He scoffs. "Everyone lies."

"No, I think in this case, it's just you."

He laughs hard and looks back at his ship. "What do you think of her?" He asks.

I tilt my head, thinking of the nicest word possible. "She's old."

"Yeah, she is." He laughs. I laugh at him as he begins to get back on it. "Do you think I'll see you again, Miss Sanders?"

"Only if you stop running away from reality."

He laughs hysterically while pulling up the anchor and closing the door. "Never."

CHAPTER FIFTY-NINE

Juliette Sanders,
London, United Kingdom

I t's been a few days since we got back from Haroux. Mum ended up having to have a few stitches as did a few of the Quinten's.

Robert refused to see a doctor, but he apparently let Alexis take a look at him. He also had to update them all on what happened and what has been happening when it comes to Clarissa.

He's ordered security details on all of us. Mum wasn't hesitant this time since we now know Rodger is involved.

Spencer is packing up a lot of his stuff in

Michigan and he and Damian will be moving over to London in the next few weeks.

Damian has been given the all clear from the hospital, but has to go through some significant therapy. He also made a really tough call and spoke to Carter's parents, who invited him to the funeral. I haven't spoken to him yet, but Peter and Spencer were there to support him, and they said he did great and supported Carter's family.

There has been no sign of Clarissa, and no one has heard from her since she left the house the other night when Serena was there.

Robert has tried to get in touch with Tommy, Clarissa's blood brother, but he is refusing to take his messages. Robert thinks that Clarissa might have given him a warning or told him a lie. So, he's taken other measures to try and get in touch with him so he can be kept in the loop.

I managed to speak to Detective Gomez for a few hours last night, in all honesty, it was great to hear his voice. He sounded tired, and he also said he hasn't got any leads.

I feel incredibly guilty for lying to him, especially since I know so much more since the situation with Rodger and Chase.

I came away from Haroux with a few scratches and a slight bump on my head that is now a lovely pink and purple bruise. I also came away with the knowledge that I will never let

Arielle treat me like that again.

Mum said she was proud of me for standing up to her, and that she's proud that I managed to get out of there without her giving me some sort of title.

She had overheard some of the other guests saying that the ball was a ceremony, crowning me as Princess Julianna. But that isn't my name, and she knows that.

Any letters I receive from her, I've been told I have to keep as evidence if I ever wanted to take her to court for harassment.

I doubt she will send any, she will have to polish her reputation since it was her and Edward who invited us over to Haroux.

In all honesty, I couldn't care less. None of us expected Rodger or Chase to turn up and set a bomb off in the palace.

I look up when I hear a slight knock at my door. It's nice being back in my old room again. I miss Robert already, although I know he's not going to come over any time soon in the hopes it saves me from Clarissa.

"You have a visitor." Mum says sweetly standing against the door. "You may want to get out of your dressing gown Juliette." She instructs and I tilt my head.

"Is this not appropriate?" I ask sarcastically,

looking down at my dressing gown.

Mum shakes her head before standing up and walking down the landing.

Curiosity fills my veins. Who could possibly want to see me? Unless it's Mikki and Katy. However, they would just let themselves in and walk upstairs.

I decide jeans and a t-shirt to be best. It's still hot in this house, so I doubt I'll catch a chill.

I put my slippers back on and proceed to walk down the stairs to see whoever is there to see me.

Hearing a familiar voice, I can't stop the smile growing on my face. "Was the Army not for you?" I ask as I get to the bottom of the staircase.

"Well since I heard that you decided to almost get yourselves killed in another country, I decided to come home and do my brotherly duties and protect you. Since your incapable or protecting yourself." Marcus mocks before walking over and pulling me in for a hug. I hug him tighter. It feels so good to see him.

"I find that rude! You weren't there, I stuck up for myself in front of one of Clarissa's crazy boyfriends." I say pulling out of the embrace and putting my hands on my hips. He follows my sass.

"You lie. There is no way!"

"Actually, she did. Protected her and her sister. Even held a sword to his throat." Mum says in my defence.

I give him a smile as he looks back over at me shocked. "Who decided to give you a sword! That is dangerous." He teases before walking around the corner and pulling out a suitcase. "You better be getting used to me. I'm here for a few weeks. If that is alright with you, Mrs Sanders?"

Mum gives him a look. "It's Amy," She reminds him. "You can stay as long as you like, Marcus." She reassures him.

The moment is very short lived when there is a knock at the door. From the look that is exchanged around the room, none of us were expecting visitors.

Marcus pulls out his gun and slowly begins walking towards the door. Because of the stain glass window at the front, you can't really see who is outside.

Marcus opens the door, slightly hiding his gun as he steps back giving me and Mum a look into who is standing at the door.

I take a long deep breath when I notice it is just Officer Bradley standing there, with a gigantic box.

"What in god's name happened to your face?" He says nodding at my head, completely ignoring Marcus standing there. He looks over at my Mum who has a few butterfly stitches on her head. "And what happened to you, Mrs Sanders?" He exclaims before welcoming himself inside.

Marcus gives me a look as if to say, 'do we trust him?' I give him a nod and he hides his gun as quick as he can.

"It's honestly nothing, Officer Bradley. We are both fine." Mum says, opening up so he can put the box on the table.

"Has this got something to do with the trip you took to that island, Haroux?" He asks, looking between us both.

"How do you know that?" I ask him and he opens up the box.

"I spoke to Q. He told me that there was a situation but, said that when I came to speak to you, you would explain it." He says pulling things out of the box. "Also thank you for telling him it was me that gave you the information." He teases. I forgot he told me not to.

"Did he tell you why we were there?" I ask him and he nods his head.

"Said you went there for a visit. He knows someone there. Is that right?" He asks, still not looking over to us.

He didn't tell Officer Bradley the real reason and that was probably to protect me. I'm sure Robert trusts him, but I also believe he didn't tell him because right now he is unsure on who he can trust.

"That's right."

"Okay, tell me what you know."

After about forty minutes of telling a few white lies, we have managed to update Officer Bradley on everything. I also introduced him to my case and gave him the contact of Detective Gomez in Michigan so they can work together on the investigation.

I'm still so curious on why he brought the box and why he hasn't said anything yet. But I can't say I blame him; we've just told him a lot of information including the situation in Michigan with Serena.

We also had to explain how we thought Chase was involved in the attack in Haroux. That raised his eyebrows as he listened carefully to what we had to say, also including some white lies.

He takes a stand and starts lifting up some of what seems to be case files and puts them in the middle of the table.

"Your yet to tell me why you're here and what

all this is, Officer Bradley."

He raises his eyebrows again and starts pushing some of the files towards us. "In the last two years, there has been quite a few children murdered. There are all from good families, very well educated and they had a good social group. They had nothing in common individually wise. They didn't attend the same schools or clubs." He explains before pointing at the pile of files in front of Marcus. "Some of which didn't even live in the same country."

My eyes widen. "Are you saying she has more victims?"

He nods as he comes over to the pile in front of me. "These are from here. The ones in front of Marcus are from France and the ones in front of Mrs Sanders- they are from some other places in America, not including Michigan." He explains.

I feel the colour drain from my face. There is more victims.

"Officer Bradley, how many victims are we looking at in total?" Marcus asks looking up from the pile of files in front of us.

"So far, 14."

I get up immediately and walk away from the table in complete disbelief. Fourteen victims. Four in Michigan, three in the UK, five in other parts of America and three in France.

How could this happen? How could she kill these children?

"Juliette, that means the reason she started doing this isn't because of you." Mum explains causing me to turn back around to her. "They said it was because you came into their life. But Robert said he didn't tell them till just before you came out there. So, you couldn't be the reason." She reassures me, getting out of her seat and pulling me in for a hug.

"What about the Williams brothers?" Officer Bradley asks. "Weren't they sent here to keep an eye on Juliette?"

"Yeah, but Robert had a meeting with them hours before the plane took off. My guess is that is when they told him."

"Unless Clarissa found out for herself?"

"But how?"

"What about projects? Like school projects? Did any of them include family histories?"

"We were home schooled, and we all come from messed up families. I doubt he would want us to open up our traumas." Marcus says sarcastically looking over at Officer Bradley.

"The only problem with trying to work out Clarissa's intentions is we would lose our minds." I say moving out of my Mum's grasp and walking towards them. "Officer Bradley, it was made very clear to us by Chase that if you and Detective Gomez don't stir your investigations in another direction that she is going to kill her two children. So, what do you say we do?" I explain.

Everyone turns to look at Officer Bradley. He doesn't stutter though, only walks round the table and breaks the space between us.

"What if I told you that we can find those kids alive and we can catch Clarissa, Rodger and Chase?"

My interest peaks. "And how do you suggest we do that?"

"By playing them at their own game."

"When you say *'we'* Juliette, I'm assuming you mean, just you and your team? Isn't that right Officer?" Mum asks calmly.

A look is exchanged between Mum and Officer Bradley that gives me and the rest of the room the indication he wasn't just referring to him and his team.

"I want Juliette to be my undercover informant over at Interpol."

TORRIE JONES

The Betrayal That Follows

The Hidden Jules Series #3

COMING SOON...

But until then, enjoy a sneak peak...

PROLOGUE

The Betrayal That Follows

Clarissa Quinten

You know what's funny? How stupid Juliette is to think that I would stop killing.

The promises that were made were only to lure her away from what I really want to do, who I want.

I want her dead.

That is the only this to feed this hate I have is to see her blood all over my hand and her body on the floor.

She's stupid. She's naïve.

All of which she knows.

The attack in Haroux wasn't thoroughly planned. I didn't think she would be able to get away, but I also didn't think that my boyfriends would be stupid enough to let her live.

Rodger being the main one. He always had

a soft spot for her. For her kindness and her curiosity.

Well, that curiosity is going to get her killed and she will be the only one to blame.

I turn over in my bed and see Chase snoring. He keeps me up most nights, always has when I've stayed with him.

I managed to create a new identity, one that's going to help me hide until Juliette follows through with what I asked.

If she decides to do that.

I would hate to give Rodger the signal to kill Sapphire.

Chase will be leaving me soon, leaving me alone with this toddler who I have no idea how to deal with.

I do like his name, however. Dracov. He will be strong, and a fighter. Just like his daddy.

I get out of the bed and pull the hoodie over me as I begin to walk to the board in front of the bed.

My vision board.

Filled with wonderful ideas and potential victims. I think of this as my own personal Pinterest board. It bothers Chase, but he doesn't mention it too much.

I place my hand over the photo of a girl riding

her bike down the street.

"Not long." I whisper, stoking my hand over the photo a few times. "You'll get what you deserve."

The Troubled Series

Hate you too.

When trouble meets
troubled...

Torrie Jones

ABOUT THE AUTHOR

Torrie Jones is a Northeast author that likes to bring the stories that do her head in to life. She has a cat named Sheldon and a dog called Penny. Her work is mainly Young Adult Mystery, Detective, and Crime. But she also writes romance with her debut novel Hate you too, book 1 of the Troubled Series, releasing in April 2023.

She is a lover of Marvel, smutty books, and all things nerdy. She started writing back in 2016 with her debut novel, The Lies We Tell becoming a number 1 best seller when released in 2022.

Torrie is active on social media! Keep in touch...

INSTAGRAM - @torriejonesauthor

Join the Troublemakers! - Trouble's Book Club on Facebook.

Tiktok - @torriemaryjones

Goodreads - Torrie Jones

www.torriemaryjones.com

ACKNOWLEDGEMENTS

To my family who love and support me no matter what.

To all of my amazing friends who give me the kick up the arse when I need it. (Which is 90% of the time.)

To my Troublemakers who have stood by me no matter what. I really hope this was worth the wait.

And to you my lovely reader. I hope you love Jules and the Quinten's as much as me.

Torrie x

BOOKS AND OTHER WORKS

The Hidden Jules Series -
The Lies We Tell
The Secrets We Keep
The Betrayal That Follows - *Summer 2023*

The Troubled Series -
Hate you too

Novels -
Dealing with the Outcast - *Autumn/Winter 2023*

Printed in Great Britain
by Amazon